P9-DUV-367

CALLIE KNIGHT

CALLIE KNIGHT

Jack Pearl

SATURDAY REVIEW PRESS/E. P. DUTTON & CO., INC.
NEW YORK 1974

Acknowledgment is made to MCA Music for permission to use portions of the song, "Alone Again (Naturally)"; Words & Music by Gilbert O'Sullivan

Library of Congress Cataloging in Publication Data

Pearl, Jack.
Callie Knight.

I. Title.
PZ4.P539To [PS3566.E218] 813'.5'4 73-17126

First Edition

10 9 8 7 6 5 4 3 2 1

Published simultaneously in Canada by Clarke, Irwin & Company Limited, Toronto and Vancouver
ISBN: 0-8415-0297-8

In memory of
Mark Van Doren and Joseph Wood Krutch
without whose encouragement
this story would never have been told

I. INCONTINENCE

II. BRUTISHNESS or BESTIALITY

III. MALICE or VICE

The arrangement of the sins
in Dante's Hell from:
"THE DIVINE COMEDY"
of DANTE ALIGHIERI

"This judgement of the heavens that makes us tremble,
Touches us not with pity."

Shakespeare, *King Lear*
Act V, sc. 3

An Ending

The girl noticed him as soon as she walked into the coach. A soldier wearing captain's bars on his cap and battle jacket. Two rows of campaign ribbons and decorations. He was young, not more than thirty. Dark and good-looking in the sullen way that females find attractive.

She looked straight at him with a smile. Touched her hair to catch his eye. But he was preoccupied, gazing out the window at the muddy Hudson River. She shrugged and went down the aisle to the john at the end of the car.

He did notice her on her way back, no way for her to see. Otherwise? Who would ever know? A whole lifetime can be redeemed or doomed for overlooking a smile, a glance, a flounce of the hand.

He admired her. She was blond, his preference in a woman, with a good figure that she carried with confidence, conscious that it showed off to good advantage in her tight pants suit.

The captain slouched in, watching her all the way to the end of the car. He wore a puzzled smile.

Women wearing suits on the street, in fashionable restaurants, even the nurses in the hospital at Clark Air Base on the dusty Luzon Plain.

Hot pants! He shook his head. When he'd left for Vietnam in 1966, no gentleman would use the term in mixed company.

Three months short of seven years. The world turns a lot in seven years. Spins off remarkable changes.

Men playing golf on the moon! A black revolution. A youth revolution. A women's revolution. "Women's Lib," his ear was still not comfortable with the sound of it, nor was his mind. It had an obscene sound like the old shocker of the forties and fifties: "Free Love."

At the Homecoming Reception Center at Travis Field in California, a girl reporter (wearing hot pants) introduced him to the term. He asked her what Women's Liberation meant.

Jesting, but with a clear invitation in her eye, she replied, "It means I can ask you to go to bed with me, Captain. Now you'll get a chance to see how it feels to be pinched in subway cars and get whistled at by drugstore johnnies. That's oversimplifying it, Captain, but you get the message."

Seven years. He felt like Rip Van Winkle when that gentleman awoke and tried to go home again. The long white beard was only a storyteller's prop. He knew all about Rip. Funny, it was along this Hudson shoreline Rip had taken his big sleep.

He had never seen the Hudson River before. Had never thought about it since grade school history.

"In 1609 Hendrik Hudson sailed his sloop Half Moon *into New York Harbor and up the river to Albany."*

A gold star, young man.

He gazed out the window again across the broad brown river, its far bank dim in mist. Misty or filthy air. There was also the Pollution Revolution.

Last night on the television in his hotel room, he had watched an advertisement sponsored by an antipollution group. An Indian with a feather in his hairband paddling a birchbark canoe down the Hudson River in sad contemplation of the contaminated waters. Dead fish with bloated bellies floating in the current. A gull mired helplessly in oil slick. Beer cans, trash of all kinds littering the shallows. Poor red man, a single tear rolled down his cheek at the atrocities his white brothers had wreaked on *his* land in a mere two centuries.

A conductor came down the aisle and bent over him. "Captain, this is it, your stop's next."

"Thank you." He looked with disapproval at the man's long hair, burnside whiskers, and handlebar mustache. A man in uniform should have a sounder sense of decorum. But why fault the conductor? Since he had checked out of the "Hanoi

Hilton," he had seen United States enlisted men and even fellow officers who looked like Jesus Christ in khaki!

He stood up and removed his small travel bag from the overhead luggage rack. Straightened his tie, tugged down his jacket, and checked the angle of his cap, his reflection in the filthy window.

The diesel engine cut its speed approaching the outskirts of the town. The captain stood in the vestibule alongside the conductor, bag in hand. He carried a manila envelope under the other arm.

"Looks like you're the only one getting off here," the conductor said with a laugh. "Haven't had anybody on this run get off at Knightsville in over two weeks."

"I guess it's not a very popular place to visit," the captain observed.

"Naw, this little burg has been dead for years, you'll see. Say, I didn't mean—that is, do you come from Knightsville, Captain?"

The captain smiled, but there was a note of hesitation in his voice. "No . . . I don't come from here. I'm from down south, Texas."

"I shoulda known by the drawl. Like John Wayne."

It was on his tongue to say that John Wayne had never been within five hundred miles of Texas, or a horse, until a talent scout spotted him on the football gridiron at U.S.C.

Instead he said, "I've never been to Knightsville in my life. Till now."

The conductor eyed him curiously. "I was wondering why you'd pick it now? There's not much doing. No good resorts. No night life. I was wondering . . ."

The captain's smile broadened. "I've been wondering myself."

There was no proper platform at the station. He followed the conductor down the metal steps and stood on the dusty right of way. He squinted against the glare of the clear June sky that spanned the circular horizon like a china blue bowl. Like the bridge spanning the river to the west.

"There she is, *her* bridge. It looks in good condition." He was speaking more to himself than to the conductor. A tone of reminiscence. He turned and looked eastward, the land side. About fifty feet off the tracks there was an ancient clapboard building, a ramshackle affair with peeling paint and a sagging roof. A wooden bench ran the length of it. Two old men sat there smoking corncob pipes and brooding silently.

The front screen door was flung open and a red-haired youth trotted out and ran down the track to the baggage car. An attendant handed him a flat canvas sack with a lock on it.

"That's the mail," the conductor explained. "Though I can't figure out why anyone would want to write to anyone in this ghost town."

The captain nodded. "I know about the mail. There was a time when the mail train came through Knightsville it was a big occasion, especially the seven-thirty evening special. The whole town turned out when it blazed through." He looked up and down the track. "Where's the rig used to hook the mail bag in on the fly?"

The conductor removed his cap and wiped a hand across his greasy thatch. "I dunno, Captain. Must have been before my time."

"Of course." The captain looked back to the building. "Alva's store, do the Lampberts still own it?"

"I dunno." He was regarding the captain strangely. "Say, I thought you had never been here before?"

The captain laughed and clapped him on the arm. "That's right. . . . Thank the Penn-Central for me, it's been a very pleasant ride." He touched his cap and moved away.

He walked slowly up Knightsville Road. At the top of the hill behind Lampbert's store, it widened into a four-lane highway. There was a traffic light at the intersection. The crossroad there was blacktop asphalt, sweating in the heat of midday. The signpost on the corner said it was "S. Knight's Drive." From where he was standing he could see the big white house, a quarter of a mile away, overlooking S. Knight's Drive. In the past the Knight homestead had been cloistered within the virgin forest. Presently the trees were cut back on both sides of the highway and the crossroad, five hundred yards he judged. He hadn't expected the region to look so naked.

There was a Shell gas station on the corner on which he stood. On the opposite corner was another station, "Pete's Chevron" the sign read.

On the corner diagonally across from him was an "amusement park," so the sign read. It was too small, seedy, and run-down to rate that designation. Mock oases like this one could be found all over the United States along major highways, usually at key junctions, where travelers could fill up their gas tanks and break the cramped monotony of the road for a half hour. The refreshment stand advertised: Red Hots with Chili. Superburgers. Pizza. Cold Beer and Soda. The amusement area covered an area of perhaps two acres. There was a carrousel, a whip, miniature cars fixed on a circular course for the smaller tots, and miniature golf. The concession doing the biggest business was the public toilets.

In the middle of the amusement park was the *piéce de résistance.* A plaster-of-paris statue about twenty-five feet high. A medieval knight astride a horse. Both sprayed with whitewash. The knight had his lance poised for battle.

The billboard on top of the refreshment stand proclaimed:

WELCOME TO THE KINGDOM OF THE WHITE KNIGHT
HOTEL ACCOMMODATIONS AVAILABLE AT THE CASTLE
COCKTAIL LOUNGE AND RESTAURANT
1500 FEET———→

The arrow pointed in the direction of the house on S. Knight's Drive. A stone retaining wall shored up the high ground on which it stood above the road and the adjacent amusement park. A recent innovation to keep the soil from eroding away beneath the house now that the trees whose roots had held it fast for centuries had been uprooted.

The Kingdom of the White Knight. The White Knight's Castle. *Christ!* he thought, the whole clan of them buried in the small cemetery behind the house must be spinning in their graves.

When the light was with him he crossed over to that corner of the intersection and walked up the blacktop drive toward "The Castle." A rueful grin spread over his face as he approached it. Distance served it more charitably than proximity. The closer he came, the more evident became the deterioration. Typical of hotels and motels in the boondocks whose livelihood is dependent on attracting the overflow from more plush public inns and a percentage of the transients who, having accommodated themselves at the amusement park, decide it's too late in the day to drive on farther. Paint peeling from the clapboards, like the horses on the dilapidated carrousel shedding their lacquered coats.

The slates on the roof, once the finest gracing any house

on the Hudson, not excepting the River Rich, were broken, chipped, a good many missing altogether. The front porch had been enclosed. A flight of steps led up to a new entrance. Above the door, spelled out in neon script: COCKTAIL LOUNGE. In the windows flashing signs invited the thirsty to try: RHEINGOLD, PABST, and ROLLING ROCK. The old ox trail at the side of the house had been widened and paved. It led up to a parking lot in what had once been the backyard. He walked up the incline and past the sparsely tenanted parking lot; he counted seven cars. A chain-link fence had replaced the hedge that had separated the yard from the cemetery.

The condition of the small graveyard was more disheartening than the other transformations he had noted which alleged progress had wrought on this poor town. Weeds, neglected grass, and wild flowers had repossessed the land. Private plots were indistinguishable, as were individual graves. The smaller headstones were overgrown. Only the commanding tombstones in the very center of the graveyard had, so far, prevailed over the ravages of nature. That would be where so many Knights had gone to their final rest. He put down his bag at the edge of the cemetery and labored through the thick vegetation. It reminded him of jungle grass in Vietnam pulling so tenaciously at his legs. Trying to tell him, it seemed, to go back.

Go back.

Probably the wisest thing for him to do right now. Wiser yet never to have come at all. He pushed the tight clumps apart impatiently with his hands and went on.

Two boys burst out of the apple orchard beyond the cemetery, the larger chasing the smaller. He had an armful of apples gathered from the ground under the trees. On the run he pitched one at the small boy. It sailed past his ear and splattered against a headstone.

The captain grinned. He had played that game himself the summer they had visited his mother's sister in Michigan. Fruit rotting on the earth after the growing season provided lethal ammunition for boys' mock battles.

The pursued took refuge behind one of the big headstones in the Knight plot. He successfully avoided a half-dozen volleys before breaking for the parking lot. He made the fence and vaulted it. A clean escape, the captain believed. But, no, he'd judged too soon, as so often he had in Nam. In midair the projectile struck the boy just behind his left ear.

Head bursting like a overripe melon. Human shrapnel of blood and brain and bone.

The captain wiped a hand over his sweaty face and shuddered. So real the illusion. A rotten apple splattering, nothing more. The boy laughing and mopping his head with a handkerchief.

"Just wait, you bastard! I'll get you for that."

He turned his back on them and continued on.

The music from the carrousel in the amusement park carried from the loudspeakers to the graveyard. The music of 1973 was as foreign to him as the new morals and manners and attitudes. This one he recognized from hearing it played over and over again on the jukeboxes in the canteens at Clark Air Base and Travis Field. Some limey rock star who couldn't even speak his Queen's English. It had a haunting quality that fitted his mood, expressed perfectly by the phrase from which its title came:

Alone again . . . naturally. . . .

The marble corner posts, marking off the plot, were submerged in greenery. The brass railings had long since been removed by vandals or souvenir hunters. He had to smile at the manner in which old Cyrus had laid out the plot.

Formal seating arrangements . . .

He inspected the two imposing headstones at the head of the plot, read the brass plaques:

Cyrus.

Emma.

And around the table.

William.

Jeanine.

Nathaniel.

Looking back over the years,
And whatever else that appears,
I remember I cried when my father died,
Never wishing to hide the tears.
And at 65 years old, my mother God, rest her soul,
Couldn't understand why the only man she had ever loved had been taken,
Leaving her to stand with a heart so badly broken.

His heart began to pound as he moved on to the grave that had brought him to this alien place. But was it alien really? He dropped to his knees and braced his hands on the top of the stone.

HAM KNIGHT
Born 1905

The date on the right side of the dash was effaced by a glob of apple butter, a wild shot dealt in the boys' fray. The captain reached out to wipe it clean with his hand.

PART 1
Incontinence

Hidden from the road, above and beyond the big white Knight homestead, the little graveyard hung on the steep rocky slope of the wooded mountainside, its pitted marble headstones tilted obliquely to the slanting earth.

About the open grave, the mourners, too, leaned toward the incline like stalks of wheat canting in the wind, black capes and coats flapping against their legs.

The clergyman, in his voluminous blowing vestments, resembled a great black bird with a white satin breast. The reading of the final invocation was a signal to the diggers. They let the ropes play smoothly through their hands and the elegant teakwood coffin sank slowly into the pit.

> *"God of ages who hast made our days few and swift on earth,*
> *Our strength fails like grass. . . .*
> *Lift us above the fret of time and ventures scarce begun*
> *Into Enduring light. . . ."*

Nathaniel Knight and his son, Ham, stood apart from the other mourners at the head of the grave. Husband and son to the woman in the box. Nate, bull-chested and erect at seventy-one. White hair and beard, wild in the wind, gave him the appearance of Michelangelo's God on the Sistine Chapel's vaulted ceiling. Ham, at sixteen, big and broad as his father, more man than many around him, yet inside the man's body a grieving boy torn by the wailing torment he was ashamed to show.

Mama! Mama, don't leave me! Dear God, don't take my mother!

A single sob escaped him as the dirt and pebbles trickled through the minister's bony fingers and rattled on the coffin's lid.

> *"Teach us by death some worthier way of life.*
> *Forsake not the work of Thine own hands. . . .*
> *O Lord in Thee have we trusted.*
> *Let us never be confounded*
> *In Jesus' Name. . . ."*

"Amen."

The mourners chorused it after him.

> *"Amen."*

Ham shook his head, rejecting the awful finality of death. The gravediggers bent now to their spades. The blades bit deep into the loose-piled soil and gravel, working in sluicing seesaw rhythm, first one, then the other, the fill falling onto the thick rock slab that sealed the crypt with a hollow drumming sound.

Ham turned away in panic as tears, just one or two, scalded his eyelids. The dam of his composure was crumbling. *I mustn't cry! Not in front of him!*

He blinked to clear his vision and was startled to find himself watched by a young woman standing between two unmarked graves in an adjacent plot. Her pale blond hair fell long and straight across her shoulders. Her eyes were green and inquisitive as a cat's eyes. Her features were small and agreeable, helped by a well-shaped head and fine bone structure well defined beneath the taut, lean flesh of her face. Her skin was very white, with a milky sheen about it that made her appear fragile. But below the tapered column of her neck, her form was all of this earth. Her breasts full, her hips and thighs molding the thin cotton of her skirt.

Ham could not make up his mind whether or not she was pretty. One thing she was not was *ordinary,* he decided. What she was most was *disturbing.* He thought she must be very young, maybe a little older than himself, yet there was a quality, wise and worldly, in her expression that insinuated age and experience. She accepted his appraisal of her with a candor rare in the shy, timid girls of the region.

The stern voice of his father called his attention back to the steadily filling grave. "This is no time or place to be making eyes at a female, Ham."

Hot needles jabbed the boy's cheeks. "I wasn't, Paw. It's just that she's strange about these parts."

Nate glanced over his thick shoulder at the girl. She was walking along the perimeter of the seedy burial plot, knee-high in weeds and grass, with long measured steps, pacing off its dimensions. Head down and very solemn.

"That's Tom Hill's plot," Nate said. "He quit the quarry ten years back to work in one of them brick kilns downriver. Not long after, they shipped his body back here to be buried beside his wife. Tom had one child, a girl, I think. Her name was Callie. That could be her. About eighteen or nineteen years old she'd be now."

There was a swell of voices around the new grave as a huge blackbird swooped down from a nearby treetop and settled on the headstone. A digger flicked dirt at it with his shovel and the bird hurtled into flight again. It flew in a tight ascending spiral above the grave until it was a speck against the sky and finally passed from sight.

It was only proper that the Knightsville Cemetery should lie close by the home of the village's founder. Two acres, squared away on the sides, bequeathed as public land in 1863 by Cyrus Walton Knight along with the inviolable right of access by way of an uneven, rutted oxcart trail that seed-and-sawed back across the thickly treed face of the mountain to the rock quarry at the summit. The graveyard was contained within the vast Knight acreage, stretching east and west, as Knight's Road ran, to the village limits and miles beyond; south to the Hudson River; and north across the thorny spine of the mountain defined against the puffs of white cloud that appeared to catch on its jaggedness like balls of cotton.

"My cemetery," Cyrus Knight liked to say. And he was accurate. He owned the slate quarry on top of the mountain. He owned the property on which sat the self-built shacks of the workers he had brought in to dig the slate. He owned the general store in the village. He owned the ground on which the villagers had built the Presbyterian church with materials supplied by Cyrus. In all but a strictly legal sense he owned the men and women and children of Knightsville for as long as they drew breath, and when the spirit had departed, their mortal shells were remanded to the earth in the two-acre sanctuary on Knight land, in sight of Cyrus's bedroom window. *My cemetery.*

One hundred years after Cyrus Knight founded Knightsville the village's population was recorded at the county seat as 321, just 150 more than it had stood when the output of the quarry was at its peak.

By the end of World War I there were more farmers in Knightsville than there were slate workers. They were the wise ones who saved enough of the fair wages paid by Cyrus to buy seed and livestock and quit the quarry before the fine stone dust had calcified their lungs. And later, when the demand for slate declined, layoffs forced many others to eke a living out of the good loamy soil along the river.

The invention of the asbestos shingle, light, durable, and cheap, had killed the mass market for slate. In no sense, however, did it mean catastrophe for the quarry owners. Smaller work crews continued to dig high-quality slate for sale at premium prices to the luxury trade, who would no more think of roofing their town houses and country estates with asbestos than they would think of buying ready-made apparel in a department store.

Still, it meant less work and responsibility for quarry owners. Inactivity did not suit Nathaniel, heir to Cyrus Knight's curtailed slate empire.

"I was not cut out to be a landlord and a bookkeeper," he told his sister, Jean.

Following the example of so many of his former workers, Nathaniel cultivated a section of Knight acreage along the river, built a barn and silo, and bought some livestock.

Even before the world war, the Knightsville graveyard had become a local landmark, attracting the historically curious from the big tourist resorts of Lake George, Ticonderoga, and Saratoga to view its crazy-quilt burial plots laid out amidst rustic disorder with the high grass and weeds lashing in the wind at the ancient markers and headstones bent strangely to the slope of the mountain. But it was a place to be visited only in the bright light of day. Its quaintness and charm dissipated fast when twilight cast the long blue shadows of the forest across the graves, and evening touched the pleasant coolness of the glade with a damp, bone-deep chill that moved the mind to brood on human mortality and quickened the imaginations and footsteps of passing schoolboys.

The sole untrue tone in the little graveyard was the Knight family plot, a large rectangular area, in the center of the cemetery, planted with thick close-cropped fescue lawn grass and segregated from the smaller untidy plots about it by a low rail barrier of age-weathered brass supported by squat marble stanchions on each corner of the plot.

The inspiration to provide the village of Knightsville with a cemetery had come to Cyrus in the summer of 1863, when he was notified by the United States War Department that his oldest son, Will, had been killed at the Battle of Gettysburg. Accompanied by thirteen-year-old Nate, his second son, Cyrus traveled by train and horse-drawn wagon to the military cemetery where the army had buried Will. With the permission of the government he exhumed the body and conveyed it, packed in ice, back to Knightsville. Will Knight became the first tenant of the graveyard.

The Knightsville Cemetery had, literally, grown around the single grave of Will Knight in the shady clearing behind the big white house. Within one week after Will's burial, Cyrus had leveled, cleared, and fenced in his own plot and erected headstones for all the living members of his family, with the date of birth engraved on each one, then a chip of a dash, and alongside that a questioning blank that carried with it an impending sense of doom.

"I never go anywhere without making reservations," Cyrus explained to his wife and son and daughter with dry humor that escaped them. "Mother and I will lie at the head of the plot. Will's at my left. . . ." He looked at his daughter. "Jean, you'll lie beside Will . . . and you, Nate, you'll lie on the other side at the foot of your mother's grave." He smiled with inner satisfaction. "By my reckoning there's room enough for seven or eight more next to you children to accommodate your own families."

The Knight family burial plot had been laid out by Cyrus in the style of formal seating arrangements at a supper table. At the "head" of the plot, on the high mountain side, there rested a huge block of the finest Vermont marble—its high furbish waning and pocking with every passing year—with a thick slab of high-quality Knight slate fixed to its smooth top surface. Inlaid in the slate were two brass plaques, side by side:

CYRUS WALTON KNIGHT
1798 – 1880

EMMA WILEY KNIGHT
1810 – 1866

Strong, unaffected, enduring, no maudlin trivialities.

Will's grave was the first one on the east side of the plot, at right angles to the graves Cyrus had chosen for himself and his wife. A plain upright block of marble bore the inscription:

WILLIAM WALTERS KNIGHT
1847 – 1863

Emma Knight was laid to rest just three years after her oldest son.

Cyrus, invalided at eighty-two, by the fine quarry dust, died in his rocking chair at a window overlooking the graveyard on Halloween of 1880.

The fourth Knight to take her appointed place in the family plot was Jean. Jean had married the manager of the village general store, Burt Lampbert, and had borne him one son, then had bled to death in the wracking delivery of their second son, stillborn.

JEANINE RUTH KNIGHT
1840 – 1885

Burt Lampbert had protested the usage of her maiden name on the headstone. "She's my wife, ain't she? It should read Jeanine Ruth Knight Lampbert."

Nathaniel Morton Knight, thirty-five, unmarried, sole survivor of the Knight clan, sole heir to the name of Knight and all its legacies, looked at his brother-in-law with shock and disapproval.

"The stone was written that way over twenty years back. It's the way our father wanted it."

Lampbert, a mild man who had escaped from the quarry to the easy job of managing the company store because of his alliance with Cyrus's only daughter, could only say again, "But she bears my name now. She's a Lampbert."

Nate regarded him with indifference. "Then buy your own plot and your own stone."

Jean was buried beneath the Knight headstone. Burt Lampbert remained on as the store manager until 1898, when he fell out of a rowboat into the Hudson River on a midnight eel hunt and was never heard of again. He was presumed dead, although his corpse was never recovered.

It was the same year that Nate married Amanda White, the new grade school teacher from Albany Teachers' College.

"I'm sorry about Burt," Nate told his bride, frankly but not with malice. "Still, I guess it's just as well this way. It'd seem peculiar as the devil to put up a Lampbert headstone in the Knight burial plot."

Amanda White Knight could never be quite certain in later years, but she came to believe that her disillusionment with life and her marriage had begun with Burt Lampbert's drowning. Not that she felt any grief for Burt, who was, after all, a stranger. The grief she felt was for Nathaniel and for all the Knights who had come before him and for all the Knights who would come after him. Their tragic opaqueness. And mostly she grieved for herself.

It did not redeem Nate with Amanda when, after Burt's death, he bestowed the managership of the company store on his nephew, Alva—Burt and Jean's only child—an old-mannish youth of twenty years with a receding hairline and a stooped back.

"Noblesse oblige," she said with a smile when he told her of his new appointment.

Nate frowned. "And what may that mean, ma'am?"

Her thin white face, framed by ponderous strands of char-black hair, showed rare color. Her pale-blue eyes absorbed the dim candlelight like perfectly facated gems and dazzled him with their unnatural brilliance.

"Bones to the serfs," she said. "That's all any of these people mean to you, isn't it, Nathaniel! They're your serfs. You own them."

Maned and thickly bearded, he towered over her frail form, not quite amused, not quite piqued, yet bound to tolerance. He placed on her thinly fleshed shoulders hands that could each lift a hundred-pound slash of quarry rock, yet his touch was as gentle as a woman's touch.

"No," he said softly, "*I* don't own them. The Knights own them. All of the Knights, my father, me, my sons, their sons, all of our descendants through eternity. Just as they own everything else in this village, Knightsville, the name says it."

She glanced out the kitchen window past the yard, at the graveyard where the tombstones were huddled phantoms in the moonlight.

"Knightsville," she said and shuddered. "To be possessed by a name, how horrible." Her eyes were suddenly bottomless. "Even you and I, Nathaniel. We are possessed maybe even more than the others."

Despite the opposition of her husband, Amanda stayed at her job as teacher of Knightsville Grammar School for six years after she was married. It was a formidable task just to maintain order in the one-room schoolhouse crowded with sixty-odd boys and girls, ages five to sixteen. The challenge of simultaneously teaching grades one through six was a contrapuntal feat beyond the ability and endurance of the average instructor.

In the fall of 1904, Nate's indulgence ended. "You start this term," he warned her, "and I'll drag you out of that abominable schoolhouse by the hair. I vow it, I'll keep you locked in your room if need be."

She reasoned with him. "Nathaniel, I can't leave without a term's notice. It will be that long at least before they find a replacement. It isn't easy to get teachers to come to a place like this."

There was a bite of resentment in Nate's voice. "What's wrong with Knightsville?"

She sighed. "Among other things, it's too far in the backwoods. Then there's the job itself. Teaching in the city is half the work and twice the pay."

Nate scowled. "No matter, you're quitting now. Let the blasted school close down until they get another teacher."

Her eyes came alive now, as they did only when she was feeling intense emotion. "That's not fair, Nathaniel! This school has been closed too many times. Most of the children are two or more grades behind their age level. If they fall back any further, they'll just give up."

"Let them," he said. "All they need to know is how to dig slate, man a plow, and beget children."

The pale eyes on him were now bright with sly satisfaction. "Now there's a thing you can't be taught in school or anywhere else, is it, Nathaniel? How to beget children!"

His face betrayed nothing, but across the knuckles of his clenched fists the flesh drew taut white, and his careful voice had the brittle tone of untempered glass.

"It has always been that way with the Knights. My father was forty-one when my mother conceived her first."

"But you're fifty-four, Nathaniel."

He held up his hands and stared at them, thickly corded, veined, the callused skin the color and texture of oak bark. The whole man solid and unyielding as oak.

"If you'd stay at home like other women and concern yourself with wifely tasks, you'd fast conceive like one," he said finally. Curiously the anger and determination appeared to have deserted him. "You give your notice to the county now and stay on for one more term." He repeated it firmly. "One more term."

"Thank you, Nathan—" Before she could finish he showed her his back and left the room.

The schoolhouse was a rectangular clapboard building, painted white, with a small belfry on the peak over the front door. At precisely fifteen minutes before the hour of nine, every weekday morning, Amanda Knight would toll the bell that summoned the young of Knightsville to classes, tugging at the bell cord, which hung down inside the schoolroom through a hole in the roof, until her arms ached.

The students who had advanced beyond the sixth form had to walk five miles, each way, to Clinton, downriver, where there was an elementary school with all eight grades, as well as a high school.

The Knightsville school, if ill equipped with textbooks and slates, was well built and soundly calked. In winter, when temperatures fell to thirty below zero and snow and wind shrieked about the eaves like demons seeking entrance, it was more comfortable in the schoolhouse than in most homes in the village. The big potbellied iron coal stove that stood on dwarfed legs in the center of the room, abetted by the body heat of the students, successfully kept at bay the chill drafts dispersed from walls and windows that were icy to the touch.

At the turn of the century, every dwelling in the village had an outhouse on its lot, and the schoolhouse was no exception. The school outhouse was situated almost a hundred feet back in the woods. The uncommon separation was disadvantageous in wintertime, when the students would resist the call of nature to the point of torture rather than make the long bitter walk to the "icebox" as it was appropriately named. However, near the end of the school year, with the arrival of the first hot weather in May and June, teacher and students alike were ready to admit that perhaps the outhouse should have been built back even farther in the woods.

The school "lavatory," as Amanda insisted her students refer to it, was a crude shack with a wooden partition in the middle, one side for "Boys," the other for "Girls."

There was a single small window in the back of each section. Some years earlier the girl's window had been painted black after repeated complaints that the boys were "peeking." But the paint did not affect the determination of the boys one whit. The walls on the girls' side of the shack were a riddle of peepholes, which successive classes of equally determined girls had plugged up with gum, tar, and other fillers.

The 1904 term was just two weeks old, and Indian summer had smothered the promise of early crisp September days with a blanket of moist, sweltering air that lay motionless in the gorge of the Hudson River and lingered in the pockets of every valley like pools of stagnant water.

It was noon recess, Friday, and Amanda sat at her desk biting tiny unenthusiastic mouthfuls from a chicken sandwich, grateful that the school week was nearly over. With few exceptions, the students walked home at lunchtime, leaving the teacher one hour of delicious solitude. Amanda took advantage of the time to correct test papers and homework while she ate her lunch, every day a sandwich, sometimes with a piece of fruit.

She looked up from a poor composition with slight irritation as a girl came running into the schoolroom with a heavy stomping of her feet on the bare boards. Amanda glanced at the wall clock and saw that fewer than thirty minutes of the lunch recess had passed.

"You're back early, Lizzy," she said more sharply than she had intended.

Lizzy Williams was a fat, clumsy child of ten with a round piggish face and stringy blond hair. She slammed her body into the front of Amanda's desk with a force that almost upset the inkwell.

"Mrs. Knight!" she exclaimed. "There's a boy in the outhouse and he's made a hole in the partition so's he can look into the girls' toilet."

Amanda leaned back in her chair and exhaled dispiritedly. Another minor crisis. "Who is the boy?"

"I don't know." Lizzy was breathless. "But I saw his eye through the peephole when I was in there. . . . It's a good thing I saw him before I went," she said with outraged primness that made Amanda want to smile. "But that's not all," the girl went on in haste, "Betty Lou Edwards is in there now! I told her there was a boy watching, but she just laughed and pulled down her pants anyway."

Amanda was thoroughly annoyed now. She sprang up out of the chair, her body tense. "You stay here, Lizzy. I'll attend to this." She walked to the door with a purposeful mannish stride.

Betty Lou Edwards was one of the brightest girls in the sixth grade. At fourteen, she should have been doing eighth-grade work and was bored and sulky with her present studies. She was dark and pretty, with a fully developed woman's body, which, to Amanda's constant apprehension, was too bountifully displayed in the short little-girl frocks she wore to school. There were boys in the sixth grade as old as sixteen.

If what Lizzy had told her was true, Betty Lou was even more precocious than Amanda had imagined. She hurried along the path to the outhouse, her footsteps muffled by the thick carpet of pine needles and forest duff layered over the earth. The pathway curled left and right among the trees, and the outhouse did not come into view until she was almost on top of it. Amanda was relieved to see that the door marked "Boys" was standing wide open, the cubicle behind it empty. Whoever the boy had been, he was gone now, she thought. If, indeed, there had been any boy at all! The capacity for invention was extravagant in the imagination of adolescent girls. She was curious to see for herself this peephole Lizzy had described.

Amanda stepped into the boys' toilet and squinted in the dim light at the partition. She was mildly surprised to note that there was a hole, a sizable hole gouged out of one board with a knife or other sharp implement, at a height of about three feet off the floor.

Without even thinking about it, motivated by nothing more than the reflex that pulls the human eye to any small aperture, she bent over and peered into the hole in the partition. At first she could distinguish nothing in the dim interior of the girls' toilet, and she decided with some amusement that boys who constructed such peepholes must gain little else but eyestrain for their efforts.

Then just as she was about to withdraw her eye from the hole, she became vaguely aware of shape and movement. The booth, she realized with gradually accommodating vision, was not as dark as first she had supposed. Pencil rays of light filtered in from underneath the door and through the seams where the boards were joined. She could see things quite distinctly now. And what she saw shocked her more than anything she had ever seen before or would ever see again.

Framed in the small aperture were two forms, male and female, visible from waist to knee. Naked from waist to knee. The girl's dress bunched up about her hips. The boy's trousers in a heap on the floor. There was no sound at all on the other side of the partition. No movement beyond the slow, sensuous pantomine of disembodied hands, searching, discovering, caressing. Amanda watched with the same helpless fascination she had experienced as a five-year-old child witnessing a magic lantern show for the first time. She could not turn away, or even shut her eyes against the ritual being performed in the girls' toilet.

The girl's hand closed on the boy's upright phallus. *Boy? No boy, a man!* He seemed grotesquely enormous to Amanda. It was the only time she had ever seen a male like this, doing this. Never once in six years of marriage had she ever seen Nathaniel without his trousers or shirt. Connubial rites were always performed in the dark, under bedclothes and voluminous sleeping apparel.

With her back braced against the closed door, the girl drew the boy toward her and guided him gently between her spread thighs.

Amanda wrenched her head to one side, rose up, and walked to the open doorway. Sunlight caught her full in the face, blinding her. She stood there swaying giddily, with her hands braced on each side of the jamb, and after a few moments she was able to go back down the path to the schoolhouse. Her fingers and her toes were numb, as was the skin directly below and above her lips.

That night, as was his custom on Fridays, Nathaniel

reached for her in the big double bed as soon as the oil lamp was out. Unexpectedly and with terrifying clarity, her mind's eye re-created the scene she had witnessed in the outhouse that afternoon. The hot young limbs, the disembodied hands, the remarkable tumescence of the male.

Not quite comprehending what was happening to her, or why it was happening, Amanda had a sensation of wonderful weightlessness. Her body was soaring up, up, up through strata of air currents like a toy balloon, through the heavens, reaching for the hot gaseous ball of the sun. Its great storms of fire were licking at her now. And, at last, she was vaporized in the white molten core.

"Nathaniel!" she cried out and arched her hips to meet his thrust with vigor equal to his own.

Nine months later, to the day, Amanda Knight gave Nate the only child she would ever give him. They named him Ham Cyrus Knight to honor his grandfather and great-grandfather.

Ham was two days past his sixteenth birthday when Amanda was buried, one of the many thousands of victims who perished of influenza in the years after World War I.

The month of June was damp and cool with frequent squalls, and mist covered the river from dusk to dawn, even on the fair days. On the Sunday after Amanda's burial, the wind blew up with such violence that it flung the shaggy crowns of hundred-year-old oaks back and forth with the ease with which a dog would shake a rat.

In the afternoon, Ham lit a match to the birch logs in the mammoth parlor fireplace, and he and Nate brought up to date the account books, calculating outlay and income of the varied holdings, matters that had gone neglected in the grim final days of Amanda's illness. When at last the work was done, Nate lit his pipe and walked up and down before the hearth, his idle stare drawn to the red and blue and orange points of flame.

"The quarry practically runs itself, so we're all right on that account. But the farm . . ." He shook his grizzled head. "The hay should have been cut weeks back. The east meadow's already sprouting seed. And that early corn, before this week is out it'll be ripe for picking."

"Don't worry, Paw," Ham said. "You can count on me full-time in one more week. Summer vacation."

Nate stopped before the ancient wooden tote chair where

Ham sat, legs spraddled, elbows resting on his knees.

"The end of school," Nate said.

The Knightsville school had added six more rooms and had a teacher for each grade from one through six, though it had no indoor plumbing, just a larger outhouse on the hillside. Ham Knight was a straight-A student at Clinton High. He had inherited his mother's love of learning, as well as her dark, unruly hair and pale-blue eyes.

Ham looked up at his father. "That's what I said. School is out next week."

Nate combed at his beard with thick fingers. "That's not quite what I meant, son. You'll be leaving school for good this term."

"No!" Ham bounded to his feet. "Why should I quit, Paw? Only one more year to go and then I'm finished."

"Oh, yes, and what of all the talk you and your mother made of college?"

"That was Maw's wish," Ham said defensively. "What's wrong with college?"

"There!" Nate flung his huge hands, spread wide, into the air and said with triumph, "That all depends. Your mother could never see things in their proper light. College may be right for some, but not for you, Ham."

"But why?" There were sparks in the boy's eyes, like sunlight playing on a pool of deep, still water.

"Because your life, your destiny is here, in this town that bears your name. Knightsville, Ham, it's yours, all of it. Or at least it will be when I die. The quarry, the farm, the land 'most all the others farm, that's yours too."

"You're wrong," Ham said with bitter sadness. "None of it belongs to me. I belong to *it!* The same way you do and Maw did, and—and—" He faltered under the old man's angry gaze.

"That's a fancy way to speak of 'responsibility,' " Nate said in an even voice. "And your responsibility, like mine, is to this town we Knights raised out of the wilderness."

There was no appeal to reason in this house, for the only truths were those of family precedence. Ham vied to gain just one small concession.

"Let me finish high school anyway, Paw. Please! It's only one more year. It's not as though you needed me here. You can hire all the hands you need to work the farm. Same as in the quarry."

Nate, eye to eye with his son, dropped both hands on his shoulders. "Ham, I don't want you here to save the wages of a hired man. Money is the least of it. Boy, look at me. I'm seventy-one years old. How much longer will I be on earth to manage all this for you? Ten years maybe? Maybe ten days? Who knows? No, you're needed here to learn. There's much to learn and no more time to frit away on schooling. That's for those who would be lawyers and doctors and bankers. Look, boy, if you want to read books that's fine for leisure time. Sundays and such. But those things which our name stands for, they must come first. You understand?"

Ham's shoulders were as broad as the old man's and sheathed with hard muscle, but his father's hands weighed on them as ponderous as stone. He imagined that unless he shook them off, those hands, he would be crushed beneath them, a shapeless blob of flesh smeared on the hard oak floor.

"I'll do what you want, Paw," he said in resignation.

"Good boy." Old Nate was elated. He loosed his hold and rubbed his palms together, the sound like sandpaper scraping sandpaper. "I'd say one step toward manhood deserves another. You'll take a drink with me, Ham."

The ratification of the Eighteenth Amendment to the Constitution, two years before, prohibiting the sale and manufacture of alcoholic beverages in the United States, had caused less stir in Knightsville than it had in foreign lands. The natives had never done much trade in store-bought liquor. Homemade applejack and corn whiskey had been the region's pride for generations.

Ham, wearily, trailed his father into the spacious kitchen. The surfaces of the ancient iron range, which had always shone like gunmetal, were dull and crusty from days of inattention.

"We need a housekeeper here now that your mother's gone," Nate said. He fetched a stone jug in from the pantry and sat two tumblers on the table, half filling both.

Ham lifted his without savor. The taste of apple liquor, green as turpentine, had brought the bitter taste of vomit to the back of his throat the few times he had sipped it secretly with boys behind the barn.

Nate offered a pretentious toast: "To the memory of my dear departed wife, God rest her soul, and to the future of my only and beloved son."

Embarrassed, Ham looked past his father through the window that overlooked the graveyard. He set the glass down hard, untouched, and said with curiosity, "Paw, she's there again, that girl."

Nate's face was stern as he moved to the window. "Well, I'll be damned!"

To hear his father curse astounded Ham. The Holy Bible and all its prescriptions and prohibitions were a way of life to Nate, inviolable. He would as soon perform a capital crime as take the Lord's name in vain or even utter lesser blasphemies. The provocation had to be extreme, and Ham was nervous.

The blond stranger he had first seen at Tom Hill's grave on the day his mother was buried was sitting, of all places, on the marble monument that marked the graves of Cyrus Knight and his wife. Sitting there with her long legs dangling, crossed at the ankles, while she turned the pages of a thick book.

Nate tipped his head back, swallowed the apple whiskey in a single gulp, then hurled the empty glass into a corner. The crystal fragments decorated the floorboards like chips of ice. He stomped loudly to the back door.

"We'll take care of that wench right now. Come Ham!"

Ham's breath came hard and his heart swelled in his chest as he stumbled across the yard behind his father. The girl saw them as they stepped across the low hedge that divorced the cemetery from Knight property, and Ham prayed that she would run. But she never moved at all, just shut the book and smiled as they approached. He saw her teeth were small and white and not too even, the dog teeth somewhat long and pointed. In the wind, the tendrils of her long blond hair curled and lashed about her face and neck.

When Nate stepped over the tarnished rail into the Knight plot, she left the marble block with feline grace. Her short skirt drew far up on her thighs, revealing for a moment more woman's limbs than Ham had ever seen before.

"Good day," she said, her voice less high and nasal than the speech natural to the women of this back country.

She stood erect with her arms folding the big book to her body, pushing it up against her breasts. The thrust of her breasts within the bodice of the wool knit dress awed Ham. A sight that came quite commonly, of late, in shameful dreams, but which he'd never hoped to see in wakefulness. Ham was fearful that his body would betray his carnality.

Hot-faced, he compelled his attention to the fresh grave

of his mother, and the tortured memory of her cold, dear form imprisoned in the earth to rot was an instant antidote for the living flesh that had begun to obsess him more and more.

The sound of his father's voice fell startlingly on his ears. Gruff, but not the expected thunderclap the girl's misdeed would seem to warrant.

"What's your business here, miss?"

Her green eyes reached scarcely to the level of his chest, but showed no fear. "Why, I came to visit my father's grave," she said.

Nate grunted and placed his fists like mallets on his hips. "You're in the wrong plot, then. And defiling the graves of my kin."

A faint ridge of vexation marked her brow. "You're cross because I sat here reading?" She touched the block of marble. "Do you really think the dead care so?"

"It's I who care," said Nate, but his censure was no longer cogent. He seemed uncertain of himself standing there with his beard and shaggy hair all lively in the wind.

The girl laughed unexpectedly, the sound of it carrying light and trilling in the air. "You could be Lear."

The old man frowned. "Lear, who is that? You're impudent, miss!"

"No, no!" she said. "King Lear." She held up the heavy volume for him to see. "A character in a play. A noble man, a king."

Nate and his son saw the title: *The Complete Works of William Shakespeare.*

"Have you never heard of William Shakespeare?" she asked.

"I have, in school," Ham said quickly. "I've read *King Lear.*"

"There now!" she said to Nate. "Ask him. He'll tell you I was paying you a compliment."

"I'm not much one for reading," said Nate with some uneasiness. "Just the Good Book. I read that."

Her laughter was thin, reedy, without substance, evaporating like smoke in the turbulent air, not fitting with her voice at all, Ham thought.

"The Good Book," she said, holding the Shakespeare against her breasts again. "I read this, the *Best Book.*"

"You are a blasphemous girl," Nate said.

Her eyes turned down upon the ground. "I'm sorry," she said quietly. "I don't mean to give offense. It's just that this is the only book I've ever owned . . . the only thing I've ever owned"—she looked around at the forlorn burial plot where Tom Hill rested—"except this patch of earth."

"You mean the burial plot?" This strange female confused Nate.

Her eyes were dull and opaque now. "My father gave me the book when he died, and the deed to the plot. The people at the orphanage handed it over to me when they turned me loose last month."

Pain caught like a burr in Ham's throat. With the sure irrationality of adolescence, he knew all the hurt and sorrow she had been afflicted with since birth. He knew he loved her.

Nate was not unmoved himself. "You're all alone," he said in as soft a tone as Ham had ever heard him speak.

"Alone," she said.

"You must live someplace, with someone, a young girl like you."

"I live alone. A room in Clinton. There was no place else to go when I left the orphanage, so I came back here. My only roots, the moldy bones planted in that plot of earth."

Nate shook his head uncomprehendingly. "Devotion to the memory of our dead is not common these days. You're to be admired for that."

"Oh no," she said, surprised, "that's not it at all. It was the piece of earth that drew me back. It's mine! True, it's small, but my own. The only tie I have to this poor planet." Her gaze was locked with Nate's. "*Nothing can we call our own but death, and that small model of the barren earth, which serves as paste and cover to our bones.*" Mischievously she amended. "The words of a king, would you believe it!"

"From your book, no doubt," Nate said. And his craggy face assumed the closest semblance of a smile that Ham had seen since the onset of his mother's illness—before that, even. Ham saw something else in his father's expression that he had never seen in all his remembrance: the way he was attentive to the youthful body underneath the wind-whipped skirt.

"I mean no disrespect to my father, lying there," she said. "He did as well as he was able, for one who lacked so many things that make a man a man. He gave me this at least." She stroked the cover of her book. "It's been father, mother, teacher, protector, friend for as long as I can remember."

Nate inclined his head toward the unseemly little plot. "But that handful of earth means more?"

"Oh, yes," she agreed solemnly. "You have to possess a piece, no matter how insignificant, of the earth to justify your presence on it." She laughed again. "Without that land, I'd fly off into space a puff of vapor."

"You're a strange girl, Callie Hill," Nate mused.

"You know my name," she said. "It's a strange name. My father gave it to me. Caliban."

"Caliban?" he said with distaste. "That's no name for a girl. No name at all."

"It is no name," she said, not offended. "It's a phantom, fairy, hobgoblin of the imagination. No matter, my friends call me Callie."

Nate cleared his throat and said with a cordiality and formality that Ham found both out of character and outlandish in the graveyard setting. "Miss Callie, I'm Nathaniel Knight, and this is my son, Ham. We're pleased to make your acquaintance."

She studied Ham, biting her lower lip with the two pointed teeth at the corners of her mouth. Not a grin, but a hint of impish amusement.

"Is that short for Hamlet?" she asked soberly.

"Hamlet!" Nate was amused. "That sounds like one of those queer ones from your book too."

Ham was overcome with humiliation, powerless to check the rush of blood to his cheeks. "Just Ham," he said savagely, all the love he had felt for her transformed to hate.

"*That's* from the Good Book," Nate said, pleased at his own little joke. Then to Ham's astonishment, he went on, "Miss Callie, Ham and I would be honored if you visited with us. Maybe you could brew us up a pot of good coffee." He directed his eyes to the freshly turned soil of Amanda's grave, planted with geraniums and pansies. "The boy and I have been helpless in the kitchen since my wife passed away."

The girl regarded the grave in solemnity, one slender hand lifting to her throat. Long fingers stroked a pale-blue pulsing vein. Ham looked away as she spoke: "*Death is a fearful thing. . . . To die, and go we know not where . . .*" Impulsively she clutched Nate's arm. "I make good coffee. Or so they tell me at the eating place where I wait on tables in Clinton."

"You're a waitress!" It was difficult to tell whether the old man was shocked more by her announcement or by the touch of her young, soft hands on the knot-tough muscle of his forearm.

Ham trailed behind them, outraged, outcast, troubled by her ambiguity. She was barely more a woman than he was a man, yet she had won his father's favor as an equal, and all the while Ham sensed, in some dark niche of the mind, that his father's wisdom was less than his and that she was wiser than either of them would ever be, than any man would ever be.

Nate waved his hand at the dirty pans and dishes cluttering sink and drainboard. "We're not good housekeepers, Ham and I. There's clean cups in the cupboard still."

She laughed. "We'll leave them there and clean up this disorder. The coffee will taste better without the dismal view."

"I aim to find a housekeeper very soon," Nate said. "There's plenty women in the village could use some extra money for part-time work."

The girl pushed up the sleeves of the dress above her elbows and walked to the sink. "A house this size, you should have a woman here full-time." She dropped her hands upon the twin water taps. "Running water, hot and cold," she said with satisfaction. "The only house in Knightsville with such convenience, I'll bet."

"You're right," Nate told her proudly. "And indoor plumbing, and a coal furnace in the cellar." He rapped hard knuckles against a grilled opening in one wall. "Big pipes, ducts they call 'em, carry hot air from the furnace to every room and out these registers. Like magic, isn't it?"

Ham was irritated with his father. "In big towns all the houses have central heating. It's nothing special."

"In Knightsville, it's special," Nate said, unperturbed. He corked the jug of whiskey, still standing on the table, and carried it back into the pantry.

While she waited for the sink to fill with steaming water, Callie Hill frowned at the glass splintered in the corner where Nate had hurled it. "I'll get to that mess when I'm done with these."

Ham protested. "No, that isn't right. It's not your work."

"Let her be," said Nate, emerging from the pantry. "I like

to see a woman toiling in a kitchen. It's right somehow."

Callie took a knife and sliced thin curls from a block of yellow lye soap that looked like cheese into the filling sink. "You need a woman here full-time," she said again.

Nate turned a chair from the table and sat down astride the wicker seat, resting his heavy arms on its high back. His eyes were fixed on her intently, bright beneath their thick white hoods. "You want the job?" he asked.

She kept on slicing soap. Ham felt a choking fullness in his throat. It had to be a joke. Yet, he knew, his father never joked.

"What do they pay you in that restaurant?" Nate asked.

"Ten dollars a week and meals," she said. She laid the knife and soap aside and faced him. Her moist red bottom lip was pinched between her pointed teeth. An unbecoming habit, Ham decided, it made her look like an animal.

"Fifty dollars a month and room and board," Nate said quickly. "Yes or no, you want the job?"

"I'll take it."

"Why?" Ham asked, perplexed. "The pay's not that much more and the work is far more than you've been used to as a waitress."

"That's so," she said and smiled at Ham. "But taking care of this house will be a joy to me."

"How's that?" Nate scratched his bearded chin.

"My earliest memory of Knightsville as a child is of this house. Big, white, sitting up here on the mountainside, with those two tall pillars on either side of the front door like sentinels, and the windows, all those windows, with their panes glittering gold in the setting sun. On my way to school each day, I'd pass here and think: I wonder what would happen if I walked right up there and knocked on the door?"

Nate laughed with delight, leaning back and slapping the heels of his hands against his knees. "And you thought that if you did an ogre would pull you in and eat you!"

"And it was true! The moment I entered this house I became your prisoner. Your scullery maid, your slave." With a graceful flourish of her hands, she curtsied, bending low and pulling her chin in tight against her breastbone so that her long blond hair tumbled across her shoulders and covered her face. "Your wish is my command, sire."

The counterpoint of her own shrill laughter with the old

man's blustery guffaw was a disturbing cacophony in Ham's ears. A stranger might easily have thought his father was a frivolous man!

Abruptly, she straightened, parted the strands of hair covering her face like a woman peering through a curtain and said puckishly to Ham, "Young man, fetch me an apron. There's work to be done."

"Yes, ma'am," he said before he could prevent it.

They sat at the big round table in the kitchen drinking strong coffee laced with thick yellow cream from fat-lipped mugs.

"It's rich as butter," Callie said, wiping the rim of the cream pitcher with her index finger and licking it with her pink wet tongue.

"You're a cat," Nate said.

She closed her eyes to slits. "I'd like to be a cat."

Nate looked at the darkening windows. "Time to light the lamps," he said.

She watched him touch the match flame to the wick of the oil lamp held in brackets on the wall above the table. "In Clinton 'most everyone has electric lights."

Nate shrugged his shoulders. "The electric company hasn't seen fit to bring their lines in to Knightsville. We lie off the beaten track. It suits me fine, though. I find the light of oil more pleasant."

He turned the wick up high and inspected the newly cleaned kitchen. The drainboard bare and dry. The iron range reflecting the mantle's glow in its shining nickel trim. The floor swept clean. "It's good to have things ordered again," he said. "It's good to have the comfort of a woman's touch around you."

She hefted the big mug in both her hands and looked across the rim at Ham. "I hope I'll please you both."

Ham pushed back his chair and stood up very straight. "Time I milked the cows," he said.

When he was gone, Callie leaned across the table and looked into his cup, three-quarters full. She sighed. "I don't think Ham likes my coffee."

"He's still a boy," Nate said. "He hasn't yet acquired a taste for man's pleasures."

"I see," she said, with an enigmatic smile.

They listened in silence as the grandfather's clock in the parlor commenced its sepulchral chiming.

"Eight o'clock," she reckoned. "I must be on my way. The milk train is the last that stops tonight."

Nate turned his chair and faced her with his hands resting on spread knees. "Why must you leave? You live here now."

"There's loose ends to tie up. I have to get my things, few as they are, in Clinton. Quit my room, my job." She dropped one slender hand upon the table.

He stared at the hand a moment, then covered it with his own large hairy paw. "Stay and cook my supper. Tomorrow's time enough for such petty stuff."

Her hand beneath his clenched and unclenched in time, strangely, with the beating of his heart.

She giggled. It had been fifty years or more since Nate had heard a young girl giggle.

"I have no other clothes but what I'm wearing. Nothing to wear to bed. I'd have to sleep naked or in my slip."

He felt the blush hot on his face, the accelerating blood in pulse and temple. His tongue felt thick and stubby in his mouth. "Upstairs, lots of fine clothing. Nightclothes. My wife's. She was slim like you. A woman who took great pride in her appearance. Everything you need."

Her eyes were wide and innocent. "You think that would be all right? I mean, they are her things. You wouldn't mind?"

"I wouldn't mind." His grip tightened on her hand.

"But her? What would she think?"

"She's dead!" He pressed her hand until she winced.

"Please! You're hurting me!"

He let go of her hand and held his own hand up before his face, staring at it, troubled by it. "I'm sorry. . . . It's just that . . . a woman's touch . . . It's been so long. . . . I'm sorry. . . . Forgive an old man. . . ."

"No!" she whispered. "You're not an old man."

"I'm over seventy," he said, bewildered. "It's been so long since I've felt like this."

"The years don't matter," she said. "It's how a thing is made that counts. That block of marble in the graveyard. This house. These walls, this floor, this table!" She placed both hands flat on the oaken table. "*My age is as a lusty winter.*"

He contemplated his upheld hand, gross, callused, knotted with veins and tendons, brown and stained with slate dust in the half-moon of the nails.

"I am an old man," he said again.

She bent toward him and took the hand in both of hers and drew it to her breast. "You speak about a woman's touch," she said. "Well, touch me!"

With one hand she unfastened the pearl buttons at the front of her dress and slipped it down off her shoulders. She drew down the straps of her slip and pulled his hand against one breast, bent forward so that its bulk nested heavily in his palm.

Nate's eyes were dazed, but his fingers trembled on the breast, then tightened, gently kneading the flesh.

"An old man shouldn't have such thoughts," he said hoarsely.

"An old man, Nathaniel?" Her smile was sweet, her manner gentle and coaxing. One slim hand reached down and undid the buttons on the fly of his trousers. He watched that moving, working hand in fascination, and then in wonder at the miracle it wrought.

"See, Nathaniel?" she said in triumph. "Not an old man. But a man. A man!"

With his hand still upon her breast and her hand still on him, she went to him, lifting her skirt hip-high with her one free hand and straddling his legs with thighs spread wide. She pressed her lips to his right ear. "I know a little of your book, too. . . . *I am the resurrection and the life!*"

It was after ten when Ham climbed the steep back stairs to the upper floor that night. A lamp, turned low, sat on the table in the hall against the wall. He stood a moment, in the silence, looking to the closed door of his father's room. And then with pain to the room across the way, the door ajar, the light within drawing a luminous line upon the floorboards of the hall. The sound of a woman's soft humming behind the door. His mother's room. Nostalgia engulfed Ham. How many nights, hundreds, thousands, had he come up like this to the comfort of his mother's light and presence in that room.

The harsh rasp of melancholy burned like a fiery coal in the tender hollow of his throat and he cried out softly, "*Mama.*" In bleak despair he went inside his room and shut the door and leaned back against it in the darkness with the hot, wet tears on his cheeks.

He lit the lamp on the table by his bed and filled the enamel basin on the washstand, in one corner, from a swan-necked porcelain pitcher. Three years before, Nate had built on to the house an indoor bathroom, with tub and toilet and running water, on the ground floor, just off the kitchen at the foot of the back staircase. Yet the nightly ritual performed at the washstand had never been diverted. A covered chamberpot sat discreetly beneath each bed, too, though it was seldom used except on bitter winter nights when it seemed more expedient than a long trek, made in nightshirt, down the drafty back stairs.

Ham stripped off all his clothing, as was his sleeping habit. Before he climbed into bed, he stood before the dresser mirror and studied with detachment his naked body. Long, muscled arms, full chest, broad shoulders, and flat belly, no hips at all. He started at the tapping at his door.

"Who's there?" he called.

"It's Callie," the girl's voice came back, muffled by the door. "May I come in?"

Her very voice was like a hot caress and with mortification, in the mirror, he watched the physical onset of desire.

"No!" he shouted. "You can't! I'm in bed."

"I heard a sound before as if someone was in distress or pain. Are you all right?"

"Yes, I—" He could not think of how to end it.

"Look, I'm coming in," she said with determination that sent Ham racing for the bed. He cupped a hand above the mantle of the lamp and blew the flame out, then lay down and pulled the thin cotton sheet up to his neck.

The door swung full back on its hinges, and she stood there on the threshold with the lamp in her hand turned up bright. It gave Ham a queer sensation looking at her, a phenomenon of body chemistry that made the short hairs at his neck's nape fur up like the tail hairs of a frightened cat. In the uncertain illumination of the oil light she might have been his mother standing there, long hair hanging straight below her shoulders. She wore one of his mother's fine silk nightgowns, modest in its full cut and high neck and copious folds that brushed the floor.

She came into the room, toward the bed, floating, it

seemed, in the full long gown that hid her moving feet.

"That was you crying out, Ham. I know it was. Are you ill?"

Ham lay rigid, staring at her, his hands clenching the cover tightly to his neck. "I—I, no, it's nothing," he lied. "I was dreaming, that's all. I get bad dreams sometimes."

She bent over the bed and looked into his eyes and smiled. The lamplight shone upon her face bizarrely, misshaping her features with planes of bright and shadow. She looked wicked, wanton, and unreal.

"Can I help in any way, Ham?" Her voice was a whisper. Then she placed a small white hand on one of his rigid legs above the knee.

Through the thin cotton cover he felt its warmth as if she had touched bare flesh. The lamp's flame reflected in her eyes, twin tongues of gold fire.

"No!" he said, drawing up his knees vigorously, shaking off her touch. "I'm tired. Let me be." He rolled onto his side facing away from her and closed his eyes. She didn't speak, nor did he hear her go. But when he opened his eyes again, the room was dark and empty.

The next day Nate took Callie up to the slate quarry through the rutted tunnel in the forest climbing steeply to the mountain's summit. They stood atop the highest prominence, a sheer stone bluff above the mammoth crater it had taken man a hundred years, with pick and chisel, to gouge out of the mountain's obdurate shoulder. In a cranny, at the low mark of the pit, a crystal pool had risen from the seepage of subterranean springs, its unmarred surface in the sunlight gleaming like a polished silver plate.

Nate curved one arm about her back with his hand fastened possessively on her elbow. "That tiny plot of soil you treasure in the graveyard, you speak of roots. Look!" He swung his free arm in an arc from east to west. "As far as you can see, the land is mine. And down below right to the river's edge. It's mine. Does it impress you?"

She upturned her face to his and slyly said, "But I can see beyond the river, *that* land's not yours. Nor is the river."

He laughed with vague uncertainty. "No man 'owns' a river, girl."

"Men control rivers, the term is not important."

"Whatever do you mean?"

"A man controls what's bounded by his land. If the valley on the other side was yours, you would, in fact, own the water that lies between."

He combed his beard with idle fingers. "Now what would I do with a river?"

"Build a bridge across it."

"A bridge?" His booming laughter was flung back to them off the quarry's walls of shale. "And why would I want to build a bridge?" He motioned to the house, large as his own, built on a distant hillside across the river. "To make it more convenient for the Majorses to cross the river when they drive to Cape Cod in their fancy motorcar?"

"That's just the point," she said in all seriousness. "Motorcars and trucks—and the many more there's going to be—heading to and coming from the four points of the compass. They've got to cross the river."

Nate was growing tired of playing silly games with a young girl. "Let them cross the bridge at Clinton, or downriver forty miles, who cares?"

She kept at him stubbornly. "The Clinton bridge was built for horse carts. Besides, the streets that feed it are narrow bottlenecks. Even now, in summer, the cars line up, sometimes two blocks, to cross the river."

"Let them," said Nate. "There's not one motor car in Knightsville. . . . C'mon, we've got to get you on that noon train."

She took his arm as they stepped cautiously down the sloping backside of the bluff, hazardous with its shifting layers of discarded shale.

"They charge a toll for every cart and motorcar that crosses the bridge at Clinton. A silver quarter," she said.

Nate grunted. "It would take a heap of silver to make up the cost of even a small bridge, Callie."

She sighed. "Are the Majorses richer than you? Do they own more land?"

"Thunderation!" Nate was genuinely outraged. "My father was a rich man when Carl Majors's father got off the boat carrying his whole poke wrapped in a red bandanna on the end of a stick."

She watched him from the corners of her eyes. "Did he dig slate too?"

"No," Nate said crossly, "he made mud pies. Bricks, old man Majors made bricks from river clay. They own the kilns down the river. I don't abide with houses built of bricks and with asbestos roofing."

She had the final word. "Nor with motorcars and bridges."

At the bottom of the bluff, he placed his hands on her waist, his fingers nearly spanning its slender girth, and lifted her with ease to the seat of the cart. She smiled when he climbed up beside her and took the reins.

"You're the strongest man I've ever seen, Nathaniel. I feel so safe with you."

He laid a hand upon her knee and said with deep emotion, "You do what you must do fast in Clinton and get right back home, you understand, Callie?"

"Home," she said in a low voice. "Home, how wonderful that sounds."

On December 10, that same year, Nathaniel Knight made Callie Hill his wife. It was her nineteenth birthday.

Pastor Saul Williams, a thin, ascetic-looking man of fifty-eight, officiated at the simple ceremony held in the Presbyterian church. Nathaniel wore a blue serge suit and a shirt with a high starched collar and a blue tie.

"I feel like a bull with a saddle on its back," he complained to Ham before the wedding. And he looked it.

The bride wore a simple black suit with a white ruffled shirtwaist. Above her left breast was pinned a small corsage of mistletoe and holly berries that she had picked and bound herself. Her long hair was drawn tight in a coiled bun behind her neck, its pale hue intense in contrast to the somber motif of her dress. She wore no hat, just a delicate white veil draped over head and face in the fashion of a Spanish mantilla. This nuance invited silent disapproval from the women. She looked much older than her years.

The gathering of witnesses at the church was small, just five aside from Ham. Not one uninvited spectator appeared, not even on the street outside the church. It was the way Nate wanted it, and this was his town.

After the ceremony the guests were asked back to the big house on the hill for a wedding supper whose sumptuousness amazed them. Roast goose, a ham, candied yams, squash and home-baked bread and three varieties of pie—all prepared ahead of time by Callie.

"A woman's wedding day is special," Nate had protested. "She shouldn't have to toil. Let Rena Lampbert attend to supper, she's offered."

"Especially not today," Callie told him lightly. "You know what everyone is thinking, you've married a child. Let today set them right. Callie Hill Knight is a woman, and mistress of her house in all respects."

Nathaniel carved and served the meat at the head of his table, with Callie sitting opposite him at the foot. At Nate's right hand sat Ham. Alongside Ham, Alva Lampbert, Nate's middle-aged nephew, who was village storekeeper and postmaster, thin, round-shouldered, and myopic, his rasping, nervous voice making loud and liberal address to "Uncle Nate" as if to call constant attention to the blood tie. Beside him his stringy wife, Rena, saying little, her sparrow eyes fixed for most of the mealtime on Callie, with envy and resentment.

At Nate's left hand sat Walter Campball, Nate's quarry foreman, a stout jolly man, with coal-black hair at fifty, and a pocked red nose from drinking his homemade applejack for too many of those years. His wife, Susan, at his left, even stouter and jollier than her husband. Old Cyrus Knight had loved Walt Campball as a son, and Walt enjoyed Nate's confidence as did no other man alive. The Campballs had a sixteen-year-old daughter, Lucy, who was not present.

The last member of the party was Carl Majors, the wealthy widower who tenanted the big gray house across the river. His presence at the wedding was a grudging concession made to Callie because the day was hers.

"You must be daft, girl!" Nate had said when first she broached the invitation. "The Majorses are no friends of mine. I've never been in his home, nor he in mine."

"Then it's time that changed," she chided with a narrowing of her eyes. "The two richest men in these parts should be better acquainted."

"I can't see why," Nate said.

She put one small hand on his massive thigh and stroked him boldly, as a wild animal trainer would soothe a restless beast. "And I can't see why not. Just last week I read in the *Clinton Herald* that Carl Majors had signed a big contract for his bricks with the state government at Albany. The buildings his bricks put up should all have Knight slate on their rooftops."

"Thunderation, girl!" Nate bounded to his feet. "Knight slate on monstrosities made of Majors's red brick! My father would sit upright in his grave."

She did not push the matter. "If you think he might not accept the invitation, it might be wiser not to ask him then."

With his white beard and hair all bushy, Nate stalked about the room like an aged, angry lion. "Not accept! Hah! The Majorses have been waiting fifty years for such an opportunity. Few men in this whole state can say they have sat down at a table with the Knights. Hah! He'll accept, don't have any misunderstanding about that!"

She caught her underlip between her teeth. "Well . . . if you think it's all right."

The invitation was delivered to Carl Majors, and he did accept. For Callie his appearance was the high spot of the day. Majors arrived in his big Mercer touring car, its brass headlamps and black enamel chassis waxed and polished for the occasion, the red-painted spokes of the big rubber-tired wheels spinning like gay Fourth of July pinwheels.

Though the first snow of winter lay crisply on the earth and the overcast threatened more, Majors rode bareheaded in the open tonneau, the canvas top folded back into its well behind the rear seat. On the seat itself rested a case of imported French Champagne, an imaginative and welcome gift to Callie's way of thought, and one that titillated the other ladies.

Susan Campball drank it as if it were soft apple cider, and by the time she had finished her third glass, the giggling girlish coquette within that mass of quivering flesh asserted itself. Carl Majors, her dinner partner on the left, bore her elbow nudges and her anecdotes of courtship, honeymoon and marriage with tolerant good humor.

Rena Lampbert, who had sipped suspiciously at her first glass of bubbling wine, was quick to accept a second, and two bright spots, like rouge, were deepening in her pallid cheeks.

Ham's glass stood half-finished at his place, while his father and Walter Campball and Alva Lampbert downed their wine quickly, anxious to be done with it so they could open the hard cider chilling in the pantry.

Of all those present the two who attended to their glasses with most savor were Carl Majors and the bride, speaking with the animation of fast friends at the foot of the table.

Carl Majors was a man of medium height, thickset, with coarsened hands and powerful arms and shoulders that were the heritage of a young manhood spent laboring in his father's kilns. At forty-eight, his light-brown hair was marked by a thin band of gray slanting back from one temple to the crown. His eyes were blue and glazed over with a watery film common to blue eyes of a light shade, which suggested weakness and mild spirit. A deception that hid the true man underneath: a man who had battled and bested bullies in the clay pits at fifteen, usurped from his father and uncle the leadership of family and firm at twenty-five, captained an infantry company in World War I and earned a silver star, and who had been loved by many women. A man who could wear a ridiculous brush of mustache on his upper lip with impunity. A sport who dressed with purpose in loud checkered suits with a four-carat diamond stickpin in his tie and who could stand off and view his own foibles with the same indulgent humor with which he viewed the foibles of others.

He picked up one of several bottles scattered about the table and filled Callie's glass to the brim and then his own.

"I really shouldn't have any more," she said, not meaning it, and he knew she didn't mean it.

"Of course you should," he told her.

Her eyes were mesmerized by the rising bubbles in the wine. "I've never had champagne before."

"It was invented for you, my dear."

Not hearing him, she chanted dreamily, *"Give me some wine; fill full. I drink—"*

"—to the general joy o' the whole table." He finished the couplet for her.

She looked at him with plain delight. "You've read *Macbeth*!"

"Several times. Are you surprised?"

"No more than you are at my reading it!"

He laughed, displaying blunt yellow teeth. "Mrs. Knight, why did you ask me here today?"

She sipped from her glass, not looking at him. "It was Nathaniel's wish."

"I'm sure of that," he said wryly.

She thrust the tip of her pink tongue into the wine like a child reveling in a glass of soda pop. "Why did you come, Mr. Majors?"

He leaned back in his chair. "Why, to see what kind of woman could cause a man of seventy years to forsake the blessed single state."

She smiled into the glass, still not looking at him. "And do you have your answer?"

"I do."

Plump Mrs. Campbell grasped him by the arm and rocked giddily toward him. "I've heard about your exploits with the ladies, Carl Majors. But shame, shame, shame! Trying to turn the head of one a bride mere hours." She winked one eye, set deep in layers of fat, at Callie. "The truth is, dear, I want him for myself."

Callie smiled. "And shame on you, ma'am. You've already got a good man of your own."

The woman laughed hysterically now and, turning to her husband, clouted him mightily on the shoulder so that he nearly lost his seat. "There's no one man good enough, child. You'll find that out in time." She looked across the table at Rena Lampbert. "What do you think, Rena? Is Alva man enough for you?"

Rena Lampbert's blush suffused the high spots of color on her cheekbones from the wine. "I think," she said primly, "that some of us are feeling our drink."

"Well, Miss Prude!" Susan Campball reared like a wounded hippo, all of her chins trembling with menace.

"Rena's right!" Nate shouted from his end of the table. He was bored and restless with the witless talk of stocks and bonds and the up-spiraling market by his nephew and his foreman, neither of whom possessed a single share of any issue. "Too much talk and drink. Now what about our pie and coffee, Mrs. Knight? It's just one hour to our train time."

She smiled in his direction. "I hear you, Mr. Knight."

"Let me," said Rena, rising swiftly. "The bride has done enough today."

Callie rose too. "I'll welcome your assistance, Rena."

"But you don't have to," Rena Lampbert objected. "I'll manage alone."

Callie ignored her, smiling to one and all. "Excuse me, please. This won't take long."

Carl Majors inclined his head toward the table's head. "Nathaniel, I'll drive you to the depot in my car."

Nate was not pleased. "No need to trouble, sir. Ham's got the horses hitched."

"No trouble at all," Majors said. "I must pass through the village. Ham will have his hands full with all this cleaning up. Besides, it will be a thrill for your bride, riding in a motorcar."

Nate glared at Majors from underneath his bushy brows and cleared his throat with a vulgar rattling noise.

"It most certainly will thrill me," Callie said, arriving with a large pie tin balanced deftly on each hand. "A perfect way to begin my honeymoon."

Alva Lampbert addressed Carl Majors across the table, an edge of ridicule in his voice. "Seems to me, Mr. Majors, it would have been a lot simpler for you to come across the river in your boat than go all the way around the mulberry bush with that motorcar."

"I expect you're right, Alva," Majors said pleasantly. "But it wouldn't have been nearly as much fun."

Callie placed the pie tins on the table, apple and mince glazed with pats of melted butter, steam rising from the even rows of knife vents in the brown top crust.

"Just how far is it from your place to Knightsville by car, Mr. Majors?" she asked in a loud voice to capture all attention at the table.

"Let me see," Majors mused. "Four miles of dirt road to the highway. Five more of highway to Clinton. Cross the bridge, then four miles back to the highway on this side. Five miles south again to your cutoff, Knight's Road." He paused to grin at Nate. "You folks have gall to call that abominable cow trail a road, Nate. . . . Then three miles over the bumps and ruts to Knightsville. Now what is that altogether, about twenty-one miles, I guess."

"There," said Alva Lampbert smugly, "you could've boated across the river in five minutes."

"Or motored across in one minute if there was a bridge," Callie said with purpose.

Nate snorted his derision. "That girl is bewitched by bridges, Carl. Know what she schemed up once? She wanted me to buy some of your acreage across the river and a right-of-way to the highway over there, and build a bridge."

"A toll bridge," Callie said.

Majors's veiled eyes examined her with curiosity. "An interesting idea."

"You think so?" Nate laughed. "Tell you what, Carl Majors, I'll sell some land on this side to you and the right-of-way up that abominable cow trail to the highway over here. Then *you* build the bridge!"

The Campballs and Alva Lampbert joined in his laughter.

"That's good," said Alva, "you'd get your name in all the local papers. A sport who puts up his own bridge so's he can cross the river in his motorcar."

When the laughing was done with, Callie said, "There'd be plenty others eager to make the crossing."

"There's something in what she says." Majors aimed his words at Nate. "Beyond our limited horizon here the whole nation is moving into the future on rubber tires. Cars, Nate. The horse is obsolete. That means new highways, thousands, millions of miles of paved road. Our location here is good, a crossroads of the northeast. Right now, a bridge across the river could link the highways, east and west, in just eight miles. Half of the distance it is at Clinton, and without the bottleneck of a heavily trafficked town."

"Bridges, roads, and such are government affairs. If they want to buy my land and build a bridge that's fine with me," Nate said. "If their price is right." He slapped his hands on the white linen cloth before him, stained with wine and gravy and brown sugar from the yams. "Now where's my pie, wife! I'll have the mince!"

The village of Knightsville boasted a single public building two stories high. The bottom floor contained the general store, its tiered shelves, on three walls, advertising canned goods, dry goods, hardware, drugs, and sundries. Beneath the counters, under glass, were meat, dairy foods, and penny candy. A partitioned stall on the fourth wall contained the U.S. Post Office and the office of the game warden. Alva Lampbert was jack of all these trades. The childless Lampberts lived in the apartment above their domain.

On one side Lampbert's store was bounded by a freshet, tumbling over a bouldered bed into the river. A wooden bench spanned the whole front of the store, where the old men gathered in the heat of summer days to smoke and reminisce and wait for mail trains.

The New York Central tracks passed twenty yards away.

And across the right-of-way and a little to the east was the Knightsville Railroad Depot, a squat, glum-appearing structure blackened with coal dust and with posters pasted on its sides urging the strangers who sped through on trains to "Smoke Camel Cigarettes" and to "Chew Wrigley's Spearmint Gum" and to dose their constipated children with "Fletcher's Castoria."

At 6:04 P.M. Carl Majors saw his hosts climb aboard the New York train, flagged down with elaborate ceremony by the stationmaster, Hector Jones. Majors was wearing his driving cap to offset the chill of evening. He doffed it now with an elaborate flourish and bowed low to Callie. "Even the mighty New York Central pays homage to your beauty, fair lady." His eyes were merry. "I'm not sure the bard said that."

She showed her pointed teeth. "What the bard said was: *That was laid on with a trowel, sir.*"

The locomotive's whistle bleated mournfully, and they climbed aboard with the sound receding down the river valley. Nate waved from the platform and called to Majors with a little bite of malice, "We'll be in New York City before you get back across the river in that fancy motorcar of yours."

Smiling, Carl Majors stood bareheaded on the platform and watched the train diminish in the blustery winter darkness.

Walt Campball and Alva Lampbert coddled mugs of hard cider in their hands before the parlor fire while their wives cleared the table and washed the dishes. Ham, without a drink, sat cross-legged on the hearth studying the colored flames.

"Well, Ham," said Alva, "how do you like your new stepmother?" The emphatic irony was not lost on either Ham or Campball.

"She keeps a good house," replied Ham evenly.

"Amen," said Campball, chewing on his cold pipe. "And a wondrous cook. That goose." He smacked his lips in appreciative recollection.

Normally a meek, quiet man, the drink had made Alva bold. He spoke now with an unexpected vehemence that startled Ham and Campball and drew their full attention to him: "Uncle Nate is an old fool!"

For the space of a heartbeat no one spoke in answer and Alva emptied his mug in one huge swallow that brought tears to his eyes and almost made him gag.

"Here, here!" Campball said in mild rebuke. "That's no way to talk about your uncle, Alva."

"It's the truth!" Alva said in a woman's waspish voice, leaning forward in his chair. "What does a man his age want with a girl nineteen? What does she want with an old man like Nate? I'll tell you what she wants—his money!"

"That's all! Alva!" Campball said severely. "You have no cause to talk like that."

"Why not?" demanded Alva. He thrust a bony hand at Ham. "I'm thinking of this boy, my kin. I can't stand by and see a conniving wench steal away his due inheritance. Old Nate has one foot in the grave as is. It won't take too much time with *her* to put his both feet in."

Campball stabbed his pipe stem at the storekeeper. "You hold your tongue! I won't hear this, Alva!"

Ham was studying his cousin with curious solemnity. With intuition way beyond his years, he said, "Alva, don't fret. He didn't change his will. She wouldn't let him. The store is yours as always when he dies."

Alva blinked his hyperthyroid eyes and stammered, "Well, now, Ham. I—I—it wasn't me I was thinking of. But—but—he *really* didn't change his will in her favor?"

"No," Ham said wearily, turning his eyes back to the fire. "He wanted to, but she laughed and told him that he was the soundest man she knew and would probably bury all of us."

Alva's titter was absurd. "She said that? She's a wag, that girl. . . . Well, now, you're right, Walt, she has a way with roast goose. And did you taste that apple pie? I must admit there's more to her than meets the eye." He bent forward in his chair and placed one hand on Campball's arm. "But you can't blame me for showing some concern. Ham's my baby cousin. I aim to see his interests are protected."

Without pretense, Campball drew back from Alva's touch and changed the subject. "Ham," he said, "you'll be alone for seven days. Come up and take your evening meal with us."

"Thanks, Uncle Walt, but I'll make out."

"No trouble," Campball protested. "Aunt Sue is bound to have it."

"Ham has his family to look out for him, Walt," Alva said haughtily. "He's welcome to take his meals with Rena and me."

"Thank you both," Ham said in haste. "But I reckon the chores about here will keep me busy from dawn to dark. I'll make out fine. . . . Er . . . er . . . Callie"—it was an awkward name for him to say—"cooked me up a mess of stuff before she left. It's in the pantry."

Walt Campball was disappointed. "We were looking forward to having you with us, Ham."

Susan Campball's thick bulk filled the doorway, dish and dishtowel in her hands. "And our Lucy will be heartbroke," she joined in. "The last time she saw you, Ham, was in the spring at Clinton High. I told her you're just playing hard to get like all men do." Her whinnying laughter grated on Ham's ears.

"I'll come up one night, Aunt Sue," he promised, anxious to end the idle talk. He got up from the floor and stretched his arms. " 'Scuse me, folks, but I got to see how things are at the barn."

When he had left the room, Walt Campball said to Alva, "Fine lad. His father should be mighty pleased with him."

"Yes sir," Alva agreed, then added slyly, "and his stepmother too."

Ham sat astride the three-legged milking stool and bent his forehead to the cow's fat silken side. He cupped the warm, full udder in his palms and let the hard teats slip between his fingers. And he felt debased to find his thoughts on Callie, his father's wife.

One August morning Ham had been shaving in the bathroom beneath the back stairs. The door was half ajar. His lathered face looked back at him from the mirror above the sink. The only sound was the crisp scrape of the bone-handled straight razor on his cheek. And abruptly he saw her image in the glass. She stood behind him in the doorway, wearing nothing but an unsashed robe, her nakedness a narrow swath from neck to knee between the parted folds. He pretended not to see her and with shaky fingers drew the thin blade down one cheek. He did not feel the bite of it in his flesh and was stunned to see the blood rise up through the white foam.

She stood there unmoving, it seemed, forever, an unfathomable smile curling up the corners of her mouth, then, unhurried, drew the edges of the robe together.

"I'm sorry, Ham," she said. "I didn't know you were in here. I was going to take a bath."

Words gagged in Ham's throat, and by the time he turned awkwardly toward her she was gone.

His fingers kneaded the warm teats of the cow. Though his breath steamed in the frigid air, his armpits and groin were damp with perspiration.

"Our Lucy will be heartbroke!" Mrs. Campball's mulish laugh and heavy-handed humor came back to him. Lucy Campball. Like a sluggish serpent, lust uncoiled deep down inside of him. The cow performed a nervous dance to and fro and bleated in protest as he gripped her with uncommon roughness. He thought of Lucy with a feeling close to anger.

Tomboy Lucy in her coveralls, with her close-cropped curly hair, who could swim the river, climb a tree, run a race as ably as any boy. Snub-nosed, lean-faced, long-legged, with a dimple in her chin. A pretty boy. The only time she wore girl's clothes was on Sundays and special holidays. Then, somehow, she was different and not much fun to be with. Their easy camaraderie had died on such a Sunday.

It happened in the apple orchard back of Campball's place, a sultry August Sunday with the drone of insects lively in the lazy air. They sat cross-legged in the shade, playing catch idly with a fat green apple, both restless with the constraints that characterized *the day of rest.*

Lucy had reached her twelfth birthday, six weeks after Ham, but there were times when he felt he was her junior. She was a big girl, as tall as he; her breasts pushed out like crab apples in her pinafore, and the flounced skirt with the starched cambric petticoat underneath emphasized the disturbing billowing of hips and buttocks that till recently had been as flat and bony as his own.

Unexpectedly she hurled the apple far over his head and leaned back a tree bole, her full mouth pouting. "Poo! That's a silly game."

Ham shrugged. "We could go down to my place and ride the new mare my father bought."

"In a dress!" she exclaimed. She clapped one hand across her mouth and snickered in the hateful private way of the older girls at school who stood around at recess in little whispering groups making fun—Ham was certain—of him. "Now wouldn't I look silly riding a horse in *this?*" She reached down and lifted the hem of her skirt and petticoat. "Oh, Ham, really!"

"Lots of ladies ride in dresses," he said in defense. "I've see pictures of 'em. They sit sideways on the horse."

"Sidesaddle, silly!" she informed him superciliously. "Anyway, they don't wear frilly clothes like this." She lifted skirt and petticoat still higher, exposing her bare knees. Her legs were drawn up and spread wide apart, in the same careless way she sat when wearing denim jeans.

Ham had seen Lucy's bare legs a hundred times in the past when they went bathing in the river. Not many years before, she and he had stripped to their underpants and waded in the quarry pool with their fathers looking on and laughing. But something had changed. Lucy had changed. Those bumps in the top of her dress, she had told him once they mortified her. Her legs, softer and rounder than the legs he remembered. Up at the quarry it had never crossed his mind what those underpants concealed. Ham had changed too.

He stared at her brazenly, aware of a warm blissful sensation building in his loins. An alien state whose uncharted shore he had touched on vaguely certain nights while on the borderline of sleep and consciousness, an unreal place that could not be defined in daylight. But suddenly on this day it came totally alive, claiming him completely and forever. Ham was mystified, awed, and a little frightened by the strange new behavior of his flesh.

At that moment the relationship between the boy and girl, almost twelve years in its duration, underwent an immutable transformation. Ham knew it instantly, and he sensed that Lucy knew it too. Her face was flushed, and there were points of sweat dotting the smooth skin of her brow. Still she made no move to bring her knees together. A large fly with a yellow furry torso and greenish gossamer wings settled on one of her bare shins and crawled down the inner side of her calf. She paid it no attention. There were no words to breach the hot, still tension in the orchard.

Ham sat with his arms locked around his knees, timid to make any move that would betray physical evidence of the bewildering awakening of his maleness. The intentness of her gaze on him became unbearable. Her serious brown eyes were wary, knowledgeable, challenging. Ham, abruptly, hated Lucy and hated himself even more. *She wants me to look at her panties and bare legs! a voice whispered. And she knows I want to look 'cause it feels good down there!*

In one quick motion he twisted his body around and stood

up and walked off without looking back at her.

"Go play with your dolls, Lucy," he said sullenly. "I'm going home to ride that mare."

"Ham Knight!" Her voice had a shrillness to it that made him wince and hunch his head between his shoulder blades. "I ain't never played with dolls and you know it! You take that back, Ham!"

"Go jump in the river!" he shouted, pulling at his pants legs to ease the tightness in his crotch. "You can't play anything else all dressed up like a sissy girl."

"I'll show you who's the sissy, Ham!" She leaped on his back before he realized what was happening. "I can outwrestle you even in a dress, Ham Knight."

"Hey, you stop that!" He staggered backward beneath her weight. She hung on to him, arms and legs wrapped around his neck and waist. "Hey, Lucy!" He teetered on his heels for one uncertain moment, then bucked his shoulders forward in counterbalance, so vigorously that he stumbled to his hands and knees.

"Lucy Campbell, I'll murder you!" he gasped. "Get off!"

She laughed and pounded up and down upon his back as if he were a hobbyhorse.

"Give up! Give up, Ham! You say you've had enough. Give up or I'll tickle you to death."

She knew his weakness, and Ham collapsed flat on the earth as her fingers clenched in the tender flesh between his ribs.

"Lucy! Stop!" He writhed helplessly under her relentless kneading hands. He did not know quite how it came about, but then the hands were in his pockets clutching at the sensitive areas around his hipbones.

They were both laughing now, piercing laughter more hysterical and wild than humorous, echoing through the leafy tunnel of the orchard and flushing coveys of nervous birds out of treetops.

"I give up!" Ham panted at last. But the fingers did not stop, their touch softer now and probing lower in the crevices of his groin. And then they closed full upon him there. There was one instant of breath-consuming panic when he struggled to pull away from her. Then sensation got the upper hand.

"Lucy!" he groaned, pushing and rubbing rhythmically against her hands so tight upon him.

The convulsions left him wet and weak, a puppet. She took one of his hands in both of hers and directed it urgently against her body. Against the silk Sunday panties, where she trapped it with her fleshy thighs.

"Now you play with me, Ham."

"No!" He pulled away from her with the loathing of one groping in the dark who touches an unseen object of unfamiliar form and substance.

"Ham! Please!" Her body trembled and her breath came quick and shallow.

Ham scrambled to his feet and began to run back down the lane and never once looked back. Four years had passed since that Sunday, and never had he visited the Campball home again.

Ham's fingers flexed with expert rhythm on the hard teats of the cow, and the rich yellow milk spurted with metallic sibilance against the tinned bottom of the pail.

The next evening after milking, Ham shaved and dressed in the dark-blue suit he had bought for his mother's funeral. He walked the mile and a half to Campball's house. It was the second-biggest house in Knightsville, fitting for his father's foreman. Walt Campball had a small barn for his one horse and two cows and a fat sow pig that guiltily reminded Walt of his dear wife, Sue.

Sue Campball fussed over Ham and pressed all kinds of food and drink on him before they even sat down to supper. Politely Ham sipped on a glass of berry wine and ate tiny sausages with toothpicks stuck in them.

"It's the latest style in the city," Sue announced with pride. " 'Horse derves' they call 'em."

Susan Campball thought of herself as Knightsville's bellwether of *bon ton*. It was a lonely service, but she was diligent, mailing to the weary wives of quarrymen and farmers invitations to cozy little afternoon teas and bingo parties. A few of the ladies accepted out of curiosity; most of them never even acknowledged the R.S.V.P. that Sue printed neatly in the left-hand bottom corner of her Sears, Roebuck formal notepaper decorated with violets around the border.

The Sears, Roebuck catalog ranked only second to the Bible in the Campball home. It was Aladdin's magic lamp. The latest wonder that the genie at Sears had provided was a Victrola.

"Our Lucy is just crazy over that machine." Sue feigned exasperation. "From the time she gets home from school till bedtime, it's nothing but music, music, music!"

Walt grunted as he packed his pipe. "They call that music."

"Dad-*dy!*" Lucy shrieked. "It's what they're playing in all those New York speakeasies. Jazz! The cat's meow!"

"Play something for Ham," her mother said. She looked at Ham. "She learns all the new-fangled dances the minute they come out."

"She'd be better to learn how to cook the old-fangled dishes," Walt declared.

"Dad-*dy!*" Lucy shrieked again. Then the syncopated dissonances of trumpet, clarinet and trombone, drums and cymbals exploded on the room, shrill and tinny in Ham's ears.

"That's the shimmy," Lucy yelled above the din, and though the tune was strange to him, Ham was quite clear why they called it *shimmy.* She came weaving across the room toward his chair, shaking shoulders, arms, and hips so vigorously they were all a blur of motion. She held out a slender hand with painted fingernails to Ham.

"Come on, Sheik, I'll show you how to do it."

Ham shrank back in the chair. "Not me. I never danced in my life."

She giggled. "I guess not. Your education has been neglected in many ways."

"Lucy!" her mother snapped. "You mind that snippy tongue. "It's not Ham's fault he had to quit school."

Laughing, the girl turned and shook her backside almost in Ham's face. "I wasn't talking about school, Maw."

Sue Campbell sighed. "Ham, you watch how Lucy does it. Later on she'll teach you how."

"Yes, ma'am." Ham was grateful for an excuse to keep his eyes on Lucy. Up till now, he had dared only to look at her with furtive sidelong glances. The tomboy who had been his playmate, confidant, and equal had disappeared forever. Lucy Campbell was a strange woman with painted lips and nails, bobbed hair, and short bangs brushed flat against her forehead. Her breasts, bound tightly in the latest fad to sweep the nation, were too full to be disguised by such nonsense. He didn't care for her dress, with the silly fringe dangling at the hemline, except that it was very short. Once she high-kicked straight at Ham and he had a glimpse of firm, round thigh high above the rolled tops of her stockings. His heart quickened and he thought of her again as she had been that hot day in the orchard. This time he would not run away!

Sue Campball pushed her heavy body out of the rocking chair and walked toward the kitchen. "Time we were eating supper. Roast beef, Ham, with Yorkshire pudding, does that sound good to you?"

Ham laughed. "Aunt Sue, you know it's my favorite."

After supper, while the woman and her daughter cleared the table and washed the dishes, Ham sat with Walt Campball in the parlor.

"Carl Majors asked me to stop by his place some day this week," Walt said. "To talk about an order of slate for those buildings of his they're roofing down in Albany. You want to come along as your father's representative?"

"Not me," said Ham. "What do I know about the slate business?"

The older man frowned. "You've got to learn, boy, your father wants it."

"My father wants too much at times."

Walt looked at the boy through the blue smoke rising from his pipe. "And always gets it."

Ham was glad when the women came in from the kitchen and the conversation ended. At nine o'clock, the mother and father bid Ham goodnight and went upstairs to bed.

"You send him home in just one hour," Walt warned his daughter. "He's a working man and needs his rest."

"Well, working man," she said when they were gone, "do you want to learn to shimmy?" She wagged her full hips in slow time, sensuously, and Ham felt the quiver begin deep down in his belly. He was impatient to finish out the game begun four years before. "Maybe the Charleston is more your style?"

"I'll try," he said, his mouth and throat as dry and rough as bark.

"Vo-do-de-o-do!" She high-kicked, affording him a peek at bare leg and panties. She set the needle scratching on the spinning record and walked up close to him and asked, "Are you really interested in learning how to dance, Ham Knight?" Her brown eyes met his, less than one foot apart. The same eyes that had belonged to the girl in the apple orchard, wary, knowledgeable, challenging.

"Well . . ." He hesitated. "Well, sure I do."

She laughed in a way that made him feel young and awkward and inferior. "You waited a long time, Ham. Four years."

Uncertain of her meaning, he answered her obliquely. "Your mother invited me to supper."

Her smile was sly. "I don't see why, considering that I wasn't invited to your paw's wedding."

Ham's face grew hot. "There were no young folks there, outside of me."

"Did *you* get to kiss the bride, Ham?"

His face grew even hotter. "Heck no! I told you it wasn't one of those regular weddings."

"I'd guess not," she said. "Your new stepmother is a real young girl. Not much older than us, I'd say."

He nodded. "She's nineteen."

"And pretty too."

"I guess she is, I haven't noticed."

"You haven't noticed! I'll just bet!" She laughed as if at some private joke. "She's lived five months at your house. I bet you've noticed plenty, Ham, about her. Your paw sure did. Nathaniel Knight must be quite a man to win a young girl like her for his wife."

"I thought we were going to dance," Ham said, uncomfortable with all this talk of Callie and his father. It made him feel ashamed of them and for himself. Even to think about them in his own privacy.

His discomfort amused the girl. "Sure, if you want to."

It required just five minutes to demonstrate that Ham had small aptitude for the shimmy, or the other frenetic dances that were coming into vogue in the early nineteen twenties.

"Let's try something slow, a two-step," Lucy told him. "When we were kids I used to think you had the biggest feet in the world." She winced. "And I was right." She lifted one red-slippered foot and massaged the instep.

"I'm sorry that I'm clumsy," Ham apologized. "If you can bear it, I'd like to try the two-step or a waltz maybe."

"A waltz!" She regarded him as if he were an alien species. "That's for old men like our fathers." Her eyes gleamed wickedly. "Well, maybe not for *your* father. He has young ideas!"

She talked with her back to him while she changed the

record on the phonograph. "Ham, the machine needs winding. The crank is right there on the side."

He walked up behind her, then hesitated. The crank was crannied in the tight angle between machine and wall. Bent over the turntable, Lucy blocked his way.

"Well, go on, Ham, what are you waiting for? I've got to change the needle, but you can wind it up and save us time."

He leaned across her back, and by stretching awkwardly he could just grasp the wooden handle. Every time he turned the crank his body would make light contact with hers, and every touch would tease the beast within him. His heart was galloping now, and the hunger of his body could be neither concealed nor compromised.

Good God! he thought frantically. *Soon she'll turn around and see me! I can't dance in this state!*

In his mind there was the image of a bewildered boy running through an aisle of apple trees. And then the matter was decided for him. She backed against him—deliberately or not he'd never know—her soft, well-fleshed buttocks, warm through the skirt, pressing hard against his rigid loins. All inhibition dissolved then in the heat of fever.

"Lucy!" he whispered in her ear. His big hands found her breasts and he held her tightly against him.

She straightened up and turned her head to look at him across one shoulder, and the expression on her face was anything but what he'd hoped to see. Shock. Outrage. Revulsion. At least she was determined to appear so.

"Ham Knight!" Her voice was as brittle as shale and pitched with indignation. "You stop that right away! What's wrong with you!" She twisted roughly in his arms, braced her hands against his chest, and shoved him away.

Ham was even more confused and scared than he had been that Sunday in the orchard. "I thought—I thought—Lucy, that time when we were kids!" He labored to explain what he could not understand himself. "Don't you remember?"

She slapped him hard across the face, the sting of it bringing tears to his eyes. "Lucy!" he said miserably.

"You dirty boy!" She hissed at him like a wildcat, her fingers curled menacingly near his face like claws.

His arms fell limply to his sides, and he shut his eyes

against the sight of her. "I'm sorry, Lucy, I really am," he said in despair.

There was a note of triumph in her voice that both puzzled and angered him. "Is that the kind of play your father's bride encourages?"

Without another word Ham went to find his coat. She followed him to the hall closet and out onto the porch where fine snow was sifting in from underneath the sloping roof.

"You think of her and rub up against me like a dirty little boy, Ham Knight!" she screeched after him, as he bent into the wind. "You never were a man, and never will be, Ham!"

When he was gone, into the snow and darkness, she went inside and shut the door and leaned against it. A feeble smile of satisfaction flickered across her white, tense face.

Do I remember that day in the orchard! The gall of him to ask! Four years gone by before he looked at me again! The high and mighty Knights! Better than everyone else! The foreman's daughter a convenient whore! Four years to get my revenge! Lucy blinked in rare self-revelation. *And I didn't get a thing at all!* She jammed her clenched fists against her eyes and began to cry.

It was a winter of despair for Ham. Snow fell almost every day from New Year's Eve through the middle of March, choking roadways, piling up in drifts, a score feet high and more, against the north walls of barn and house. The quarry road was blocked for weeks, all work closed down. It was a major adventure to journey to the village store and back on snowshoes. Day after day the shriveled column of mercury in the thermometer outside the kitchen window stayed degrees below the zero mark. The ice on the river grew so thick that on the first day of spring Carl Majors drove his Mercer car across the Hudson to Knightsville.

There were days of inactivity, too much time to think and stare out windows at the dreary albino landscape or into the hypnotic fire burning on the parlor hearth. Too much time to brood about his mother's dying; the pain of her loss full upon him now, the excruciating knitting pain so much more intense than that inflicted by the open wound the day she died. Too much time to resent his father for betraying the memory of his mother. Not six months, even, had he waited! Her house, her bed, the very clothing she had worn next to her dear flesh defiled by the wanton flesh his father lusted for.

Too much time for Ham, himself, to dwell upon that same flesh. Lecherous imagery, the old man and the young girl rocking on his mother's bed.

Day and night he hated both of them, which one the worse he could not tell for sure. And least of all could he tell why he hated either of them!

In the months since Callie's coming, his father had more to say to him than all he'd said in all the years before, and said it more benignly. The old man had toiled beside him all summer in the fields, culling corn and stacking the mowed grass; toiled beside him in the winter in hip-deep snow, plowing the trails to shed and barn. He had praised Ham as his son and treated him as a man and as an equal—as equal as he'd ever treated any man. Ham hated him for it.

He could find no overt fault with anything the girl who was his stepmother did or said. As housekeeper and cook she was equal to his mother. Ham could find no single fault. He hated her for it.

And as a wife? Well, what fault could be found with any woman who pleased a white-haired, bearded man who'd always had the sour disposition of a prophet? A woman who had peeled the wrinkled mask of discipline and restraint from his features and inspired him to whistle lively tunes all day and cry out in rapture in the dead of night, what fault could be found with such a woman? Ham hated her for it.

She mended Ham's clothes, sewed on his buttons, baked his favorite buns and pies. And offered consolation in his deep depressions.

"You yearn for education," she said once, when she found him brooding over an abandoned schoolbook. "It's a tragic thing to be deprived of things we so hotly desire. Don't give up hope, Ham. *The sea hath bounds but deep desire hath none.*"

Ham sneered. "You've got fancy words for everything, Callie, but they're not your words."

"No matter," she said without offense, "the feelings are mine. He frequently borrowed other people's words himself."

Ham frowned. "He? Who, Shakespeare?"

"Of course, there are those who claim none of the plays and poems are his creation. But it matters little who said them, wrote them. They do exist, they are beautiful and truthful, and that's the end of it. They speak of things the whole world feels and understands. They help us, you and I, to better understand the world, and in understanding others we can better understand ourselves and rid our brains of guilts and doubts that otherwise might lead to madness." She placed one white hand gently on Ham's arm. "There are many things you'd like to understand about yourself, Ham."

"Me?" Ham tried to laugh, but his mouth and throat were dry as straw. He wanted to pull away from her touch, but the warm hand on his sleeve held him like a magnet.

There were golden points of pigment in the fluid of her irises that swirled in everlasting motion like particles of dust in a beam of sunlight, lending to her eyes a look of mercurial enchantment. Enchanted eyes with the power to strip his mind and body naked, exposing all his sins of deed and thought.

"Your father can stop you from going to school, Ham," she said. "But he can't stop you from learning. Books, Ham, we'll fill this house with them, all you desire. For a start I'll give you my book."

Ham was truly startled. In the evenings he had watched her by the fire with the Shakespeare volume cradled lovingly in her lap, transported beyond the prison of the room, the house, her own body by the magic of printer's ink on paper. How he envied her! How badly he wanted to feel that book in his own hands, turn the pages, discover its magic for himself. Yet he never dared. She guarded her Shakespeare the way a mother guards her firstborn, returning it, after each reading, to a repository in her bedroom.

Now she was offering this treasure to him freely. For the interval it takes a star to flash across the evening horizon and die, the love he had known for her briefly in the graveyard, on the day they met, he knew again.

With emotion he said to her, "Thank you, thank you, Callie. I'd like that very much."

And then with her next words, his horizon was dark again. "Maybe you'd like me to tuck you in your bed at night, as a proper stepmother should, and read you to sleep with a Shakespeare sonnet?"

He had the urge to smash his fist against her delicate face, to see red blood streaming from her whimsically smiling mouth where the sharp teeth pressed into the wet cushion of her lower lip. Barely able to speak, he turned his back on her and walked away.

"I can read well enough," he mumbled.

She gave him the book and he read it through, and through again, plays, sonnets, everything, in the bleak days and never-ending nights that stretched out from January until the end of March. He came to love Shakespeare, he believed, as greatly as did Callie Hill—he never thought of her by any other name—yet the understanding she had promised never came to Ham. Each time he finished reading *Hamlet,* he understood less about the tragic prince than he had the time before, and had less understanding of Ham Knight than Hamlet had understanding of himself. He would have died before confessing his dilemma to Callie, so smug in her omniscience of the mortal world. And the more he pondered, the less he understood about anything, and his mind rebelled against the pain of all this unaccustomed use.

He hated Callie for putting that book in his hands.

But after the day she saved his life, he hated her most of all.

It was a muggy day in early June, past noon before the sun broke through the shroud of river mist. The mowed grass lay in rippled swaths in the south meadow waiting for the haymaking crews to stack and bind it into ricks. Old Nate was troubleshooting a work lag at the quarry. His son Ham, seven days less his seventeenth birthday, was working with the field hands, making hay. At one o'clock Callie drove into the field in the buggy rarely used except to go to church on Sunday. The men all straightened up from their work to watch her as she reined the small honey-colored mare expertly to a halt.

Ham's face, already crimson from the sun, flushed redder still when he saw her. She wore a pair of faded denim trousers that he recognized as ones he had outgrown years before. They were immodestly snug about her hips and thighs. Her hair, tied with a red ribbon at the back of her head, trailed behind her like the tail of the honey-colored mare.

Slut! Ham thought, angry and humiliated because she was his father's wife, or so he told himself. No decent female past the age of twelve would dress in man's clothes.

The other men did not share Ham's displeasure and stared with open admiration. Callie smiled and called to them, "Here's your lunch, boys. It's extra-special good today. Fried chicken, hot bread, and iced coffee."

Loudly voicing their appreciation, all but Ham rallied around the buggy to take the hamper and jugs she handed down. She looked across their heads at his lone figure standing ankle-deep in hay.

"Don't take all day, my boy, or you'll be left with only crusts."

"I'm not hungry," he replied. Sullenly, he turned away and walked to the near side of the meadow where a low wall of odd-shaped slabs of slate, piled one on top of the other, marked off the boundary of a neighboring field.

He started to sit down, his full weight not yet settled on the stone ledge, when the strident warning charged the quiet summer air with high tension. The field hands, clustered around the buggy, cursed, jostled one another like frightened cattle, coffee spilled, sandwiches were dropped. The blond mare reared, whinnying, high on her haunches.

It was a sound unlike any other sound to those who knew and feared it. Ham had heard it described variously as "a swarm of angry hornets" and as "a locust fighting mad" and as "a buzz saw striking through a knot in oak."

The truth was it sounded like nothing else but what it was: the singing of hemp across a tree bough at a lynching. The rattling descent of the guillotine's blade. The blunt clatter of the firing squad cocking rifles. It was the sound of death.

"It's a rattler!" screamed a field hand.

Ham looked down between his spread legs and saw the flat-wedged weaving head, the black beaded eyes, the dappled torso, thick as a man's arm, the faded neutral coloration of its skin camouflaged against the earth and stone. The timber rattlesnake, North American cousin of the venemous pit asp.

Without feeling—fear and pain were strangely absent—Ham saw the blurred motion of the head, the white flash of fangs, unbelievably large, fasten on his thigh through the denim trousers. *A rattlesnake can't strike without first coiling, so much for old wives' tales like that!* he thought with calm detachment.

He was aware of the rhythmic convulsions of the sinuous muscular body, the spurting venom. Sensuality and the serpent, biblical allegory.

Fear and pain struck simultaneously, belatedly. Crying out in terror and revulsion he leaped from the wall, spinning like a dervish, beating at the snake with his hands. It clung fast to him, the length of it, six foot at least, whipping and writhing around his legs. In desperation, he grasped it with both hands about the fragile neck, just behind the flat hammer head, and tore it from his leg.

In his grip the snake was helpless, lashing at him with its rattled tail, helpless but still defiant, fearless, full of fight, the venon dripping from its yawning mouth. He held it up at arm's length and, for one unforgettable moment, looked directly into the serpent's bright hooded eyes, malevolent, burning with hate and fury.

With a scream of savage gratification, which fell on his own ears as a voice from some faintly remembered dream, Ham ripped the snake's head from its body and flung the dismembered parts away from him. He looked up and saw Callie's white face and staggered toward the buggy.

"I've been bit," he said matter-of-factly. "Will you ride me back to the house?"

The light buggy swayed from one side of the dirt road to the other as Callie kept slapping the reins sharply against the mare's hindquarters, until the frightened horse was fairly galloping.

Ham clung tightly to the buggy's seat. "Slower," he warned her. "You want to tip us over?"

"You want to die from that bite?" She glanced at his pants' leg where the snake had struck; the jagged edges of the torn denim were wet and bloody. The thigh was swelling fast, the faded blue material taut as sausage skin around it. "Do you have a knife?" she asked him.

"Not on me."

She nodded. "Every second counts. We'll get you into bed and phone Dr. Murphy across the river, he's the closest, right away. But there's no time to sit and wait for doctors. We'll start treatment on that leg at once."

"What do you know about treating snakebite?" Ham asked her dazedly. Each heartbeat was a throbbing agony in his swollen thigh and in his head. His throat was alum-dry and he had a terrifying sensation that he was slowly choking.

She whipped the reins down hard on the horse's back. "I know you've got to bleed it, get out all the venom you can."

Ham was silent, closing his eyes against the dizzy sight of the landscape sweeping past the onrushing buggy. He felt sick to his stomach.

Neither of them spoke again until Callie halted the mare

in the graveled drive before the house. She jumped lightly to the ground and came around to his side of the buggy. "Can you make it by yourself?"

"I think so." Gripping the buggy's hand rails, Ham lowered himself gingerly on the fulcrums of his elbows. "There's pins and needles in this leg." He winced as he put his weight upon it.

She slipped one arm about his waist. "Here, lean on me."

"No!" He pulled away from her. "It's all right. I can manage."

When they were inside the house, she told him, "You go right upstairs and take off your clothes and get into bed. I'll call the doctor and be right up."

Leaning heavily on the banister, he climbed the long staircase step by painful step. Callie went straight to the wall phone in the hall and lifted the earpiece from its hook. She turned the metal crank on the side insistently to summon the operator.

Ham undressed, and he was badly shaken by the appearance of his leg. The thigh was swollen twice its size at least, the flesh around the angry festering fang wounds mottled with an ugly purplish bruise. He climbed shakily into the bed and drew the covers over his body. He lay there, frightened by the relentless pumping of his heart, each constriction moving the venom deeper into the labyrinth of his circulatory system. In his imagination he saw an X-ray picture of himself, like the one on the frontispiece of a biology textbook he had read in high school, all the blood vessels red on the right side and all blue on the left side. He wondered how long it took for the poison to reach the heart, or brain, or lungs, wherever it had to reach to kill you.

In his lifetime, Ham had seen many timber rattlers, most of them at the quarry where the slate workers dynamited the rocky dens in which they hibernated all entwined like spaghetti in a bowl. Those that were not destroyed by the concussion stayed stunned long enough for the workmen to beat them to death with rocks and sticks. Generally, though, the villagers avoided rattlesnakes and the snakes avoided them.

But periodically the big timber rattlers would invade the lowlands, in dry spells when they were seeking water, and inevitably they would encounter man. Such encounters usually ended in death for the snakes. But there were enough cases on record where the outcome had gone the other way to lather Ham with the sweat of fear and make his bones shake.

When he heard the quick footsteps in the hall, for one moment, in his disordered thoughts, he imagined it was his mother coming to help him, as she had done so many times when he was ill or hurt. He almost called out to her, *Mama! Mama!* Then he saw Callie in the doorway.

As she approached the bed, he saw that she was gripping an open straight razor in her right hand.

"What's that for?" he asked her anxiously.

"I'm going to bleed that bite," she said. "Take off the covers and let me have a look at it."

"I don't want you to cut me," Ham objected. "I'll wait for the doctor."

"It may be too late by then," she argued. "We've got to begin emergency treatment right away. Just look at you! You're getting more feverish by the minute."

"But I don't have any clothes on!" Ham clutched the blanket to him with both hands. "I'm naked under here."

Her face was solemn, but her green eyes reflected deep inscrutable mirth. "I've seen naked men before. Don't be such a baby, Ham."

Before he could protest, she turned the covers back from the foot of the bed, exposing his legs to the midpoint of the thighs.

"God, that's awful!" she said when she saw the bite, two oozing cavities, an inch apart, on the inside fleshy part of his left leg about two inches above the knee. She sat down beside him on the bed and touched his hot face gently with the back of her hand. "Does it hurt very bad?"

Her hand felt cool and smooth against his flaming cheek, and he was comforted, yet at the same time disconcerted by his muddled emotions.

"Not too bad," he said. "I just feel kind of sleepy. It's hard to keep my eyes open."

"Shut them then." She patted his cheek. "You don't want to watch this, anyway."

He kept his eyes open, nonetheless, staring at the spiderweb of cracks in the plaster ceiling and thinking about his mother. *I might be with you soon, Mother!* And the idea of death no longer frightened him. He was dimly conscious that Callie was doing something to his leg, a series of numbed impressions without continuity. He was aware of the razor's thin steel blade slicing into his flesh, not painfully but with brief fire. He was aware of the wet flow from the wound. Then a bewildering sensation, a soft, warm, moist pressure against the wound. He rolled his eyes downward from the ceiling and saw her crouched over him, cradling his leg in her arms. Her open mouth was covering the snake bite, working in rhythmic suction to draw the venom out of the fang punctures in his swollen, mottled thigh.

He watched her, at first, with the same calm detachment as he had watched the snake fastened to him. Fear and pain were close behind, and then revulsion. His impulse was to strike out at her, beat her away as he had beat away the serpent. He lay there enfeebled by the ferment of contradictory passions. Then a lethargy, not unpleasant, took possession of his mind and body, a subtle anesthesia that wilted his bones and sapped his will.

He watched in fascination the girl with her mouth pressed tight against the wound on his thigh. It was as if she were kissing him. Her hands on his bare flesh. Her lips on his bare flesh. Her breasts through the thin cotton shirt warm and heavy against his bare flesh. The numbness was gone. The pain was gone. His body was intoxicated with feeling, excitement whose swift ascent and certain course he could not have checked or altered had he wished to do so. He could not control the violent trembling of his body, the thrashing of his legs. He was delirious with lechery.

"No, please!" he groaned as she took her mouth away from his leg and sat up. "Don't stop!"

His nakedness was exposed to her and so was his desire, but he was shameless. He could not see her face clearly, it was as if he were seeing her though pale, green, shimmering seawater, a white wraith with hair of seaweed floating out behind it, the only vivid details the wanton smiling mouth and wanton eyes.

The water darkened suddenly as if a cloud had soared across the sun high above the sea. Blinded, drowning, gasping, he reached for her.

"Save me, Callie! Save me!"

Her laughter bubbled in his ears, muted, fading.

"I'll be back, Ham. I'll save you."

"I hate you, Callie. I hate you!"

Blackness. Nothing. Sweet death.

When he opened his eyes, he was wrapped snugly in the sheet and blanket and they were clammy with his perspiration. Dr. Willis Murphy was standing at the foot of the bed, his pink cherubic face uncommonly stern. Two tufts of white fuzz poked out on each side of his head behind his ears; for all that his pate and cheeks were hairless. The doctor never revealed his age, but Nate claimed he had been in practice when he himself was a lad in knee pants. Doc Murphy had been threatening to retire for twenty years, the moment he could find some altruistic graduate of med school to take his place. In 1922, he was still the only general practitioner in a radius of twenty miles from Knightsville.

"How you feeling, lad?" Doc Murphy asked in his high, old-woman's voice.

"Pretty fair," Ham answered weakly.

He saw them, then, one on each side of the bed, his father and Callie.

Old Nate laid a gentle hand upon his shoulder. "You're going to make it, boy. Doc says so." His voice was touched with a reverence Ham had not heard since the night his mother died.

"You're lucky, laddie," Doc said. "It was the quick thinking of this little lady that saved your life. She bled the wound clean." He looked approvingly at Callie. "You're a plucky girl."

"She's *my* wife, Willis," Nate said, as if somehow that entitled him to share praise meant for her.

When she started to speak, Ham wished himself dead on the spot. *She was telling them all about it!*

"I lanced the punctures with a razor, two crisscross slashes in each one. I let it bleed for a time to cleanse the wound, then twisted a pair of suspenders around his leg above the bite to stop the flow of blood."

Ham stared up at her with incredible relief. She had not told them how she sucked the wound clean, nor of his insane, obscene ravings. He had to be insane to say the things and do the things that he had done that day. And to his father's wife! *God, how I hate you, Callie!*

With fear he met her gaze. Her face was serene, unfathomable. Pure, virginal in a white dress, her hair brushed out long and tumbling about her shoulders, the first time she had worn it that way since her marriage to Nate. Her eyes a green enigma.

"Poor Ham," she continued with her eyes steady on him. "He fainted when I cut him with the razor. How delirious he was, moaning and thrashing about, mumbling things I couldn't make head nor tail of." She smiled at him sweetly.

"He's tired," Doc Murphy said. "We'll let him rest."

Alone at last in his room, Ham could reach no clear conclusion about his father's wife. Why had she lied? Or *had* she lied? Maybe the entire episode had been a figment of delirium. Ham knew the world of dreams could often preempt life in realism. It was an explanation he was eager to accept. His confidence flowed back. Of course it had been a dream! Just another of his tantalizing dreams. Weak and grateful, he lay back on his pillow and closed his eyes and said a prayer of thanks.

"Father, forgive me my sins.

"Father, give me strength to overcome temptation. . . ."

And he mumbled his interminable penitence until he fell asleep. Restless sleep, tortured by dreams.

Ham, spreadeagled on the featherbed cloud, his naked body warming to immense life in the blood-red glow. She is hovering over him in his mother's silken nightgown. Her streaming hair is touched by a fragile luminous halo. Her lips are parted and her cat's eyes gleam as they behold the turgid upward thrust between his thighs.

Her fingers are working at the pearl buttons that fasten the front of the nightgown. In one swift motion she bares her breasts and shoulders and peels the silk down over her hips, lets it billow to the floor. She stands before him naked, and smiling her sharp-toothed foxy smile. Ham has never seen an unclothed woman and he is filled with wonder at the near-faultless symmetry of her body, with its harmonious sheathing of bone in flesh, fluid continuity of form, contrasting so acutely with the crude angularity of the male body. Round, lush, warm, sweet, rich, fertile. Mother earth. The womb of man's eternity.

Ham cries out to her in his unbearable yearning.

"Please! Please! Please!"

She moves with panther grace onto the bed astride his knees.

And the illusion ends.

Ham pushed himself up from the pillow on his elbows. It was not a dream! He was lying in his own bed in his own room and there was an oil lamp with a rosy globe upon his dressing table.

The sight of the white bandage binding his swollen thigh startled him back to full reality.

"Callie, why are you here?"

"Because you want me here," she answered softly.

"No! You're my father's wife!"

"Shh! We musn't wake your father."

"Go 'way, go 'way! I don't want you."

"That's not true. You're a man, Ham. A man wants a woman. And you want me." She laughed quietly. "No need to hide it any longer, Ham. I saw how badly you wanted me this afternoon."

Ham squeezed his eyelids shut against the sight of her and against the sight of his own lust, shamefully exposed.

"It was a dream. I was delirious."

"Poor Ham." She şighed.

Knees going far apart, she descends upon him and he gasps with pleasure as she enfolds him in her flesh and just in time. He reaches for her and pulls her down upon him, burying his face in the perfumed hollow of her throat, and her long hair tumbles in a fan across his pillow, closing him in a warm, protective tent of darkness.

Afterward he lay face down on his pillow, the painful aftermath of sin as unrelenting as his pleasure had been in the sinning.

"Is it better, Ham?" Her lips were soft against his ear, and she caressed the broad muscles of his back.

"Stop it, Callie!" Her touch was loathsome to him now, as loathsome as the touch of the snake had been. He rolled away from her and sat up in the bed, his eyes fixed straight ahead so that he would not have to see her nakedness.

"Look at me, Ham." Her voice was firm.

"No!" he said hoarsely. "You best get out of my room. If my father ever finds out what we did tonight, he'd kill us both. And we'd deserve it."

"Why should he find out, Ham? There's no one but us to tell him."

"You're evil, Callie." His hands trembled. "Why did you do this to me? Why did you come here tonight and tempt me?"

His scorn amused her. "Who sins most, the temptress or the tempted?" she asked him lightly.

"But you're my father's wife!"

"And you're his flesh and blood."

"Get out of here!" he said in rage. "Don't speak to me unless my father's present. Don't set foot in my room again."

In silence she rose and stepped around the bed to where her gown lay crumpled on the floor. He saw her briefly with the lamp's soft sheen on her smooth, nude flesh. The moist feel of her still on his fingertips. He closed his eyes and waited until he heard the soft closing of his door. And he fell back on the pillow, alone with his guilt in the darkness.

The next morning, his father brought up his breakfast to him on a tray. Ham stared at the ceiling, afraid and ashamed to meet the old man's keen eyes.

"I'm not hungry," he said firmly.

"You'll eat," Nate said more firmly. "Doc Murphy wants it that way. You need the food for strength."

"I'm fine."

"I know your game, young fellow," his father bantered gruffly. "It's pleasant playing invalid with a pretty nurse like Callie to attend you."

Ham glanced at him quickly, his belly knotted up in terror.

Nate frowned. "What's wrong, boy? You've gone all white."

Ham shook his head. "It's nothing, Paw. A spell of dizziness, that's all. It's past now."

"You're starving!" Nate diagnosed. "It's as I told you. Now sit up and eat this mess of eggs and bacon."

Ham propped up his pillow against the backboard, and Nate laid the tray across his knees.

"The doc will be in this morning to have a look at that leg of yours. I think the swelling's down."

"It is." Ham's eyes fell upon the book at the side of his breakfast platter. "How did this get on here, Paw?"

Nate shrugged his massive shoulders. "It's Callie's doing. She says you asked for it last night."

After his father left, Ham opened the Shakespeare volume to a place marked with a slip of blank paper. His gaze wandered down the page to a selection underlined in light pencil. He read it:

But O strange men! That can such sweet use make of what they hate
When saucy trusting of the cozen'd thoughts
Defiles the pitchy night: so lust doth play
With what it loathes. . . .

He set the food aside untouched and closed the book.

That afternoon, Callie appeared in the doorway of his room, her face scrubbed clean and pale and pure, her green eyes wide and innocent. Her hair was bound across the crown of her head in two thick gleaming braids in the style of a farm girl. She wore a long-sleeved shirtwaist, modestly loose across her breasts. Her skirt was straight and long, unflattering to her figure.

"I've brought your lunch," she said tonelessly. "Is it all right to come in?"

"Come in," Ham said, his face hot with the memory of the night before. Powerless to stop himself, he thought about the body concealed beneath the ill-fitting, shapeless costume.

Without a word or glance in his direction, she placed the tray across his lap and walked away.

"Thank you!" he called after her.

She did not reply.

"Callie! I . . ." he faltered.

In the doorway she turned toward him and waited.

His heart was racing. "Callie—where's my paw?"

"He's up at the quarry," she told him. "He'll be back in time for supper."

"For supper." His voice was flat.

She was staring at him, silent, impassive.

"Callie . . ." His face was burning, and he jammed his hands beneath the sheet to hide their trembling. "Callie, my leg—it doesn't feel so good. . . . I was wondering, maybe—"

"Yes."

He blurted it out then in humiliation. "Would you change the dressing, Callie. Please, Callie! Please!"

He lay back in hopeless misery as she walked back to his bed, smiling her wise, sharp-toothed, green-eyed smile.

It was autumn, and the hay stacks mounded high in rolling fields gleamed like spun gold in the morning sunlight. At Knight's farm, the hands had begun to pull apart the ricks and cart the sweet-smelling straw to the barn for winter storage.

It was October when Callie told Nate that he would become a father. He folded her in his arms without a word and laid his grizzled cheek against her perfumed hair. When he did speak his voice was humble and his beard was salt-wet where it brushed her forehead.

"My darling . . . I am grateful for all you've been to me. All you've done for me. . . . And now this, this miracle. . . . I thank God for his generosity. The signs have pointed to a good harvest, but now! This makes it the richest harvest of all time."

His laughter boomed through the great house, and he kissed her. Then he stomped out of the house and spread his arms wide and lifted his craggy face to the blue sky. Warmed by the sun, with his white beard and hair wild in the wind off the river, he breathed deeply and gratefully.

"Nathaniel!" she called to him from the porch. "Where are you going?"

He looked to her and laughed again. "To the fields. To tell Ham. To tell everyone. Nathaniel Knight is going to have a son."

It was after dark when Ham brought his father home in a horse-drawn wagon, the old man sprawled in deep sleep on a bed of hay. Ham left him snoring in the stable back of the house and went inside.

Callie was waiting in the kitchen. "It's late," she said, "I was worried."

"You were worried!" he said with bitter irony.

"Where's your father?"

"I left him in the barn—drunk!"

"Drunk? Your father?" A playful smile curled up one corner of her mouth.

"You bitch!" Ham raised a heavy arm as if to strike her.

She did not cringe or even blink her eyes. "What's that for, Ham?"

He dropped his arm, his shoulders slumped. "No, the hate I feel for you is only the reflection of the loathing I feel for myself. God, how I wish I was dead."

"But why?" she asked curiously.

He sat down at the table and rested his head in his hands, looking at the clean plate she had placed there for his supper, now cold and juiceless in the scorched pots on the range. Looking at nothing.

His voice was lifeless. "All afternoon, he's been spreading the good news. Nate Knight's planted a child in the belly of his young bride. Up and down the river, every tenant, every farm, and drinking toasts with everyone." He laughed a short, hoarse laugh. "He used to preach against the sin of pride."

"He should be proud. It's not every man of seventy-two years who can make such a boast," she said.

He whirled suddenly in the chair and grabbed her by the wrists and pulled her to him. Her gaze was steady before the fury in his eyes.

"You! You hypocrite! You cheat! It's not his child you're carrying, we both know that."

The lamplight flickered in her eyes. "I know nothing, Ham, except there *is* a child. I have no inkling whether you're its father or its brother, Ham."

He flung her arms down as if the touch of her was poisonous and he cursed her. "God damn you! What a thing to say! It really pleases you, doesn't it, woman! Hell, you're not a woman, you're a witch!" He beat the table with his fists, sending silverware and china crashing to the floor. Rage spent quickly, he slumped forward on the table with his face buried in his folded arms.

Callie bent over him and put her arms around his shoulders. "I am a witch, Ham. And you're bewitched."

He tried to shake her off. "Don't touch me!"

She smiled on him with tolerance, the fond tolerance of a mother for her misbehaving child. "Come upstairs with me, Ham," she coaxed. "I'll bewitch you."

He raised his head and stared at her with speechless disbelief.

"Your father's drunk. He won't wake till morning. Come, Ham." She turned low the oil lamp in its bracket on the wall and walked to the doorway. She stood there looking back at him, a pale wraith against the darkness of the room behind her. "I'll be waiting for you, Ham."

He sat there in a stupor for how long he did not know. Finally, he stood up and walked toward the staircase, the excitement already rising inside his body.

That was the first week of October. By mid-month, from the high point of the quarry, the forest was spread out below in its warm mantle of red and brown and gold forearmed against the approaching winter. Even on clear days, when the sun was at its zenith, the heat of the afternoon was abated by crisp drafts blowing down the river valley from the north. And the nights were chill, and there was the good sleeping again under blankets.

Nate spent more of his time around the house after Callie made her announcement to him. "A man should be close to home when his woman is carrying," he told her when she suggested that he was neglecting his business affairs. "I'll leave other matters to my son."

He looked at Ham with a father's pride. "It's just this year that Ham has become a man. Last autumn he was a boy. He behaved like a boy. He looked like a boy. Now suddenly he's a man, with a man's looks and a man's behavior. Soon he'll know enough to do it all by himself. The quarry, the farm, he'll be able to manage them alone. And I can sit here on the porch rocker in the sunlight and watch my second son grow up."

"The child may be a girl."

He took her fragile head between his huge brown hands and examined her with a strangeness she had never sensed in him before.

"One waif like you around this place is all I want. The child will be a boy," he said with finality.

Callie had always slept in her own room, and, when he wanted her, Nate would come to her bed. Now, to her dismay, he decided that she would sleep in his room until the baby came.

"No, Nathaniel," she argued, "I'm restless. You'd bother me and I'd bother you."

"Then we'll just move your bed into my room and we'll not disturb each other," he insisted. "I want you close to me now, Callie."

In two weeks there had been no chance for Ham and Callie to be together as they had been. Ham was relieved at first. The temptation had been removed, he thought. But as the days went by, his hunger grew ravenous. His nights were spent in sleepless torment, despairing of his outrageous need for Callie, hating her, hating himself, and hating his father with vicious, murderous hatred.

On a Sunday morning, Ham whispered to Callie in the kitchen while Nate was in the graveyard visiting the family plot. "I've got to see you. It can't wait. Today, this afternoon, I'll wait in the hayloft for you."

She smiled at him. "I'll be there. Three o'clock. Your father likes his nap on Sunday."

Ham nodded and went out into the air. He stood there a moment, watching his father across the ancient headstones. Nate was kneeling at Amanda's grave, praying, his white mane tousled in the wind. Angrily, Ham looked away and stalked around to the front of the house.

The hayloft was a hive of warm silence, humming with the voices of the flies that teased the cows and horses below. Ham climbed the ladder swiftly, pausing on the final rung until his eyes accommodated to the dimness. There were no windows, just the wide loft door, shut now, but light aplenty sifted in through the wide cracks in the side boards. Ham lay down on a pile of straw at the back of the loft. When all the tame hay was in, the loft would be filled up almost to its vaulted roof.

She didn't keep him waiting long. When he saw her, at the top of the ladder, his longing became so intense that he began to unbutton his trousers even as she stepped bare-legged across the loft floor.

She understood his need—it was plain to see—and she laughed and hurried to him. "Here, let me help you, my love," she whispered. Her hands were on him.

"Callie, love," he gasped.

She kissed him with mouth wide open, teasing the inside membrane of his mouth.

They fell upon the hay. "I'm naked under this," she whispered. She helped his shaking hands undo the buttons at the front of her dress. He cried out with delight as he uncovered her. His child! It had to be his child!

Impulsively, he rolled her skirt above her hips and bent his face to her bare, soft belly, kissing it tenderly, *kissing his child!*

They were spent but still locked in tight embrace when the old man discovered them.

Nate stood over them with his fists clenched, a massive vengeful figure. *I am looking into the face of God on Judgment Day!* Ham thought, and he was terrified as he had never been terrified in all his seventeen years.

Nate reached down and grabbed Callie by her long hair, dragged her to her feet, and shook her like a doll.

"Whore!" he spat in her face. "Fix your clothes and get out of here. My son and I have things to talk about and do alone." He said to Ham. "On your feet!"

Ham scrambled on hands and knees toward his trousers cast aside on the straw. His father aimed a kick at his bare buttocks and Ham went sprawling, gasping from the hot pain of the heavy boot. He rolled away from a second kick, found his feet, and backed away.

The old man advanced on him. "What kind of a son would lead his father's wife into adultery! What kind of monster have I spawned! You're depraved, debauched, no immorality too vile. Even incest!"

"She's not my mother, you dirty old bastard!" The sound of the word in his ears shocked Ham. No man had ever insulted Nathaniel Knight to his face. He experienced the thrill of fear he had felt as a child standing at the church altar, before the cross, and thinking blasphemies.

Nate rushed at him in wild rage and clubbed him on the side of the head with a heavy horny fist. Ham fell sprawling on the hay.

"Seducer!"

Ham evaded the cruel boot again and stumbled to his feet. "Stay away, Paw!" he screamed, the pain and indignity of his treatment dispelling fear with anger.

"Don't call me that again! I'll not be a father to a lecher!"

"Lecher!" Ham shouted savagely. "You're the lecher, old man! "My mother not cold six months when you slaver all over a girl young enough to be my sister!" Ham stood fast against the bull charge this time. He blocked one blow with his elbow, but the power of it numbed his arm all the way up to the shoulder. He struck out with his right hand and hit the old man high on the right cheekbone. It was a good blow, and it made Nate back off, but only briefly. His fists beat down Ham's defense and bludgeoned him to the floor a second time. Stunned, badly hurt, he stayed down on his hands and knees.

"All right, I've had enough, Paw!"

"An eye for an eye . . ." His father's voice came to him, chanting as if in a dream. "You've robbed me of my manhood. It's only fair you should lose yours!" The words fell like hammer blows on his brain. *My manhood?*

The torture of the boot driving up between his legs made his father's intent manifest. Ham writhed soundless on the dirty boards, powerless to breathe, doubled up and clutching at his groin, the unrelenting agony carrying him to the brink of unconsciousness. Only his fear held him back.

Mutely he saw his father walk to a near corner of the loft and grip a pitchfork angled there. He started back to Ham. Ham tried to speak, plead, beg for mercy, but his lungs were still burning for air. *God, dear God, help me! God! Strike him dead!*

Nate stood over him, the fork in one hand, and bending low over Ham's contorted body he tried to pry his knees apart with the free hand.

Ham was powerless before his father's murderous rage and iron strength. He stared up at a mask of hate in terrified submission. And all at once, while he braced to endure the vengeful thrust, Nate's iron grip slackened and the fire in his eyes dimmed. Died. His expression was surprised. No longer looking at his son, but seeing past him, past this moment, this day, beyond all worldly time and space.

He straightened up, letting go of Ham, letting the prongs of the pitchfork clatter to the planks with the handle resting loosely in his flaccid fingers. His other hand clutched at his throat, slipped down to span his breastbone. He backed off, stumbled, canted to the side like a drunk. Fell to his knees, still holding on to the pitchfork, gripping it with both hands now. Trying hand over hand to pull himself up to his feet.

Ham knew from the dead eyes, even before his father pitched forward and lay still with his face buried in a clump of hay. Nathaniel Knight was ready for his place within the brass rectangle at the center of Cyrus Knight's austere little cemetery on the hill.

Silence. Silence, disturbed only by the humming of the flies in the stable below and his own rasping breathing. She materialized out of a dark corner of the loft like a wraith, walking soundlessly on her bare feet. She stood over her husband, looking down at him in silent solemnity.

Ham got to his feet cautiously, clenching his teeth against the fire in his belly. If his innards had come tumbling out on the floor, he would not have been surprised. Somehow it seemed wrong that he should be standing here looking down at his still father. It was an act of God, surely, that he was alive.

"He's dead," Callie spoke finally, without any emotion.

Ham walked past her without a word.

God, dear God, help me! God! Strike him dead!

She went after him and grabbed his arm as he turned to descend the ladder.

"Ham! Answer me. What are you going to do?"

He spoke then in a lifeless voice. "Phone for the doctor."

"No use of that. Your father's dead. I know."

"The law then. I killed him."

"You're insane, Ham. It was his heart. He's had spells before. When you got the snake bite, he had a bad one. He didn't want you to know."

"I wanted him to die," Ham said.

"That's not the same as killing him. Your father's terrible temper was what killed him."

"The crime is in the heart as well as in the deed. I murdered him in my heart."

"That's nonsense. Such talk will get us nowhere. Look, we've got to tell a story about what happened. There's always an inquest into sudden death like this."

"What happened?" He shrugged. "We know what happened. We don't have to make up stories."

He started down the ladder with Callie behind him. He glanced up once, seeing beneath her skirt. He looked away, feeling nothing.

Outside the barn he strode through the tall grass toward the house with her clinging to his arm and devising tales to tell the law and the neighbors.

"You and he were working in the loft, Ham, after dinner. That's logical, you're far behind in harvesting the hay, I heard him say it. Look!" She cast one arm behind her, pointing. "That wagon by the barn's half-full of hay from yesterday. It was hot up there. He'd had a heavy meal. It happens to men his age every day. He just collapsed with the fork still in his hand. Do you understand, Ham?"

He stared at her with a strange new regard. "What took him to the barn? I heard him snoring in his bed before I left the house. What stirred him?"

Her eyes were slitted, wary. "We never can predict the habits of others. Your father was fickle in his habits."

"He's napped two hours each Sunday for as long as I can remember," he said and looked at her with speculation.

Her voice was tense. "You don't imagine I told him I was going to the barn to lay with you?"

"I could believe almost anything about you, Stepmother." His gaze was cold upon her.

"Stepmother!" It startled her. "What kind of joke is that?"

He began to recite with strong accent on the meter:

"Murder most foul as in the best it is,
But this most foul and unnatural."

She looked at him from narrowed eyes. "The ghost of Hamlet's father."

"My father's ghost," Ham said quietly.

PART 2

Violence & Brutishness

One year and four months had passed since this same assembly had huddled against the bluster of late spring while Pastor Saul Williams intoned the invocation over Amanda Knight's coffin.

"God of all ages who hast made our days few and swift on earth . . ."

On this event the sun shone brightly, the woods around the tilted graveyard pulsing with songs of birds and insect life. Life. It filled the eyes and ears and nostrils.

And this time it was Nathaniel in the box, and Callie Hill was within the realm placed apart from the other common graves by the green mildewed brass railing.

And Ham was dry-eyed, his heart as empty as his soul. He looked across at the sad neglected plot with the single grave of old Tom Hill and saw her as clearly as he had that day, fairy-like, unreal, with her golden hair, pale flesh, and luminous eyes.

His eyes cut back to Callie in her black, billowing widow's weeds. Her face inscrutable behind the veil. The same one she had worn at her wedding, dyed black.

Not a fairy was she. Witch was what she was. Black widow.

Behind the veil, the eyes took it all in. The hypocritical cleric mouthing his lifeless homilies.

"Cancel the hurt we may have done to him by hasty work or unkind deed.
Hold him in perpetual light from grace to grace, from strength to strength . . .
O Lord in Thee we have trusted.
Let us never be confounded.
In Jesus' Name . . .
Amen."

When Nate and Callie would pause at the door to pass a courtesy to the reverend after Sunday services at his poor church, Saul Williams would caress her hand with his cold bony fingers as if it were a sexual fetish. Wetting his thin lips with his wet, glistening tongue.

"The Lord has truly blessed you, Nathaniel."

"Amen."

The mourners cried in chorus.

Walt Campball teetering under the dead weight on his arm of his fat, weeping wife. Susan Campball's tears were real enough, Callie guessed, but her grief was more for herself than for the corpse. The passing of one's contemporaries is a yardstick of one's own mortality.

Alva and Rena Lampbert looked like two scarecrows in their funeral finery. Rena made a show of dabbing at invisible tears with a black lace handkerchief.

Callie had observed Ham gazing at her father's plot, knowing what he was thinking. Of the first time he had seen her. And desired her. Yes, even that day she had sensed his need while it was yet a mystery to Ham.

She breathed in deeply, recording this moment in all of its dimensions on the same scroll of memory that contained *The Complete Works of William Shakespeare:* at least a commanding cross section of his plays and sonnets.

The smell of rich loam mounded behind the grave. Sweet grass cuttings, the scent of cut flowers, the smells of death. Red, orange, yellow of autumn foliage and blue sky assaulting the optic nerve with their vibrant intensity. She turned her face upward and let the sun warm her face through the veil.

For one intoxicating instant she was the center of the universe, she knew religious ecstasy. Callie opened her eyes to reality. She was at the center—of this ceremony. The widow of the dead man. Mrs. Nathaniel Knight. Successor to the patriarch of the Knight clan. The village and all its domains stretching north and south and east along the river belonged to him. Nathaniel was a rich and powerful man, kin to the feudal noblemen who inhabit the bard's poetry.

And she was heir to it all. Well, not all. Her hand came up and gripped Ham's arm when the minister nodded to the diggers leaning on their spades. She and Ham. Stepmother and stepson, side by side. Bound together by an ever-closer tie. She placed her other hand gently on her belly, taut with the child it carried though still not prominent to any eye but hers.

When they turned away from the diggers bending to the last grim task, filling the hole, Ham tried to pull away from her, but Callie's grip on his arm was iron.

She looked up at him and smiled. In a voice meant to be overheard by those around them she said, "You're the man of the house, Ham. Now that your father is gone, it's you I'll have to lean on."

Walt Campbell fell in on the other side of Ham and patted him on the back. "You have nothing to fear, Callie," he told her. "Age means nothing. Ham's a Knight. Ham's a man. You're in good hands."

To Ham: "This is a bad time for your stepmother, expecting the child and all. Take good care of her and, remember, you got me and your Aunt Susan. We'll help all we can in any way you need us."

Ham grunted unintelligibly. Callie spoke across him to Campball. "Thank you, Walt. I don't know how we could have gotten through this awful week without you and Susan. We want you to come back to the house with us now for a little lunch. All of Nate's loved ones," she added, noting the anxious faces of the Lamperts. "He'd want that. Just before he passed on, Nate said to me—" She broke off, diverted by the sight of Carl Majors.

Standing outside the railing in the uncut grass. Dressed in a light Palm Beach suit, and a sporty tie, and he carried a straw hat in his hand. He offered his hand to Callie.

"Terribly sorry I'm late. I was in Baltimore when I received the tragic news. My son phoned me there. I cleaned up my business as soon as I could and drove all night to get back here and—" He ran one hand down the front of his suit in a self-deprecating gesture and apologized. "Please excuse my appearance, but I didn't have time to change."

Callie put him at his ease. "There's nothing to excuse, Carl. Ham and I are grateful that you came at all. Isn't that so, son?"

With a strangled sob, Ham pulled loose from her and ran down the trail. Callie sighed. "Poor boy, he's been rock, rescue, and refuge for me all week, I knew once he'd seen us through our trial he was bound to break down. He idolized his father. It's been a stunning blow to him, as well to me."

Carl Majors nodded soberly. "An awful tragedy, losing both his mother and his father so close together. He's fortunate to have you."

She brushed her veil aside and smiled at him, a green-eyed enigma. "We're fortunate to have one another."

She offered him her arm. "You'll join the family in our mourning luncheon, of course?"

"I'm honored." He grasped her forearm with one hand and fitted her frail elbow into the callused palm of his other hand. It was the only time he had touched her other than a casual handclasp greeting. To his surprise she was not as frail as her appearance hinted. Her arm was firm and strong and warm through the long black sleeve.

There was no sign of Ham when the small party entered the house. Callie cast her eyes up the broad stairs.

"He's probably in his room," she said. "I'll go to him. . . . Susan, I'd be obliged if you and Rena put the coffeepot to boil." To Campball: "Walt, you know where Nate kept his apple brandy in the pantry. Perhaps you and Alva and Mr. Majors would like some spirits."

She ascended the stairs, gathering up the long black skirt with both hands at her knees. Carl looked after her, admiring the shapeliness of her ankles and calves in the dark, unflattering stockings.

Callie entered Ham's room without knocking. He lay supine on the big fourposter bed, staring at the cracked ceiling.

"Ham, are you ill?"

He said nothing.

"You should come down and show your appreciation that they took time to come here and pay their last respects to your father."

Slowly he sat up and put his feet down on the floor. He sat

there with his head in his hands. "I'll be down," he said. "Just give me a few minutes."

"We'll expect you, then." She turned and left the room. She went to her own room and removed the hat and veil. Inspected herself in the dresser mirror. The cosmetics, lip rouge, perfume, powder that she had always kept hidden from Nathaniel lay openly on the dresser top. She touched the puff to her nose and forehead, reached for the lip rouge, then thought better of it. Not today, in the presence of his kin.

Ham came down soon after and was civil through the cold meal, meat, cheese, and salads contributed by Susan Campball and Rena Lampbert. He ate nothing and spoke only when someone spoke to him. No one was offended. They applauded the display of grief by Nathaniel's devoted son.

As he had at the wedding feast not long before, Carl Majors sat between Susan and Callie. This time there was no levity. The Lampberts and the Campballs ate methodically amid small, strained conversations. How well the corpse had looked. How hot the summer had been. Post–World War I prosperity.

Just before he had died, Nathaniel had added five more men to the quarry crew. The demand for slate had never been so great since the turn of the century. Carl Majors' brick kilns downriver cast a crimson halo into the sky all night long.

"Two shifts around the clock," he bragged. "Build, build, build, everybody is building. Homes, factories, office buildings, you name it, someone is building it. There's money everywhere, it seems."

"It seems," said Walt Campball. "Where does all this money come from?"

"The stock market, of course." Carl was in a patronizing mood.

"It just growed, like Topsy," Walt replied with a smugness of his own.

Carl laughed, showing hard yellow teeth. "It's difficult to explain to one outside the Market."

Callie's green eyes were deep and quizzical. "I don't trust things that are difficult to explain."

He met her gaze. "I pay accountants and brokers to understand such things for me. I expect your husband did the same."

"To some degree. He had a lawyer and a broker, but Nate told them what he wanted. They didn't tell him."

His pale eyes were getting rheumy from too much applejack. He patted her knee under the table. "That's why Nate wasn't as rich as I am."

Callie smiled and let his hand linger on her knee. "We'll see if it stays that way." She changed the subject. "How are your children, Carl?"

"Oh, they're fine, I think. I see them so infrequently, I can never be positive." He laughed. "Children, indeed. Bruce is twenty-four, a junior partner in the firm. Chris is seventeen and spends most of her time in Albany or Saratoga with friends or cousins. Can't say I blame her. This section is no place for a young woman of marriageable age."

Susan Campball clucked. "Exactly what my Lucy says. She's set on going to New York and becoming an actress soon as she graduates."

"Over my dead body," Walt grumped.

"It could come to that," Carl jested. "They must have their way, come hell or high water, this younger generation. You must meet my boy and girl, Callie." He glanced down the table at Ham. "You know my daughter, Chris, from school, isn't that so, Ham?"

Ham's ears reddened. "I know who she is."

Indeed he did. Blond, beautiful, aloof, regal, strutting around as if she wore a crown. "Princess," the other girls called her with undisguised envy.

"Then you must get to know each other better," Carl said. "Callie, why did Nate turn down all my invitations to visit us across the river? I even offered to come and pick you up in my car."

She shrugged her shoulders. "Nathaniel was not a social person. He liked his home and his privacy."

"Well, now that you're alone, I insist you and Ham come over and have dinner with us. What about next Sunday?"

She glanced at Ham and caught his eye. "What do you say, Ham? I think it would be healthy. There's just the two of us now, alone together in this big house. We should get out and see other people."

"Anything you say," he agreed and dropped his eyes.

"Soon the two of you will be three," Susan reminded Callie.

Callie laughed and spanned her belly with both hands. "That's right. I forgot all about little Nate."

The Campballs and Lampberts regarded her with good humor and affection. Susan said, "Little Nate, it's a dear thought, but it may turn out to be a girl."

Callie smiled confidently. "Oh, no, it's a boy all right. And my fondest wish is that he'll grow up to be exactly like his older brother."

"Hear, hear." Carl lifted his applejack glass. "Let's drink to it. To the splendid sons of Nathaniel Knight. May the unborn son become as much of a credit to his father as his son Ham."

Ham shoved back his chair, almost tipping it over. He mumbled. " 'Scuse me, I got chores to do down at the barn."

"A fine lad," Carl said after he had fled. "He won't let grieving interfere with his responsibilities."

"He's a Knight," Walt Campball declared with familial pride; after all, Nathaniel had been a father to them all in Knightsville. "They carry on an important tradition."

Carl slumped in the chair and gazed wryly into his glass. "I won't deny it. I may have more money than Nathaniel Knight possessed. Yet no one ever considered naming a town after Carl Majors."

It was their first night alone in the house. Old Nate had been a very real presence even dead in his coffin in the parlor. Callie was excited at the prospect.

She had cooked the beef stew and dumplings that were Ham's favorite dish. Instead of the bright oil lamp, she lit two tapered candles on the kitchen table.

"It's all over, Ham," she told him when at last they faced each other across the table. "Really over. What's done is done, is over and best forgotten."

He looked at her strangely. "Best forgotten? My dead father's blood on our hands and you expect me to forget? You and I are Macbeth and his Lady."

Her mouth curled down in pique. "That's nonsense. We never laid a hand on your father. It was his heart."

"His heart," he said bitterly. "We destroyed his heart as certainly as if we had used a dagger. The end's the same."

She studied his face, dark and brooding in the flickering candlelight. He looked older these past few days. More a man than he'd appeared when measured against his father. She wanted him badly the way a woman wants a man, breast to breast, mouth to mouth, loin to loin.

"You will forget," she said. She knew how to make him forget his father. The same way she had made him forget Nathaniel in the past. No room for any other consideration in the mind and heart but the all-consuming passion for the flesh. Ham would find his redemption in the carnal fires.

He stared down at his untouched plate, his hands on the table alongside the knife and fork. She reached over and put her hand on one of his.

"Eat your dinner, you'll feel better. It's your favorite, stew and dumplings."

He shook his head. "I can't. I'd choke." He pulled his hand away and dropped it in his lap.

"Suit yourself." Callie bent to her own plate with gusto. She was ravenous. The sense of something important accomplished always gave her an appetite.

"I don't understand you, Ham," she said, chewing the tender beef and biscuit. "Your father's time had come. If it had not ended in the loft, it would have come about the next day, pitching hay, as they think. Or even in my bed. That sport can be as fatal as brawling or laboring. Think how you would have felt if it had happened that way."

"Stop it." He braced elbows on the table and covered his face with his hands in shame.

"It was best this way, believe me." She licked the grease off her fingers with curling tongue. "Admit it, isn't this what we always dreamed of? You and I alone in this house. Man and wife. Waiting for the birth of our child."

"I won't hear any more of your evil talk." He clapped his hands over his ears and leaped up, toppling the chair. He threw open the back door and ran out into the night.

Callie wiped her sticky fingers on a napkin, stood up, and walked to the open door. He was loping up the overgrown cart trail that went to the quarry. That led nowhere; he'd soon be back.

She hummed softly to herself as she washed and dried the dishes. Pleased with herself. Pleased with the way things were going. She patted the unborn child in her belly tenderly. He—it was a boy, she knew—had worked the magic. Fulfillment beyond her widest expectations. One year ago plus four months a slavey in a dirty beanery, smiling and curtsying to country bumpkins for their nickels and dimes.

Today a lady of the manor. A widow of means far in excess

of what she had believed before Nate's death. She'd read the will while the undertaker was draining out his congealed blood on the kitchen table. She'd wisely never pushed him on that score. He'd been a cautious and suspicious man in matters of finance. Time enough after she told him she was with his child.

"Pray, have no concern for me, my husband. I'm young and strong and able to care for myself. But our baby . . . your son, Nathaniel . . . he'll be your heir as well as Ham. . . ."

The next day he took the train to Clinton to meet with the lawyers who'd drawn his first will. The new will partitioned his estate, cash and stock and all his vast land holdings, into three equal parts. His wife, Ham, and the unborn child presumptuously named in the text as "Nathaniel Knight the Second."

Standing at the sink she looked out across the yard toward the graveyard. The white marble ghosts in the graveyard glowing eerily, keeping patient vigil over Cyrus and Emma and Will and Jean and Nathaniel. That afternoon the mason had chipped the final date on the face of his stone.

1922.

"Amen," she sighed.

A comet blazed across the sky and dipped behind the mountain. A pleasing omen. She was not thinking of Nathaniel. But of his son, Ham. Her gaze wandered to the dark, disheveled patch of sod where her father's bones resided. And she made a note to herself to speak with Walt Campball next day. She wanted Tom Hill's plot mowed and tidied. And after that there'd be a headstone and, yes, a brass railing like the one enclosing his rich relatives. She had to laugh, the way her father would have laughed. Relative to the high and mighty Knights! Well, now, it was true! There was a link. His daughter. Caliban Hill Knight.

Caliban . . .

As a child she'd been teased and tormented by the other children, and even her teachers said the name with disguised disdain.

"How on earth did you get that name, child?"

How indeed?

Tom Hill's passion for the Bard of Avon and his bizarre sense of humor. Or was it humor?

She'd complained bitterly to him once, and Tom had laughed and swung her up onto his big knee.

"It's a perfect name for you, love. Caliban was the offspring of a devil and a witch. Which is pretty much how I'd describe your dear departed mother, and she would me. Outsiders saw only her ravishing beauty. A mask, to be sure. I soon saw past that. But we all wear masks, Callie."

She'd laughed and pulled playfully at his cheeks. "You don't have on a mask."

He'd held her close against him in a rare show of paternal devotion. "Oh, Lord, my love. How little you know."

It was true, she learned. Nathaniel Knight knew more about her parents than she did. He was reluctant to speak of them at all, but Callie prevailed.

Tom Hill was born and raised in Knightsville. His father, uncles, and brothers split rails, tarred ties, and hammered spikes for the New York Central Railroad. It was better than working in the quarries and spitting blood from lungs calcified with rock dust before a man was thirty. But it was not good enough for Tom.

The Spanish-American War gave him the chance to get out of Knightsville. He enlisted in the army and was assigned to the engineers. His three years in the corps provided him with the background to go into the construction trade after his discharge. He got a job in Albany with a contractor who had won bids on government projects, erecting state buildings and laying roads. It was there he met Kitty Slade. She was a wench, he knew, but it was the wench in her that he found irresistible. At first.

Tom had a dark, perverse side to him. He was a drinker and liked to brawl. He had been charged with the attempted rape of a Clinton high school teacher before he ran off to enlist in the army. The jingo-minded politicians of the era had the case against patriotic young hero Tom dismissed.

When Kitty became pregnant he moved her back to Knightsville and went to see Carl Majors, the brick tycoon across the river, about a job. Tom Hill brought with him a formula he'd devised, a fast-setting, cohesive mortar for laying bricks.

Carl was impressed with the formula and the man. He hired Tom and put him to work at the big Majors kilns in Newburgh. Far enough from Knightsville so he could only come home on weekends.

It was best, Tom and Kitty decided, for her to stay with his mother and father in Knightsville until the child was born. A bad decision, as things worked out. When the time came to move, the new mother had a change of heart. She liked things as they were. Free of her husband from Sunday until Friday. Free of the responsibilities of motherhood: grandmother was mother to her child. Free to come and go as she pleased. Flirting in the speakeasies at Clinton, the kind frequented by a certain caste of woman.

A bartender once inquired of Kitty, "What kind of future is there in hanging around dives like this? You're a beautiful girl. You got class."

She gave him her vague, enigmatic smile so like Callie's smile and told him, "Seeking pleasure for myself and giving pleasure to others. What better goal is there to living?"

Live she did.

And then there was an abrupt change to her life-style. She stopped her weekday trips to Clinton. Made one overnight trip each week to Albany. "To visit family and friends," as she explained it to the Hills.

One Thursday while he was in the state capitol on legal business, Nathaniel Knight saw Kitty Hill riding in a horse-drawn carriage with Carl Majors. He had never mentioned it to a soul until he told it to his young wife, Callie. She had a way of worming the deepest secret out of a man, even a tight-lipped man like Nate.

The revelation did not move her. It was like hearing scandal about a stranger.

"My father knew about her and Carl Majors?" she asked.

"I expect he found out. There was one grand row, oh, I guess you were about three. He came near to choking her to death. They lugged him off to the county jail. When they took him up before the judge the next week, she never appeared to testify. She'd packed her bags and left without a trace and was never seen or heard of again. Just as if she had gone up in a puff of smoke."

Callie sank her teeth softly into her lower lip. "Like a witch."

"There was a rumor going around that Carl Majors had driven her away. He denied it to your father and to the police. No one came forward to say he was lying, and the matter was dropped. Right after that, Carl transferred your father to a smaller kiln at Buxton so he'd be near you. Your grandparents cared for you until they both died in the terrible winter of 1907 from the flu. Then your father took you back to Buxton to live with him."

Tom Hill had passed on before his time, knifed in a brawl when Callie was ten. After that, the long, dreary years in the orphanage with no surcease except from the Book. Escape from the institution and from the prison of her body into the magic world of Shakespeare's plays.

All the roles she had played. Lived, not played. She *was* Lady Macbeth.

> *Here's the smell of blood still: all the*
> *Perfumes of Arabia will not sweeten this little hand. . . .*

She was Lear's monstrous daughter Goneril:

> *. . . See thyself, devil*
> *Proper deformity seems not in the fiend*
> *So horrid as in woman. . . .*

She was Hamlet's adulterous mother, but never the mad Ophelia:

> *To her sick soul as sin's true nature is,*
> *Each toy seems prologue to some great amiss.*

She *was* Caliban.

And the true play guise was the mask of golden hair, emerald eyes, and fair complexion she wore on the earthly stage.

She played the role of Orphan Hill as well as any other of her roles. Accepted with reservation by both her peers and the surrogate mothers, nuns, who cared for and taught them. Others behaved and spoke guardedly in Callie's presence as if she were an uncomfortable stranger met for the first time. Too many facets to her, ever turning and casting disconcerting reflections into the eye of the beholder. Too many surprises. Nothing to seize on and embrace, devoid of the solidarity vital to deep and lasting relationships. Full of affectations, or what they took to be so. Her recall of Shakespeare too often employed as a weapon, flailing away all around her with confounding elliptical passages to answer any argument or challenge.

"Must you always speak in parenthesis, Callie?" a sister

once chided her in class. "I'd like a simple statement out of you just once in your life."

Callie smiled her sly smile and a veil descended over her eyes. She replied:

> *"You would play upon me; you would seem to know my stops; you would pluck out the heart of my mystery; . . ."*

There was laughter all around her; Callie was smugly serene in her small triumph.

They all breathed a sigh of relief at the orphanage when, in the late spring of 1921, Callie left them, clutching the Book and the deed to her father's burial plot to her bosom. There was a new ten-dollar bill in her pocketbook and a carpetbag containing her few possessions carried in her left hand. Prior arrangements had been made for her to board with a religious family in Clinton and to wait on tables in a small, respectable restaurant.

On her first day off she bought a bouquet of violets and took the train to Knightsville. She walked from the depot to the small cemetery on the hillside behind the big white Knight house.

It was almost impossible to make out her father's resting place among the high weeds that glutted the poor plot. She pulled out handfuls of tall, wiry grass until the small perimeter of the grave was cleared. Then she scattered the blossoms on it and blew an affectionate kiss to his ghost.

It was on that day she first set eyes on the dark, brooding, grieving youth who so reminded her of the Prince of Denmark.

Later, when she learned his name was Ham, it seemed natural to her. A portent of the true beginning for Callie Hill.

She wiped the drainboard, hung the dishrag up to dry, drew the curtains across the moonlit landscape of the cemetery. She blew out the lamps and lit her way up the back stairs with a candle.

She undressed by the dim light of the single candle, standing naked before the mirror. Pleased with her body in the candlelight's magic glow. The carnality of her woman's flesh subdued by provocative shadows. She wished Ham could see her like this. He'd soon forget the death of the old man in the pulsing life of the young woman.

She wrapped a clinging negligee around herself, picked up the candleholder, and went to Ham's room. She opened it without knocking and walked slowly toward the bed. He lay on his side curled up in the fetal position. Pretending to sleep, she knew that.

"Ham," she called softly. "I've come to you. I need you, and you need me, you know you do."

His eyes remained shut, but she saw his body quiver under the blanket. She placed the candle on the small table beside the bed and took off the robe.

"Look at me, Ham," she whispered; more loudly when he still did not respond: "Look at me. Do you dare?"

With fearful hesitation his eyelids opened. He stared at her mutely. She bent low over him and looked into his eyes.

"Ham . . ." Her voice was a caress. She put a knee upon the mattress and drew the bedclothes down off him. He slept raw, as she did.

He held up a hand to fend her off. "Callie, please. . . . Go 'way and leave me be."

"You need me. You want me. As you did that day, mad with wanton lust." She took his outstretched hand and kissed the palm. Lay down beside him. Slipped her thigh between his thighs.

He moaned and shuddered. "As I did that day. O God!"

She smiled and put her arms around his neck. It was as good as done. He was seduced, she thought. Soon discovered it was a misconception. His lips were cold and unresponsive, his manhood lifeless.

"Oh, my love," she breathed in his ear. He might have been a stone statue. So hard. So cold. So rigid and unyielding. She touched the thick vein in his throat with her tongue. It pulsed with turgid rhythm, denoting the dispassion of his heart. She nuzzled the thick dark mat of his chest. His belly. But rejecting all the coaxing of her hands and lips, he remained impotent.

"Why are you doing this to yourself? To me?" she chided. "Stop sniffling like a child and be the man again I loved so well before this business."

"Love?" He gave her a short, brittle laugh. "Love had little to do with what you and I did together behind my father's back. Our treacherous lechery, that's all we had together, Callie."

"Don't be a fool! A maudlin, spiteful boy is what you are. Do you think to punish me with coldness? This pretending you don't want me as a woman any longer."

He sat up and took her hands off his body. Gripped her wrists tightly and fixed her with an unwavering gaze.

"I'm not pretending. You must know that by now. Nothing you can do or say can change what's happened. The fierce yearning I had for your flesh is dead. Your naked body repels my sight."

"You bastard!" She slapped him hard across the face.

Ham was shocked. He'd never seen her temper, or heard her shout an angry oath at anyone.

Callie was surprised herself. Not given to outbursts of undisciplined emotion of the kind she'd always rued in her own father, she regretted this lapse.

"I'm sorry, Ham. Even if you did deserve that."

Ham pulled up covers. "I'm sorry too. I truly am. I don't blame you, Callie, for my father's death. It was I who begged on hands and knees for you to come to me in the loft last Sunday. The burden of guilt lies on my conscience."

She put on the negligee and wrapped it tight around her. "All this talk of guilt and conscience, it sickens me. '. . . *Conscience it makes cowards of us all* . . .' I do believe, Ham, you take pleasure in suffering. If you'd been born in an ancient age, you would have kissed the Roman centurions' feet as they threw you to the lions. The trouble with your kind is you spend so much time agonizing over what's to befall you in the next world that you don't live at all in this world. This great God of the Good Book your father worshiped. If he's up there somewhere in that infinite sky above us, he's fixed our short stay here on this planet. He's the author of our destinies as surely as the bard foredoomed Hamlet even as he first put his quill to the paper."

"I can't abide with that."

"Then you're blind. There is no way your father's death could have been avoided. Even if he had banished me from your lives that first day we met in the cemetery, another woman would have come in my place. And you would have lusted after her in the loft one day, and old Nate's death scene would have been played out as it was ordained.

"There was a king in ancient Greece who was told by an oracle that his son would murder him and marry his own mother, the king's wife. Vowing to prevent it, he ordered the infant be abandoned in the mountains, where the wild beasts would devour him. But the boy was saved by shepherds and raised to manhood. He became a mighty warrior and leader, and later when he did battle with his father, they met as strangers. And Oedipus—that was his name—did triumph over the father and took his life. And just as the oracle had predicted, he took the king's wife along with his kingdom. It came to pass that Oedipus learned the truth of what he had done and in anguish stabbed out both eyes with his mother's brooch. That's you, Ham. Killed your father and bedded down with his wife. And now you're blind as well. Poor fool. I'm going to bed."

She picked up the candle and walked to the door. Before she left the room she turned and looked back. Her feelings about Ham were complex and ill-defined. She had no love for him—any more than she had loved his father—or, for that matter, her own father. Callie had never experienced the hyperbolic emotion that poets described as "love." Ham was right on that score. The pleasures of the flesh they had consumed together had little to do with "love." Her one regret was that his impotence was depriving her of the sweet experience. Otherwise Ham had served his purpose. She clasped both hands across her tight abdomen, felt life there stirring.

Ham was a dim shadow in the background of her ruminations as Callie lay in her bed making plans for the future. In the foreground of her thinking loomed Carl Majors, vivid and real as life in the darkness. His presence in the house that day lingered on long after his departure with the insistency of musk. A swaggering male animal, that was Carl, every inch a man. She smirked at the inadvertent pun. He'd never be incapable in bed with a wanting female.

On Sunday Carl Majors arrived before noon in his big black Mercer touring car. It was a late Indian summer day, more like July than October.

"A perfect day for driving," said Carl as he helped Callie into the front seat. "It can be windy, though, on the highway at high speeds. Do you want the top up?"

She laughed. "Please, no, I love the wind. It sings to me."

The heavy lips beneath the brush mustache curled wryly. "So tell me, miss, what song is that?"

"Oh, there are many songs. Of life and love and ecstasy and pain and hate and death. Of all there is under heaven on earth."

"I'm glad I don't have your imagination," he said as he took his place behind the big steering wheel, made of pure ivory. "It's trial enough to deal with what I can see and hear, much less your fairies and spirits."

"The wind's no spirit or fairy. It's a force."

"You're a strange one, Callie Knight." He looked over his shoulder at Ham, stiff and uncomfortable on the back seat in his suit, tight collar, and tie, the garb he reserved for weddings and funerals. He wasn't certain in which category the mood of this occasion fitted.

"You think so too, Ham? Have you ever known a female like this one?"

She turned to read Ham's expression when he answered. "No, I reckon not, sir." A pause as he and Callie gazed into each other's eyes, then: "Still, I'm not sure I know her at all."

Her green eyes mocked him. Turning around further, she reached over the seat back and patted his knee. "A fine thing to say to your stepmother, as close as we've been this past year."

Carl shook his leonine head. "Stepmother. I swear Ham looks more like your older brother."

She chuckled softly and patted Carl's knee. "Such flattery. Nathaniel always said you had a way with women."

"Idle rumor."

"I'm told you knew my mother?" Her voice almost too casual.

It caught him by surprise. His head snapped around and he stared at her an instant, eyes wide, mouth open. She was grinning at him like a fox.

"Well—yes—I think I did."

"You think? She couldn't have impressed you, then?"

"I said that wrong." His florid complexion heightened. "Your father was in my employ. A good man, Tom Hill—"

"When he wasn't drinking and fighting and feeling sorry for himself," she added lightly.

He coughed in embarrassment. "Well, all of it is long past. What I meant to say about your mother was, I scarcely knew her at all."

She studied him with head tilted to one side. "How odd.

Almost the same words Ham used about me. Was she pretty?"

He shifted his eyes back to the road. "A handsome woman. A handsome couple the two of them made. To tell the truth, you don't bear much resemblance to either one."

"Then I'm not handsome, is that it? A crone is what you think of me?"

He laughed. "Whoa there, miss! Hold on! You have a knack for twisting words."

And minds and hearts, Ham's expression said.

"You're a very beautiful woman," Carl said. "And you know it very well."

"I thank you, sir." She leaned back in the seat and gave her attention to the road. Knight's Road, a three-mile stretch of potholed dirt hardly more than a trail and barely wide enough for two cars to pass.

The car lurched through a waterhole that was deeper than it appeared. Its occupants bounced high off the seats and came down hard. Sound springs and soft leather cushioned the descent. Nevertheless, Callie was jarred. She turned pale and clasped her hands to her belly.

Carl stopped and reached out to her in alarm. "Good Lord! That was stupid of me. Are you all right, my dear?"

She took a deep breath, gingerly probed her body. "I—I think so. I'm a hardy mother, never fear. It came as a shock, that's all." She laughed and made light of it now.

But Ham had observed something in her brief unguarded moment. She possessed a vulnerability he had never before suspected.

Carl let the car creep forward in second gear for the remainder of the trip on Knight's Road.

"It's a disgrace for such a poor ox path to bear the name of Knight," Callie declared when they finally reached the paved highway. "Ham, we really must do something about it. I'll speak to Walt Campball about hiring some men to level this road."

"I'll tell you what you ought to do," Carl suggested. "You said yourself on the day you wed Nathaniel that the horse and buggy would soon be obsolete. It's true. Knight's Road should be paved, and the Knights should have a motorcar of their own. What do you say to that?"

"I say 'aye.' How about you, Ham?"

Ham had been trying to persuade his father to buy a car

like the Majors one since he first set eyes on the black enameled beauty with the brass headlamps and the sporty red-spoked wheels. Now, contrarily, he felt obliged to take the dead man's stand.

"I don't know." He was unenthusiastic. "Don't seem much sense to build a three-mile road for one motorcar."

"Why does it have to be for one?" Her pupils went to pinpoints as she looked up at the sun and stretched her arms wide to the brilliant azure sky. "If there were a bridge across the river at Knightsville and a paved road here leading to the highway . . . ?"

Carl broke in, "You know, I've given that idea of yours considerable thought since you first broached it. My son, Bruce, he thinks well of it too. We'll talk more about it after we get home."

She teased him. "Home? I just left home."

"There you go again," he said jovially. "Playing anagrams with everything I say. All right, I want you and Ham to think of Wheatley as your second home."

Callie turned to him and clapped her hands together in a child's wonder. "Wheatley? Your house has a name? Like Elsinore Castle?"

"The land was given to my father by his father-in-law, Tobias Wheatley. The estate bears his name in honor."

"How charming." She turned back to Ham. "Shall we honor your father in like fashion?" It gave her satisfaction to see him cringe.

She shrugged and said to Carl, "I don't think Ham approves. I suppose he's right. 'Knight' doesn't sound right for a house; in any case, it's always been called the 'big Knight House' for as long as I can remember. No mind, we thank you, Carl, for your generosity. Our second home, Wheatley. It's a warm feeling."

Her hair was done up in a severe bun at the nape of her neck. When they were on the highway, picking up speed, she reached back and removed the pins that held it fast.

She let go with a peal of wild laughter as the hair unfurled like a golden flag, whipping out long behind her in the slipstream of the Mercer, flashing, fluttering.

"I've always wanted to do that," she announced. "I saw a girl in a motion picture show in Clinton. She was standing at the prow of a sailing boat with her long hair flying in the wind.

It looked glorious, but I never thought I'd have the opportunity to try it. Sailing on a big expensive boat. Or riding in a marvelous motorcar like this one."

Carl looked at her and laughed. She sensed his growing affection for her. "I tell you, Callie, you make a list of all the wonderful things you've ever wanted to do, and we'll see what we can arrange."

"I warn you, I'll do it. I enjoy being spoiled."

He reached over and covered her hand on the seat between them with his gloved hand. "You were born to be spoiled, my dear. You know, more often there's greater joy in making others' dreams come true than in realizing your own."

"Dear Carl . . ." She pressed his hand and gave him her sideways smile.

The main street of Clinton, feeding Sunday traffic to the narrow bridge that spanned the river there, was clogged with horse-drawn buggies, carts, and automobiles, the drivers shouting and blowing horns at indifferent pedestrians and children frolicking in their path.

"It seems to worsen every day," Carl told them.

The traffic jam was a personal vindication for Callie. Smugly she observed, "Like I told Nathaniel. They could be crossing our bridge at Knightsville and happy to pay for the privilege. Not hampered by this narrow street and heavy population."

"It makes sense," Carl agreed. "It might be well to widen Knight's Road when you have it paved, with the future in mind."

"A wider bridge too," Callie said as they moved at a snail's pace across the Hudson, held back by the foot traffic on the span. "One with walks for pedestrians so the cars could cross at their normal rate."

"And not so rickety as this one," Carl muttered through chattering teeth, the big Mercer rumbling over the loose boards.

Callie looked down on her side. "The boards are hopping up and down like piano keys. Is it safe?"

"Oh, it's safe enough. Just old and outdated. Built before I was born."

"Outlived its usefulness."

His yellow teeth showed briefly. "The bridge or me?"

She laughed and covered her mouth and nose with one hand in a winsome feminine gesture. Her green eyes danced.

"The bridge speaks for itself. How do you say for yourself?"

"Actions speak louder than words, they say, so keep a keen eye on me, my girl, and you'll soon have your answer."

She realized he had thrown down the gauntlet, but the time was wrong for her to pick it up.

"I have a keen eye, Carl," she said lightly. "And you can depend it will be fixed on you."

Across the river in Saratoga County, Carl made up for lost time, driving the big touring car at speeds of fifty to sixty miles an hour. The ride took Callie's breath away, and her first sight of Wheatley left her even more breathless.

"It's magnificent," she gasped, clapping her hands together. "How different it appears from the other side. So much smaller. Don't you think so, Ham?"

"I've been here before," he answered sullenly. With boys from school who were sniffing after Christine Majors. Skulking around the low wall that ran around the grounds, hoping for a sight of her.

Not daring to venture beyond the NO TRESSPASSING signs.

In summer, when she came down to the private Majors beach with its white sand brought by barge from Long Island, they would row across and exchange banter with Chris and her girl friends. Offshore. They were never invited onto the beach. She kept them in their place.

Ham hardly ever spoke, never to the girls. His preoccupation was covertly watching Chris. She had been his secret lust object until Callie came into his life.

The two were alike in that they were blond and fair, with slender figures, desirable women. Chris was taller and her eyes were as blue as the sky. That said it all, he felt, the eyes. The wide-open blue sky with nothing to hide. In Callie's eyes you gazed down into fathoms of deep, dark green sea. There was the lure of mystery. Excitement. Promise of unimaginable treasure. And menace.

Ham was sitting in the boat once when Chris pulled herself out of the water onto the float, scant feet away. The white jersey suit clung to her body so tight that he could make out her nipples and cleft.

That memory sustained Ham during the hot restless nights of summer and the cold lonely nights of winter when desire got the better of shame.

Carl drove slowly up the long circular drive that ran in front of the mansion so that Callie could feast her eyes. It was a large gray house of simple, harmonious Georgian design adorned by majestic pillars in front and balancing porticoes.

"Do you like it?" Carl asked. It was a jest, for he was well aware that she was childishly impressed by symbols of wealth and power. In a paradoxical way it was her greatest weakness and her greatest strength. A weakness in her character. A strength of will and determination nursed continually by her ruthless obsession with acquisition. Not mere material acquisition. She reached out for the flesh and the soul of those close to her.

Carl Majors was a deep man who had always been fascinated by the mind and nature of *Homo sapiens.* A mystifying, stupefying, terrifying, unspeakably terrible species. It impressed him the first time he opened a Bible as a boy and read with awe of Cain and Abel, Saul and David, Lot's wife, and the Crucifixion.

Man.

Fashioned by God in his own image.

That thought caused Carl, not a religious man, to question the ancient theologians' version of the Fall and wonder if perhaps it was the Dark Angel occupying the high and mighty universal throne.

He had no illusions about this pretty little creature. Not since the day he had seen her standing at the altar beside old Nate wearing the white lace mantilla on her fair head. An angel she'd looked like. Angel, ah, yes, but which one?

The preacher could have saved the time and read the Invocation over Nathaniel Knight right then and there!

Callie was a fascination in all respects, mind and body, heart and soul. A rare treasure to possess. What a challenge for a man to be bound to such a one as she. For poor Nate it had been no contest. For Carl Majors, now that was quite another matter. No man, or woman, had ever come out on top of Carl Majors in any endeavor. Callie the Acquirer. What an acquisition to acquire her!

They were admitted by a uniformed maid into a huge center hall. Callie gaped at the diamond crystal chandelier bathed in the sunlight streaming through the round skylight above it, blinding her with its multifaceted brilliances and splashing spectrums on the marble floor. Twin stairways, following the contours of the hall on either side, curved up to a second-story balcony.

"It's elegant," she said, clapping her hands again in the common gesture that gave him a sense of power over her. To keep her in this state of imbalance, dazzled by new magics he would conjure up for her, now that was the way to keep her. And even as he hoped for it, he knew the absurdity of such a hope. For her appetites fed a bottomless maw. And, in the end, even a conjurer with the stamina and ingenuity that Carl Majors possessed must be brought to his knees in sheer exhaustion.

Yet hope is what every human being lives for. For without hope life is meaningless. Carl hoped.

"I've never been in any place like this," Callie said, eyes cutting this way and that way, missing nothing. "It's a palace." She was the first to note the presence of the girl on the balcony above. Her blond hair was done up in serpentine braids and she wore a simple white skirt and a blue shirtwaist. She reminded Callie of a perfect manikin she'd seen in a fancy ladies' shop window when her father had taken her to Philadelphia. Self-consciously Callie smoothed back her wind-tangled hair with her fingers.

She smiled and Callie smiled back, mistrusting her aristocratic manikin beauty. A cameo face reflecting nothing of real experience. An empty page in the book of life.

"There you are," Carl called to her. "Come down and meet our guests."

She came down the stairs with grace, the fingers of one hand brushing lightly over the banister, the genteel smile set on her oval face.

"We didn't expect you back so soon." Her voice went well with her face and style. "Traffic must have been light?"

"To the contrary," he replied. "There was a bad tie-up at the Clinton Bridge. But my expert driving skill more than made up for it. Ask Mrs. Knight. Callie, my daughter, Christine."

"Mrs. Knight, how nice to meet you." She came straight to Callie, her hand held high with the wrist delicately curved in the manner prescribed by the English governess who had reared her.

The faint intimidation Callie had felt on first seeing Carl Majors's daughter was gone. Like a hothouse orchid she'd wilt and wither at her first brush with frost.

"My dear, you're even more lovely than your father claimed." Callie took the girl's hand in both of her hands, embracing it warmly, the way an older woman would greet a young girl. "But please call me Callie, I do hope we'll grow to be good friends."

She glanced at Ham squirming in his dress-up clothes and shifting from one foot to the other to ease the pinch of his shiny black shoes. "I believe you know my stepson, Ham."

Chris was flustered. She'd heard the talk when old Nathaniel Knight had married Tom Hill's orphan girl. His housemaid, no less, a slattern young enough to be his own granddaughter.

"Old fool!" "Slut!" "Conniving bitch!" were some of the kinder sentiments voiced in Saratoga County. Across the river in Washington County folks were silent about the union. Nathaniel's wrath was notorious, and it was his domain.

This pretty slip of a woman with the elfin face and affable demeanor did not match at all the bleached, brassy, uneducated tart she'd pictured.

"We went to the same school," Chris said aloofly. "But we've never been formally introduced. How are you, Ham?"

He cleared his throat. "Hmmmm . . . I'm fine. Pleased to meet you."

Carl lit a cigar and grinned around it. He had known what his daughter imagined Callie to be, never made an effort to dissuade her view. He stood back and relished the moment.

Callie had genuine style; he admired style in men and women. She navigated the currents of life like a weather vane, her direction always true. The way she had clasped his daughter's hand. Referring to Ham as "my stepson." Perfection. Invalidating convention with two deft strokes. As far as age went, the two were contemporaries, the few years separating them. Chris had girded herself to play the lady of the manor to Callie's uneducated sluttish kitchen maid. Those roles had altered fast. Here was his stuck-up brat flushing and ill at ease; she might have been confronting the wife of Governor Al Smith herself!

Carl chuckled and placed a hand on the small of each woman's back. "Shall we go into the parlor and have something cool to drink? It's been a hot, dusty drive."

Callie had never been exposed to luxury of the sort she was encountering in Wheatley. The Knight home was well appointed in colonial decor. The Majors manor—she could not think of it as a plain old house now that she had seen it—reflected the tastes and talents of a legion of decorators and unlimited funds invested. Rugs, furnishings, draperies, the pictures and tapestries that adorned the mahogany-paneled walls in the parlor impressed Callie with their permanence. A rock of ages, this home. An enormous bronze eagle spanning the brick facade of the fireplace seemed to be scowling contemptuously at her.

"He doesn't take to strangers, does he?" Callie said feyly in the act of sipping lemonade, which the maid, Annie, had served to her and Chris and Ham. The tumbler half-filled with dark bourbon whiskey on the table next to Carl Majors's chair kept eliciting disapproving looks from his daughter, she duly noted.

The three of them stared at her in bewilderment.

"What are you talking about?" Carl asked, and then he saw the direction of her stare and broke into laughter. "Oh, you mean old Sam. Uncle Sammy has been guardian of these rooms and corridors from the beginning. Even before the interior was completed, they mortared and riveted him into place. I tell you, Callie, he doesn't have much use for us either. Pathetic mortals pretending otherwise. Wasting our whole lives collecting money, objects, other people to insulate us against the irrevocable fact of death. We're hardly brighter than the Egyptian pharaohs who built temples to celebrate their immortality and were sent off to their imaginary other world with food and gold and even doglike servants who went trustingly to their own wasteful ends."

Chris had still another worried look at the dwindling whiskey in his glass. "It's much too early in the day for you to get so philosophical, Father."

"I like to hear men speak of life and death," Callie declared. "It's why I have so much love and appreciation for Shakespeare."

"*You* read Shakespeare?" It slipped out, no barb intended.

Callie knew it, but it pleased her to show up the girl's clumsiness. "Does it surprise you that one brought up in an orphanage can read?" She mitigated the sharpness with a smile.

"Oh, no. Not at all," the girl protested, cheeks spotting pink. "It's only that—"

Carl came to her rescue. "Read it? I believe she wrote the damned limey's works. She's memorized Shakespeare forward and backward."

Callie licked the side of the straw where the sweet liquid had run down. "Backward," she mused. "I've never thought of that, we'll see." Adding with mischief: *"Men have marble, women waxen, minds.* It takes a hammer and chisel to make an impression on marble. Wax absorbs impressions easily and naturally."

They all laughed, with the exception of Ham, who alternately glared into his glass and stole shy looks at Chris. He found her as attractive and appealing now that he had met her as when he had pined after her from afar. Dim hope sparked. Could he through Chris escape from Callie's spell?

"Touché, Callie," Chris said, really warming to her now. "Marble minds, you hear that, Father?"

Carl rubbed his mustache, smiling; he enjoyed being the butt of clever gibes. "Now what's that from, Miss Wax Head?"

"The Rape of Lucrece. . . . Line, let me see, oh, halfway through the twelve hundreds."

"That is remarkable." Chris was full of admiration. "I wish I had one quarter of your talent. Why, in school, I couldn't even memorize a simple five-line poem."

"You've finished school?"

"Clinton High. Father wanted me to go to Vassar this year, but I wanted to travel. Europe." She tilted her head and touched a hand to her braids, an affectation, a princess calling attention to her tiara.

Callie smiled. "When you pass through Stratford on Avon, you must remember to send me a picture postcard."

Chris blinked. "Stradford? Is that in England?"

Carl roared with mirth and got up to refresh his drink.

Chris knew he was laughing at her, and being ignorant of the reason made it worse. Callie passed over it quickly and beamed at Ham. She patted his knee.

"Ham would have finished high this past year, but for his father's health. He left to take some of the load off Nathaniel. He was fortunate to have a son like Ham."

Ham pressed his tight-clenched fists into the soft cushions

on either side of him, staring as hard as he could at the cruel beak of the bronze eagle.

Carl called to them from the serving cart inside the big bay window at the front of the parlor. "Speaking of sons, here comes mine. He's been riding."

Bruce Majors made his entrance. Taller than his father, but not as imposing. His sandy hair was thinner than Carl's, his chin was weaker. A nice-looking young man, Callie thought, an altogether eligible bachelor. He wore a polo shirt that flattered his tanned muscular arms and good chest, and riding breeches with muddy boots.

Bruce was captivated by Callie and showed it. "If I had known there were girls like you in Washington County, I wouldn't be a bachelor. Where did Nathaniel Knight find you?"

Golden specks danced in her eyes like dust swirling in bright sunlight. "He didn't find me. I found him."

Carl Majors stood outside the scene, observing, amused by her irony.

Bruce sat down on a chair across the coffee table from Callie. "My father tells me you have some interesting ideas about a bridge here?"

"Yes, and my convictions are stronger than ever after driving through that bottleneck at Clinton today."

"I'm all the way with you. In fact, I've done some research on the project. Would you care to look at my figures and some rough diagrams?"

"I can hardly wait." She clapped her hands together. "Carl! Ham! Did you hear that? We're as good as begun building our bridge."

"*Our* bridge?" Carl's mouth was awry. "You move fast, Callie Knight."

"Time's too precious to waste. Let's see your notes, Bruce."

She stood up and Bruce offered her his arm, but his father pushed between them. He winked at Callie as he tucked her elbow into the snug hollow of his large rough hand and said to Bruce, "Sorry, son, the little lady's in my charge. In her delicate condition, she needs the touch that only a man of my infinite wisdom and experience can provide."

The younger man's jaw trembled, and for an instant Callie

thought he might contest his father's claim. The instant passed and Bruce looked down at the floor and tried to dismiss the incident on his own terms. He held out his hands, palms up.

"I clear forgot I've been riding. I'm filthy and covered with horse sweat. Forgive me, Callie."

"You'd be surprised how much dirt I've touched in my life." To Carl: "You wouldn't. You knew my father."

He led her off to the study with Bruce following.

Callie was wearing black only because the mores of the region dictated it; Nate had been in his grave less than one week. But her simple dress, high-necked and long-sleeved, was contoured to her figure.

As an undergraduate at Yale Bruce Majors had gotten two New Haven girls in trouble. His father had arranged for their abortions and financial settlements.

"Christ, boy, can't you be careful if you can't be good?" Carl admonished him. "One more like this and you're on your own."

Bruce was more careful after that, except for one close scrape when he went to work at the eastern sales office of the Majors Brick Company in Philadelphia. The office manager tipped off Carl that Junior was sleeping with a secretary. The girl was fired and Carl issued an ultimatum.

"Even a dumb animal knows better than to soil his own nest. That tool between your legs stands up every time you see a pair of boobs or a comely backside. All right, that can't be helped at your age. But if you ever stick it in a cunt anywhere in Saratoga County or in Philadelphia, I'll kick you out without a cent. I understand these things. I've taken my lumps. It'll pass, and then you'll settle for this." He tapped a bottle of bourbon on his desk.

Bruce had been faithful to the vow he'd made his father, for three years. There were plenty of willing ladies in Albany and New York City. In Saratoga County he had a reputation as pure as a priest's.

Watching Callie, he was not as confident about his willpower as he had been before he entered the parlor a half hour earlier.

Ham experienced a wave of panic being left alone with Chris Majors, but she soon put him at his ease.

"Ham, would you like to walk around the grounds? See the stables? Or we could go for a spin in Father's Chris-Craft?"

All summer he'd watched the Majorses' big inboard planing up and down the river, with her nose pointing skyward, water arcing off her curved prow in graceful spumes on either side.

That morning Ham had vowed no one or thing would penetrate the wall of his reserve. Yet here he was grinning broadly.

"Say, I'd like that fine."

Chris laughed and grabbed his arm. "You're actually smiling. I was beginning to think you had no teeth. Come on."

They walked down a grassy slope in the direction of the beach and boathouse.

"Your stepmother is quite an interesting person, isn't she?" Chris asked.

The mention of Callie constricted his throat. The most innocent question or mention of her in context with himself and he was overcome with paranoia. They *knew!* Everyone knew or had strong suspicions. Ham Knight had been fornicating with his father's wife. The child she carried was his child. The sight of the sinners in the very act was the weapon that had struck down Nathaniel Knight.

"Quite interesting," he mumbled through teeth clenched so hard they ached. His armpits were wet with sweat.

"She's very sweet. So different from what I had expected she would be. Of course, I've only met her. What kind of a person is she?"

He shoved his hands in his pockets to hide their trembling. "Oh, she's all right. She cooks fine. Keeps house. You know. And she reads a lot. Not just Shakespeare, either. My mother's books she found up in the attic."

"Yes, the way she talks and acts, you'd think she was a highly educated woman."

"She's smarter than I'll ever be," he said with an inflection that went deeper than the meaning of the words.

"Do you like her, Ham?"

"I never said I didn't."

Her eyes held his. "No, but you still haven't said you do."

He looked away. "I like her fine."

She sighed. "Think of the fun you'll have when your little brother is born. I'd love to have a baby in our house."

He remained silent.

"You know," she mused, "I think Bruce fancies your

young stepmother. Did you notice how he looks at her?"

"No," said Ham. The idea was incredible. She couldn't be serious.

"Men," she said airily. "Women are sensitive to such things."

She was serious. He could only look at her, speechless.

Chris was intrigued by her observation. Bruce and Callie Knight. True, her background did not match up to the Majorses'. She'd wed a man old enough to be her grandfather, by what suspect design Chris chose to overlook. Now she was a widow carrying the old man's child. However, Bruce was not untarnished himself. Too often she had been reluctant witness to angry clashes between Bruce and their father precipitated by his misdeeds. Less frequent during the past year. Chris rightly attributed the truce to the good sense Bruce showed in pursuing his vices more circumspectly. Not that he'd reformed. How many times she'd heard Father say, "What you need, my boy, is to find the right woman and settle down."

The "right" woman. Certainly not one of the callow peasant girls in Saratoga County. Ever since the trouble at Yale, at Carl's advice, Bruce had been avoiding the girls in his own society. His circle of female acquaintances was made up mainly of New York show girls, Albany shopgirls, and the high-class camp followers who always showed up at Saratoga for the racing season.

In company such as that, Callie Knight came off with high marks as an eligible mate for her brother.

When they reached the beach, Chris stooped to remove her shoes and walked through the white sand in stockinged feet. The boathouse, a small bungalow, sat at the river's edge. It housed two berths, one for the big speedboat; in the other berth a handsome sailboat bobbed at anchor. She led him up a circular staircase to the upper story, where there was a small sitting room, a galley, and two dressing rooms. The front wall of the room was solid glass, so spotlessly clean Ham had the illusion that he was on an open porch looking out across the river.

Chris indicated one of the dressing rooms. "You can change in there."

"Change?"

"Of course. I'm going to give you the ride of your life.

You'll need a bathing suit. There are plenty of spares on the shelf. You'll find one that fits."

Chris went into the other room and closed the door. The notion was still very much on her mind. Callie and her brother. It was right somehow. An alliance of the Majorses and the Knights, the two "first" families of the region.

She undressed and examined herself in the mirror on the wall. Her figure was good. She stood sideways and drew in her tummy, ran a hand over the generous curve of her buttocks.

The thought intruded without any warning. *I wonder if Ham thinks I have a sexy body?*

It shocked her as much as if a stranger had posed the question. She blushed, felt the heat spreading down over her neck and bosom.

She'd been preoccupied with Bruce and Callie.

But what about Ham and Chris? Her best girl friend in Clinton High had had a crush on Ham the year before.

"He's *so* handsome," she'd sigh. "And those *shoulders!*"

Chris thought so too, but would never have admitted it. She went out of her way to ridicule him. "Oh, Nan, he's a big dumb lummox. You hear how he talks in class, all mumbles, so nobody can understand him."

"He always knows the answer."

"Oh, Nan, really. He's crude and uncouth the way he always walks around with his hands in his pockets staring right through you or scowling at the floor. He never smiles or says hello."

"Oh, I know he doesn't know I'm alive." Nan's smile was teasing. "But he knows *you* are, Chrissy."

"What are you talking about?" Pretending to be exasperated.

"Last week at Wheatley when those boys were rowing around the float and flirting with us. You came out of the water with your sexy suit, all wet, you should have seen his eyes bulge."

Chris thrust her thin aristocratic nose into the air and sniffed. "He's probably a sex maniac on top of everything else. An animal."

The study smelled of old leather, cigar and pipe smoke, and spirits. A pungent blend that tickled Callie's nose.

"What a fine place to sit with a good book before the fire on a wintry night," she said. She walked about, laying her hands on the brick mantle, the dark paneling, the carved chair-backs.

"You shall do it on a night this winter," Carl promised. He poured himself a fresh drink from a decanter on the desk.

Bruce removed a folder from the top drawer and spread out sheets of paper on the desk top. Callie sat in the big chair behind the desk and the men stood on either side.

Bruce bent over her, so close their heads were almost touching. Her fragrance titillated his nostrils. He pointed to a rough sketch of a bridge.

"An engineer from New York came up here last week and looked the situation over. It's his advice that in the interests of economy and practicality, it should be a simple truss bridge. Three piers here, made of stone and steel, sunk deep into the river's bottom. Supporting the spans here, the trusses."

"It must be wide enough to accommodate two-way traffic," she said.

"Of course, with ease. Here, this sketch from a bird's eye viewpoint. The oblongs represent the width of an average motorcar, done in scale."

Callie frowned. "There's no footpath."

Bruce was amused. "Why should we indulge pedestrians who pay no tolls?"

"That's not the point. They're a nuisance, in the way of vehicles, they tie up traffic."

Carl baited her. "Where will all this traffic come from?"

"You'll see. Someday motorcars will be moving across our bridge in a steady procession, night and day."

"It's customary to close toll bridges to traffic at night," he reminded her.

"Not this bridge," she said adamantly.

In the beginning the Majors men were indulgent of her zeal for affairs that were properly the concern of knowledgeable males.

Let them patronize me, she thought. *My turn will come.*

She possessed a keen and analytical mind that absorbed information like a sponge, and the rare talent of being able to select out of the random storehouse those facts pertinent to the solution of a given problem.

"There's ground to be plowed before an ambitious plan

like this one can be sowed," Carl reminded her. "A thorough study must be made of state and local ordinances. Here in Saratoga County and across the river in Washington County. Taxes. License fees. Other considerations. This is a politically sensitive state; that's to say New York has sensitive politicians."

"What he means"—Bruce smiled—"is that we may have to grease some palms to hurdle some of the obstacles in our way."

Carl sat down on the edge of the desk and lit a cigar. "Wayne Harrison is about due for a visit to Wheatley. He's a state senator, and an old, true friend. I'll see if I can get him up here next weekend. Election day is only a few weeks off. Wayne will be out beating the drums for campaign contributions. I'm certain we can depend on him, as he can depend on us." He winked.

"I've heard Nate mention him," Callie said.

Carl grinned. "So naturally you'll be interested in contributing to his campaign?"

"I am indeed. You may tell Senator Harrison that I intend to match whatever you contribute."

"Are you sure that's wise? I realize Nathaniel left you well off. How well I don't know. But a young widow with an unborn child to look after must be very careful how she disposes of her assets."

Callie smiled. "Don't worry about me, dear Carl. I've learned a good deal about business and finance from Nathaniel the past year. The income from the Knight estate will see us all through this life. The baby and me. Ham. We're well provided for and then some."

"I'm pleased to hear that. I should have known. Your husband was a prudent man. I'm sure he invested wisely in gilt-edged securities. Utilities. Government bonds, that sort of thing."

Callie frowned. "Too prudent in many ways. As soon as his will's been probated and the estate is settled, I'd like your advice, Carl, about my investments."

"I'll be honored to be of assistance. And you do have Nathaniel's brokers to advise you."

She wet her lips. "That's the point. I don't approve of the way they advised Nate. They are so—oh, what's the word?—such cautious men."

He smiled. "Conservative is what you mean. Yes, Bartlett Limited will never set the financial world afire with the feeble sparks they strike. You plan to shift the emphasis of your investments, then?"

"I want to sell off at least 50 percent of our present holdings and reinvest in the future."

Carl's left eyebrow lifted. "The future?"

"Yes, in rubber and oil and real estate, things that are bound to grow with this country."

Carl looked to his son. "What do you say, Bruce? Do you agree with her?"

"I think so. If the automobile industry grows half as much again in the next ten years as it has in the past ten, there's pure gold in oil and steel. And as for real estate, that Florida oceanfront land we've been considering appears to be a good investment in the future."

"We'll see," Carl said. "I'm not so sure. Miami is a splendid place to visit in winter if you happen to be very rich. The real profit is in goals that are accessible to everyone. Florida beach land for the poor and middle classes? You may as well sell real estate on the moon. How would they get to it?"

"In their automobiles," Callie answered.

"Across the sand dunes? There's no way overland to reach most of the ocean frontage that's selling so cheaply. You have to go by boat."

"Then build new highways, bridges. People will always find a way to get where they want to go."

"Some do, like you, Callie." His expression was amused and enigmatic.

She studied him, uncertain of his meaning. Then her white teeth fastened on her lower lip and she nodded. "Yes, I usually get where I want to go. Don't you?"

He reached for her hand and clasped it in both of his big paws. "I do . . . perhaps you and I can find a common destination and travel there together?"

She smiled at him. Looked up at Bruce standing at the other side of her. Erect and rigid, arms held stiffly at his sides. Face averted. With her free hand she touched his arm and said, "Perhaps the three of us can travel there together."

In the weeks and months ahead, the child grew in her belly. Winter came, record snows clogged the valley, for six weeks the temperature held below ten degrees. Carl Majors drove his car over ever-thickening river ice to visit the Knight place two and three times a week and almost every weekend

Callie would be a weekend guest at Wheatley. Her world expanded.

Some of the most influential and affluent men in the state visited Wheatley that winter, and Callie charmed them all. She captivated Senator Wayne Harrison, a tall, lanky man with a profile like a blade and eagle eyes. A displaced Westerner, he spoke in a lazy drawl that was misleading. His mind was as alert as Callie's.

"So you're the bridge builder," he told her the first time they met. "I've heard a good deal of you."

"And I of you, sir."

He examined her with frank admiration. "You're a very beautiful woman."

She was the outstanding presence in the room. The other women at the party, even lovely Chris, were pale shades in the background. Callie glowed. Her long, loose white Grecian evening gown had been designed by the personal dressmaker for the governor's lady. It bared her back and shoulders and plump crescents of her bosom, bigger, as the months went on, with milk, and it was draped in such a way over her swollen abdomen as to make her pregnancy provocative.

Her hair was a golden beehive, a labor of love by Chris Majors. In those early days she worshiped Callie as an older sister. Sister-in-law was what she had in mind, blind then to the game Callie played with the father and son, believing the hugs and kisses Carl bestowed on Callie were the same as the hugs and the kisses he favored her with.

Callie tilted her head to one side and curtsied to the senator. "Thank you, sir. And you're a very beautiful man."

Wayne Harrison's prominent ears turned fire red, and he laughed to hide his mortification. "Ma'am, I've been called a lot of things in my lifetime, but beauty was never one of 'em. I think you're pulling my leg." He ran a nervous hand over his craggy features.

She pointed to the great bronze eagle over the fireplace. "There's all kinds of beauty. Like Uncle Sam there. He's a beauty. For that matter, there's beauty in the metal itself. I love the look of bronze. When you put your tongue to it, it even tastes exciting."

His laughter this time was relaxed and genuine. He locked her arm with his. "I'll drink to that—if you'll join me."

"With pleasure."

"By the way, I want to take this chance to thank you for your generous contribution to the party."

Her eyes were bright and hard. "Oh, it wasn't for the party. I don't hold with any party. Just the man. I like you."

The senator ran a finger around the inside of his tight starched collar. She was an unsettling woman. "Well then, thank you, ma'am. From me, and all my loyal campaign workers and staff. Now let me hear about this bridge. . . ."

With the Majorses monopolizing so much of Callie's time, Ham experienced a sense of freedom such as he had not known since before she invaded the Knight home. There was a mountain of paperwork to be done that winter after his father's death. The will itself was simple. Nathaniel in the final declaration had divided the estate into three equal parts, including the house and all the property in Knightsville. One third to his wife. One third to Ham. And one third to his unborn heir. He had designated Callie as executrix. Ham's inheritance and the unborn heir's share of the estate would be held in trust until each one reached the twenty-one majority set for males in New York State. In every sense Callie was in absolute control. Ham cared little. He had his hands full running the farm and the quarry with his able foreman, Walt Campball.

There were trips to Clinton and Albany, made in Carl Majors' car. Lawyers, brokers, revenue agents to confer with. Documents to be signed. Ham never read a word of what he put his name to. He did what Callie and Carl told him. When Callie explained her intention of revising his father's investment plans, he listened with numb ears, number brain.

Municipal bonds, shares of railroad and utility stocks durable as the cornerstone of the capitol building or the iron rails the locomotives pounded, dependable as the flow of water from the state reservoir, all converted into volatile investments that fluctuated like the quicksilver in a thermometer. The Detroit motorcar industry. Beach and desert wastelands on the barren coasts of Florida and California. Guided by Carl and Bruce in her first uncertain steps into the complex and precarious world of high finance. Avidly learning all they could teach her. Reading investment tomes Carl had in his library, back issues of *The Wall Street Journal.* Soon able to pick her way through the labyrinth of the Market with unerring instinct and manipulate big money with greater daring and facility than her teachers.

When she invested heavily in an audacious scheme to organize an airline to fly commercial passengers coast-to-coast from New York to California, the Majorses and even her new aggressive brokers were aghast. Carl lectured her: "This Howard Hughes, no one's ever heard of him, and in all likelihood, no one ever will again. That goes for your money too."

Ham didn't care what happened to the money, as long as Callie left him alone. The long weekends she spent across the river at Wheatley were the best times for Ham. He was always included in the invitations, but he used the excuse of his considerable responsibilities at the farm and the quarry to decline.

His social diffidence exasperated Chris Majors. One Sunday afternoon while Callie was visiting Wheatley, she skated across the ice and intruded on his solitude. Her unexpected arrival flustered Ham. She was bundled up, gloved, and swathed in scarves against the bitter February cold, her skates slung over one shoulder.

"Well, don't just stand there gawking at me," she snapped. "I'm freezing to death. Let me in."

Later, thawing her frost-numbed toes and fingers by the big fire in the parlor and sipping steaming coffee laced with applejack, she chided Ham: "Do you know it's been five weeks since you've been to Wheatley? No, don't tell me how busy you are. Callie says the quarry's been shut down since after New Year's. And the farm's in hibernation. So what is all this work you have to do?"

She reached for his hand, but he stood up too quick for her. He braced the butts of his hands against the stone mantel and stared into the red and orange flames.

"There's the books to keep. Walt Campball is helping, but I'm slow."

"Callie says you have everything in order, Ham. Why don't you speak the truth? You don't like us, do you?"

"That's not so. I'll always be grateful to Carl and Bruce for all they've done for us since *he* died." A biblical "He." His father frowned down on him from the tintype on the mantel.

"Then it must be me. Have I offended you some way?"

"You're the nicest girl I ever met, Chris."

"I don't believe you. Or do you mean 'nice' as opposed to 'attractive'?"

He turned his head and looked down at her sitting on the

raised hearth. Her blond hair fell in soft waves about her shoulders, haloed by the firelight.

"I think you're beautiful, Chris. I always have."

It was more than she'd expected from shy, withdrawn Ham, and it made her shy in turn. She smiled and looked down at her hands clasped in her lap.

"Why, thank you, Ham. I—I'm truly flattered." In a small voice: "I wish you'd show it then and stop treating me as if I had the plague."

"I don't mean to, honest." He sat down beside her and looked straight into her wide-set blue eyes. "There's things about me you don't know, Chris. I'm all mixed up inside my head."

She put a hand over his. "You're not the only one. There's mixed-up heads at Wheatley, mine as much as any. Life's full of problems."

"It's not the same, what you're thinking, the devils that have hold of me."

"Tell me about them, Ham. I want to help."

He shook his heavy head. "I can't, what's done is done, and no amount of talking is going to change anything."

"Please, Ham, trust me. I want so much to be close to you. It hurts me when you push me away."

Ham wanted to express what he felt toward Chris. Wanted to touch her. To take her in his arms. To love her. But he was cut off from her forever, imprisoned within his father's tomb.

He reached out and grasped her shoulders. "Dear Chris," he cried. "I want to come to you but I can't."

"Then let me come to you." She tried to move into his arms, but he held her off. "See! You're doing it again. Ham, what's wrong?"

He shook his head. "I don't want to hurt you, Chris. But a small hurt now is better than a big hurt later."

She pushed back a lock of hair off her forehead. "Ham, I swear you sound like Callie, talking in conundrums. That's what it is, all right, it's Callie's influence that's made you so melodramatic, acting and talking like some tragic Shakespearian hero."

Bound to his stepmother by common guilt. He overreacted. "Callie? What has she got to do with anything? Christ! I hate her!"

Chris was shocked. Less by the blasphemy than by his attack on Callie.

"Ham Knight! What are you saying? You hate your father's wife? Oh, Ham, you don't mean that?"

She was staring at him strangely. Suspicious. Probing. Fearful that she would read the truth on his guilty face, he put his arms around her and drew her close, his face in her hair.

"Damn Callie!" he said gruffly and stilled her lips with his mouth; no more questions.

"My darling," she whispered when the kiss ended and pressed her cheek against his shoulder.

He held on to her very tightly, not wanting to let her go, not ever. Chris could be his haven. In her embrace he was safe. In her tenderness he might find salvation. Chris, all light and beauty.

So different from Callie. Hot, violent pounding of flesh and blood in darkness, blinding mind, heart, and soul. Blind, burning voluptuous sin.

Callie was all darkness and evil.

He could hear her laughter mocking him as if she were present in the room. He deafened the sound of Callie by calling out to Chris: "Chris, Chris, I need you."

"Ham, I need you too. I love you, Ham."

He kissed her with tenderness, that was all he felt for this woman. Not the brutish passion with which he had lusted after Callie.

"I love you, Chris." It was easier to say than he'd expected. He gave no thought to the future commitment it implied. For the present it was enough to say it: *"I love you."*

She spent hours in his arms on the sofa in front of the fire. They caressed and kissed, it was all wonderful and innocent. Chris was grateful for the respect Ham showed her. She knew about the facts of life and the urgency of sex in men. Strong, virile men like Ham. She loved him and he loved her, and in truth there was no favor she could have denied him if he had made it clear he wanted her. Ham would be shocked to death, she thought, if he knew just how badly she wanted him.

"I can't wait to tell them," she murmured.

"Tell them what? Who?"

"My father and brother, silly. And Callie. About us." She

felt the tension in him. "Ham, what is it? You haven't changed your mind about me, have you?"

He laughed uneasily. "Of course not. You're the one who's being silly. I do love you, Chris."

"All right." She sat up and faced him. "When two people love each other, it's customary for them to be engaged, and later married."

Ham was stricken. Marriage! The idea had never occurred to him. He and Chris belonging to each other. Forever. *"Till death us do part . . ."* For him tonight had been the fulfillment of their relationship. Why couldn't they go on like this? Seeing what was in her lovely face, he knew why not. Chris wanted him in every way. Companion, protector. Husband. Lover. Father to her children. He looked down her body and undressed her in his mind. Pictured her naked on the bed, arms and legs outstretched to receive him. Sweat beaded on his forehead and wet his armpits. Not the heat of lust. His loins were cold and empty.

"We must tell them we're going to get engaged," Chris said, then, sensing his reluctance: "Ham, why don't you want to tell anyone? You're not ashamed to be in love, are you?"

His answer came in a split second's inspiration. "I'm surprised you'd have to ask why, Chris. My father dead less than four months, it just wouldn't be right. People in these parts expect long mourning from the Knights."

It slipped off her tongue before she could prevent it. "Your father didn't think so, Ham." He grimaced as if she had slapped him. She touched his cheek. "Oh dear, I didn't mean to say that."

He turned his head so that his profile was dark against the flames, inscrutable.

"It's all right, Chris." His voice was pious. "I'm sure where he's gone now, he regrets what he did. No matter, one disrespect can never justify another. I'm mourning, that's all there is to that."

"I understand, darling." She was contrite. "We won't tell anyone till you feel right about it."

"Thanks, dear Chris." He bent his lips to her head, kissed the golden crown.

Nathaniel Knight the Second was born on March 21, 1923, in the big Knight house. Carl Majors had failed to persuade

Callie to have the child in Clinton General Hospital. Her one concession was to let his personal physician make the delivery. Carl spent the night and day in Knightsville, pacing the floor and drinking whiskey, mounding ashtrays with his wet cigar butts.

"You'd think he was the father the way he's carrying on," Chris said to Ham.

Ham had two drinks, more than was his custom. It made him reckless. "Maybe he is. Who's to know?" He laughed.

Chris was not amused. "Ham Knight! What a terrible thing to say. You must be drunk."

"I'm joking. These solemn occasions need some leavening."

He thought: *She could have been with him as well as me. I saw his car pass this way weekly last summer while we were working in the fields.*

Willing to grasp at any outrageous chance to ease the burden of his sin. The improbable was put to rest the first time he saw the child.

A boy, as old Nate had foretold. "Little Nate," the mother whispered the first time she suckled him.

At the door of her room Ham's brain screamed at him to turn and run. Escape the house. Escape Knightsville. Put half the world between him and the witch inside. With his hand on the knob, he looked back. They hemmed him in, Chris, Carl, and Dr. Haley.

"Go on, lad," James Haley urged. "She asked for you before anyone else. She wants you to be the first to see your brother."

Like a condemned man climbing the scaffold he entered the room and closed the door behind him, leaned back on it to brace his trembling legs.

Callie had never looked more beautiful. Or more evil. Birth wracks women. It made Callie glow. A point of fever put a flush on her cheeks and green fire in her eyes. She lay propped up in the big bed like a queen, with her hair fanned out across the pillows, holding the baby to her bare breast. The blue nightgown was pulled off her left shoulder. Her round milk-white breast, larger than when his lips had tasted there. The tiny mouth fast on the teat, the tiny fingers straining at it. Ham wiped an arm across his eyes.

He'd come in so quietly and she was so intent on her occupation that he went unnoticed, or so it seemed to Ham. She rocked and sang to him in her arms.

> *"I have given suck and know*
> *How tender it is to love the babe that milks me."*

Then, without looking up at Ham, she smiled. "You know that lullaby, Ham?"

His throat was dry. "Macbeth, I think, and it's no lullaby."

"She was a loving mother and a loving wife, the lady. Your vision is so narrow, Ham. You look at a barn and only see the one side." Her eyes and mouth were sly. "Come over here, Ham, and pay a welcome to your . . ." Deliberately she let it hang there, delighting in the torture she was inflicting. Laughed softly. "Well, Ham, suppose you tell him? Your brother . . . or your son."

"Stop it." He ground his teeth.

She touched the baby's fat chin with a finger. "The dimple matches yours, that's true. Then your father also had a clefted chin. The points are even. Ah, there are the eyes. Cryptic and sullen like yours. The shape as well. Oh, I don't think there's any doubt."

The singsong cadence of her voice over the hungry sucking noises of the child mesmerized him.

"But wait, we can't be sure," she said. "After all, he could be your father's son. Your spitting image, as Alva says you were to Nathaniel when he was young. No, this sweet angel has arrived and will depart this world as the mystery of the ages." She pressed her lips to its downy head.

He turned away and put a hand on the doorknob. Her voice stopped him, the quality of it so changed that, with his back to the bed, she could have been another woman speaking.

"Ham, wait . . . one more thing. . . . I won't have you laying your guilt on this child. We're all born naked and innocent. Whatever you think of me or of yourself, don't hate the child. Son or brother, he's your blood kin, Ham, remember that." Building to genuine fervor now: "I'm his mother. He's my love. Love him too, Ham. You owe your father that, at least."

He fled the room.

The doctor, Chris, and Carl were startled by his appearance.

Chris came to him, all concern. "Ham, you're so white. Are you ill?"

He tried to smile, thought his face would shatter like untempered glass. "It's nothing. I've never seen a one as young as him before. So small it doesn't look human."

The men laughed while Chris pouted: "That's a terrible thing to say about your baby brother, Ham. The doctor says he's beautiful."

Dr. Haley was an erect, distinguished man with red burnside whiskers. He wore a pair of rimless pince-nez spectacles on a black cord around his neck.

"Indeed he is, Miss Majors," confirmed the physician. "Why don't you and your father go in and see for yourselves."

They entered, and the doctor snipped his glasses onto the high bridge of his nose and studied Ham.

"I knew your father, a nodding acquaintance, we met sometimes in Clinton and in the capitol," he said to Ham. "A fine man, we all mourn his passing. He was a patient of Dr. Murphy, a close colleague. Murphy was confounded by the seizure that took him, his heart wasn't all that weak. Your father must have pushed himself that fatal day beyond all normal endurance."

Ham hung his head. "He was that way. A strong man all of his life."

Haley nodded. "The strong ones, it's always them that go quick. They don't know when to stop until it's too late."

Ham mustered courage and looked up, met the doctor's lensed eyes squarely. "Do you think, sir, that the attack which felled my father could ever have been brought on by a shock?"

Haley's forehead furrowed. "A shock? What kind of shock? Bad news such as hearing about the loss of a loved one? Oh, to be sure, unforeseen tragedy has triggered heart attacks in healthy men."

"Loss of a loved one," Ham repeated. The guilt was worse than it had ever been before. The child at Callie's breast was a living indictment of his crime. As it grew, so would guilt grow.

While Carl and his daughter were visiting with Callie, the nurse came in for the baby. She had attended Carl Majors's wife for three years before she died.

"Jane Hathaway, she's the best there is," Carl had assured Callie. "She's semiretired, but she'll put on her cap again for me."

Miss Hathaway had boarded a train the day after he phoned her and made the two-hundred-mile trip to Knightsville. She was a large woman, built straight up and down like a child's drawing, sexless, but with a pleasant, homely face. She looked ten years younger than her fifty-five years.

"You'll be staying on here with Mrs. Knight for an indefinite period, Miss Hathaway," Carl told her as she stooped to take the child.

"For as long as I'm needed," the nurse replied. With practiced casualness she swung little Nathaniel out of his mother's arms and onto her shoulder, patting his bottom gently to dislodge the gas.

"I'll be on my feet within the week," Callie asserted. "Dr. Haley says so."

"You'll still need help," Carl said and teased, "What do you know about taking care of a baby? You're scarcely more than a girl yourself."

Her eyes rebuked him, not a girl's eyes. "I'm a mother, his mother, that's all I have to know. I could take care of my child if we were put down in the middle of the wilderness."

He smiled. "She wolf, heh? I'll bet you could, but then you'd have time for nothing else . . . such as driving into New York City with Chris and me come May. Would you believe it, there's motion pictures going to play at the Rivoli Theater in which the actors speak? They actually speak, right up there on the screen. It must be spooky."

She was a girl again, her mouth agape in wonder. "I read about that in last Sunday's *Times.* Oh, that would be something to see! Aren't you excited, Chris?"

"I suppose so." The younger girl turned down her eyes.

"Well, you don't sound very enthusiastic," her father complained. "What's changed your mind?"

Chris smiled, a strained smile. "Nothing has. Of course I'm enthusiastic. I've been looking forward to this vacation for a long time."

Callie smiled with a hint of malice. "It must be me, Carl. Of course, and I don't blame you, dear. You see little of your father as it is, you don't want to share him with another woman. And you won't. Thank you, Carl. Maybe some other time."

Carl ridiculed the idea. "That's nonsense, Callie. Chris adores you, we all do. Tell her she's in error, child."

"Father's right, Callie," Chris said obediently. "I'll be

disappointed if you don't come with us to New York."

But her blush gave away the lie. The longer Chris knew Callie, the less she knew Callie, and the more impossible it became to sustain the direction of her feelings for her. Her emotions were as inconstant as the wind vane on the boat house.

At first she had viewed Callie as the perfect wife for Bruce and a devoted older sister. But to her surprise and consternation their father became the more determined suitor. Worse, Chris became convinced that Callie was playing son against father. One moment running her hand through Carl's thick hair, taunting Bruce: "How is it you didn't inherit your father's beautiful hair? Glorious mane, O King of Beasts."

Bruce's expression said he'd like to have Carl shorn like Samson. Then he'd mope around abysmally until Callie made some gesture to reestablish an intimacy with him.

Impulsively grabbing his hand and pressing it to her swollen belly: "Oh, Bruce, he's such an impatient lad. Here, do you feel him kicking?"

Livid with envy, Carl would pour himself a double whiskey.

Chris resented Callie for instigating this rivalry between her father and her brother.

Other times she'd ask herself more impartially, was it really Callie's fault that two grown men behaved like schoolboys? Self-doubts insinuated by her conscience after a generous warm act on Callie's part.

One Sunday she presented Chris with a cameo brooch and matching earrings. Not the ordinary carving of a woman's profile, but of a man and woman in powdered wigs dancing the minuet, an exquisite and delicate work of art, painstakingly conceived and executed.

She hugged Chris and kissed her cheek. "You spoke of a set like this you'd seen on Mrs. Vanderbilt at the governor's inauguration ball. I've been trying to locate a match ever since."

Chris was overcome with gratitude. "I've tried everywhere, even in New York. I thought they must be unique and gave it up."

Callie smiled. "They were unique. I wrote Mrs. Vanderbilt about them, and her secretary replied promptly and with courtesy. They were custom-made by Caldwells. I simply phoned Philadelphia and ordered them to duplicate the set they'd made for her."

Carl was delighted by the episode. "I wonder how Mrs. Vanderbilt is going to like that? You are the most provocative woman I've ever met."

As cunningly as she played Carl and Bruce against each other, she played Chris against herself.

"It's settled then," Carl declared. "The three of us are going to New York."

"I can't wait." Callie smiled sweetly and reached for Chris's hand. "Dear, that blue taffeta gown you're set on, I'm sure we'll find it in Saks."

Chris brightened, her resentment at Callie's intrusion dissipating fast. Her father would never squire her around to all the exciting shops and department stores she was so eager to see again after so long; her last shopping spree in New York had been the spring before. With Callie along, she'd have a companion, young enough to share her enthusiasm for the feminine ritual.

"Miss Hathaway will stay on with you indefinitely." Carl settled the issue.

Callie shrugged. "If you say so. I suppose she will be a boon. She seems very capable."

"The best." He rubbed the gray stubble on his chin. "Well, I'd best get back to Wheatley. I need a bath, a shave, and some sleep. It's been a long day and night."

Callie, still holding Chris's hand, reached out her other hand for his. She squeezed both hands hard. "You can't imagine how comforting it was knowing you were here. Caring about me the way a family cares. How much that means. With Nathaniel gone, there was only Ham until you dear friends rescued us. I love you both." She paused before adding a postcript. "And Bruce too. I love you all. How is Bruce, by the way? I haven't seen him in over two weeks."

"Bruce has been busy. Very busy," Carl mumbled, avoiding his daughter's accusing stare. Since the New Year, Carl had seized every opportunity to send Bruce on the road "to promote business," as he put it, despite the fact that the Majors brick kilns were hard put to keep up with the backlog of orders. The roaring boom of the nineteen twenties was building fast. Contractors were clamoring for bricks. Carl's flimsy excuse to keep his son away from Knightsville and Callie.

"I'll phone him tonight and tell him you and little Nathaniel are fine," Chris promised.

Carl grabbed her arm roughly. "Come on, Chris. We've overstayed our welcome."

He ushered her to the door and into the hall. "There's one more thing I must say to Callie. I'll be right along." He went back inside and closed the door, walked to the bed.

He put his hands on her shoulders, bent down to kiss her brow. "You behave yourself and do what Miss Hathaway tells you. We want you sound and strong for our trip to New York."

"I'm ready now," she said, laughing.

He looked into her eyes. "New York is only the beginning. The places we're going to go, you can't imagine the plans I have in mind for you. For us."

Callie drew her bed jacket closed in mock modesty. "Carl Majors, if you don't stop looking at me that way, I'm going to blush."

A hot flash of desire made him pull back from her. Carl was ashamed of himself. Lusting for a woman who had just given birth to another man's son. An old man like himself, who would not be lying six feet under today if he had not succumbed to her temptation.

They were good days for Ham when Callie was in New York with the Majorses. The more miles between them the better. The child was another matter. Nathaniel both repelled and attracted him. Each time he passed the bedroom that served as a nursery, his eyes were drawn to the crib. If the baby was asleep he would enter quietly and stand over the crib, studying the serene cherubic countenance for some clue.

Brother or son? Ham was obsessed by his uncertainty. Once, as he hovered over the infant, Nathaniel's eyes had opened wide. Dark solemn eyes like his own. Wise, knowing little eyes, transfixing Ham. Ever so slowly, the tiny petal mouth had curled into a smile. The chubby arms thrust out toward him.

Ham shivered and backed off.

"What's wrong, sir?" Miss Hathaway's voice startled him from behind.

Ham whirled, swallowed, struggled to compose himself. "I thought I heard him cry so I looked in at him."

She went past him to the crib. "He wants to be picked up and played with, that's all. He frightens you, doesn't he?"

Ham stiffened. "Me? Frightened of a baby. You must be joking."

She picked up Nathaniel and kissed his forehead, smoothed back his fine hair, jiggled him on one arm. "There there, my darling, did you have a nice nap?" To Ham in earnest: "It's not uncommon, Mr. Knight, for grown men to fear a child. They think of them as Dresden dolls that'll break if you drop them. Let me tell you, I've handled scores like this young man here, and they're not as fragile as you'd imagine."

Ham was quick to agree with her. "Yes, that's it, they're so small and helpless-looking. My mother had a china platter so thin it was transparent. I dared not touch it. I knew in the hands of a clumsy oaf like me, it was bound to break. The one time she let me put it away for her, sure enough, I dropped it."

Miss Hathaway laughed. "In that case, we had better not take chances with Master Nathaniel." She raised her heavy eyebrows when the baby cried out to Ham and lifted its arms again. "What do you know about that? He disagrees. He wants to go to you."

Ham retreated. "I'd best get to my chores." Down the stairs pell-mell he fled to the barn.

On the way he ran into Walt Campball.

"Whoa there, lad!" Walt stopped him with a stocky arm. "Who's chasing you, a ghost?"

Perhaps, Ham thought.

He said, "Going and coming are a total waste of time. I get them over with as quick as possible."

Walt looked like a dark-bearded Santa Claus in his red mackinaw and tassled wool cap. "I admire ambition, Ham, but it seems to me of late that all you do is work."

"I read."

"Same thing. I mean, you should get away from here more than you do, be with young people your own age. Lucy says they never see you at the Saturday night barn dances anymore."

"I never did care much for dancing."

Waly nudged him with an elbow and winked. "Well, me neither, lad. But it gives a young buck an excuse to hold a girl, and that introduction can lead to other things, if you know what I mean?" He guffawed.

Ham's strained laughter was lifeless. "I know, Uncle Walt, but I don't get on too well with girls."

"You're shy, Ham, that's all. Why, a good-looking feller like you could have any girl he wanted. I know because I hear Lucy talking with her friends, not meaning to, you understand? But the girls these days have so much brass, they don't care what they say, nor who hears them." He shook his head in sorrow. "My daughter talks to her mother about things that I would never broach to Sue. No matter, there's more than one female in this town who has an eye for Ham Knight. Say, why don't you come over for supper some night this week? Now, don't say no. You've put us off long enough."

Ham was backed into a corner; the last time he had visited the Campballs had been the week his father married Callie, more than a year. With reluctance he agreed.

"I'll come, Uncle Walt. What night?"

On Wednesday night he took a bath and put on his one formal suit. It was fitting, he thought, as he battled with the tie. He had no more heart for this event than he did for funerals or weddings.

To his relief, Lucy was not home when he arrived. Ham dreaded having her greet him at the door after the way he'd played the fool on his last visit. By the time she did come home he had two apple brandies under his belt and felt light-headed and "don't give a damn."

Lucy made a grand entrance bedecked in the flapper uniform of the day. Boyish bob, cloche hat, long-waisted dress with short pleated skirt. Rope beads rattling on a bosom bound so tight she could have been a boy.

Susan Campball hurried over to pick up the deep-crowned, floppy hat Lucy tossed carelessly on a chair.

"Is that how you take care of your nice things?" she reprimanded. To Ham: "It's the very latest style from Sears, Roebuck."

Walt scowled and chewed on his pipe stem. "You're late. We've been waiting supper."

The girl fluffed up her hair with one hand and sat down across from Ham, crossing her long legs with a high flourish that let him glimpse her bright-red panties.

"Sorry, but Tillie and I went for a spin in Jake Spencer's new Dodge. Would you believe he had it up to sixty miles an hour on the highway, and it wasn't opened up all the way?"

"Sixty miles an hour?" Her mother gasped. "You must be out of your mind riding with a maniac like that."

"I don't want you seeing the likes of that Spencer boy," Walt warned her. "He's a bad apple, him and those cronies he hangs out with."

She rolled her eyes in sufferance. "Don't be so highfalutin, Pop. Jake is okay if you know how to handle him."

"Where did Jake Spencer, or any other Spencer for that matter, get the money for a Dodge motorcar?" Susan wanted to know.

Walt grunted. "Running whiskey down from Canada for that bootlegger uncle of his."

In upstate New York, the Volstead Act had scarcely affected the drinking habits of the populace. Among the River Rich—the Rockefellers, Morgans, Goulds, Harrimans, Astors, Vanderbilts, and Majorses—their bars and wine cellars were stocked with premium whiskeys and vintage wines procured from "suppliers," many of whom, despite the fact that they were felons and murderers, were socially acceptable to the elite they served. Or, more appropriately, who served *them,* for it was the tolerance and permissiveness of wealth and power that enabled bootlegging to flourish as an national institution that usurped much of that same wealth and power for organized crime. Judges and politicians were heard to boast they had drunk toasts in the mansions along the Hudson River with Al Capone himself!

The poor and not so rich didn't have bootleggers. They got their "moonshine" directly from the illegal stills infesting the mountains of New York. Applejack was the favorite drink in this section of the country. To Ham's knowledge no revenue agent had ever been seen in Knightsville. Back in the hills to the east of the quarry there were half a dozen distilling operations making wine and beer and whiskey, months before Prohibition became a national edict.

"That's not true!" The girl denied it. "Jake has a job in the new paper mill up near Hudson Falls. He only comes home on weekends."

Walt shook his head, deploring the present conditions in the Hudson Valley. "Won't be long before this country is as bad as Philadelphia and New York, what with all the factories going up along the river. Carl Majors has opened two more kilns, did you know that, Ham? One in Westchester, that's fine, keep 'em downriver. Soon big industry will be pushing the farmers out of the valley."

"What do you have against national prosperity, Pop?" Lucy demanded. She got up and poured herself a drink of brandy.

"If it is prosperity," Walt growled. He held out his glass. "Here, give me and Ham another nip of that, and who told you you could drink whiskey? You're still a minor."

"Oh, Pop." She giggled. "This is 1923. Keep up with the times."

"And what times they are," he lamented. "Females running around the streets wearing less than my grandmother wore in the privacy of her bedroom. Drinking and debauching and howling and shaking to that terrible music. 'A return to normalcy,' the Republicans call it. Harding normal, I ask you, what kind of a man is he to be sitting in the White House?"

"I hear the president is ailing," his wife murmured.

Walt knocked out the pipe ash into a big copper ashtray. "Ailing, is he? Small wonder. That Ohio gang of his is even too much for his stomach. Whole damned cabinet is corrupt. Smith, that phony Colonel Forbes. His one crony killing himself before the law could do him in. The president himself, playing cards and boozing and wenching right there in the White House. He's a national disgrace."

"Oh, Walt, it isn't right to say things like that about anyone, much less the president," Susan protested. "Pastor Williams was only speaking about it last Sunday. *Let him cast the first stone,* Jesus said. It's the Democrats who started those ugly rumors. Nobody knows for sure they're true."

"Let Pastor Williams believe what he wants to. I never liked Harding. And neither did your paw, Ham, and the Knights have been Republicans since before Abe Lincoln. 'Walt, I don't like the looks of that man,' he said to me last election."

"I think he's a swell-looking guy," Lucy observed. She lay back on the couch and gazed at the ceiling. "Gee, imagine how those young girls must feel being invited to the White House. *By the President himself!* Just like the harem girls those old Turkish sultans used to keep."

"*Lucy!*" Her mother was shocked. "I won't have that kind of talk in my house. And in front of a young man at that."

Lucy winked at him. "Ham's heard worse than that, haven't you, Ham?"

Ham ran a finger around the inside of his collar and

changed the subject. "Two men quit the quarry to go work in the Majors kiln at Haverkill. Are we going to replace them, Walt?"

The dour foreman scowled. "Won't be easy. There's too many easier jobs around at better pay. I hear the New York Central Railroad is hiring for their road gangs. They're going to redo the beds, lay new rails, and spruce up the right-of-way. Make the old line the fastest, smoothest-riding, fanciest railroad in the USA. Them gandy dancers get top money."

"Then we must pay top money too," Ham said with an authority that made Walt sit up with new respect for his benefactor's son. Like everyone in Knightsville, he would forever respect the old man's memory in the archaic feudal meaning.

"I meant to talk to you about that very thing," Walt admitted. "It's strange, this new prosperity and progress. Business booms, stocks go sky-high, everyone has money to burn, yet the pair of boots I bought in Clinton last weekend took a greater part of my pay than the pair I bought three years back. Now what's the good of having twenty dollars to the ten you had in 1920, if it buys you less?"

"That's inflation," Lucy said with the smugness of a girl who had just earned a high school diploma.

"I know what it is," her father snapped, getting up to fill his glass again. "It's a fake just like those moving pictures. An optical illusion. The light burns out and all the pretty pictures and people disappear in a puff of smoke."

Ham put his hand over his glass when Walt stooped to refill it. "No, thank you, Uncle Walt. I'm dizzy."

"We'd best eat right now, the roast will burn," Susan said. "Or Walt will be too drunk to carve." She hauled her bulky body out of the deep chair with great labor and waddled off to the kitchen.

"You've never seen me drunk, woman," he yelled after her.

Susan had the last word. "If I haven't, then God forbid I ever do!"

On the way into the dining room, Lucy took Ham's arm and whispered, wickedly, "I hope you do get drunk, and then I'll take advantage of you." She pressed her hip against his.

All during the meal of golden-crisp fresh ham and candied yams and sweet red cabbage, Lucy teased him about Chris Majors, her envy ill disguised.

"Ham's got himself a fancy girl friend." She tilted her head back, made a haughty face. "Her long nose sticks so high in the air, she hasn't seen her feet in years."

"You stop that, Lucy," her mother reprimanded. "She's a very nice girl, I hear."

"Who told you? Ham? He's prejudiced."

Ham's face was redder than the cabbage. "She's not my girl friend, and she's not stuck up either."

Smirking: "Well, you're her feller, not to you she's not. I hear she has so many clothes, she changes dresses every hour."

"I wouldn't know about her clothes."

"Oh, wouldn't you?" With a lewd smirk: "Doesn't she wear clothes when she's with you?"

"That will be enough, young woman!" Walt was genuinely angry now, and she knew she'd gone too far. "You apologize to Ham. Right now."

She sat up straight, hands folded in her lap, and tried to look penitent. "I'm sorry, Ham. I was only joking, you know that."

"It's all right, Lucy." Ham was blushing furiously.

After the main course, when her father left to check the stock, and her mother went off to fetch the pie and cream, Lucy resumed her goading.

"Chris Majors is thick with your stepmother, isn't she, Ham?"

"All the Majorses have been kind to us since my father's death."

"Is Chrissy kind to you?" Her dark eyes mocked him. "Or maybe it's Carl Majors that Callie's getting thick with? She's off with him in the city now, isn't she?"

Not looking at her, pushing a crumb around the white tablecloth with his teaspoon in solemn concentration.

"The three of them, Carl, Chris, and Callie."

"Do you miss her?" Purposely not defining "her."

"Not particularly."

"Mama and me were up to your place just the other day to see the baby."

"I know. I was in town buying feed."

"He's adorable, little Nathaniel."

He shrugged. "All babies look alike."

"Not this one," she said. "Nathaniel looks just like you."

He shut his eyes and saw the hoary god of vengeance

standing over him with the pitchfork. Driving it home this time. The cruel steel prongs shredding guts and genitals. Her voice brought him back.

"Ham, are you all right?" She was looking at him curiously.

He touched the white napkin to his forehead. "Yes . . . I guess I shouldn't have had that last applejack, that's all."

"Oh?" A note of skepticism. "I said the baby looks like you."

He was in control again. "Does he now?" He took a sip of water. "Well, who should he look like? You? It's my brother."

"That he is," said Susan from the kitchen doorway, coming in with the immense lattice-work apple pie and jug of cream. "The sweetest little darling born in Knightsville. I tell you truly, Ham, I don't know how *she* can go off and leave him with a stranger."

Ham looked up at her and stated, "He's better off with Miss Hathaway than with anyone, in my opinion."

He felt no concern at all about little Nathaniel being alone with Jane. While with Callie fussing over him and carrying him around with the careless abandon she'd tote her book, *the* Book, Ham was always nervous she'd drop him.

The realization jolted Ham. He cared.

In the months that followed, Ham escaped from Callie and the baby, and from himself, in work. The quarry, farm, and dairy filled his days, and nights, exhausted from the days, he'd sink into dead slumber.

In January of 1924, Senator Wayne Harrison phoned Carl Majors from Albany.

"The state's granted the charter to build your bridge. Are you and the Knight woman in this venture together?"

"A partnership."

"Just in business?" the senator inquired slyly.

"I hope to improve on that, but for now, just business."

"You old dog. By the way, what would you say about taking in a third partner?"

"You?"

"No, New York State. The state would subsidize half the cost in the public interest. Do you realize how many new projects are on the drawing boards of the Highway Department? We won't be able to build 'em fast enough, it looks like, at the rate vehicular traffic is on the rise in this state, all over the country. Right now the arteries of communication between New England and New York are too few and too inadequate. This proposed bridge of yours would divert a lot of cars and trucks away from Clinton and Troy."

"That makes sense to me," Carl agreed. "Bridges and paved roads don't come cheaply, as I keep telling Callie Knight."

"Another thing, this road that will link the bridge to the highway on the east bank. The bureau of land deeds claims that road is on her private property. You see the difficulty here, Carl. The state can't build a road to channel public commerce on private land. What the department proposes is for the state to purchase that land from the Knight estate. I don't have to tell you the price will be far greater than its present worth."

Callie was impressed by the unexpected windfall when Carl told her, but she was suspicious of the state subsidizing the bridge.

"What do we need the government for? It won't be our bridge."

"Of course it will. That's what the free enterprise system is all about, the Republican doctrine. The government wants this bridge and road built. Sooner or later it would have to build a bridge somewhere. More than one bridge in time, automobile traffic is on the increase every year. So it puts up government money to encourage private capital and initiative to fulfill the project. It's the same thing makes digging for oil so attractive."

"They wouldn't interfere and we'd get to keep the tolls?"

"Every cent."

Her smile was satisfied. "Then we'll do it, Carl."

That spring, construction on Knight's Road was commenced under the supervision of state engineers. She might have sold the title to the land it ran over to the government, but it would always be "Knight's Road" all the same, as far as Callie was concerned.

That summer she took it upon her self to oversee the grading and widening of the country lane in person. Riding her chestnut gelding back and forth from Knightsville to the highway. Once she came close to being sideswiped by a felled tree. The foreman cautioned her.

"You stay clear of this area while we're working, that's an order, ma'am. You get hurt, it's my responsibility. You hear?"

She measured him thoughtfully. A squat, porcine man; his gaze wavered first. At last she said, "I hear you, but I have no intention of 'listening' to you. No one tells a Knight to stay off Knight's Road. Do *you* hear me?"

He whirled around and retreated, muttering to himself.

The men looked forward to her visits, this pretty blond young woman, sitting erect in the saddle. Local workers for the most part, they all knew of Callie Hill, the orphan girl who'd married old Nate Knight and then "fucked him to death," so the popular version went.

She was an object of curiosity, some erotic, at first. But she soon won respect. A young surveyor who had a way with Clinton's ladies laid an imprudent hand on her thigh. Her riding crop slashed down. Next thing, he was kneeling on the ground nursing a sprained wrist and howling in pain. Her gaze challenged a circle of grinning faces. The men working on the opposite side of the road sobered fast. She wore her newly gained wealth and power as if she had been born to it.

In time they came to like her. She was a thoughtful and generous patron. In the August dog days she daily sent a hand on horse and wagon up Knight's Road to bring iced lemonade to the construction crew.

Each winter Ham and a work gang would cut blocks of ice out of the frozen river and bury them in sawdust in the old Knight icehouse at the bank below the Lampbert general store. Except for record-breaking summers the supply would last the villagers through fall.

In the summer of 1924 Callie Knight received an invitation to attend a ball at the governor's mansion in Albany. The Majorses, of course, were on the list. Callie was delighted.

"Now, don't tell me that the governor said to Mrs. Smith, 'We mustn't forget to invite Callie'?"

Carl chuckled. "Not that Al wouldn't leap at the chance to have a beauty like you decorating the state house, but you owe this honor to Wayne Harrison."

"I am honored, then. The senator is quite a man." Amused by his casual reference to Governor Smith: "Do you call him Al to his face?"

"Certainly. We're old cronies. Not out in public, though, as long as he's in office. Then it's 'Governor,' of course. Al is a good man for a Catholic and a Democrat."

She laughed. "Pray tell me, Carl, do Catholics and Democrats worship a different God than yours? Is he some special deity, your Presbyterian Lord?"

"You're daft, girl," he scoffed. "It's them that thinks their God is special, not me. Poor Al. He plans to be reelected, and then in '28 he wants to run for President. A pipe dream. Even if he wasn't Catholic. The reins of government are back in the hands of the sane and responsible Republicans."

"Where God intended them to be," she said mischievously.

"By God, that's right!" He laughed. "If the will of the people is any indication of his determination, then it's the truth. Old Harding was a sorry mess, rest his soul, but he still got 61 percent of the vote. And now that honest Cal is the president, the ship of state will soon be back on course. The way I see it, the two-party system is finished. The people will never give those Democratic warmongers another chance to drag America into a foreign conflict."

She rumpled his hair. "You know, Carl, I think you'd make a fine president. Have you ever thought of going into politics?"

He seized her hands and pulled her down into his lap. "I'd rather make a fine husband than a President. Callie, dear, will you marry me? No, don't put me off again. Time enough has passed since Nathaniel died. Your mourning's over."

She put her hands on his shoulders and looked into his slate-blue eyes. "Give me a little more time, dear Carl."

It was the most she had given him up until now, and he was elated. "You're not saying 'no,' that's something."

"I am not saying 'no.' Neither am I saying 'yes' to you."

"You will. You must." He was getting passionate. Her bottom was warm, yielding in his lap through the thin summer frock. "I want you so badly, my darling."

She took one of his big hands and placed it over her left breast. His fingers trembled, flexed tenderly.

She smoothed back his thick hair, which she had mussed. "Carl, dear," she whispered. "If you want me you can have me. You don't have to marry me for that."

They were in the Japanese gazebo that sat on a bluff overlooking the river, screened from the house by a tall hedge of Russian olive.

"Where? When?" he asked with urgency.

She looked out across the lawn and garden. They were alone. She slipped off his lap down on her knees and undid the buttons on his fly.

Carl was hypnotized by her busy fingers. Her touch was exquisite. With one hand she lifted her skirt. She was wearing a lavender chemise. She unfastened the crotch buttons and pulled the flap aside. The sight of her naked genitalia fanned desire the like of which he had not experienced since his youth. He could no longer control it, his spasms commenced. Callie snatched the white handkerchief out of his breast pocket and covered him.

It was over quickly.

Spent, Carl lay back in the chair, eyes closed. "I'm sorry," he said in shame. "I haven't failed a woman since I was a very young man."

Callie smiled. "There, and that's because you are a young man again. You haven't failed me. Failing comes at the end, and this is only the start."

"I love you with all my heart." He put his arms around her and pulled her hard against him. His mouth buried in her spun-gold hair. Unseen was Callie's smile. Sly and secret. Pleased with herself and the way things were going.

Callie Knight and Chris Majors were the belles of the governor's ball in gowns one of rose, one of lime, cut low in front and back, with matching headbands. Carl was his daughter's escort. It had been his intention to squire Callie, but Chris had threatened to stay home.

"It's proper etiquette for me to be on your arm, not my brother's," she insisted, and finally he gave in. It was a small point; he'd still be with Callie.

A small point, but a turning point. The irony. Carl lost the chance to prove himself to Callie. He lost Callie. He lost everything.

The high point of the evening for Callie was dancing with Al Smith. He was impressed with her knowledge of politics and her keen mind, and told her.

"Not many women your age understand what's going on in government," he said. "Take Harding. That plurality the Reps are touting don't mean a thing. He got the overwhelming female vote because of his silver hair and Barrymore profile. Now, that's what I don't like about you girls poking your pretty noses into politics. You're all heart and no head. Present company excepted, of course. If the apple looks rosy and shiny, you'll take a big bite without even considering that the inside could be wormy and rotten."

Callie smiled. "If it's wormy, spit it out."

"Easier said than done in politics. It's an apple like the one Snow-White bit into. The voter is stuck with what he bites off. If it turns out to be bad, he chokes on it. So tell me, Mrs. Knight, how is it that you're so well informed?"

"I read a good deal. The *Times* and *Journal* and that new magazine they call *Time.* But I learned about politics long before I ever saw a copy of any of them."

The governor's eyebrows lifted. "Oh? And how is that?"

"The Book, it's all in there. All of life and love and death. And politics."

"What book is that?" he said, patronizing her. "I surely must read it."

"Shakespeare's works. *King Lear. Macbeth. Julius Caesar. Richard III.* Everything's said in the histories and the tragedies that's happening today and will happen tomorrow. The names and places may change, but the human qualities are all the same for all times. Courage. Cowardice. Treachery. Ruthlessness. Immorality. Murder. The things that make the world go round."

He laughed. "I can see you don't have a high opinion of politicians."

She shrugged. "Everyone is a politician in his own way. We're all born into this world questing for money and power. It's just that the politician makes a career of the drive."

"Where's my counterpart in your book?" he said, humoring her.

She wrinkled up her brow in earnest thought. "Let me see. . . . Oh—you do resemble Richard II."

He grinned ruefully. "It's probably just as well I don't know the gentleman."

"Perhaps." Her smile was cryptic. "To my mind the ideal ruler was Richard III, a deformed and ugly man with a will of steel. Utterly ruthless, he destroyed anything or anyone who got in the way of his lofty goal. To be the king of England. Stranger and kin alike. He knew how to use people, how to exploit their strengths and weaknesses. He bent everything and everyone to his own designs."

"That must be our dear departed Harding?" he joked.

"No, not Harding," she said seriously. "His corruption grew out of ignorance and indifference and weakness. Richard is redeemed by his courage, wit, and lack of self-delusion. Whatever had to be done to gain the throne he did without regrets."

The governor frowned. "Do you believe that philosophy? That the end always justifies the means?"

She looked him in the eye and said, "It's never been any other way from the day the first man got off all fours and reached out for the stars."

The orchestra stopped playing then and he led her back to where Bruce Majors was waiting on the edge of the dance floor.

"My compliments on your excellent choice in women, Bruce," the governor told him. "I found Mrs. Knight's views on politics so entertaining that I forgot how much I hate dancing."

He acknowledged her curtsy with a dapper bow and returned to his place on the dais.

"Even the governor of New York is smitten with you, Callie."

"He won't be after he reads Richard II," she said.

"What the devil are you talking about?"

"A private joke. It's nothing. Where did Chris and Carl go?" she asked as they approached their empty table.

He looked across the ballroom. "They stopped by Senator Harrison's table. Dad wanted Chris to meet Wayne's latest flame. He's sending her abroad next fall until the elections are over to keep her out of his hair. The opposition could build a dandy scandal around the senator and that little redhead. Wayne's idea is for Chris to accompany her. I guess he wants some one to keep an eye on her."

"She'd be good company for Chris," Callie said.

Bruce was dubious. "It depends upon what you mean by 'good.' It would not be my description of the lady."

"Wayne Harrison is a ladies' man."

"In the plural. It's a wonder some of the affairs he's been involved in haven't tarnished his political image. Married women, that kind of thing. Old Wayne is as fast on his feet as that classy young boxer Gene Tunney. He's had a lot of punches thrown his way, but none of them have landed. I hope his luck holds out. He's a good man and one hell of a senator."

She looked across the room at the table dominated by the massive figure of Wayne Harrison. At their first meeting she had been attracted to him. And the attraction became stronger each time she saw him. When he danced with her earlier, he had whispered in her ear, "You're the most beautiful woman here, Callie. I wish we could get to know each other better. Too bad the Majorses own you. I wouldn't step on Carl Majors's toes over a woman, even one so desirable as you. He's a power in this state."

Callie had to strain her neck to look up at him, he was that tall. "I agree with most of what you say. Just one mistake. The Majorses don't own me. Nobody owns me." She laughed. "Though when I was at the orphanage the sisters sometimes told me I was possessed by the devil."

His eyes narrowed on her pensively. "I wouldn't be surprised if they were right. . . . Now what did you mean, you agree with most of what I say?"

"Just that. It's not the time for you and me. It would be pointless to begin. Not now at any rate." She purposefully left the subject ajar.

"What are you thinking?" Bruce asked her.

"Senator Harrison isn't sending that girl abroad just because of the elections. He's getting rid of her for good."

"Did he tell you that when you danced with him?"

"He didn't *tell* me. Odds and ends of chatter I put together form a picture. You'll see. Has he been seeing another woman recently? A lady? One suitable to be mistress of the state house someday?"

Bruce leaned forward and folded his arms on the table. "It's funny you should ask that. United States Senator Hubert Clement has a daughter. Homely as sin, but eligible. Wayne's made several trips to Washington in past months, residing at the Clement home in Arlington."

She was satisfied. "That's it. A man like that can have any woman he wants." An afterthought: "Almost any woman. . . . It's more political for him to marry for advantage rather than for love or desire."

"It works the other way as well." His hand slipped under the tablecloth and came to rest on her thigh.

"Yes, go on." She would hear him out before denying that soliciting hand.

"A woman who can have any man she wants should only marry for advantage. It's you I'm talking about, Callie. He's asked you to marry him, my father?"

Her eyes held fast on his eyes. "He has."

"What was your answer?"

"That I'd consider the proposal."

"And have you decided?"

"I think so. The answer is for your father, not you."

"You are going to marry him."

"I may."

"Then change your mind. There's no advantage to it. I want you to marry me."

She approached it craftily. "I thank you, sir, but what's the advantage marrying you and not your father?"

His fingers tightened on her thigh. "Five years back Carl had a big row with Kelly of Philadelphia, the other big brick manufacturer. I won't go into the sordid details. The end was a five-million-dollar lawsuit filed against my father. He settled finally out of court for what amounted to a pittance. Kelly didn't really want the money, he's rich enough. It was the victory he was after, rubbing Carl's nose in the mud. Another man, he might have gone to court and won a big judgment. Right after that, my father took his name off the title to the company. He transferred full ownership to Chris and myself. The agreement provides that he will be employed for the remainder of his life as president at a salary. That way, if he's ever in another scrape like the one with Kelly, the best they can get out of him by law is a portion of his income. The business is safe."

All the while he was speaking, Callie was attentive, her fleet mind digesting the confidences he was unfolding. Racing ahead, so that she surmised the objective of his brief before it was presented. However, it suited her to play the game out to its end.

Her smile was sugar laced with arsenic. "Do you think I'd marry your father for his money? From what you say, it's the other way around. If I choose to marry Carl, he'll be getting himself a well-off widow."

A muscle fluttered at the side of one eye. His weak blue eyes watered under the intensity of her hard, bright gaze.

"And you'll soon be a widow again, Callie. He's an old man." Spitefully, he threatened. "If you marry him, you'll never build that bridge. This house, this land is in my name. All the Majors capital."

"You wouldn't dare defy your father," she taunted. "Old he may be, but he's a man. He could break you in two."

His face flushed. "You think I'm weak. All right, that may be. But in this one thing, I'd risk his wrath. What I don't understand is why would you force it to that point? You don't love my father."

"I don't love you either."

"I know that. But as you said before, it's a matter of advantage rather than love."

She smiled and laid her hand on top of his hand on her leg. "When will we start work on the bridge, Bruce?"

A warm flood of relief swept through him. His voice broke. "The day we get back from our honeymoon. Dear, darling Callie, you do mean it? I know you love to tease. But you are serious, you will marry me?"

"Yes, if that's what you want. I'll marry you, Bruce."

"My wife." He was shaking with emotion. He bent in her direction. "Kiss me."

"Here? Now?" She was amused. A shy man, he was not given to baring his emotions in public.

"I want them to see. I want them to know." He placed his hands on her shoulders and drew her face to his. Callie put her hand on the nape of his neck and kissed him lightly on the lips.

When she looked up she saw Carl and Chris. Carl swayed and held on to the back of an empty chair. His face was gray, his eyes glazed.

Chris clapped her hands in glee. "Hey! What is this, you two? Smooching in the middle of the governor's ballroom? What's come over my bashful brother?"

Bruce squared his shoulders and looked at his father. He had never challenged Carl before on anything. And Carl had never backed down from any man.

"Your bashful brother is not as bashful as you think," Bruce told his sister. "Your not so bashful brother has just proposed to Mrs. Knight, and Mrs. Knight has consented to marry him at the earliest opportunity."

"That's wonderful!" Chris rushed around the table and stood behind their chairs with an arm around each of them. She kissed her brother first, then Callie. "I'm so happy for you both. I don't want to brag, but I must claim some small credit to this happy occasion. I've been pushing you two together since that first day Callie came to Wheatley."

Callie smiled and reached up to pat her cheek. "My sweet little sister. You'll be my maid of honor."

"Father, did you hear that? And you can give the bride away—" She looked around for Carl and broke off.

Carl was gone.

Carl was lost.

After four double shots of bourbon from his flask in the coatroom, Carl found the resolve to salvage what he could of his lost pride and dignity after his ignominious retreat from Bruce's triumph.

He went back to the ballroom and took the governor aside. "This has turned out to be a doubly happy event, Governor," he explained. "My son and Mrs. Knight have just announced their engagement."

"Well, well, that certainly is a surprise," the governor said, although he was not all that surprised. In his brief encounter with Mrs. Knight, he had come to regard her as a complex and fascinating woman. He studied Carl. It was plain how "happy" this sudden news had made him. He looked like warmed-over death. "I'd like to congratulate them myself."

"I had something like that in mind." Carl's gaze wavered. "Do you think you could find a bottle of champagne in this hallowed hall? I'd like to toast their happiness."

Al Smith winked and put an arm across Carl's sagging shoulders. "I wouldn't be a bit surprised if the former tenant left a few bottles in some dark corner of the cellar. I'll tell you what, you bring the happy couple into my private study right now. It's more fitting that the toast be intimate, don't you think?"

Governor Smith had always been a staunch foe of Prohibition but was too discreet to use the prerogatives of his office to flaunt the law.

Chris flew out of her chair when Carl reappeared at the table. "Daddy, why on earth did you run off like that? You didn't even congratulate Bruce and Callie!"

He rubbed his hands together and forced himself to smile, not looking at either Callie or his son. "Well, I had something more elaborate in mind than a handshake and a kiss. Come on, all of you, the governor wants to propose a toast to the happy couple."

Bruce was relieved and showed it. He'd girded himself to deal with his father's predictable anger, sooner or later. Waiting made it worse. Now here Carl was, beaming at them and calling for a toast to their happiness. He had underestimated the old man and told him so on the way to the governor's study.

"I'm sorry if this has caused you pain, Father. You're a good sport."

"No, you're wrong," said Carl. "I'm a good liar."

Governor Smith's toast was simple and gracious. He lifted his crystal goblet to the light. Infinite chains of bubbles swirled to the surface of the liquid gold and popped into the air, forming a shimmering halo above the goblet's rim.

"To the most radiant lady in Albany tonight and to the luckiest gentleman. May your life together be as sparkling as this fine old wine."

After the toast, Governor Smith placed his hand on the small of Callie's back and bantered, "Bruce, my boy, if I were single, you wouldn't have won this lady's hand without a fight."

Carl's mouth curled up on one side, a travesty of a grin. "She's had her fill of old men, Governor."

Callie smiled at him across the rim of the glass, sipping the wine. "There's no truth in what he says, Governor. After his handsome son, there's no man in the world I'd rather be a wife to than Carl Majors."

The governor and his wife laughed. "Your maiden name was Hill, I think?" the governor asked. "It could be English, but I'll wager your father came from the Old Sod from the easy way the blarney rolls off his daughter's tongue."

Carl turned to the window and looked out into the black night. Past the twinkling lights of the capitol. Into the past. The day in the gazebo. Callie warming his loins. With the promise of all that was still to come. Shattered dreams.

He turned around and looked at her talking animatedly with the governor's wife. Not really a beautiful woman. Nose too sharp. Forehead too high. Her eyes more feline than human. The way she always bit her underlip with two pointy teeth was unattractive. Her neck was too long.

His gaze dropped to her breasts.

He wanted her so badly. He didn't know how he was going to endure the days and weeks and months ahead of him without her. Her presence in the house constantly reminding him of his loss.

Two years passed, his agony was unremitting.

The long lonely hours of the night were the worst for Carl. Knowing she was so close, with his son, the two of them lying together naked in embrace. His nights were filled with images of Callie. For the first time since he was fourteen, Carl masturbated. Afterward he'd go down to the study and drink himself into a stupor. It became his habit to stay in bed until noon and later.

The manager of the firm's main office in Troy complained to Bruce: "He comes in here twice a week, closes himself in the office, and drinks. His secretary says he hasn't dictated a letter in ten days. Up and down the river, the kiln foremen are screaming at me, and so are the district sales managers. There are a hundred and one executive decisions we've been waiting on. I swear I'm going to resign if this goes on much longer, Mr. Majors."

Bruce was grim. "I'll take care of the mail on his desk, Gardner. Tell the foremen and sales people that the Majors Brick Company will be back on course by next Monday morning."

He worked steadily all that day and night and through the weekend to meet his deadline.

"But I can't keep on doing his work and my own," Bruce lamented to Callie when he returned to Wheatley. "Where is he now?"

"He took little Nate down to the river to watch the construction workers sink the piers."

"Are you sure you can trust him with the boy?" Bruce asked anxiously.

"He's sober. I don't worry about the baby with him, Bruce. I believe he loves Nate as if he were his own grandson."

He took her in his arms. "I love Nate too, darling. Still, I'd like to see him with a baby brother before long."

She touched her fingers to his lips and smiled. "Patience, dear Bruce. I think there should be the space of at least four years between children. The doctor told me that. I'm not a brood mare, you know, like some of the hardy ladies in this county."

What the doctor had said was that Callie was as healthy as any woman he had ever examined and that she could have another child whenever she cared to, and as many more as she cared to have. His prognosis didn't suit her fancy or her plans. Nathaniel was all the child she wanted or needed.

Bruce held her tenderly. "You're small, but you aren't frail by any means. How well I know."

She slapped him playfully. "Keep your mind on your business. What are we going to do about Carl?"

He shrugged. "I don't know what to do. I cleaned up the backlog in his office, but by the end of the week his desk will be piled high again."

"There's only one thing to do," she said firmly. "You take over his job as president and turn your work over to Gardner. It would mean promotions all down the line. That's good for morale. This company can do with a good shaking up."

He shied away. "I can't relieve my father just like that. He's been running this company since he was twenty-four."

"Then it's time he took some rest. Every good workhorse deserves a green pasture in his old age."

"Carl's not all that old. It's the drink." He shook his head. "I don't like what's happening to my father, Callie. A few years back he was a two-fisted drinker who could match men half his age tot for tot, and at the end of the evening he'd still be fresh enough to take the others home and put them to bed."

"That's how it is with drunks. I know from my own father. It hits them all at once. He's declining, Bruce, and you must face up to it. The company is your responsibility now."

"I suppose you're right. I wonder how he'll take it?"

"He'll be relieved, I think."

He sighed. "I hope so, because I have no choice." He went over to the liquor cabinet and mixed himself a scotch and soda, Johnny Walker Black bootlegged from Canada. "Can I fix you something, dear?"

"A light sherry, if you please."

Callie took her knitting from the sideboard and sat down on the couch in the parlor. "I'm making a sweater for Nathaniel. Would you believe he's already outgrown the ones we bought for him in Albany?"

"He's a Knight. They're all big men."

Resentment clouded her face. "Well, I'm not a Knight and I'm not big, and he's my own flesh and blood. I don't imagine Nate will be all that big."

Bruce laughed and brought the drinks over to the cocktail table. "You're jealous because Nate's a Knight through and through. Why, he's the spitting image of Ham."

"He has my coloring and bone structure. Delicate."

"Whatever you say, my sweet." He sat beside her and put an arm around her. "By the way, how is Ham these days? I haven't seen him in weeks."

"Chris says he's fine. She's over there now, taking him some preserves the cook put up."

He made a face. "It's always her that goes to him. Not that I have anything against Ham. I like the lad. It's just that it should be the other way around, it seems to me. The boy should court the girl."

"I told her the same thing, and now she's angry with me."

"Chris angry with you?" He was astonished. "Why, she adores you."

She looked up from her knitting. "I only wish you were right, Bruce. I've always loved Chris like a sister. But since I married you and came to live here at Wheatley, her feelings about me have changed. I think she resents me, Bruce."

"In what way?"

"Countless ways. I don't blame her, I suppose. Before I came here, Chris was the lady of the house."

"That's not so. Chris was, is, a child. She never lifted a finger around this house. The maid and cook ran the place by themselves."

She put down her knitting and needles and faced him. "The maid, now that's another reason Chris has been quarreling with me. I had to discharge Annie."

"You discharged Annie?" he said in disbelief. The tic began to work at the side of his face. "Annie Stone is the best maid we've ever had. She's been with us since she was eighteen years old. Ten years of faithful service. I don't understand, Callie. You should have consulted me before you did a thing like this. What did my father say?"

Callie stood up, walked across to the doorway, and slid the doors shut. She came back and stood behind the couch. Placed her hands on his shoulders, kneading his taut back muscles.

Her voice was low. "Bruce, this is not an easy or a pretty tale to tell. Not to you, his son."

He shook off her hands and got to his feet. "What the hell are you trying to say?"

She lowered her eyes and folded her hands in front.

"When Carl drinks, the heavy drinking he's fallen into of late, he loses control."

Bruce was pale, his voice high-strung. "In what way?"

"He becomes amorous."

He was outraged. "Has he been bothering you? Goddamn-it! I've seen the way he looks at you. He always has. I'll break his drunken head if he ever lays a finger on you. Has he?"

She came around the couch and clutched his arms. "No, darling, calm yourself. He hasn't touched me, not—" It was an artful incompletion.

"Not yet! Is that what you were going to say?" he shouted. She could feel him trembling.

"It was Annie he touched. More than touched." She shook her head sadly. "Poor Carl, why is it that as men grow older they always lust after younger women?"

"Tell me about my father and the maid," he said with dread.

"They were together in the boathouse. In the carnal sense. She denied it, of course, but I found the money he had paid her stuffed in her bodice. I had no choice, Bruce. I had to dismiss her. For everyone's sake."

"Yes, naturally. You did the right thing. The only thing." He was dazed. "My father and the maid. All these years, he's treated her like a daughter. And now something like this. I'm so ashamed for him. Paying a young girl like some dirty old lecher prowling the red-light district in Clinton."

She patted him in consolation. "It's pity we must have for him, Bruce. Pity and understanding. Poor Chris, I couldn't tell her why I had to let Annie go."

"My God! No! What *does* she think?"

"I can't imagine. All I could think to tell her was that Annie was untrustworthy and disrespectful. She won't accept that. In her eyes I'm the villain of the piece."

"I'll have a talk with that young lady."

"No, Bruce, it would only make matters worse. She'll come around, you'll see." She pushed him down gently on the couch. "Now sit down and have your drink. We'll talk about something more pleasant. I telephoned Handly, the broker, this morning."

He gulped the strong whiskey. "What for?"

"I ordered him to sell another five thousand shares of Majors Brick."

Bruce's thin, sallow face registered dismay. "I told you when we last discussed the matter that my father wouldn't approve of selling off more shares of company stock. It reduces our holdings to less than a controlling interest. We could be taken over."

"That's not likely. It's a good solid stock, but in performance it's not bullish enough to attract that kind of investor. Bricks are too tame for speculators."

"How did you re-invest the returns from the sale?"

"Warner Brothers. All the movie stocks are good, but the Street likes Warners and so do I. Two-thirds into movies. The remaining third I sank into Dodge Motors."

He snorted. "You 'sank'? You know the jargon of the market better than Handly. Next thing you'll be wanting a seat on Wall Street."

"I might. There's a woman governor down in Wyoming. Why not a market seat for me?"

He grabbed her hand and pulled her down beside him. "You're a mad woman, but I worship you." He kissed her eyes and nose and mouth, filling with desire for her. He could escape from his wordly cares into Callie's sensuous body the way his father escaped into the bottle. "Let's go to bed, darling."

"If you want to." She ran her small white hand up the inside of his thigh and caressed his hard penis. Casually she began to unbutton her blouse.

"What are you doing?" he demanded.

"You're ready now. Why not take advantage of it? You know what happens when you think too much about sex, Bruce."

Since puberty Bruce Majors had been sensitive about his masculinity. His initial sexual encounter had been with another boy at camp. He had left the camp the next day, and for months he had been wracked with guilt and fear, fear that he was homosexual. His promiscuity in college was an extension of that guilt and fear. Each new conquest over a female was an absolution as much as it was an act of lust. His sexual drive was not as powerful as his performances pretended. One week of marriage had revealed to Callie how fragile Bruce's desire could be. Even small distractions could render him impotent.

Since inheriting Carl's shirked business responsibilities, he had made love to Callie only once in four weeks.

"We'll do it right here, darling, on the couch. Chris is across the river. Nate and your father are out. Annie's gone, and Cook went to visit her cousin for the afternoon. *Strike now or else the iron cools.*" She laughed and went on undressing.

It was calculated cruelty on her part, reminding him of his inadequacy, making a joke of it, laughing at him.

Bruce slumped forward, cradling head in hands. As full and eager as he had been a moment earlier, so was he empty and unfeeling now.

"Oh, no, it isn't happening again, is it, darling?" she inquired with false solicitude. She went over to him and pressed his head into her soft belly, stroked his hair. "It's all right, my dear Bruce. It's only because you're so tense all the time. I'll make you another drink; it'll help you relax."

She picked up his glass and carried it over to the server in the bay window. Humming softly. Poured a generous measure of scotch in his glass, grinning at herself in the gold-framed mirror on the wall.

Carl sat on the beach with little Nathaniel nestled between his legs. Sheltering the child with his body against the cool north wind blowing down the river valley. It was a bright day, but the sand was gray and damp from a week of rain.

His hair was whiter than it had been a year before, and shaggy. His habit for twenty years had been to visit a barber every Friday. Five-, six-week intervals satisfied him now, if he happened to think about it or Bruce reminded him. There was white stubble on his jaw and cheeks and he was tieless. A caricature of the dapper sport who had prided himself in turning the heads of women half his age when he strutted into a hotel lobby or a fashionable restaurant.

The two big steel and stone piers on either bank were dark, foreboding monoliths against the white clouds. In the middle of the river a work gang was submerged in a caisson on the muddy bottom, laying a concrete foundation for still another pier. On the Knightsville side a crew was constructing the first truss for the bridge. When it was completed, the Knight-Majors toll bridge would have a span of 1,600 feet with four 400-foot trusses.

Nate shifted restlessly in his embrace, complaining in a

piping voice that was precocious for his three-and-one-half years, "Grampa, can we go over there?" He pointed a small finger at the men working across the river. "I can't see good from here."

"Not today, son. The boat's laid up, and Grandpa's too tired to make that long roundabout drive through Clinton. It won't be long, though, before you'll be able to walk over to Knightsville all by yourself."

Nate clapped his hands the way his mother did when she was elated. "Hurray! Then I can go see Ham any time I feel like it."

Carl smiled and hugged him close. He loved her child as dearly as if it were his flesh and blood. To think, he could have been Nate's stepfather instead of Bruce. The thought chilled him and he took from his pocket the silver flask that once had sparkled like a jewel. He didn't bother to polish it anymore. Tarnished, like its owner, it served its purpose. He drank long from its crusted mouth.

Nate, plump and rosy-cheeked, smiled up at him. "You drinking that old cough medicine again, Grampa? You sure must love medicine." He made a face. "Ugh! I hate medicine."

Carl patted him as he put the flask away. "This is bad medicine for little boys like you, Nate." He grimaced in repentance. "Bad medicine for anyone."

The nagging grief. The boy addressing him as "Grampa." Rumpled, white-haired, jolly grandfather. Well, not so jolly. But otherwise he suited the role only too well.

What's in a name? He could almost hear Callie mocking him.

What indeed? If Nathaniel called him "Daddy" he would have been a relevant, vital man instead of an old man, unshaven and unwashed, brooding on this barren beach.

Dirty old man . . . She had called him that, and it was the truth.

He had gone to her room that morning to tell her he was taking Nate for a ride in the car. He knocked on the door.

"Callie, it's—"

"Come in," she called back.

He entered the bedroom and saw no sign of her.

"Callie?"

"In here." Her voice came from the bathroom door, a foot ajar. There was the sound of water running. He expected she was drawing her morning bath.

"I'm going for a drive with little Nate," he said loudly.

"You'll have to come in here. I can't hear you."

Innocently he did her bidding. Though later he admitted to himself it was that same innocence of a man who finds a diamond ring and blinds himself to the lost-and-found advertisements thereafter.

He pushed open the bathroom door and stood on the threshold gaping at her. Callie was naked in the tub, soaping her breasts with her hands. It took his breath away.

"I'm sorry. I—I didn't think you—I—I—" Stumbling over the words. Yet he made no move to retreat. He could no more have torn his gaze from her body than he could have willed the blood to stop pounding in his loins.

Unperturbed, she covered herself with the small washcloth. His enthrallment amused her. "Stop gawking at me like a libertine, Carl. You've seen women unclothed before, and a good many from what I hear. I thought you were Bruce."

"Bruce left for Kingston." His mouth was dry.

"Oh, yes, I'd forgotten." Her green eyes were cunning. "Well, now that you're in here, you can make yourself useful. Here, scrub my back." She held out the washcloth to him and made a pretense of hiding her breasts behind her other arm.

Carl, knowing he was playing pawn to her sadistic humor, was unable to retreat with his dignity intact. Entranced, he approached the tub, took the cloth from her hand.

She was temptation. "Not too rough, my back is tender." Head cocked to the side, watching him coyly out of the corners of her eyes. He wiped the rag across her shoulder blades. Slippery with soap, his nervous fingers let it fall. It sank in the water, up to her midriff, to the bottom of the tub. He looked down at the cloth where it lay by her buttocks.

"Well, pick it up, Carl," she coaxed. "I don't have all day to bathe."

He bent over and put a hand into the water. It was trembling. As he picked up the cloth, the back of his hand brushed her body. A spontaneous reaction over which he had no control. He turned his hand and cupped her buttocks. Shaking with soft laughter, Callie lay back in the tub, her full weight on his arm. Her lathered breasts were buoyant. He could not take his gaze away from them. The hunger in his eyes excited her. "Poor Carl. Touch me, go ahead. Get over with it quickly like the last time. Incontinence seems to be a family trait in the Majors men."

"You bitch!"

"Dirty old man!"

Emotions all ran together like the colors on an artist's palette. Love. Lust. Hate. The hand in the water moved up her back and gripped the nape of her neck. The fingers of his other hand closed around her throat. Tightened.

There was no fear in her. Only contempt. The ridiculing smile.

"Do you really think you can do it, Carl?"

He looked deep into her eyes.

"What do you see, Carl?"

"Fire and ice. There's only one place in the universe where those two complement each other. The core of hell itself."

"You believe I'm Satan, is that it?"

"I don't know. You might be."

"There's a way to find out. Strangle me. Push me under. If I perish, you'll know I was human after all."

"I'm tempted." His strength was waning. It was he who was strangling.

"Yes, you're tempted and know not which way to go."

She reached up and clasped the hand at her throat. Urged it down her body, laid it on her right breast. "Now here's the way, dear Carl." She opened her arms to him.

"Black magic," he muttered. He took his hand from her breast and slipped it under her raised knees. She put her arms around his neck. With the ease of youth he lifted her out of the tub and carried her out of the bathroom to the big double bed. Her imprint on the sheet and pillow was still warm and fragrant from sleep, musk, and violets. He laid her down and gazed at her naked body, the vision of so many tortured dreams. Pale blue veins marking her breasts and belly and thighs like the gossamer threads that run through fine Italian marble. The golden triangle opened to him. And this time Carl did not fail her.

The price of his attainment was high, as it must be in all such bargains. What Carl Majors had lost before this day, dignity, self-respect, zest for living, all were nothing compared to what he would pay now.

Remorse and self-loathing set in quickly. "My God! What have I done? My son's wife! Callie, I swear, it will never happen again."

She jeered at him. "That's a pity. I thought it was rather nice myself. I wonder, if I had married you instead, would Bruce have tried seduction on his father's wife?"

He sat on the edge of the bed and covered his face with his hands. "It's bad enough for a son to betray his father, but when a father betrays his son, he's less than human."

"I had the same thought reading the New Testament. Jesus on the cross crying out to his Father, *'My God, My God, why hast thou forsaken me?'* "

He turned to her in despair. "You wanted it to happen. You've been planning for it to happen from the first day you moved in here as my son's wife. I see that now. Even as you nursed your baby you were tempting me."

She laughed. "You were envious of Nathaniel, is that it? Shame on you, Carl. You could have left the room."

"Damn you! Always leaving your bedroom door ajar when you're dressing. Flaunting your body at me."

She sat up and pulled the sheet up to her neck. "There, does this make you feel more comfortable? Carl, a gentleman does not skulk around a lady's bedroom door, with his eyes to the crack."

"But why? Why do you want to make me suffer, Callie? I was your friend. I wanted to be more than friend. I offered you my name. Haven't I suffered enough, losing you to my son, having to look at you all day and knowing you're with him all night."

She ridiculed him. "You make no sense, Carl. All your suffering because of me, isn't this what it was all about? Your lust for me? Well, now I've taken pity on you, let you have me, and still you rail and carry on."

"Pity? You make me despise myself. I'd rather pay a whore. At least that's an honest and equitable transaction. There's no lower condition to which a man can sink than in a well of pity."

"Then stop pitying yourself. Self-pity is what plagues you most."

An idea intrigued her. She clasped her hands together as in prayer, thinking aloud. "Wouldn't it be odd if I were to become pregnant? You or Bruce could be the father. I wouldn't know."

"My God! That's monstrous!" He was appalled.

The symmetry of coincidence appealed to her. Old Nate cuckolded by his son. And here was the father putting the horns on his son.

"It's a common happening when a man and a woman lie together. This week I've lain down with two men. So you see." She threw up her hands to chance.

He began to dress. "I should have drowned you before when I had the opportunity."

"It was your choice."

"You're an evil woman, Callie. The brilliant, burning evil that the candle flame is to the moth."

"I'm flattered. It's nicer than being thought of as a crone on a broom." Her eyes were ferociously bright. "What *is* evil, Carl?"

"Evil is. A force unto itself. Do you know who Count Dracula was?"

She laughed. "Some silly fairy tale about a man who turned into a bat at night and sucked blood out of pretty young girls."

"That's fiction, but there was a real Dracula. Vlad the Impaler. His favorite sport was to hold banquets in the palace garden where his enemies and others in disfavor were impaled on pointed stakes. They died a slow, torturous death while Vlad and his guests wined and dined."

She screwed up her face in distaste. "I knew a boy who stuck pins through butterflies."

Carl shuddered and combed his fingers through his shaggy hair. "There are ways to impale a man, crucify him, that make the stake and nail seem merciful."

A knocking on the bedroom door ended it. Carl was alarmed. "My God! I can't be found in here."

Callie threw back the sheet, leaped out of the bed, and grabbed a wrapper from the chair by the window. "Quick! Into the bathroom, behind the door."

She donned the robe, tied the sash, called out, "Yes? What is it?"

"Annie, ma'am," was the reply, muffled by the thick oak door. "Have you seen Mr. Majors?"

"Come in, Annie."

When the maid entered the room, Callie was sitting on the edge of the bed, shaping her fingernails with an emery board. She looked up at the girl indifferently. "What about Mr. Majors?"

Annie Stone was a plain, plump girl with short black hair that fell straight about her round face. Her best feature was her wide-set eyes of an intense violet hue owed to her Celtic heritage.

"Master Nathaniel has been all dressed and waiting for him in the car for a half hour."

"I'm sure I don't know where he is. Probably he's puttering around the garage or down at the boathouse."

"No, Sam has looked in both places."

"Then I suppose he's gone for a walk. He often goes down to watch the work on the bridge."

Annie was skeptical. "Not without Master Nathaniel, he wouldn't. He promised the lad a ride in the automobile and said he was coming up here to tell you."

Callie yawned. "Well, he changed his mind. Or forgot. That's not surprising, though, Annie. Mr. Majors has been getting more forgetful lately. I'm sure you've noticed."

Annie's cheeks pinkened. "I can't say I have, ma'am." Her gaze slid away from Callie to the half-open bathroom door. "I see you've had your bath, ma'am. Shall I clean up in there now?"

"Later on, Annie. After you find Mr. Majors. I think for now you had better fetch Nathaniel in from the car and take off his coat."

"Yes, ma'am." She kept on staring in the direction of the bathroom.

It irritated Callie. "What are you looking at, Annie?" she snapped.

The wide violet eyes came back on her, and Annie smiled. A smile with just a hint of impudence. In her voice too. "Nothing special, *Mrs.* Majors."

"That will be all, Annie."

"Yes, Mrs. Majors." The girl turned and walked to the bedroom door. She looked back before she went out into the hall, eyes darting from Callie to the bathroom and back to

Callie. Still smiling, she closed the door softly.

Curious, Callie got up and walked around the bed. She looked toward the bathroom from Annie's point of view. Her expression became grave.

"So that's it," she mused. All of the doors at Wheatley closed over high, snug thresholds built to block the circulation of icy air in the large, drafty house in winter when temperatures dropped commonly to zero and well below.

With the bathroom door ajar, there was a gap between the bottom of it and the tiled floor of an inch or more. Under it the toes of Carl's brown shoes were visible.

When he emerged from his hiding place, he frowned at Callie standing with her hands on her hips, feet spread wide. A defiant posture.

"That was close," he said. "What's wrong with you? You look so strange."

"It's nothing, nothing at all," she answered. "You'd better leave now."

"I'll go down the back stairs and say I've been up in the attic."

She nodded. "That sounds reasonable. Here, let me see if the hall's clear before you go."

She opened the door a hair and peered up and down the long hall. "It's all right." Before she let him out, she added casually, "Oh . . . next time, Carl dear, we must be more discreet."

"There's not going to be a next time," he declared with finality as he fled.

Callie shut the door and leaned back against it, thinking. That damned Annie! Had she seen the shoes? In all likelihood. She might have thought they were a pair of Bruce's shoes lying behind the bathroom door. Not so likely. The subtle change in her behavior, the smile, the tone of her voice.

". . . *Mrs.* Majors . . ."

Annie knew it was Carl behind that door, all right.

The shoes, the tub, the disheveled bed, even a simple river girl like Annie Stone could add up the one, two, three of that composition. The question mark in Callie's mind. What would she do with her knowledge?

In all probability, nothing. Ten years she'd worked for the Majorses, good years that had inspired a family loyalty in Annie. For Carl, Bruce, and Chris. She knew the maid did not consider *her* or Nate "family" and never would. She was certain Annie would never use her new weapon to hurt any of the Majorses. As a consequence it could not be employed effectively against her either.

The logic was all on her side, but Callie was not satisfied. Annie had resented her from the day Bruce made her lady of the house. The jezebel Callie Hill. Rankling at the memory of the occasion when Callie had waited on *her* in the café where she'd worked in Clinton. The Annie who had been with a soldier that night was a world removed from the prim little Pollyanna who served the Majorses. She had been giggly from drink, twitching and squirming with pleasure while the soldier worked his hand up under her dress. One face for the Majors world. A different face for her private world. Callie could not tolerate the situation as it stood. The sense of disadvantage she would feel every time Annie put on her taunting smile that said, "My drawers are cotton and yours are silk, but when we kick them off, we're both sisters under the skin!"

She resolved to do something drastic about Annie.

Carl vowed that he would never again covet his son's wife. On the day he had lain with her in his son's bed, he avoided her like the plague. Hating her. Hating himself. The next day she appeared at the breakfast table looking like a sweet, freshly scrubbed, demure child, in a short jumper and prim shirtwaist with a small bow at the collar. Her long blond hair was tied back in a ponytail. She kissed Bruce on the cheek and then kissed Carl.

"Good morning, Dad," she said.

All of his vows crumbled to dust. He wanted to tear off the chaste jumper and blouse. Strip her naked as he had seen her the morning before. Possess her. He could no more divorce himself from this woman than a consumptive could will away his fever.

"Why don't you come into the office with me today, Father?" Bruce asked Carl. "There's a mountain of work to be done."

Carl carried his coffee over to the sideboard and poured a generous measure of rum into it.

"Let Gardner do it," he told Bruce.

"Gardner has all he can manage with his own work. And frankly, so do I." Bruce glared at the bottle. "You're starting even earlier than usual today, I see."

"Not really," Carl said indifferently. "I haven't stopped from last night. I'm sorry if I've made life difficult for you and Gardner, Bruce. Tell you what, next week I'll turn over a new leaf and go in every day until my desk is cleared. I'm just not up to it today."

"That's obvious." Bruce threw down his napkin and stood up. "There are matters that won't keep until next week. . . . Callie, don't expect me home for supper. I'll be working late. In fact, I may have to stay over and work the weekend. I'll phone you when I know for sure."

Callie walked him to the door and kissed him good-bye. As she shut the door, Carl came out into the hall.

"He'll be away tonight," he said, his implication clear.

She grinned like the Cheshire cat, pinching her bottom lip with her sharp teeth. "You said there'd be no more next time, remember?"

"Do you want me to get down on my knees and beg you?"

"That would be a sight. You're shameless, Carl. Bruce is halfway down the steps and you can't wait to seduce his wife."

"That's right," he said bitterly. "I'm a rotten bastard, and that's all there is to it. I should have known better than to let you into this house to begin with. I saw what you did to Nathaniel and to Ham, and yet I let it happen. I thought I was strong enough to deal with you. What a fool! I've seen it with holy rollers back in the mountains who handle rattlesnakes. They may get away with it once, twice, more, but they're doomed at the start. All that's undetermined is the time and place."

The smile dissolved into sullenness. "What do you mean, you saw what I did to Nate and Ham? I was a good wife to Nathaniel. I gave him a child. Not many men his age could boast they've sired a son."

His pale watery eyes were in that moment clear and canny. "Dead men can't make boasts. I wonder."

"You can wonder all you want. I must bathe Nate." She pushed past him with annoyance.

"Wait, I'm just a blabbering old fool," he whined, his moment past. "I must be with you tonight."

"We'll see."

"Callie, please."

She looked back across her shoulder. Calculating. "All right, Carl, but we can't risk it in the house after yesterday.

Annie suspects us as it is. The boathouse, that's an ideal place. At eight o'clock."

It was all Carl could do to get through the day ahead. He wanted to stay sober, but it was not to be. Callie saw to that. When he returned from his daily outing with young Nate in the afternoon, she had a tumbler of bourbon waiting at the side of his chair.

"You need some warming after that walk. Your ears are red from cold," she said. "I'll join you." She had poured a glass of sherry for herself.

"It's the wind," he said, holding out his hands to the fire. "I can't remember a fall as cold as this one. Feels like snow."

"Did you take Nate down to see the bridge today?"

"For a while. It's going well. Grayson, the chief engineer, says it will be open to traffic by September of next year."

She finished her sherry and rose to pour another. "Can I refill your glass, Carl?"

He looked uncertain.

"Come on, drink up, this is a celebration."

"What are we celebrating?"

"Your retirement."

He was displeased. "I'm not retired. I haven't been going to the office as much as I did, that's true, but . . ." He fell silent, trapped by truth. For more than a year, his position as president of Majors Brick had been a title only. He had taken charge of the company when it consisted of a single kiln and expanded it to a baker's dozen with sales offices in twenty states. Now he was a figurehead to his empire.

He drained the glass and handed it to her. "Here, fill it up. I want to propose a toast."

When she returned with their glasses, he lifted his and said, *"The King's a beggar, now the play is done. . . ."*

Callie laughed. "How clever, Carl. Do you know what play it's from?"

His smile was crooked. *"All's Well That Ends Well,* and if that isn't a joke, I've never heard one."

He ate no supper. At seven he put a fresh bottle in the pocket of his overcoat and left the house, telling Callie, "I'm going down there early to light the fire and make things comfortable. You will come?"

"I'll be there. At eight."

One hour later, she went up to her bedroom, put on the ankle-length mink coat Bruce had given her for her last birthday and tiptoed down the back stairs. The kitchen was dark. Maude, the cook, and Annie retired to their rooms soon after the supper dishes were washed, Maude to sleep, Annie to read the trashy romance magazines she was addicted to. Callie let herself out the back door and walked down the grassy slope, bathed in moonlight, to the boathouse. Carl had fastened the shutters so that the lights would not be seen from the house.

She went in and up the short flight of steps from the mooring slips to the room above it. The boathouse was furnished in good taste, like all the other rooms at Wheatley. It was designed like the stern castle of a Spanish galleon, with the curved bay window overlooking the river. An officer's cabin with pegged decks above and below. Double-decker bunks on one wall. A Franklin stove in a corner, its metal sides cherry red from the wood fire blazing inside its potbelly. Carl was sprawled out on a studio couch opposite the stove drinking from a half-empty bottle of bourbon. His eyes reminded her of the blue-glass marbles the children had played with in summer at the orphanage. His speech was slurred.

"I was 'fraid you wouldn't come." He placed the bottle on the floor and got to his feet unsteadily.

"I told you I would and I'm here." She pulled the coat tighter around her body and held out her hands to the glowing stove. "It's a cold night for this season. There's frost on the ground."

He came up behind her and put his arms around her. "I'll soon warm you up. A li'l'a this." He opened the front of her coat and clamped his hands over her breasts. "You smell good." He nuzzled her neck. "You're bad for me, like the booze an' cigars. Don' give a damn. I need you." He pulled her over to the studio couch.

Callie laughed. "You're drunk, Carl. Too drunk to do what you want to do, no doubt."

He roared. "Carl Majors, too drunk to love a beau'ful woman. Oh no, you'll see."

She offered no resistance when he drew her down on the cushions and kissed her. Opened her mouth to his tongue, feigning ardor. Without waiting for her to take off her coat, he began to paw at her body with the overeagerness of a schoolboy embarking on his first sexual experience.

His libido was remarkable, considering his age and the quantity of alcohol he had consumed that day.

"I want to undress," she said when he tried to take off her underwear. "You too. Here, help me make up this bed."

She removed the coverlet from the studio couch and turned down the blanket and sheet beneath it. Carl was undressing at a feverish pace, casting his clothing to all parts of the room. In spite of his dissipations his body was in good shape except for his paunch and the rolls of fat over his kidneys. He climbed naked into the bed and pulled up the covers.

Meanwhile Callie had taken off her coat and nothing more. She assumed a pose of remote detachment, shoulders slumped, the coat hanging from one hand and dragging on the floor. Her concentration was turned back toward the house.

"Whassa matter?" Carl demanded impatiently. "Why're clothes on?"

"I just remembered something," she said with concern. "I left the oil stove on in little Nate's room."

"Oh, hell! The oil stove will keep, but this may not." He pulled down the sheet and exposed himself to her.

Callie smiled and walked over to the bed. She bent and stroked him with a deft and sympathetic hand.

"I'm not worried about an old bull like you. You'll be as ready in five minutes as you are now. That's all it will take. It wouldn't be any good for me with that worry on my mind. Just last week two tots were burned in their beds when an oil stove exploded. I must check it, Carl."

"I guess you must," he conceded. The boy was precious to him. "But hurry. I want you so bad right now, it's a madness."

She picked up the bottle of bourbon and handed it to him. "Here, this beauty will keep you company until I return."

He took it and tipped it to his lips, drinking half of what remained. Callie put on her coat and walked to the stairs. She hesitated, looked back at him.

"I'm going to put out the lights. The stove is all the illumination we need. I'll come back to you in the darkness like a wraith, the way the Queen of Sheba came to David's couch."

He laughed and lay back on the pillow with the bottle resting on his chest. "It's all games with you. Living. Loving. Life itself is a game to you, I sometimes think."

She snapped off the wall switch and descended the stairs

to the lower level. She found a flashlight on the utility shelf alongside the door and snapped it on. Played it on the back wall until the switchboard was spotlighted in its beam. She opened the metal cover and pulled the master switch so that the lights upstairs could not be lit. Deliberately took the flashlight back with her to the house.

She walked through the hall to the guest closet in the foyer and took off her mink coat. From the day Bruce had presented her with the coat, it had never hung anywhere else but in her bedroom wardrobe. Tonight she would make an exception. It was that kind of night. After she'd hung up the coat, she went upstairs, to her room, and undressed. In nightgown and robe she went down to the servants' quarters at the rear of the first floor. There was light spilling out from under the maid's door.

Callie rapped softly with her knuckles on the panel. "Annie, it's Mrs. Majors."

The girl regarded Callie with suspicion when she entered. She was sitting up in bed reading a book, wearing a woolen nightgown.

"What do you want, ma'am?"

"I want you to put on a robe and a shawl and go down to the boathouse. I'm worried about the elder Mr. Majors. You know the way he's been drinking all day. He could fall asleep down there with a lighted cigar and burn himself to death."

Annie glared at her, making no pretense of hiding her resentment. "The boathouse? In my nightclothes? At this time of night?" The words were forming in her throat: *"Do it yourself!"* But she swallowed them. She was too obedient a servant to treat the mistress of the house with open disrespect. Even a mistress such as this one! She was paid to oblige, even if it meant getting out of a warm bed and abandoning the heroine of her novel on the very brink of seduction.

"I would go myself," Callie assured her, "except I'm waiting for a phone call from my husband."

"Liar!" the maid's sullen expression said.

"Yes, ma'am," she said and kicked off the covers. "What do you want me to do? Suppose he's angered by my intrusion?"

"Don't be silly. You know how fond Mr. Majors is of you, Annie. He was saying to me only the other day, 'It's a lucky thing for Annie Stone that I'm not twenty years younger. She wouldn't be safe in this house.' "

Annie was putting on her slippers. One slipper on, the other held in her hand, she straightened up in surprise. "Mr. Majors said that?" She didn't trust the compliment coming from this one.

"He said even more, but I don't intend to tell you what. You'll be getting a swelled head."

Annie Stone was a hard-working country woman who had been treated to scant flattery in her twenty-eight years. She was easily disarmed, even feeling as she did about Callie.

"It must be the drink that's affecting his eyesight," she said shyly. "He's a fine gentleman, Mr. Majors, he is. There's lots of girls wouldn't mind being chased by one like him. He's not that old." And with a meaning look at Callie: "Isn't that right, Mrs. Majors?"

Callie sidestepped the pitfall. "You must tell him that, Annie. Men love flattery, especially one his age. He might even raise your pay, you'd like that, wouldn't you? All right, now hurry to the boathouse and see about the fire in the stove and the ashtrays. The way he's been at the bottle, he may be insensible at this late hour. Throw a shawl over him if he's sleeping, Annie, so he won't catch his death. It's bitter outside." She protested when the maid started to put on her cloth coat over her gown and robe. "Your coat would be adequate if you were dressed, but you should wear something warmer over your nightclothes."

"It's the only coat I own," Annie told her.

"Then you'll use mine, the mink. It's in the downstairs closet. Here, this won't do." She took the coat from Annie and hung it back in the closet.

The maid's eyes were wide with wonder. "Your fur coat, ma'am? You want me to wear your coat to the boathouse?"

"Of course. It's just the thing for a night such as this."

There were times when Annie would sneak into the mistress's room and touch her cheek to the lush, dark silky pelts. She hankered so to feel the treasure around her body, but dared not.

"Oh, I couldn't, ma'am."

"You will. Come on." Callie moved around behind her, placed her hands firmly on Annie's shoulders, and marched her out of the room.

A false note sounded dimly in Annie's mind when Callie removed the precious mink from the common guest closet in the hall. It was lost in the thrill of being caressed by all that fur and silk.

"It feels so wonderful, ma'am." She was intoxicated.

Callie turned the high collar up so that half of Annie's face and head were buried. "There, that will guard you against the night winds. There's a scarf in the pocket. Tie it over your head."

Annie giggled. "It tickles my nose." She did as she was bid about the scarf. Callie put an arm on the small of her back and ushered her along the hall to the back door. "I won't wait up, Annie. If my husband phones, I'll take the call on the bedroom extension. I'll trust you to hang my coat back in the closet."

"Yes, ma'am, I'll be very careful of it." She held more respect for the coat than she did for its owner.

Callie stood by the pantry window watching Annie move off across the lawn toward the boathouse. She walked proudly with her head high and shoulders back, hugging the coat tightly around her. She would be a queen for a spell in the dead of night, though there was no one to see her.

After God the highest power in the universe was the dramatist, the rare one such as the Bard of Avon, Callie mused. Creating and peopling his own private world. Manipulating life and love and death to his own will. Pulling the strings on flesh-and-blood puppets.

Yet the vain intrigues presented on stage were pale excitements compared to the infinite dramas being staged within the audience. They were the real players. The power of the playwright was pallid opposed to the player in life's drama who held the power to control the machinations of the plot and manipulate her fellow characters.

"Her" fellow characters. Not the banal "him." Men, the bastards!

Annie hummed to herself as she went down the sloping lawn, silvered with frost in the moonlight. She'd have walked clear to Clinton if she got to wear this dream coat.

She reached the boathouse and opened the side door slowly. It was black as pitch below. In the room upstairs there was dim illumination from the fire in the stove, too faint to see anything more than indistinct outlines. She paused a moment for her vision to adapt to the dark, and then started up the creaking stairs.

At the top she stopped and felt for the light switch on the wall. It was dead. She scanned the room, squinting hard to penetrate the black murk over everything.

"Mr. Majors . . ." She whispered it lest she wake him. Again. "Mr. Majors . . ."

She thought, he may have left the boathouse by his own accord. Well, she'd do what she'd been sent to do and be on her way. The Franklin stove was banked and the glowing coals in the pit were waning. She walked around the perimeter of the room, bumping into objects, running her hands over tabletops and counters. She found one ashtray an enormous one in the form of a binnacle. It was filled with cold cigar butts. On around the room until . . .

Her knees bumped against the side of the studio couch.

The sound of Carl Majors's voice startled her, but not with fear.

"Goddamnit, I thought you'd never come. I finish a whole stinkin' bo'll waitin'!" He hurled the empty bottle at the stove. It splintered and the residue inside sizzled on the hot iron sides in myriad puffs of steam.

Annie had seen him drunk before but never in anger. But she was not frightened. Drunk or sober, Carl Majors was a gentle man. She could make him out sitting up, a faceless silhouette.

"I came down to see if you were all right," she said. "Mrs.—"

He was deaf to anything but his own voice, loud with vexation. Shouting.

"You took so long, I went to sleep waitin' for ya. Whatcha pussyfootin' aroun' like that for? Come over here!"

She had responded to all of his summonses obediently for ten years. So she obeyed him now. She walked around to the front of the couch and stood before him. His hands clamped down on her arms.

"Take off that damned mink," he said.

"She said I could wear it." She tried to pull away, but it was too late.

"C'mon, I'll take it off for you . . . take it all off. Tha'll be fun." He pulled her down on the couch, bent her back across his legs.

"Mr. Majors, this is Annie!" She said it loudly, but she didn't scream. Not at the master of Wheatley.

His drunken laughter overcame all of her pleas and protests—resistance manifested in words and deeds that lacked conviction.

She put up a feeble struggle as he took off the mink coat and tore open her robe. She had a free hand. He had to release it to work her nightgown up above her hips. She pushed and pulled at his arms and hands and shoulders. She whimpered. When he mounted her, she turned her mouth away from his hot kisses and lay inert. When he entered her she moaned and a shudder ran the length of her body.

All at once the heat caught her up and her arms went around his neck. Her mouth came around to meet his. She arched to meet his driving.

They were asleep in each other's arms when the light went on. Carl snored on in his intoxicated, satiated stupor.

Annie squawked like a cat whose tail's been trodden on and sat up. Stricken at the looming presence of Callie, she frantically tugged the nightgown down to hide her nakedness.

"What have we here?" Callie derided the maid. "I instructed you to cover Mr. Majors if he was asleep, but I don't recall telling you to get under the covers with him."

"He was drunk." Blushing furiously, she sat on the edge of the bed, pulling on her slippers.

"Not too drunk, from the looks of things."

"He raped me. I don't know what he thought. It was dark. I couldn't put on any lights." She rattled on, defensive and confused. "Then he grabbed me in the dark and—and—" She let out her breath, surrendering to the irrefutable evidence. "He did it to me."

"And you let him?"

"I tried. I tried to talk to him. He wouldn't listen to me."

"Did you scream?"

Her head drooped, eyes fixed on the floor. "I—I did. I screamed."

"You're a liar!" Callie ridiculed her. "If you had, we'd have heard you up here at the house. Old Sam in the back room, he always sleeps with his window open. To paraphrase: 'You did protest, but not too much.' Am I right?"

Annie retreated into silence as she put on her robe and tied the sash.

"No matter, I don't imagine you'll be pressing any charges against the old goat when he comes out of it. That wouldn't be wise, now, would it?"

Annie struck out at her finally in her desperation. "I *do* know what he thought when he grabbed me in the dark. He thought I was *you* in this coat. He was expecting you."

Callie scoffed at her. The advantage Annie had gained the previous morning was discredited in the light of what had occurred tonight.

"If it had been me, he'd have gotten his face slapped like the naughty boy deserved and a smart tongue-lashing to go with it."

"I know he was in your bedroom yesterday morning. I saw him in the bathroom."

Callie smirked at the absurdity of the girl. "A woman who's as easy a mark as you are would think so, naturally. That I had asked him in. The truth is, he's a dirty old man, always prowling about peeking in bedrooms and bathrooms. I try to hide his perversions from young Mr. Majors. He'd have him committed. That's why I protected him yesterday when he came sneaking into my bedroom while I was in the bath."

"You're a liar! Mr. Majors isn't like that at all. You're evil! God, how I hate you!"

Callie stepped forward, took Annie's chin firmly between her thumb and first finger, and tilted it up so that the maid had to meet her eviscerating glare.

"That's fine with me. After what's happened here tonight, I wouldn't have you around here another day. You whore!"

Annie began to cry.

"Stop that slobbering and get back to the house. You are to be out of Wheatley, off the grounds, before noon. One more thing, I might remind you that you have two brothers employed by the Majors Brick Company. And your Uncle Tod is assistant foreman at the Knight quarry. Oh yes, I'll provide you with a reference and two weeks' salary in addition to what you're due now." She smiled. "That's for the services you provided to Mr. Majors here tonight!"

Annie covered her ears with her hands and ran sobbing down the steps and out of the boathouse in her robe and nightgown.

Callie picked her fur coat up from the floor where Carl had thrown it in a heap. Carefully she brushed off the dust and smoothed the mink's nap. She folded it over a chair back and walked to the little bar and galley in the alcove. She filled a pitcher with cold water and carried it back to the couch. Leaning over the sleeping man, she emptied the contents into his face. The shock brought Carl to his senses. He opened his eyes, then squeezed them shut again against the painful light.

"Oh, Jesus . . ." he groaned. With a great effort he pushed himself up on one elbow, staring baffled at the sodden sheet and pillow.

She stood over him with menace in her voice and eyes. "You drunken sot, now you've gone and done it."

He looked up, wary of her. "What are you talking about? Why did you do this to me?" He ran a hand through his wet hair. The cold bath had sobered him.

"You know very well what you did, Carl. You raped Annie."

Dazed, he shook his head. "Raped Annie? That's a poor joke, Callie. Unworthy of your rapier wit."

"It's no joke, Carl. I sent her down to make sure everything was in order here at the boathouse before we went to bed."

"*No!* Stop tormenting me like this!" He shrank away from her, back to the wall. "You're trying to befuddle me, but my mind's clear on that at least. You went back to the house to—to—" He pounded a hand against his head to clear the idea. "To turn off the heater in Nate's room. That's it, then you came back to me and . . ." Small doubts began to insinuate themselves.

The voice, it was not like Callie to cry out the way she had. "*Mr. Majors . . .*" It echoed back from the labyrinth of his mind. The feel of her body under his hands, the skin's texture coarse. Callie was all satin.

"I didn't come back to you, Carl. I had no intention of coming back and submitting to your drunken pawings. I sent Annie."

A violent chill seized him, he wrapped the blanket around his naked body. The stink of sweat was acrid from his armpits. This ague was not from outer cold. The ice lay deep within.

"You lie! The mink coat. I felt it. Your coat." Feeble protesting.

She took the coat from the chair and draped it around her shoulders. "Yes, my coat. I let Annie wear it."

His head snapped back and thumped the wall. He shut his eyes. His voice was calm, resigned. "You let her wear your coat.

. . . Yes . . . I see it now. . . . Well, what do you have planned for me, my sweet daughter-in-law? Is Annie phoning for the police? I can see the headlines now: BRICK BARON JAILED FOR RAPING MAID. Is that my lot?"

"Don't be maudlin, Carl. I've taken care of everything. Annie won't speak of what happened to anyone."

He opened his eyes and saw her with dawning insight. "Ahhh . . . I should have known better. . . . You are far more inventive than that. The rack is more your style."

"Stop raving nonsense, Carl. Get up and put on your clothes. Go back to the house and sleep it off." She turned to leave. "By the way, you don't have to worry about facing Annie. She'll be gone by noon. For good."

She started down the steps to the door.

Carl's head fell forward on his breast. "For that I'm grateful. Poor Annie."

Carl shivered as a cloud contoured like a greyhound raced across the sun. He hugged the boy closer to him.

"Are you cold, Grampa?" the piping voice inquired. "I'm not cold a bit. You keep me warm."

"I'll always see that you're warm and protected, son." His arms tightened around Nate.

The boy laughed. "Hey! You'll hug me to death, you big grizzly bear!"

"That's what I am. A bear." He made ferocious growling noises. "I ate up your grandfather as the wolf ate Little Red Ridinghood's grandmother, and I put on his clothes."

Nate wriggled out of his grasp and leaped up, running down the beach screaming and laughing, waving his arms.

"Help! Help! A grizzly bear's after me!"

Carl got up stiffly and walked after him, casting one backward look at Callie's bridge.

Nate ran all the way to the boathouse. Chris had just returned from across the river and was kneeling on the dock securing the inboard's mooring line. The boy threw himself on her.

"Auntie Chris! A grizzly bear's after me. Save me!"

She sat down hard on the wooden planks and caught him up in her arms. "Hey! You want to push me in the river?" She kissed his cheek, grimaced at the reek of liquor on his baby skin. She watched her father trudging through the sand, old and weary, angry at him for inviting pity. Her father, all of her life he'd been next to God in her eyes.

"How is Ham?" Nate asked, his dark eyes shining.

"He's fine," she said, but her heart was troubled for Ham.

"Why didn't you tell me you were going to see Ham? You promised I could go with you next time." His small mouth was petulant, small jaw thrust out in imitation of Ham.

She pressed her cheek to his hair. "I'm sorry, honey. Your mother said you wanted to go with Grandpa and watch the men building the bridge."

He sulked. "She knows I would rather have gone with you, Aunt Chris."

Chris was silent. She couldn't lay the blame for *that* on Callie. Callie had suggested she take Nate to see Ham, and Chris had said she'd think about it. Then she sneaked off without him, feeling like a fraud.

How could she tell darling little Nathaniel that his brother didn't want him at the Knight house? How could Ham be so cruel and insensitive? The boy idolized him. Dogged his footsteps on the rare occasions Ham gave his grudging consent for Chris to bring Nate across the river. Imitated all of Ham's mannerisms. Why was Ham so cold to his own flesh and blood? Was he jealous in some unnatural way? Bitter that his father had sired a second son who would share his inheritance? No, that was not like Ham, he was indifferent to worldly goods.

Once she asked him outright. Ham got sullen. "I don't care much for young'uns, that's all."

Nate tugged at her skirt. "Aunt Chris, what's the matter?"

She smiled at him. "Nothing is the matter. Why?"

He frowned, eyes and mouth screwed up tightly. "You had a mad face. Like Ham, only his face is always mad."

She sighed and took his hand. "Let's walk down the beach and meet Grandpa."

When the three of them came back to the house, Bruce met them in the hall. He had a drink in his hand. Nate ran up and threw his arms around his stepfather.

"Papa, what did you bring me?" he asked excitedly.

Bruce rumpled the boy's hair and stroked his cheek. "I'm sorry, Nate, but Papa was so busy with his work all weekend, he didn't have time to buy you a present. Next trip, I promise. Two presents, that's what I'll bring you next time I go away."

"Two presents. Wheeee!" He ran down the hall to the kitchen where Callie was preparing dinner in the cook's absence. "Mama! Mama! Papa is going to bring me two presents next time he goes away. Can I have a cookie, I'm hungry."

Bruce greeted Chris and his father with stiff reserve.

"How did things work out at the office?" Carl inquired.

"I managed to clean up your desk," was the cold reply. "I'll tell you about it later. Right now, I'd like to have a few words with Chris. Alone. Will you come into the library with me, please?"

Carl's bushy eyebrows lifted as he contemplated the dark color of the drink in his son's hand. "Is that for me?" he asked.

Bruce glared at him. "No, this drink is mine. And for your information, it's my third since I arrived back."

"Well, there may be hope for you, after all, my boy," Carl murmured and retreated into the parlor to mix his own drink.

Bruce led his sister into the study and shut the door. "Sit down, Christine."

The girl braced herself for the hard words she knew were coming. He only addressed her by her full name when he was angry or displeased with her. She perched gingerly on the chair beside the desk. Bruce sat down in his high-backed chair behind the desk to show her it was to be a formal meeting. He cleared his throat with self-importance.

"I won't have you being disrespectful to my wife," he said.

The blunt attack unsettled her. "I've never been disrespectful to Callie. If she told you that, she's lying."

"Callie didn't tell me. She tried to defend you, as she always does. I surmised that something was wrong between you two."

"Do you mean her dismissing Annie? Yes, I'm very dismayed about that, Bruce, and I told her so. If that's rudeness to speak my mind, then I'll confess to it. She had no right."

"She had every right. She's the lady of this house."

"All right, she had the right. But not the cause. Annie has served this family faithfully for ten years. Have you or Father ever had reason to be dissatisfied with her work or her behavior?"

He put down his glass on the blotter, drummed on the desk with his fingers. Avoided looking at her.

"That may be true, Christine, but people and situations change."

"Yes, since *she* came here a lot has changed."

"Ah!" He pounced on her. "You give yourself away, my dear sister. Your bias against Callie. I've sensed it before, but you're usually more subtle."

"That's not true! You're the biased one." There was a tremor in her voice as she fought back tears. "I admit before I met her, I may have judged her unfairly. But all that changed. I loved Callie like a sister in the beginning. I wanted her to marry you, you know that's so."

He gave a little, reached out, and laid a hand on her arm. "Yes, I do know that, Chris. I'd like to know why. What happened to change your feelings toward Callie? Oh, I realize it was only natural for you to harbor some resentment when I married her and brought her to this house. Our house. *Your* house, where you were born and brought up. You felt she was an usurper."

"No, no, you're wrong." She denied it vigorously. "I wanted Callie here. I'm too young to think of myself as Wheatley's lady. I want my own house someday."

"Then you must tell me what's gone wrong between you two. Now, leave Annie out of it. There are circumstances about Annie you don't know."

"Then I want to know and judge for myself."

"I can't tell you, Chris," he said wearily. "It's very painful for me to talk about. Much less to you."

"It has to do with Father?"

He was silent.

"Father and Annie?" It was apparent to her all at once what he was insinuating. "Oh, *no! Bruce!* You're not saying that—" She could not put the thought into words, it was too loathsome.

"I told you I don't want to talk about it."

"Oh, Bruce, I don't believe it. It isn't true. Callie's lying." She covered her face with her hands in shame.

Bruce stood up and went over to her, put an arm around her shoulders. He spoke gently to her. "Dear Chris, do you believe that if Callie dismissed Annie out of spite Annie would have left the way she did? So abruptly and without a word to you or to Father? You pointed out she's served us faithfully for ten years. Annie is a girl with spirit. She has a tongue and she's not afraid to use it. If she felt she'd been unjustly treated, you can rely we would have heard about it."

"Not even a good-bye," Chris said dispiritedly. "I expressed it to Father the day she left, how odd it was."

"And what did Father think?"

"He said he didn't abide with long-drawn-out farewells himself."

"And *you* believe him?"

She wiped her eyes with a handkerchief. "I don't know what to believe." She clutched at him, pressed her face against him. "This once was such a happy house. We were a happy family, Father, you, and I. Now look at us! If it isn't you and Father shouting at one another, then it's you and me at odds."

"And you blame this on Callie?"

"It must be her."

He ridiculed her charge. "Really, Chris, are we going to blame our father's present disreputable condition on Callie too? The man's been a sot for years."

"Not like he is now. He could hold his drink."

Bruce stroked her silky hair. "When he was young. Age takes its toll on every one of us. I can't play six sets of tennis the way I did in college. We all must learn to pace ourselves in all of our endeavors and appetites. That's his weakness, he can't pace himself. Instead of cutting down his drinks, the old mule drinks more than he ever did. Chris, Father is no longer capable of performing his duties as president of the company. He's an ineffectual, irresponsible lush. If he gets any worse, we're going to have to put him in an institution."

"Don't say that, Bruce," she cried. "He's our father."

"Yes," he agreed with bitterness. "He is our father. And I love him. But I wish he hadn't forfeited the esteem and respect I held for him as a man. The pride that such a man was *my* father." His voice cracked now. "Oh, Christ! Sis, I know what you are feeling. I feel it too. But we can't rationalize his faults and our faults and the inevitable attrition that every family falls victim to in time by pretending that Callie is a sorceress who's cast a spell upon us."

Chris stopped crying and looked up at him. Her blue eyes were vacant, empty of anger, empty of resentment, empty of hope.

Her voice was vapid. "Yes . . . that must be it. She's bewitched us."

Callie regarded the following summer as the crux of her life, of greater moment than her marriage to Nathaniel Knight and her subsequent alliance with Bruce Majors. "Alliance" was appropriate, for, on her part, there was no emotion involved in taking either spouse.

The family spent the month of June in Saratoga, where Carl lost heavily on the races and lapsed into alcoholic despair so extreme that Bruce had him spirited out of their hotel in the middle of the night and driven by ambulance to a private sanatarium in Ballston Spa. Friends and associates received the family explanation that Carl was at the spa in the hope of curing his gout in the mineral baths with urbane pretense.

"I must take the health cure myself next year."

Callie spent August with Chris, little Nate, and Jane Hathaway at the Sagamore Hotel on Lake George. Bruce motored up on weekends.

They were lazy, hot, dog days at the lake, monotonous for Callie. The nights were the worst. Sitting on the broad hotel veranda overlooking the black menacing water beneath the Chinese lanterns. Listening to the fat rich hens, middle-aged and old, cackling about their children and grandchildren, complaining about their servants and gossiping in whispers about "that Majors Woman."

On weekends when their husbands joined them there was a little more excitement, although the men like to clique up at the bar and assess world affairs.

Al Smith had been elected to his fourth term as governor of New York.

One-thousand United States Marines had landed in China on March 5, 1927 to protect American property and nationals in the Chinese Civil War.

The most sensational news story of the year was the trial of Ruth Brown Snyder and Henry Judd Gray for the murder of her husband Albert Snyder.

But the biggest story of the year was the non-stop flight by a United States air mail pilot Captain Charles A. Lindberg from New York to Paris in his monoplane *The Spirit of St. Louis.*

The economy kept climbing to impossible peaks, one glorious high succeeding by another even loftier. The slogan of the day was: *The sky's the limit.*

And one cliché topped the other: *The end of the rainbow still's not in sight.*

The talk would diminish whenever Callie passed by the bar on her way to the dining room. The men were as aware of *"that*

Majors Woman" as their wives. Some were furtive in their interest. Some were brazen in their longing admiration. Callie was aloof and unapproachable.

She had emerged from the family crisis of the spring and winter past, unconditionally victorious. She was at dead center of the nucleus. Carl, Bruce, and Ham were her satellites, resigned to their roles.

Chris was outwardly submissive, but she continued to challenge Callie in subversive ways. Her insistence on being present at the weekly business conferences attended by Callie, Carl, Bruce, Ham, and the Knight foreman, Walt Campball, was intolerable to Callie. Chris made it plain that she was looking out for *her* interest in the Majors wealthy estate.

"She's impudent!" Callie fumed to Bruce.

"Chris isn't a child," he reminded her. "She's a twenty-two-year-old woman. She's entitled to participate in the meetings and have her say on matters settled in them."

There was also the matter of Chris and Carl. The girl exerted influence over her father only second to the power Callie held.

Callie made up her mind, she had to get rid of Chris. Marriage seemed the logical way to dispossess her from Wheatley. While they were at the lake, Callie contrived to match her up with one of the young bachelors who came to visit mothers and maiden aunts on weekends.

One afternoon on the hotel beach Chris coolly refused an invitation to go dancing with a handsome blond young man that evening. Callie reproached her. "Why were you rude to that boy? Do you know who he is? A nephew of the Harrimans."

Chris lay back in her lounge chair and pulled down the awning to protect her fair complexion. "I don't care who he is. He's rich and spoiled and thinks he's God's gift to women."

"You're rich and spoiled, what's wrong with that?"

"I suppose I am. Oh, he's not bad really. It's just—" She lowered her gaze and blushed. She said it softly. "Other boys don't interest me."

Callie measured her shrewdly. "*Other* boys? Then what boy does? It's Ham, isn't it?"

The girl nodded. "I'm afraid so."

"Afraid?" She had tried to encourage that match herself, but their relationship, it seemed to her, could never progress beyond a brother-sister duet. For three years Chris had been courting Ham without pride. He never visited Wheatley anymore. She had to go to him.

They had every opportunity to exploit their privacy. A village woman came in to clean and cook for Ham and left at dusk. Callie was certain that Chris was willing, eager, to yield her chastity to Ham Knight; she had her father's hot blood. Each time the girl returned from a protracted visit across the river, she would come under Callie's wise scrutiny. There is a subtle nuance that marks the passing from maid to mistress. A mystery in the eyes. A glint of Eve in the smile. The very movements of her new uninhibited body. Callie's female intuition would have kenned it. No, Chris retained her purity, if reluctantly.

She had thought her continence might be rectified the summer Chris spent in Europe with Senator Wayne Harrison's paramour. However, when she returned after two months in London, Paris, Rome, and Lisbon, it was plain to Callie that neither the company she'd kept nor the continental *joie de vivre* had altered Chris's chastity. Or cured her of Ham.

"Afraid, you say? Afraid of what?"

"That Ham doesn't care for me. Oh, he likes me well enough." A wishful sigh. "Once I thought he really cared, but I was wrong. Not in that special way a man should care for a woman."

Callie had no patience with the Gordian knot that always fettered feminine tongues when sex was mentioned.

"You mean he's never asked you to go to bed, is that it?"

Chris's pale face turned scarlet. "It really isn't something I care to discuss. What happens between Ham and me is a private matter. If you'll excuse me, I think I'll take a dip in the lake."

Callie watched her run down to the lake's edge and test the water with her toes. She was a pretty, healthy girl with a good body. A woman's body well regarded by the young males on the beach.

"What happens between Ham and me is a private matter."

"Only nothing happens," Callie mused. She smiled. Ham was still hers. Hers alone. Chris loved him, but she could not have him. Of all the women in the world, only Callie had known him in the ultimate way a man and woman can know each other.

Love? What was love? They had possessed one another. The bond of flesh was a nexus in the form of little Nathaniel.

"Mama, Mama!" Her son ran up to her, swinging his shovel and pail. "I met a nice man. He's coming to see you."

Callie brushed sticky sand off his sturdy little shoulders and plump belly with her hands. "You had better put on your shirt, you've had too much sun as it is today, Nate." She frowned. "Now what's this about a man?"

"He's a friend of yours and Papa's. Here he comes now." He pointed down the beach.

Callie shielded her eyes against the sun and followed the direction of his arm. She saw a tall tanned figure wending his way among the brightly colored umbrellas, chairs, and blankets decorating the sand. He was as imposing in a bathing suit as he was in tie and tails, she decided, inspecting his broad shoulders and muscular arms.

"Senator Harrison," she greeted him as he came up to them, and held out her hand. "What a delightful surprise."

He took her hand in both of his hands, held it longer than mere courtesy required, with firm, warm pressure.

"I am delighted, but not surprised," he advised her.

"Oh?"

"I met Bruce last month in Albany and he told me you and the family would be at the Sagamore in August. So the next day I booked reservations for my wife and me."

"I'm sure you'll enjoy it here. It's so—so—"

His eyes shone with merriment. "So damned dull, that's what you were really thinking."

The two of them laughed. Sharing a conspiracy directed at the wealthy, self-important dullards cooking their blubber in the hot sun.

"May I sit down?" He looked at the chair abandoned by Chris.

"Please do."

He did and swung young Nate up onto his knees. "Your son is growing up to be a fine young man. We had a nice talk, didn't we, Nathaniel?"

"Yes, sir!" Nate turned excitedly to his mother. "Senator Harrison is going to take me for a ride in his speedboat tomorrow."

"I'll bet you'll love that, dear. Now see if you can find Miss

Hathaway and tell her it's time you had your bath and dressed for supper."

"Yes, ma'am."

Harrison put him down and gave him a playful slap on the backside. "Don't forget tomorrow, son. We have a date."

They watched him run off, chubby legs flailing sand over irate sunbathers.

"Pretend we don't know him," Callie said.

"He's a handsome boy. And bright. I hope my son turns out as well."

Her look was oblique. "I didn't know you had a son."

"I don't, not yet, but that's to change in three more months. My wife is pregnant."

Wayne Harrison had married Julia Clement, the daughter of United States Senator Hubert Clement, the year before. The Majorses had been invited to the wedding and reception in Washington, D.C., and they had declined with regret. Carl was in no condition to make the long train trip and Callie and Bruce were reluctant to leave him and little Nate alone at Wheatley with the servants.

His flinty eyes bored into her eyes. "It's been a long time since we last met. The governor's ball. The night you became engaged to Bruce. I was disappointed you didn't invite me to your wedding."

"It was a quiet family affair."

He reached over and laid a hand on her arm. "Do you remember what we talked about that night?"

"Very well." Her eyelids flickered. *"It's not the time for you and me. . . . Not now at any rate."*

The flint in his eyes sparked. "I think the time may be right now. What do you think?"

Callie withdrew her arm from under his hand. The prospect of an affair with Wayne Harrison made her blood race as she had not been aroused since her wild, lusty orgies with Ham behind his father's back. She'd keep him guessing for a while.

"I'll have to think about it."

"Not too long, I trust?"

Her smile was artful as she rose to leave him.

> *"Upon the heat and flame of thy distemper*
> *Sprinkle cool patience."*

His strong yellow teeth gleamed in the sunlight. "They're pretty words, but I'm a politician, not a poet."

"All the more reason for you to heed it. A politician must learn to bide his time."

"True enough. All right, I'll bide my time. . . . Until tomorrow."

Callie was pleased with the day's events. She nodded to the pompous females rocking on the porch and turned a saucy hip to the gentlemen in the bar.

That evening in the dining room, Senator Harrison and his wife stopped at the Majorses' table to pay their respects. Julia Harrison was a stout, coarse blond woman with a loud nasal voice. Six months of pregnancy did nothing to improve her appearance.

Harrison repeated his invitation to little Nate to go boating with him the next day. He included Chris and Callie. Chris declined.

"I get seasick in a rowboat."

"I do too since I've been expecting," said Julia.

"Then I had better go along and keep an eye on this young rapscallion," Callie declared. "So you can keep your mind on boating."

Senator Harrison had rented a sleek power launch for the duration of his stay at the lake. All highly polished teak and gleaming brass.

Nate sat between his mother and the senator at the wheel, looking every bit the gentleman yachtsman in his white duck slacks, blue blazer, and skipper's cap.

Callie wore a linen dress with a floppy hat to shade her fair complexion from the sun.

The senator steered for Pilot Knob. The ride was bumpy on the choppy water and the wind slammed scud in their faces with a force that took the breath away. Nate screamed in delight. Callie gasped.

"It's more like the ocean than a lake."

"You should see her when it's storming," he shouted back over the roar of the engine. "There're waves five feet high."

She was dazzled by the panorama of blue water, green forest, and bluer sky sweeping by them on all sides.

"It's like stepping into a picture postcard."

"I wish Daddy was here," Nate said. "And Grampa." He thrust out his lower lip like Ham. "Wait till I tell Ham about it. He'll be sorry he wasn't here having fun with us."

From Pilot Knob Harrison went south to Shelving Rock. "It's said two Indian lovers leaped to their death from that ridge," he told them.

"What for?" Nate demanded.

"So they could be together forever."

"That's dopy!" the boy crowed. "Who wants to be dead?"

They moored the boat at Lake George village and went ashore for lunch. From the restaurant they saw a red and white excursion steamer docking after her voyage around the lake. Her paddle wheels rotated slowly, tossing a rainbow spray into the sunlight.

"Can we go for a ride on that ocean liner?" Nate begged.

His mother laughed and hugged him to her. "Some other day. We still have two more weeks here, sweet."

"She's a paddle-wheeler, not a liner, son," the senator corrected him humorously. "Though I'm sure her captain would be flattered by the compliment."

They cruised back to the Sagamore by way of Bolton Landing. "We must come over here for supper some evening. The French cuisine is superb," Harrison told her.

Jane Hathaway was waiting for them when they got back to the Sagamore's landing, seated on a camp chair in the shade. She put aside her book and hurried out onto the dock.

"I was beginning to worry," she scolded. "I hope he didn't get too much sun." She helped Nate out of the boat and hugged him to her.

"Jane is the original mother hen," Callie teased. "You have my word of honor Nate had the best of care."

"I didn't exceed the speed limit once," the senator joked. "But that's about to change."

"Senator Harrison wants to show me how fast his boat will go, Jane," Callie explained. "You take Nate upstairs and see he has his nap."

"Yes, ma'am." The governess jumped as Harrison revved up the powerful engine.

Nate giggled. "Don't be scared, Miss Hathaway. There's a fierce lion inside the boat, but he won't hurt you."

Callie waved over her shoulder as the cruiser turned sharp and nosed up as Harrison opened the throttle wide. Higher, higher, higher the prow lifted. Two waterfalls curled off her gunwales.

Callie shrieked. "This is exciting! I feel as if we're going to take off like an airship."

"Have you ever been up in an airship?"

"No, but I intend to soon. I'm a shareholder in two commercial aviation ventures and I should see what I've put my money into."

"You're due to strike a gold mine one of these days. It's the travel of the future, by air. Do you want to drive?"

"Not especially. Where are we going?"

"A secret place. A paradise isle."

She clapped her hands. "Do you plan to shipwreck us there?"

He reached over and laid one big brown hand on her thigh. "If that's the only way to get you ashore there, I'll do it."

She put her hand on his. "I think I prefer to take off my shoes and stockings and wade ashore."

The island lay in a small cove whose only access was a narrow channel obscured by heavy foliage on both sides. A snug private harbor where the water was a shimmering glass mirror. Callie peered over the side.

"It's so clear I can see the bottom. Look at that big fish! It must be a shark!"

Harrison laughed. "Lake bass. They grow large." He reduced the throttle and, at idling speed, pointed her in toward the lee side of the island. A thickly wooded hummock rising out of the water, not more than one acre. He cut the engine when the hull scraped the muddy bottom, and let the anchor over the side.

"We'll walk the rest of the way."

Callie turned her back to him, pulled up her skirt, and unfastened the hooks on her garters. Rolling down the silk stocking, she looked over her shoulder and saw him watching her, hunger in his eyes.

"I can't think of anything that excites me more than seeing a woman undress," he told her.

"Even more than when she's undressed?"

"Then the time for looking has passed." He removed his sneakers and socks and rolled up his slacks to the knee. He stepped out of the boat into the shallow water and helped Callie scale the gunwale. He waded to the back of the boat and removed four cushions and a car robe from the stern locker.

They went ashore. The beach was a narrow strip of bleached sand two yards wide.

Callie stood spraddle-legged, hands on hips, wriggling her toes in the coarse sand. "I feel like Robinson Crusoe."

Harrison pointed out the ashes of a fire and other items discarded by past visitors. "It's hardly virgin property, but it will do. Anyone approaching the channel can be heard well ahead. In time . . ." He let it trail off.

"In time for what?" she questioned.

He laughed. "Come on, we'll strike inland."

She followed him along a winding path through a grove of fir trees, inhaling the fragrance of pine.

"Sugar and spice and everything nice. . . . Oh, it's so lovely in here I'd like to stay forever."

"A garden of Eden," he suggested.

"And you and I are Adam and Eve, is that what you have in mind?"

They came out into a clearing that bore the evidence of other trysts. Callie wrinkled up her nose at the sight of a shriveled condom.

"Pigs! They should be forbidden to come here."

Harrison laughed as he disposed of the offensive rubber in a thicket with a stick. "So much for Adam and Eve."

He threw down the cushions and the robe and grabbed her roughly.

She winced. "You hurt me."

He relaxed his grip. "I'm sorry. It's been so long since I've had a woman, I must seem crude to you."

She ran her hands up over his biceps to his shoulders and pressed her body against his. "Sex is a crude business. When it's carried out in too mannerly a fashion, it loses a good deal. You see, it's been a long time since I've had a *man.*" The emphasis conveyed her meaning better than words.

He kissed her. Deep kisses tongue to tongue. She broke the kiss finally, breathless. Pushed him away.

"Here, let me take off my clothes." She unfastened the pearl buttons running down the front of her dress. He undressed facing her. She did not turn away. It excited her to have him watching her. To see the desire building in his hard, strong male body. When they were stripped naked they contemplated each other with candid appreciation. Then without a word they came together.

She spoke once when they were lying on the cushions and he bent to kiss her breast.

"I don't need that, Wayne. I'm ready now. Hurry!"

They were on the island for two more hours. Harrison experienced three orgasms to Callie's five. Afterward they went down to the lake and washed. While they were dressing he told her, "I've never had a woman like you before, and I've had many."

She gave him a sly, sideways smile. "And you tell the same thing to every one."

He didn't like the joke. "I've never told it to any of the others because they've all been alike. That wife of mine—" He shuddered. "It's like fucking a corpse."

Callie relished earthy talk in its natural place, it was salt and pepper to any tongue, but she pretended to be shocked.

"Senator Harrison, what a thing to say in front of a lady."

He came over and embraced her, clamping his big hands over the cheeks of her buttocks. Huskily he told her, "If you were a lady, I wouldn't have wasted a trip out here. I've had my crawful of *'ladies.'* " The word sounded more obscene than what he had said before.

When Harrison put in near sunset at the Sagamore's dock, Callie was seated in the stern, looking cool and aloof in her white starched dress, every hair in place.

The "ladies" on the veranda leaned forward in their chairs, all eyes turned on the dock. Throats were cleared for gossip. A few sighs rippled over the assembly. More than a few shameful urges were buried under all that taffeta, whalebone, and fat.

They saw the distinguished Senator Harrison leap lightly onto the boards. Extend his hand to Mrs. Majors. She alighted gracefully and thanked him with a small curtsy. He bowed stiffly in acknowledgment, smiled, and said a few gallant words to her. She smiled appreciatively, and they parted.

It was too dull and prosaic for the sluggish imaginations assembled on the Sagamore's deck. A score of chairs creaked as their occupants settled back to vegetate once more.

Not one could have imagined what Senator Harrison's parting salutation to Mrs. Majors had been: "I hope it doesn't rain, because I'm going to take you out to the island every day and fuck the ass off you!"

It was not all that simple for the two of them to slip away

together every day. Callie had Nate, Chris, and Miss Hathaway to think about. Mrs. Harrison kept a sharp eye on the senator. They were able to manage two more assignations that week, by a series of complex machinations.

On Wednesday Callie went by taxi to Lake George village and bought a new hat. There she bought a ticket for a guided tour around the lake. At Bolton Landing she disembarked with the other passengers to browse in an antique shop, and remained behind when the tour resumed.

Harrison picked her up in his cruiser and took her to the island. The return trip was almost as complicated. He took her back to Lake George village, where she took a taxi back to the Sagamore Hotel.

The following Sunday Callie arranged for the four of them, she, Nate, Chris, and Miss Hathaway, to make the grand tour of the lake aboard the paddle-wheeler. Senator and Mrs. Harrison accompanied them.

The senator drove them to Lake George village in his Dodge sedan. During the ride, Callie complained of stomach cramps, which became very severe by the time they were due to board the steamer. The senator expressed his concern.

"I hate to alarm you, Mrs. Majors, but you could be coming down with appendicitis. I don't think it would be wise of you to make this tour. I think you should see a doctor."

"Oh, I wouldn't hear of it," she objected. "I refuse to let a little tummyache ruin this day for all of you. I'll go back by taxi and consult the hotel physician. The rest of you go ahead as if nothing had happened. Honestly, I know it's nothing serious. Please do as I say."

The senator resolved the dilemma with masculine incisiveness. Mrs. Majors was right. There was no reason to spoil the fun for little Nate and the others. Mrs. Majors would *not* take a taxi back to the hotel. *He* would drive her straight to the home of an Albany internist he knew who had a summer home on Lake George.

He assisted her into the car and they drove off as the *Mississippi Queen* cast off from the landing with a melancholy toot of her whistle and her stacks belching black smoke.

They drove around the lake to Bolton Landing, where Harrison had moored his boat the previous evening. Less than one hour after they had bid bon voyage to the others, Callie and Wayne were making love on their island of paradise with the blazing August sun warming his naked back and her heaving bosom and wide-spread thighs. After the second time they bathed in the serene pool behind the island.

"It reminds me of a tropic lagoon," she decided.

"You've bathed naked in tropic lagoons before?"

She splashed water in his face. "Don't make fun of me, Senator. If your constituency could see you now, the laugh would be on you."

He pulled her tightly to him in the waist-deep water and kissed her. "I wouldn't give a damn what they thought," he said with fervor. "I'd like the whole world to see us now. I'd be so proud. There isn't a man in this state has a wench like you. In the world."

Her laughter was hot and husky in his ear as she whispered, "I think all politicians should campaign in the nude. Then the lady voters would always be sure who the best man was."

He slapped her wet rump. "You are a hussy. God, what will I do after this summer is over? I'll go mad with nothing but that old cow of mine."

She looked up at him with her shrewd thin smile. "Wayne, you don't have to lie to me. Julia isn't the only woman you have. I heard all about your exploits when you were a bachelor."

He was honest with her. "There have been girls, yes, it's true. But, I swear to God, none of them meant, or mean, anything to me the way you do. Callie . . . I'm tempted to give up my career, my marriage, quit it all for you." He took her hand and kissed the palm.

Callie smiled sweetly. "That's pretty talk and it makes sense when we're standing here loin to loin. In passion's heat you can dance to a dirge, Wayne. My darling, you've got your star. I've got mine. Our courses don't collide."

"I suppose you're right," he said with melancholy. "You generally are. Still . . ." His gaze swept over her to future visions. "There may come a day when we . . ."

She covered his mouth with her hand. "Some day," she said, and glanced up at the setting sun. "We've tarried here too long, Wayne."

They dressed and started back. Harrison took out his gold pocket watch. "There's just time for me to take you to the Sagamore, then drive back to the village and meet the steamer."

The Dodge pulled up in front of the main entrance of the hotel at a quarter to five. Putting on a good show of concern and solicitation, he helped her out of the car and steadied her elbow as she climbed the steps. Callie acted her role to perfection. Head down. Lashes lowered. Fanning herself with a handkerchief.

Senator Harrison turned his charm on the porch tenants. "Mrs. Majors had a bit too much sun, I'm afraid." He tipped his yachting cap to a group of beaming women.

He guided her across the lobby to the desk and ordered the clerk to send a bowl of ice and an ice bag to her suite. "I'll see Mrs. Majors upstairs myself, she's feeling poorly."

They rode the elevator up to the third floor and went down the hall to her door. Inside, he kissed her and fondled her breasts.

"You keep that up and I will have a fever," she warned him. "Go, now, before the bellboy arrives with my ice and bag."

He laughed. "You can mix a drink. I could use one myself. Let's have cocktails in the lounge when I get back?"

"I'd like that, but we've taken such pains to invalid me, it would look suspicious."

"Yes, I suppose so. Well, I'm off."

He strode briskly down the hall, paused a moment at the elevators, before deciding it would be quicker to use the stairs.

Minutes after, there was a knock on Callie's door. It was the bellboy, military-looking in his jaunty cap, natty brass-buttoned tunic, and tight trousers with a razor crease. He carried a tray. On it were the bowl of ice and a gray-rubber ice bag. And a third item that made her very curious indeed. A letter.

"Special delivery for Senator Harrison," the boy explained. "It came this afternoon, but the new clerk on duty didn't know about it until after you'd come upstairs."

"I'll see the senator gets it," she assured him. "Put the tray over there."

After he'd gone she picked up the letter and examined it. The handwriting on the front was feminine script. It was odd, she thought, there was no return address on the sealed flap on the back.

Chewing on her bottom lip, Callie took it over to the window and held it up to the light. The sun was low, an enormous orange fireball teetering on the mountain ridge across the lake. The envelope glowed translucent, and she could make out a single sheet of writing paper inside. It was covered with the same script that had addressed the envelope, thrice folded so that the words were a mélange of unintelligible characters.

She was able to decipher one line, the last line at the bottom of the page, where the sheet had been folded unevenly.

Yours, always, in all ways,
Evelyn

She walked away from the window, frowning at the letter in her fingers. Tapping the envelope absently on the knuckles of her other hand. Turning it over. Over again.

She pressed it against her forehead, closed her eyes. Callie believed in clairvoyance. If she had the gift, it failed her in this instance. She gave up and put the letter down on the tray.

Callie went into her bedroom and undressed. She loathed the idea of going to bed so early on such a hot night. But the charade she had put on for Nate and Chris and Mrs. Harrison, not to mention the old hens on the porch, required it.

When Chris brought Nate in to see her later, she was playing possum. Her eyes came open slowly.

"Oh, I must have dozed. How long have you been back?"

"We just got back. How are you feeling?"

"Much better, thanks." She held out her arms to Nate. "Darling, did you have a good time on your boat ride?"

"It was lots of fun, Mama. I wish you and Uncle Wayne could have come with us."

She pressed her cheek to his. "Oh, yes, Uncle Wayne, he's been so good to me. Would you do me a favor, darling? There's a special delivery letter came for Uncle Wayne after he went to the village to drive you home from the boat landing. It's on a tray on the coffee table. Would you please take it to him right away?"

"Yes, ma'am!" He ran out of the room, whooping at the top of his lungs. "Here comes the mailman. Special delivery for Uncle Wayne."

She watched Chris covertly from behind the curtain of her half-closed lashes. Her stepdaughter was standing at the foot of the bed with her arms folded, regarding her intently. Too intently. As if she were studying a specimen under a lens.

"Did you enjoy the tour?" Callie inquired.

"Yes, it was very scenic. And how was your day?"

She contrived a wan smile. "Hardly scenic, unless you'd call the bottom of the toilet bowl and the Sagamore's cracked ceiling scenery; depending on which plague was upon me. Nausea or exhaustion."

The wide-set blue eyes appraised her coolly. "It was late when you and the senator got back, I hear?"

"I guess it was. The doctor Wayne took me to is an old friend. It was a reunion of sorts. I must admit I was put out that he stayed so long. But after all, he's been so kind to all of us, and what with the inconvenience I've caused him today, I had no complaint."

"It would seem you don't." There was the air of the inquisitor about Chris. "Which doctor was it you saw? What part of the lake does he live at?"

Callie's laugh was feeble. "Oh, really, Chris, I was too sick to notice. Wayne must have mentioned his name, but it eludes me. He called him Jack, Jack something or other."

"Something or other."

"Ask him. I'm very sleepy. I think I'll nap some more." She rolled over on her side, away from Chris.

Brooding as the room filled with darkness. We mustn't underestimate Chris. The brat was dangerous. One way or the other she must get rid of her, or pull out her fangs, at the very least.

Callie ate supper in her room that evening, an insipid chicken salad prescribed by Nurse Hathaway.

"After a spell like you had, ma'am, you shouldn't be eating solid food at all."

Such petty deprivations were a trifling price to pay for the rapture she had known with Wayne in the afternoon.

Wayne. Since the arrival of the letter, every time she thought about him, the words came to mind read through the translucent envelope:

Yours, always, in all ways,
Evelyn

She wasn't jealous of this faceless rival. It was the mystery of her that obsessed Callie. She slept until nine on Monday morning, and awoke refreshed. Threw open the window and stretched up on her toes as high as she could reach. The wind off the lake was cool in the morning, whipping her nightgown around her legs and fanning her pale hair. She took a deep breath. Every part of her was alive. Every filament of flesh and blood and bone was vibrant. What a metamorphosis! Before Wayne Harrison had come to the Sagamore, each day had confronted her like a crusade. Now, she'd stir fitfully in early-morning sleep, impatient for the sun to rise on each new day.

There was a tapping at her bedroom door. Jane Hathaway called to her. "Mrs. Majors, ma'am, will you be coming down to breakfast with us?"

"I just woke up, Miss Hathaway. I think not, but thank you anyway. I'll take a later breakfast, something light as you've suggested."

After her bath she pinned her hair up in a bun at the nape of her neck. A style that made her appear sedate and older than her twenty-five years. She chose a green silk frock that Wayne had admired the first time she wore it. She sang a popular folk ditty of the region while she dressed:

"Around the corner, and under a tree,
A handsome laddie made love to me,
He kissed me once,
He kissed me twice,
It wasn't just the thing to do,
But, oh, it was so nice. . . ."

She ordered juice, coffee, and pastry in the near-deserted dining room. From her table at the front window she saw Chris and Miss Hathaway playing ball with Nathaniel on the beach.

After breakfast she strolled around the open porch that ran around the hotel. Off in a corner Julia Harrison knitted and rocked. Alone. Callie approached her.

"Good morning, Julia. Isn't it a splendid day?"

The senator's pregnant wife did not share her enthusiasm. "When you have morning sickness the way I do, it's hard to find splendor in any day. But how are you? You certainly look none the worse for your dyspepsia yesterday."

"I'm fine again. Thanks to your kind husband. And, of course, that wonderful doctor he took me to." She kept throwing furtive glances around the porch, the lawn, the beach. There was no sign of Wayne.

"How is the senator this morning? I do want to thank him again for all he did."

The woman dropped her knitting in her lap, what little lap the burgeoning fetus in her belly spared her. She acted annoyed.

"I regret that you won't have the chance, Mrs. Majors. At least, not here at the Sagamore. Wayne left last night."

Her voice and expression were carefully composed.

"He's left the Sagamore? He didn't mention he was leaving yesterday."

"He didn't know until that special delivery letter came. A political crisis of some sort. The party is having trouble with an alderman in Troy."

"I see." She massaged her throat.

An alderman in Troy? She could see the graceful feminine script on the envelope.

"He won't be coming back," his wife went on. "He'll go home to Albany when he's done in Troy. It's just as well. I hear they're forecasting rainy weather for the remainder of the week. Sit down and chat a while, Mrs. Majors."

"I'd like that very much," Callie lied. "But I have to see what my son is up to. I'm afraid he winds his nurse and aunt around his chubby little finger."

Julia Harrison smiled. "He's a beautiful boy. I hope my child is half as handsome."

Callie smiled. "Thank you. I'm sure he'll be a very handsome boy." She almost said, "With such a handsome father."

Julia evidenced disapproval. "You said 'he.' I'm hoping it's a girl."

Callie touched her shoulder for reassurance. "Then I hope 'he's' a girl. You must excuse me."

"Yes, good-bye, Mrs. Majors." Julia stared after her in befuddlement. *That* Majors Woman was an odd one.

"*. . . I hope he's a girl.*"

Callie went down to the beach, but not to seek Nathaniel. She walked in the opposite direction, away from the hotel, along the narrow, uncultivated shoreline festooned with rocks, branches, and jetsam washed in off the lake.

She pondered the question of Wayne's impetuous departure from Lake George. Not a word of farewell or explanation.

He could have written her a note. No, he would never incriminate himself or her in writing.

"A political crisis," he'd told his wife. An alderman in Troy. She recalled that the postmark on the envelope had read Troy. But no alderman in Troy or any other city could boast of a such graceful script. No, rule out the alderman. That left a crisis in Troy. What kind of crisis?

It had to be a grave business to compel the woman to such a desperate measure. An urgent summons by mail, calling further notoriety to the letter, having it delivered by special delivery to the Sagamore hotel where he was vacationing with his wife. On the Sabbath. The risk! A man of Wayne's prestige and celebrity, the foremost legislator in the state. Suppose the letter had fallen into Julia Harrison's hands instead of her own? Then what?

The letter could only mean bad news for Senator Wayne Harrison. A matter of such importance it outweighed all other considerations, including his passion for her.

Callie retraced her way along the beach and entered the hotel by the side entrance. She went up to her room and rang for a maid.

"I notice the guests at the Sagamore read a great variety of newspapers?" she said to the girl.

"Yes, ma'am. There's a lot of retired businessmen come to the Sagamore for the whole summer. They like to know what's happenin' back home. Some of the papers sent here even come from out of state."

"When they're done with them, I suppose they throw them away?"

"Yes, ma'am. Mostly in the wastebaskets in the rooms. The maids collect 'em and sell 'em to the junkman. There's good money in old papers."

"Do you remember seeing any Troy newspapers this past week?"

"Oh, sure, ma'am. Mr. Hastings in 416, he's from Troy. He gets the *Herald* regular."

"That's fine." Callie took a five-dollar bill out of her purse. "Here, Mary, this is for you. I want you to save Mr. Hasting's *Herald*s for me from now on."

That evening, and for the next three days, the maid delivered a copy of the Troy *Herald* to Callie when she made up the beds.

She pored over the Monday and Tuesday editions from front page to back page, scanning every article, no matter how insignificant. She read nothing she could relate to Wayne Harrison.

She found what she was looking for in the Wednesday edition. A full column on the second page with a bold heading:

DAUGHTER OF STATE SUPREME COURT JUSTICE
DIES UNDER SUSPICIOUS CIRCUMSTANCES

It went on to relate how at 5 A.M. on Tuesday morning Miss Evelyn Hardy, daughter of State Supreme Court Justice Edward John Hardy, was deposited on the steps of the city hospital in a state of unconsciousness. Examination disclosed that she was suffering from severe internal bleeding. An emergency operation was performed immediately, but Miss Hardy expired four hours later. An autopsy had been performed, but the results were being withheld from the press and public until a coroner's jury considered the findings. Reliable rumor had it that Miss Hardy had undergone an "illegal operation" prior to her appearance at the city hospital. . . .

Callie didn't bother reading any further. She folded the paper in half and laid it down on the couch. Tapped a finger against her front teeth, dissecting the account of Evelyn Hardy's tragic death.

A crisis in Troy.

Yours, always, in all ways,
Evelyn

Chris interrupted her contemplations. "Callie, what are you looking so smug about?"

Neither her voice nor her expression revealed the exhilarating sense of power surging through Callie.

"Smug? Do I look smug? That's odd. As a matter of fact, I'm feeling rather distressed after reading about a young woman who was murdered in Troy."

"How terrible!"

"Her name was Evelyn Hardy, she was the daughter of a judge."

Chris was shocked. Her hand went up to her mouth. "Oh!

Evelyn Hardy! I met her once. Her father did legal work for my father before he was appointed to the bench. Poor Evelyn, do they know who killed her?"

"Not yet. She had an abortion."

Outraged, Chris beat her fists against her thighs. "An abortion! How dreadful! The poor girl. I hope they find the butcher who did it and try him for murder. You're right, Callie, people like that are murderers!"

The corners of Callie's mouth curled up. "I don't mean the abortionist, my dear. I was speaking of the man who got her in trouble and arranged the operation. He's the real murderer." She stood up. "I'm going for a walk before I turn in. Good night."

It was hard to contain the elation she felt, the sense of omnipotence. The destruction of Nathaniel Knight and Ham—what was impotence but living death?—had given Callie her first taste of the power she had hungered for as long as she remembered. The taste of blood. Her power expanded when she married the Majors. Yes, it was the family she was pledged to, not one man. Manipulating Carl and Bruce and Chris, one against the other, like puppets in a Punch and Judy show. The wealth, the real estate, the lives she controlled: it was a heady wine.

The passion she and Wayne had shared on the island was diminished by the fulfillment of what they shared tonight.

A secret whose worth one day could dwarf her present wealth and powers.

Senator Wayne Harrison.

Governor Wayne Harrison.

President Wayne Harrison.

Was it such an extravagant fantasy?

President Wayne Harrison mentor to her son. Nathaniel Knight the Second. The vowels and consonants rolled off the tongue like melted butter, rich with flavor. A statesman's name, it was written in the stars.

Senator Nathaniel Knight the Second.

Governor Nathaniel Knight the Second.

President Nathaniel Knight the—no, the office was title enough.

Restored to the real world again by a voice.

"Mrs. Majors, wait!"

She cried out in disbelief. Her feet were wet. Looked down and saw the dark lake water lapping at her ankles. A man materialized out of the night.

"Mrs. Majors, are you all right?" A match flamed in his hand. Her pupils contracted against the glare. She recognized the assistant manager.

"Yes, I—I'm all right." Her voice was weak. She was confused at finding herself on the beach. Had no notion of how or why she'd come here. Walking straight into Lake George!

Small wonder for his concern. "Mrs. Majors, I think the affliction you had on Sunday has relapsed. Your eyes, your cheeks, they're raging with fever. Come, I'll help you up to your room and summon the hotel physician."

"Yes . . . you're right. . . . It's the fever. But don't bother yourself, Mr. Adams. There's medication in my suite. I can manage by myself. Thank you."

He watched her walk slowly back across the sand toward the Sagamore Hotel. In her present state she appeared uncommonly frail and worn and commonplace. Not *that* Majors Woman they whispered about on the veranda and in the bar. He shook his head, a trick of match light. He blew it out.

That fall Chris entered her Junior term at Wellesley. The headlines in the *Times* and *Journal* celebrated the fact that Germany had been admitted to the League of Nations. Prohibitionists in their zeal to combat the evils of alcohol were spawning an even greater menace. Gang wars had replaced the shooting in Europe. In Chicago, New York, and Miami, Italians, Germans, Jews, and Irish, petty felons who for years had preyed on terrified immigrants of their own kind for small blood money, were infected by the new spirit and freedom of the Roaring Twenties. Life was short. Live it big and live it fast. Crime expanded along with the rest of the American economy. Bootlegging was the catalyst that finally brought the motley warring factions together. The logistics of supplying a nation of over 105 million people with illegal booze became a common cause. A cause ironically subsidized by virtually every law-abiding citizen. Organized crime was born, a monster created by its future victims.

Capone and "Mr. Lucky," Diamond, Coll, Schultz and Lansky, O'Banion: the gangland politicians won bigger headlines than Al Smith and Silent Cal.

Saturday night dances had been a tradition in the Hudson Valley country since the first settlers sank the corner posts for their log cabins in the rich black loam. Square dancing in barns. The atmosphere aromatic with the smells of their dispossessed tenants. The country folk took dancing seriously, the elders did. Stepping through complex and variegated patterns sung out by the caller with the concentration noble gentlemen and *grandesdames* of King Louis's court brought to the minuet.

> *"Honor your own partners,*
> *Now salute your corners all . . ..*
> *Grand right and left around the hall. . . ."*

Stone-faced all the while, the ragtag band beat out the rhythms of "Turkey in the Straw" and "Old Zip Coon." Fiddle, saw, Jew's harp, and mouth organ.

Tradition suffered in the Roaring Twenties. During the intermissions the young Turks would bully the members of the band and have their way. While it was true that the "black bottom" and the "shimmy" and the "Charleston" had not been scored for harmonica, fiddle, and musical saw, the musicians performed with a gusto and volume that carried them through.

While the elders sat at the tables drinking cider and needle beer, shocked by the immoral (some said ungodly) antics of their sons and daughters. Wild shaking of hips and bosoms. Simulating wanton acts none of them cared or dared to contemplate. There was one night, etched indelibly in the memories of all the males, young and old alike, the dance at Sawyer's barn, when Mary Lou Westover, highkicking in the Charleston, split the crotch of her chemise.

The twenties were roaring to their final crescendo, but for Callie the end of the summer was an anti-climax. She was bored to death with life at Wheatley. One day was a replica of the other.

The day measured off by the level of liquor in Carl's bourbon decanter. His "cure" at Ballston Spa had lasted one day past his return to Wheatley at summer's end.

The week measured off by the metronome precision of Bruce's schedules. Mondays and Tuesdays were the days he made the rounds of the kilns. Wednesdays he traveled to the Philadelphia office and spent the night there. Thursdays and

Fridays he worked in the president's office his father continued to boycott at the plant in Troy.

On Saturdays, Bruce and Callie sat down with Walt Campball at the big dining room table and reviewed the account books for the Knight holdings, prepared by Campball and Ham on Friday night. Later on, Carl would join them for scrutiny of the Majors' books.

Bruce kept complaining it was double effort for Walt, that Ham should meet with them on Saturday as he had in years past and get the job done in one sitting.

And Walt's eyes would dart to Callie and down to the books again. Quietly asserting: "I don't mind, sir. He's busy Saturdays."

Sundays had a unique distinction. On Sunday nights Bruce would make love to her. Or try, at least. Afterward, unfulfilled, Callie would lie in the darkness and remember the summer days spent on their island of paradise, she and Wayne. Then she'd think of Evelyn Hardy, and the sensations she experienced dreaming of what lay in their future, hers and Nathaniel's, made sex seem inconsequential.

Months marked off by the same old seasons, the reds and golds and browns of autumn, white winter, spring green and wet, summer dry and hot. Bank statements. Stock dividend reports. Market peaks. The monotony of existence at Wheatley did not weigh too heavily on Callie. She was a patient woman.

There were two inspirations, the bridge and young Nate, that told her the clock and calendar were moving ahead. The boy was growing as fast as the cattails on the river bank, his strong young body leaning away its baby fat. The bridge was fast coming into its maturity. Every day and every week she could discern less daylight through the metal skeleton. Trusses, reaching out to each other, joined at last. The river breached. Her towers stark against the blue sky like the masts of a clipper ship. From the little summerhouse on the point, if she looked toward the bridge and turned away quickly, she retained an illusion it was a great ship moored in the Hudson, sails unfurled.

A workman gave Nate a souvenir, a length of cable thick as a man's bicep.

Summers Chris came home. She had a woman's legal rights now, as well as a woman's body. And she asserted them impertinently, particularly with regard to the inheritance she shared with her brother, even before their father was in his grave. She took increasing interest in the management and administration of the Majors' business and estate. She didn't challenge Callie's self-assumed stewardship simply because it was an axiom her father had taught her, never to argue with success. But the defiance was there, inert just beneath the surface.

Callie's patience faltered when it came to Chris. Chris disgusted her. Yearning shamelessly for Ham. Not yearned for in return. They saw Ham on rare occasions when Chris was home from school. And on important holidays. At Wheatley he always sat on the edge of his chair, fidgeting, anxious to be on his way from the moment he arrived. His restlessness annoyed Bruce.

"For God's sake, man!" Bruce snarled at Ham one Sunday. "If it's such an ordeal for you to visit here, then don't bother."

Ham had come to dinner to please Chris; it was her last weekend home before returning to school.

Ham turned scarlet. "I'm sorry, Bruce. I don't mind visiting you."

"Well, *thanks!*"

"What I mean is, it has nothing to do with you all, my skittishness. It's that I feel guilty taking time away from my work."

"Oh, come on, now!" Bruce scoffed. "Walt Campball runs your farm and the quarry."

"I work as hard as Walt does," Ham said quickly. "Maybe harder. And there's my studies."

"Studies, Ham?" Callie looked up from her sewing.

"Ham is taking correspondence courses," Chris informed them with a note of pride.

"What kind of courses?" Bruce asked. "Accounting? Animal husbandry?"

Ham answered for himself. "No, I can get that kind of learning from Walt and the farmhands who've been working at it for years. No, I'm studying literature and philosophy and I'm learning French."

"Literature?" Callie was pleased. "Well, you've had a start on that, haven't you, my boy? The Bard. Do they teach him at this correspondence school?"

"There's a good deal of reading Shakespeare in my classical literature course." One of the rare occasions that he'd let his eyes meet her eyes. "I thank you for that, Callie. I'm way ahead of the others in the class, they say. I got a ninety-four on my essay on *King Lear*."

"That's swell, Ham," Chris complimented him.

" 'Swell' is what the ocean does," Callie said tartly. "And boils."

"And balloons!" Nate thrust his arm at Chris and teased. "Has King Lear got a boil?"

They all laughed and the tension between Bruce and Ham was forgotten.

Nate came over and sat down beside Ham on the sofa. "What's a correspondence school, Ham? Mama says I'm going to school next year. Can I go to your school?"

Chris explained, "Ham doesn't go to school, honey. The school comes to him."

"I want that kind of a school, Mama." Nate bounced up and down with furious energy. "I want the school to come here."

"I'm afraid not, Nate. Correspondence schools are for people like Ham who can't go to ordinary schools because they have to work. Ham does his studies after he's finished his job."

"What do you want to be when you grow up, Ham?"

Ham looked foolish as the others howled with glee.

Bruce lit his pipe. "Ham's grown up, son. He's not studying to learn a trade. He has that already. He wants an education, that's all. What do you want to be when you grow up, Nate?"

Without any hesitation, the boy turned, placed his hands on Ham's arm, and answered, "I want to grow up to be like Ham."

Ham licked dry lips with tongue almost as dry. "You want to be something better than me, Nate," he mumbled.

"I do, I do!" Nate said stoutly. "I want to be big and strong like you and work on a farm. I like horses and cows and everything. Ham, when I get big, can I live with you? I'll help you with your chores. Then you'll have more time to see Chrissy."

"Oh, he'd just find some other excuse to stay away," Chris said with a smile, but her look to Ham was sad.

"I think every boy should look upon his father as a hero," Callie said matter-of-factly, not looking up from the button she was sewing onto one of Nathaniel's shirts.

There was an instant of silence, perfectly timed, that came near to shattering Ham's heart. His lungs were strangling for air before she completed her thought. "But if his father's dead like Nate's, then there's no more fitting hero for him than his big brother. Don't you think so, Ham?"

Ham couldn't endure her company and her rapier wit any longer. In desperation, he made an unusual overture to Nathaniel.

"How about that swimming lesson you've been pestering me for?" he asked the boy.

Nate was thrilled. "Oh, thank you, Ham. I never thought you'd do it, you always promise and then you make excuses."

"Excuses, he's full of them," Chris said. "You give it to him good, Nate."

Nate didn't want Ham to think he was siding with Chris. His jaw thrust out belligerently. "If you stay home, Chris, that'll be just *swell.* We don't want any girls along, do we, Ham?"

Ham looked to her to put Nate straight, but Chris was so delighted by unaccustomed kindness to the boy that she was quick to concede to Nate.

"I don't want to swim today, anyway, Nate. You two big strong men can have the whole river for yourselves."

Callie watched the two of them go off, her son clinging to his father's hand. The scene struck chords in her emotions, a song she did not recognize. She was troubled.

"Ham, don't take him out too deep."

The way a mother would caution a father.

Bruce and Chris were regarding her attentively, their expressions hinting they sensed a somewhat baffling tie between the two, her and Ham. No matter, they'd never break that code, never in a million years.

Ham and Nate changed in the boathouse and went down to the beach. Out in the channel the Hudson River was icy in the fall, but close to shore where the sun's rays penetrated to the sandy bottom, the water was temperate with just the proper bite to invigorate.

Nate had been paddling in the river for two summers. He could stay afloat like a puppy. So it was no great feat for Ham to teach him the basic swimming strokes. Within the hour, he was leaping boldly off the end of the dock into deep water. Kicking and slapping his way back to the ladder. His form was wretched, but it got him there safely.

Ham stretched out on the warm planks sunning himself. Cautioning the boy. "Not too far out now, Nate, you heard what your mother said."

Nate was full of bravado. "Girls are all sissies. They're scared of mice and spiders and snakes. They're scared of everything."

With an irony that was lost on his companion, Ham replied, "Not your mother, she's not scared of mice and spiders and snakes. Not much of anything can daunt your mother."

The dark, serious eyes, so much like his own, studied him intently. "Did you know my mother, Ham, before I was born?"

Ham closed his eyes. "I knew your mother," he said. A bleak tone.

"You know what would be funny, Ham? If you called her 'Mama' like I do. She *is* your mother too."

"Stepmother. Not my real mother. My real mother died. Then Callie married my father."

"I wish she'd married you, Ham."

So guileless, he couldn't know the cruelty he was inflicting.

"Suppose you go back to your practicing, Nate. You've got to practice if you want to race me someday."

"You mean it, Ham? You'll race me? Oh, don't worry, Ham. I'll practice. All day and night."

Ham heard the slap of the boy's bare feet on the dock. The splash as he hit the water. He kept his eyes closed, pretending to doze. It was painful for him to look at Nathaniel, to be with him, to constantly see himself in the boy. And his aversion filled him with more guilt. To blame an innocent child, to put the mark of Cain on this sweet boy who was so full of love for everyone and everything in this world seen with his chaste and charitable vision. It was odious of him. Yet it could not be denied that this angel was the unwitting instrument of his grandfather's death. The murder weapon forged with the anvil and hammer of their loins, his and Callie's. And guilt compounded guilt. Quicksand, sucking him down deeper, even deeper into the dark despair.

"Ham!"

Nate's voice was lost to him in the background sounds of the river country. The screech of a hawk across the water. The thunder of the freshet pounding over its rocky bed in the gulley alongside Lampbert's store. The hum and honk of automobiles on the distant highway. A banjo.

"Ham! Help, Ham!" A scream of jarring urgency.

He jerked upright, looked for Nate in the water around the dock. There was no sign of him.

"Ham! Help!" Fainter now.

He traced it this time, far out in the channel. A small dark head and pale face lost in the immensity of the river. A thin white arm, waving frantically. The carelessness that comes with repetition had taken Nate within reach of the treacherous current. He was being swept downriver like a leaf.

Ham sat motionless, how long he didn't reckon. Detached. The fiction he read had more reality for him than this living drama playing before his eyes.

The boy's terrified scream before his head went under galvanized him finally. Fear filled the vacuum. In a single unbroken motion, he sprang up and dove, hit the river in a flat body slap. Arms windmilling with a frenzy that left white water churning in his wake. Interrupting the rhythm twice to look for Nate and keep to the right course. A glimpse of a bobbing head. A hand clutching at heaven for life. Ham closed the distance swiftly. When he was perhaps twenty yards away, the boy went under and did not reappear. Ham jackknifed, kicked hard, and dove deep into the water. Clear and green with the sun's rays slanting at angles like so many brilliant, luminous spokes. A bass glided past him, the bubbles from its gills tickling his nose. He could see all the way down to the bottom, forty, fifty feet below him. An eerie world alien to the world of fresh air and blue sky above.

He saw Nate. Motionless, knees drawn up, head turned down, a curled fetus floating in the womb. Ham surged toward him with redoubled exertions. He reached Nate, hooked both hands under his armpits, and propelled him to the surface. Kicked up and broke into fresh air a yard from the boy. His eyes were closed, his color an ashen gray. No time to feel for a pulse, to see if he was breathing. Ham rolled him onto his back, cradled his chin in the crook of his left arm so that his nose and mouth were high out of the water, and swam for the bank. They beached far down from the Majors' dock, a rocky stretch. He put his ear to the boy's mouth. If his lungs were active at all, his breathing was too shallow for Ham to discern. There was a thready flutter in his wrist, so erratic it might have been a twitching muscle. He rolled Nate over on his belly, tilted his head to the left, cheek resting on the back of his own left hand and straddled his hips.

During the war the schools had taught compulsory first-aid courses to prepare young and old alike for that dire, if unlikely day when the Kaiser's pointed-helmeted Huns goose-stepped ashore in America. Ham had considered first-aid a monotonous joke at the time, but now he was grateful for the instruction in artificial respiration.

He pressed his palms against the boy's small back just below the rib cage on either side. Bore down. Released the pressure. Pressed again, counting to the cadence of his own breathing.

Deep in concentration he was dimly aware of shouting and screaming coming from the direction of the house. Once he looked briefly away from Nate and saw them. Callie in front, with Bruce and Chris not far behind, running down the beach. Bringing up the rear at a slower pace, Sam Perkins, the aging handyman.

Callie reached them first, threw herself down on her knees, and tried to embrace her son. It was the only time since he had first set eyes on her the day his mother was buried that he realized she was capable of anguish or prey to any human vulnerability.

"My baby! My God! My baby's dead."

He had to interrupt his ministrations to hold her away from the boy. "Callie! For God's sake! Leave us alone or he will die. I'm trying to save him."

Bruce ran up and put his arms around her to restrain her. "Let him be, Callie," he said gently. "He's giving Nate artificial respiration. What happened, Ham?"

Ham answered haltingly while he worked over the boy. "He was doing fine. . . . Swimming real well . . . off the dock . . . then . . ."

"You didn't watch him!" Callie screamed. "You let him drown!"

"No!"

"It's true! You didn't care if he died! You never wanted him to live!"

Bruce and Chris were stunned at the charge, by Callie's vehemence.

"Callie, what a terrible thing to say," Bruce reproached her. He had all he could do to restrain this slight woman, to keep her from attacking Ham with her fists, teeth, and nails.

She became hysterical. "You've murdered him, my son, my love, my life!"

Ham reared upright on his knees, his eyes blazing with murderous hate. "Bitch!" he gasped and dealt her a mighty blow on the side of the head with his big open hand. He felt he'd torn her head off and hoped it was so. He couldn't waste any more attention on her. It was the boy who meant everything now.

Ham's slap dazed her. She'd wear the imprint of his hand on her bruised and swollen cheek for a long time. The outburst served a need in both of them. Callie was sober again, in control of her words and deeds.

"I'm all right, Bruce," she spoke quietly. "You can let me go. Ham, I'm sorry for what I said. Is there anything we can do to help?"

"Phone Doc Haley. I think he's got a pulmotor."

Callie turned to Chris. "Chris, will you do it? You can get back to the house faster than Sam."

The handyman looked away with a red face as Chris gathered up her skirt around her waist and raced back up the beach.

Ham was fast reaching the end of his endurance. Sweat ran in torrents down his face and body, dropping like rain onto Nate's white, still back. And still he did not respond to Ham's frantic efforts to resuscitate him. No sign of life.

"Bruce, you're going to have to spell me for a while before I drop," he said in a voice that was thin and unsteady from exhaustion.

"Let me have him." Callie put her hands against Ham's chest and shoved him away from Nate with gentleness.

"Callie, you don't know what you're doing," he protested, but he was too weak to prevent her. He collapsed on the ground and lay there watching her.

"No, he's my love," she said. "And if he's to die, then he'll die in my arms." She turned the child over and gathered him up in the cradle of her arms.

Bruce made a move to intercede, fell back on his haunches. There was about her an aura, a mystic wall that held him off.

A vision of the Pietà. Mary clutching her dead son. Serene confidence behind the mask of grief.

Oblivious of Ham and Bruce, she whispered to Nate, "I'll breathe life into you, Nathaniel. My breath. My life."

She put her mouth tenderly on his mouth. Forced warm air into his lungs. His chest rose. Fell as she breathed in. Once more. Again. Again. And again.

Ham and Bruce looked on. Speechless. Immobilized. Awe prickling at the nape of his scalp, Ham saw the pallid eyelids flicker. A spasm of limbs. Blue lips moving.

"*Mama . . .*"

It had to be his imagination. He struggled up on his knees and bent over the boy. No, he had not imagined it. The dark eyes slowly opened.

His eyes. In their mirror he saw himself.

"*Ham . . .*" The sound more beautiful and wondrous than all the poetry written by Shakespeare.

"Nate, Oh God! Thank you, God!" He embraced the child, unmindful of the mother. His arms around the two of them. His cheek pressed to hers, their tears mingling. Their son nestled in the warm cocoon of their close bodies.

"Mama . . . Ham . . . why are you crying?" Nate's muffled voice rose up between them. Ruptured the spell.

Ham undid his arms from around the two of them. Gingerly. Pulled back. Moving with the caution of the blasters at the quarry withdrawing after they had fused a charge in the rock. All it required was an accidental spark of static electricity to beckon calamity.

"We're crying because we're happy, darling." She told him. She kissed his eyes and nose and lips, stroked his damp hair, hugged his cold, shaking, naked form to her feverish flesh. All the while cooing to him in a language that held no meaning for the intellect. Soothing sounds to appease the heart and soul. Nate whimpered and buried his face in her bosom. His taut, trembling body softened and quieted.

"I'm tired," he sighed. "I want my bed and my teddy bear."

She patted his backside. "That's where I'm taking you, my sweet. To your bed. You'll have a good, long sleep, and when you wake up, you'll be as good as new again."

His head came up, he looked around. "I want Ham to come with us. Where's Ham?"

Ham was already far down the beach, a dark diminishing silhouette against the white sand Carl Majors had hauled up the Hudson on barges, scooped from the south shore of Long Island.

The year 1927 was memorable for Callie because that was the year her bridge was completed. The opening ceremonies on October 23 were attended by a party of Albany officials headed by Senator Wayne Harrison. Among dignitaries was a vice-president of the Delaware and Hudson Railroad, one Franklin Delano Roosevelt. At the ribbon-cutting he had to be supported on each side by aides and Callie could see he was in great pain. At the conclusion of the ceremony, he was carried back to his limousine. Callie, Bruce, and Nathaniel rode with Senator Harrison in the state limousine that made the maiden crossing of the Hudson River from the Knightsville side. It was an open car and the day was windy. The gentlemen held fast to their hombergs, and Callie's hair was a golden banner whipping in the sunlight. Nate did lose his cap. They all laughed as it went sailing over the rail, zooming up and down, this way and that, like a bird, and they never did see it strike the water.

"Who was that crippled man?" Callie asked Harrison.

"Frank Roosevelt, you mean? He's a Hyde Park lawyer. He was invited because he's a V.P. of the Delaware and Hudson."

"Yes, of course, I should have recognized him. I've seen his picture in the papers."

"He's dabbled in politics. Unsuccessfully. He was assistant secretary of the navy under Wilson. He was Cox's choice for his running mate in the 1920 presidential elections and Harding beat them badly. There's a rumor he'll declare himself a candidate for governor next year if Al Smith throws his hat into the presidential ring."

Bruce shook his head. "Poor bastard. Who wants a crippled governor?"

"Oh, I don't know." Callie disagreed. "Look at Richard III. Crippled, deformed in mind and body, yet he conquered England when all the odds were on the side of his foes. There's a fire burns in the hearts and minds of the crippled, intense as the sun itself. A power denied the sound of limb. . . . This Roosevelt, he has a special quality about him. I can read it in his face, his suffering eyes."

Senator Harrison patted her arm with an indulgent laugh.

"My dear Callie, for the sake of the Republican party, let us hope that your political judgments do not match up to your instincts for the stock market."

"We'll see." She turned to Bruce. "Speaking of stocks, I think we should pick up more shares of Douglas Aircraft. I read the government has issued a charter to some pioneer to start a commercial airline."

"I hope his first service is between Albany and Washington, D.C.," Harrison declared. "I fly that route at least once a week, and these private pilots charge you an arm and a leg."

"It's a fad like the Charleston." Bruce debunked the idea of commercial aviation. "And a dangerous one. I'm surprised at you, Wayne, a responsible legislator, risking your life in those flying egg crates."

"We poor mortals, Bruce, we risk our lives and more than life, life's cheap, on ambitions far more precarious than flying." The senator stole a glance at Callie. "What do you say to that, dear lady?"

"I agree with Henry IV," she said. *"The purpose you take is dangerous; why that's certain: 'tis dangerous to take a cold, to sleep, to drink . . ."*

"I don't care much for poetic wisdom," Bruce said dryly. "I still say a sane man keeps both feet on the ground."

Callie sighed. "But think how the birth rate would decline, dear."

Bruce was mortified. "Callie! What kind of a remark is that to make before a senator and your son?"

Harrison, choking on suppressed laughter, hugged Nathaniel. "It's plain now what your father thinks of senators. Fit company for four-and-half-year-old boys. Well, I'm flattered, Nate. You're a fine young man whose company I enjoy."

On a more serious note, he asked, "I thought that Carl would be on hand today for the ribbon-cutting? After all, it was his initiative that got the project rolling. Ham Knight too, where is he today, Callie?"

"Ham was there, with Chris. They kept in the background. I think he's afraid to have his picture taken with her." She smiled. "It might be construed as a permanent commitment."

"Grandpa's drunk again," Nate said with a candor that left Bruce more stricken than Callie's risqué statement had.

"Nathaniel!" he chastened his stepson. "That's a terrible thing to say about your grandfather."

"You say it all the time, Papa."

Bruce's eyes and mouth flew open, he couldn't speak. Wayne Harrison reached across Callie and the boy and patted his arm. "It's all right, Bruce. We're old and good friends. We all love Carl."

"Thank you, Wayne." Humiliated, he slumped in the seat and turned his head, gazing upriver.

"Will you take me up a plane with you someday, Uncle Wayne?" Nate begged him.

"Indeed I will."

"Indeed you won't," Callie contradicted.

The senator was surprised. "Why, Callie Majors, what's come over you? A minute ago, you were all for air travel."

"For you and me, Wayne. Not my jewel." She squeezed the child to her breast. "We almost lost him last month to the river."

Harrison's right eyebrow went up as he reminded her, "*'Tis dangerous to take a cold, to sleep, to drink.*"

She had no ready answer for him, but kissed Nate's forehead.

It was an answer in itself, that kiss.

As they approached the Majors side of the Hudson, Callie gripped the senator's arm: "Don't you think you're going to get off just because you're a senator, Wayne. This car paid no toll when it drove onto the bridge." She held out a hand, palm upturned.

Harrison threw back his head and his booming laughter echoed through the valley. He rummaged in his pockets and came up empty-handed. Tapping his chauffeur on the shoulder, he asked, "Samuel, would you care to lend the state of New York a quarter?"

There was a single tollbooth on the Knightsville side. Two Knightsville men were employed as toll-takers. They worked ten-hour shifts. Contrary to her own view, Callie had given in to Bruce's persuasion that the bridge should be closed from 2 A.M. until 6 A.M. The sparse traffic in the middle of the night, he argued, would not justify the salary of a third attendant.

Few local workers had heard of unions, minimum-wage laws, or the eight-hour working day. The quarrymen, farmhands, and gandy dancers who kept the railroad tracks in repair put in ten hours on weekdays and eight hours on Saturdays.

"I'll work from two to six myself," Callie declared on the night the bridge was opened.

And she did, over the protests of Carl and Bruce. Endured four hours of inky isolation with only the katydids and gnats for company. When the sun rose over Knight's Mountain the next morning, her net was a single quarter. And that from a milk truck whose driver confessed he had taken a detour "just to get a gander at that Majors woman's newfangled bridge."

"She'd be pleased to hear it," she told him with a wooden expression.

He snorted. "She must be a cheap one, even with all her money."

"How's that?"

"Plain as day. Hiring a female to take tolls. Slave labor." He shook his head as he drove onto the bridge. "A woman sitting all alone this time of night, it's disgraceful."

"You're right," she shouted after him as the truck rumbled onto the span's steel apron. "It is disgraceful."

After that the bridge remained closed from two until dawn's light.

The bridge was everything that Callie claimed it would be and more. On weekends and holidays the flow of cars and trucks and horse-drawn wagons went on uninterrupted through the daylight hours and late into the evening. The first year grossed the Majorses $75,000 in tolls!

In the 1928 elections Al Smith went down in ignominious defeat as Herbert Hoover's landslide victory won forty states. Franklin Delano Roosevelt was elected governor of New York.

"I told you about that one," Callie reminded Bruce. "He has the look of kings. I'm glad he won."

She was soon disillusioned with F.D.R. Six months after the new governor took office, Senator Wayne Harrison drove to Wheatley. It was not a social visit.

"The state is having second thoughts about your bridge," he advised the Majors. "The governor doesn't think it's democratic for private individuals to share revenues with the state of New York. He feels that the money is properly the people's."

Callie was outraged. "A pox on Governor Roosevelt! A bargain's a bargain. The title is irrevocable. The bridge is ours, and ours alone. The state needn't worry. At the rate we're collecting tolls, we'll pay back its investment with interest within five years."

"You miss the point, my dear," Harrison explained. "It's the principle Roosevelt doesn't like. He says it smacks of feudalism for the Majorses to exact a fee from American citizens traveling in their own land."

"Oh, but it's all right for the state to collect taxes from Americans living on their own land. Hypocrite!"

"The crippled bastard is a traitor to his own class!" Bruce ranted. "He talks about feudalism! Ha! The Roosevelts have been squires in Hyde Park for generations. What do you think we should do, Wayne?"

Carl brought over the decanter and refilled their glasses. "I know what Wayne thinks, we don't have any choice."

The senator crossed his legs and contemplated the long white ash on his cigar. "It's not something that Mr. Roosevelt can resolve with the scratch of his governor's pen. If you choose to contest his stand, you'd get some support in the legislature. You could make a fight of it. Roosevelt hasn't been in office long enough to consolidate his executive powers."

"We do so choose!" she fumed.

"Don't be hasty, Callie. There's a positive side. New York State will pay handsome compensation to you if you assign control of the bridge to the Public Works Commission. You'll turn a profit of 300 percent on your original investment."

"Well, I'll be damned!" Carl said. "He's no thief, this Roosevelt, I'll say that for him. We could hardly ask for a better return on any of our investments."

"No, I won't tolerate it!" Callie was adamant. "The bridge belongs to me. It was my dream. My perseverance made the dream reality. There's too much of me in that span to let the state steal it from me!" She spied the gleam in old Carl's eyes. *The joke's on me!* it said. And because Wayne Harrison was witness to her egomania, she amended, "Carl and I and Bruce, we three watched the bridge grow, day by day, the same way we watched Nate grow. It's part of the family. No, they won't take it away without a fight!"

Harrison rubbed the deep furrows in his forehead. "The point is, Callie, even if you do make a fight of it, in the end you'll lose out. Nobody beats the state."

"Damn the state!"

"Remember, you sold New York the property that Knight's Road is on and the approach to the bridge. Legally, you may own the bridge, it might stand up in court. But there's a technicality on the state's side. Your bridge is on public land, property of the people of New York. The people can file an injunction compelling you to remove your bridge from their property."

"Damn the people! It's an outrage. It isn't fair!" She turned on Harrison. "Damn you, Wayne, for persuading us to sell that land!"

"Callie, you're the one who's not fair," Bruce reproached her. "Without Wayne there'd be no bridge."

Wayne Harrison had a politician's thick skin. Unperturbed, he assured Bruce, "It's all right. Callie's upset. I understand how badly she feels."

"Do you now?" she responded curtly. Then, abruptly, her whole manner changed. She smiled at the senator, a foxy smile that put him on his guard. "Wayne, you said before we would have *some* support in the legislature?"

"Some support. But not enough to permanently block the governor's intent."

"How do *you* stand on the issue? Personally, I mean?"

He shifted his big frame in the chair, tapped his cigar in an ashtray, took out his handkerchief, and patted his lips. All diversions, he wasn't deceiving Callie.

"Naturally, I'm opposed to Roosevelt's political philosophy. You should hear him rave in private. The man's a radical. It's a damned good thing he's only the governor of New York and not sitting in the White House. He'd drag the country down into socialism." He paused. "However, I'm inclined to marshal the Republican forces of the legislature on more important fronts. As I said, you don't stand to lose anything from the transaction."

Callie rose and stood over him, challengingly. "In other words, Wayne, you do not choose to be our champion in the legislature?"

Harrison's smile was tense. "Aren't you overdramatizing the issue, Callie?" He appealed to Carl and Bruce. "I'm sure you two understand my position."

"What the hell!" Carl grunted. "If we don't take the carrot now, one day the governor will arrive with a stick and simply commandeer it. Damn the bridge! I say we take our profit and bow out gracefully."

"I have to agree with Father," Bruce conceded.

"Never!" Callie snapped. "Well, I guess we've reached an

impasse. There can't be any settlement without our three signatures, and I won't sign. So the next move is up to Governor Roosevelt." She held out her hand to the senator. "No hard feelings, Wayne?"

He tried not to show how enormously relieved he was. The senator had come to Wheatley dreading this confrontation with Callie Majors. Nevertheless, he could not shake off a lingering premonition when he took her hand and pressed it, distrusting her crafty smile.

"Dear Wayne, what a harpy you must think me, railing at you this way. Of course, you must do what you think is right."

He stood up and linked her arm with his arm. "You, a harpy? That's not true. You're a strong woman with a will of iron, a rare breed. And beautiful. I can't think of another woman whom I admire more, Callie."

"Thank you, Wayne. Friends again?"

"Friends." He looked into her eyes; the veil was drawn. He wondered if those precious interludes they had shared together at Lake George haunted her the way they haunted him. Two years had passed, yet he could not make love to a woman since without shutting his eyes and envisioning Callie.

She received his vibrations, strong and clear.

"Wayne, are you going back to Albany on this side of the river or by the east highway?" she asked him at the door as he prepared to leave.

He laughed. "What a question for you to ask. You know I wouldn't do you out of that quarter toll."

"Good. I'll ride with you to Knightsville. I want to look in on Ham. With Chris away at school, we don't know what he's up to. I'll walk back, it's such a lovely day."

"Callie, tell Ham to be sure and send over his due bills with Walt next Saturday," Bruce reminded her. "The slate dealers are as bad as our brick debtors. It seems nobody's paying bills these days. And no reason for it either. The economy has never been richer."

"Richer?" Carl mused. "I wonder. There's a lot of paper money changing hands. I don't mean bank notes. I mean *on* paper. Like children playing store with soap coupons."

Harrison clapped him on the shoulder. "It's not as bad as all that, old friend. Since when did you become a pessimist, Carl?"

"It isn't pessimism, Wayne. It's a pragmatic observation

from the protracted viewpoint of old age."

Callie rode with Harrison across the bridge. He paid his toll, winking at her. "Those quarters build up, don't they?"

"Yes, and if you were honest, you'd admit that's the real reason Governor Roosevelt wants my bridge. The revenues are higher than any of your myopic legislators in Albany ever dreamed they'd be. Now you want to steal it away from me to line the coffers of the state treasury. Don't you fleece us enough on property taxes as it is?"

He held up a hand, warding her off. "I thought we had declared a truce?"

"We did, and I apologize."

Harrison drove up the dirt road from the village to the big white house on the hill and parked in a clearing on the far side.

Callie inspected the house and barn. "Needs a coat of paint. I'll tell Walt to have one of the local men do it. Art Frisbie, he can use the work. Come in and say hello to Ham."

He hesitated. "Well . . . all right, I'd like to see Ham. How is he?"

"As I said before, we scarcely ever see him or hear about him when Chris is away."

He shook his head. "He's a fine lad. Has so much in his favor. Looks, intelligence, a sizable inheritance. Yet . . ."

"You think there's something flawed about him?" She led him on.

"It's not a flaw exactly. A strangeness is more accurate. It isn't normal for a man his age to be a recluse. Even his relationship with Chris is strange."

"You think so?"

"Yes, I think so. And so do Carl and Bruce. They've hinted at things to me, not with any malice aimed at Ham. It's just that they love Chris and feel there's no future in this attachment she has for the lad."

She smiled. "I thought we two were in agreement that relationships between men and women should exist from moment to moment."

"I do agree. But it's my distinct impression there's no relationship between those two at all."

"That's their concern, not ours." She took his hand and led him up the stone steps at the side of the house and around to the front porch.

They entered the house. No door had been locked in this

house, in any house in Knightsville, since Cyrus Knight had founded the town.

Harrison removed his derby and looked around the main hall. The parlor and dining room were deserted. The house hummed with silence.

"It doesn't look as if Ham's home," he said.

Callie removed her gloves and jacket. "Make yourself comfortable. Light the fire while I make us a drink. I think old Nate's jug is still in the pantry."

Bewildered, he asked, "Where's Ham?"

"In Clinton with Walt Campball. They went up in the truck to buy feed today."

"Then what are we doing here? I don't understand why—" He stopped as Callie moved close and slipped her arms around his neck. Her voice was soft and wanton. Understanding now, before she told him, "I thought you'd want to be alone with me. It's been over two years since you and I. . . ."

He silenced her with a kiss.

They made love on the fur robe spread out in front of the fireplace, the pelt of a black bear that Cyrus Knight had shot back at the quarry in 1875. Callie pulled it over them as they lay in close embrace afterward. Wayne kissed her throat.

"Good women are like good wines. The older they get, the better they become."

She stroked the back of his neck. "By that reckoning, how will I be when I'm fifty?"

He laughed. "It's just as well I won't be around to find out."

"You're not that old, darling."

"I'm old enough to be your father."

"You're not as old as Nathaniel was, and I married him."

He ran his hand down her back and cupped one buttock in his big hand. "You know, when we were back at Wheatley, I never dreamed we'd be like this now. You were so angry with me for my stand on the bridge."

"It was a weak moment I had. *Never anger made good for itself.* It puts one more speedily into the enemy's power."

He stopped caressing her. Wary suddenly. "I'm not much for Shakespeare, but I'm sure his art must have some equivalent for this homespun homily: You can catch more flies with honey than you can with vinegar. Is that why you brought me here today, Callie? To catch flies?"

She studied him, bemused, through drooping lashes. Sex made her body drowsy. Her mind never slackened. "You believe that, Wayne, that I'm resorting to what you men like to call 'feminine wiles' to get my way with you about the bridge? Oh, Wayne, you goose, I have too much respect for you as a man and as a statesman to believe you would be swayed by such drollery, even if it was my way."

"I'm sorry," he said sheepishly. "I should have known better."

She pushed herself up on one elbow and leaned over him. No longer the warm, responsive love partner who had submitted to him moments earlier.

It flashed across his mind, which of them had submitted? She acquainted him with the answer fast. Gripped his jaw firmly between her thumb and fingers, in complete authority.

"Wayne, you are going to be my champion in the legislature. You're a power in that body. A power who can make my challenge to the governor stand up. You'll see to it I keep my bridge."

He tried to struggle up to a sitting position; she shoved him back. "Callie, be reasonable, you said you understood my position. I will not fight Roosevelt on a matter as picayune as your damned bridge!"

She made the kill with the same unconcern she had invited him to lie down with her. "Consider your position reversed as of now, Wayne. I've been curious ever since it happened, Wayne—did you take Evelyn Hardy to the hospital that night yourself? Of course you didn't, you're much too circumspect, it would have been an unwise risk."

She could see the blood draining out of his face, she'd hit the jugular.

"What the hell are you talking about? I don't know any Evelyn Hardy." He looked and sounded so enfeebled she could have pitied him. She did not.

"*'Yours, always, in all ways, Evelyn.'*" The sight of him crumbling to pieces was intoxicating.

"Good God!" he croaked. "That letter! It was sent to your suite, I remember now. *You—you opened my letter!*"

"Don't look so terrified, Wayne. Your secret is safe with me."

He was thoroughly demoralized. "You monster! I've always believed the rumors about you were exaggerated. Strong and determined people like you and I must be ruthless sometimes when things and people get in our way. But this, it's unspeakable, Callie! To sink to the level of a waterfront whore who picks her clients' pockets while they're spending their animal lust in her! To read my mail! To violate my private life! You unscrupulous bitch!"

She yawned at his pathetic affronts. "I was speaking to Judge Baker about Evelyn Hardy last week. Bruce and I had supper with the Bakers." She let it hang.

His jaw trembled so, he could barely speak. "Callie . . . you spoke to . . . Judge Baker . . . about *her?*"

She patted his cheek. "Relax, dear Wayne. You'll take a fit if you don't compose yourself. Yes, I spoke to Judge Baker about *her!* About Evelyn, not *you,* silly. The judge told us that the police are working on this case relentlessly, even after so many years. Her father is an influential man in the state and he won't rest until his daughter's murderers are brought to justice. But don't you fret, dear Wayne, you and I are the only two people in the world who'll ever know. It's our secret, dear." She sat up and stretched. "We'd better tidy up here before Ham returns and finds us in this compromising posture."

When she let him out the front door, Callie put her hand on his arm. There were creases in her brow. "Wayne . . . one thing, I don't want you to leave here under the unjust impression that I would open and read your personal mail. You're right, that would be unspeakable behavior. Thoroughly dishonest."

He could only stare at her with incredulity. What further sadism was she concocting?

"The truth is, Wayne, I did not read Evelyn's letter, nor did I as much as even lift the flap." She held up a hypothetical letter in one hand. "See, I succumbed to a mischievous impulse to hold the envelope up to the light like this. It was thin paper. The salutation at the end showed through clearly: '*Yours, always, in all ways, Evelyn.*' That's all there is to it. Now I hope you'll think better of me, dear Wayne!"

One week later Bruce came home from work, waving a copy of the Albany *Post.* "You won't believe this, Callie, but Wayne Harrison had a change of heart. The governor's motion to appropriate our title to the bridge has been shelved indefinitely. Thanks to the eloquent speech Wayne made Tuesday before the legislature. Here, listen to this." He opened the paper and read an excerpt:

> The issue is not one of people's rights versus private property, as the governor erroneously maintains. The issue here is human rights opposed to state house autocracy. Poor man or rich man, wealth or lack of it does not diminish a man's civic rights nor his freedom of choice in our democratic society. A man's home *is* his castle, that's a constitutional guarantee. No official of the state or federal government can violate his home or any private property to which he holds title unless the government can show just cause in a court of law that such action is in the best interests and welfare of the public.
>
> In the issue under our consideration, neither Governor Roosevelt nor any man present today in this assembly can submit a valid justification for the state's intent to confiscate the bridge at Knightsville from its rightful owners. . . .

He broke off. "There's more, but that's the heart of it. I wonder what possessed Wayne to back our cause when last week he was dead set on us accepting the state's offer to take over the bridge?"

She bared her teeth, an unattractive smirk. "Yes, I wonder what possessed him?"

The year 1929 was a year for the prophets of doom. A year of infamy christened in blood in February with the Saint Valentine's Day massacre when Capone mobsters, disguised as lawmen, cut down seven rival gangsters with machine guns in a Chicago garage.

The year the Mexican revolution erupted in a bloodbath that numbered fifteen thousand casualties.

A bizarre year. Joseph F. Crater, a distinguished justice of the state supreme court in New York City, set out for his office one morning in robust health and full of zest for life. He was never seen or heard from again, vanished from the face of the planet.

Harbingers of the Apocalypse, intoned the prophets of doom. Indeed, the worst was yet to come.

Carl smelled it coming; the whiskey hadn't dulled his economic acumen. "I don't like the looks of the market," he said to Bruce and Callie one morning early in September. He was making one of his rare appearances at the breakfast table, with a full glass and the last day's copy of *The Wall Street Journal.* "There's over $8 billion in outstanding loans to brokers floating. Just barely floating, I'd say." He tapped the paper with a finger. "And hear this: new issues of common stock exceed $5 billion, it's unprecedented."

Bruce belittled his apprehensions. "Stop worrying, Father. You can trust Hoover, he's got an engineer's head for figures. If the President says the day is in sight when poverty will be banished from this nation, I believe him."

Carl sighed. "Well, our money is already bet on the Republican administration. But I wish we'd laid some of it aside to bet on Babson. Roger says there's a crash imminent that could send the Dow-Jones plummeting sixty points, maybe more."

"Roger Babson is a horse's ass, pardon the language, Callie," Bruce scoffed. "Take Professor Irving Fisher of Yale, now there is one fine economist. Fisher says Babson is an irresponsible fearmonger. That stock prices in this country have reached what appears to be a permanent plateau. What do you say, my dear? Your sensitivity to the market is keener than any layman I know of."

"Lay*woman,* dear," Callie corrected him. "I don't know what to think, truthfully. I've been hoping for the past year to see the economy stabilize. As things stand now, the way it's been expanding year after year, the market is like a child whose glands have gone awry. He keeps growing until he's as tall as a man. Yet it's still a boy inside the giant's body."

"A boy sent out to do a man's errand." Carl liked the metaphor. He put aside the paper and drank from the glass of whiskey. "Well, we can only pray that the lad will rise to the occasion."

"Rubbish!" Bruce wiped his mouth with a napkin and stood up. "In any case, if there was a crash and we lost everything we have except our shares of AT &T, General Electric, and General Motors, we'd still be disgustingly rich."

Callie picked up Carl's *Journal* and studied it solemnly, tapping with her index finger on her front teeth.

On October 23 dire news bulletins from Wall Street sent

Bruce back to the scotch decanter for the fourth time that afternoon. The Majorses were gathered around the Stromberg Carlson console radio in the den. Bruce and Carl each held lists of the combined Majors-Knight investments. Callie was keeping the tally sheet on a clipboard.

They kept the vigil through the night. The volume of trading that day had been so high that the final count went on into the early hours of the twenty-fourth.

"How do AT&T and GE and GM look to you now, rich man?" Carl rubbed salt into his son's wounds.

Bruce got up unsteadily and turned off the radio at 5 A.M. He was dizzy from too much whiskey and the shock of disillusionment. He felt he had witnessed the disintegration of the Rock of Gibraltar.

"Tomorrow, it'll swing back the other way," he predicted hoarsely. "Maybe this is what's been needed all along. A catalyst that will stabilize the economy and set us on an even keel finally."

"Or sink the ship," Callie observed blithely.

Bruce glared at her. "My God! How can you joke at a time like this? Aren't you concerned at all?"

"Oh, I'm concerned, make no mistake about it, but I concur with Saint Matthew: *'Which of you can add an ell to his height by troubling about it.'* "

He raised his hands and wiped his face in weariness and despair. "Please! Spare me your shibboleths this once, Callie." He staggered out into the hall and climbed the stairs, holding on to the banister with both hands.

The next day Bruce phoned his secretary and ordered her to cancel all of his appointments.

"I'm sick."

It was true. He languished at the radio all of October 24. Black Thursday. It would be etched on the consciousness of those who lived through it for the rest of their lives. On the tombstones of those who did not survive.

When the final count was in on the morning of the twenty-fifth, it showed that in that single day over 13 million shares had changed hands.

Bruce was on his knees amid the lists and tally sheets. Hollow-eyed, the color of the cold ashes in the fire pit. Carl sat slumped over in a leather chair staring down into his glass dejectedly. His eyes out of focus. Staring down into a deep well. He saw himself down there through the clear whiskey at the bottom of the glass. No reflection. It was Carl Majors down there, trapped in a well of loneliness, hopelessness, and despair.

Four days later marked the date when an era died. October 29. The day the stock market crashed for good. Pandemonium and chaos on the Floor. Wild, unrestricted short selling. A record 16-million shares of stock changed hands that day. The decline in value in the seven days of crisis from October 23 through October 29 was over $15 billion.

The Roaring Twenties had ended.

The Great Depression had begun.

It was the day Chris arrived home from school for a long weekend holiday. She was excited and bursting with anticipation on the long train trip. Ham had written her a letter, one of his precious letters that she treasured, tied with pink ribbon. She kept them in the drawer with her lingerie in a sad endeavor to infuse them with an intimacy lacking in Ham's prose.

In this last letter, he invited her to a square dance to be held in the basement hall of the big Presbyterian church outside Clinton on Halloween. Considering that Ham Knight had never asked her out on a "real" date before (she didn't count the Saturday night movies and sodas afterward, particularly not the uncomfortable rides in his unromantic pickup truck), Chris elected to interpret his invitation as a breakthrough in their unfruitful relationship. An affirmation that he was ready to respond to her as a desirable—so long desiring—woman. It was a good deal to read into such a small promise as Ham had made.

She was ill prepared for the pall that hung over Wheatley when she arrived on Friday night. Bruce and her father sulking about in morose silence. Snarling at each other like animals when they spoke at all. The son guzzling whiskey with a vengeance matching Carl's.

The girls at Wellesley were insulated from the distasteful realities of the world. It was the birthright of young ladies of breeding and means that they should be spared unpleasantness. Chris had inquired of her history professor, "Is it true what they say on the radio, that the United States is in the grip of the worst economic crisis in the nation's history?"

He had replied, "Miss Majors, every day is a crisis on Wall Street. Take my word for it, it will soon blow over as all financial crises do."

She repeated his remark to the family at supper her first night home.

"And he'll soon be out of a job," Bruce growled.

"Professor Sloan doesn't invest in stocks."

"But the rich little bitches he teaches have fathers who do," her brother enlightened her. "And right now, scores of those fathers are leaping out of their office windows or doing it messily with a gun."

Chris put down her fork in dismay, her appetite lost. "Are matters really *that* bad?" She hesitated. "For us, I mean?"

"We're in the same boat as all the rest. Our General Motors stock alone has dropped more than 230 points. Do you have any conception of what that means? We are wiped out, my dear sister. . . . Here, let me have that bottle, Father. Might as well enjoy it while we can. Won't be long before our cupboards are as empty as Old Mother Hubbard's."

"Now stop exaggerating, Bruce," Callie admonished him. "Our position isn't as bad as your father and brother pretend it is, Chris. It's true our financial situation is grave. For the time being our assets are frozen. Wall Street is in for a long drought. But it will pass away, as everything does in life."

Bruce poured himself a drink, shoved his untouched plate aside. "And just how do you think we are going to subsist, my dear wife, while this long drought goes on? In the past ten days, orders have dropped off 50 percent. Bricks are piling up in the warehouses as fast as unpaid bills for orders already shipped on credit. Construction is at a standstill all across the country. It's the same with the Knight quarry. There'll be no more need for slate than there'll be for bricks. We'll have to sell off shareholdings in order to keep up this place and feed and clothe ourselves."

Callie's appetite was not impaired by the imminent calamity. She had not gone to pieces as had her husband and his father.

"She keeps her head when all around her are losing theirs," Chris thought. It was a grudging compliment. Cool, serene, corporeal Callie.

"We have the bridge," she said, licking butter off her fingers. "Our revenues will see us through until business picks up and the market rallies. We'll sell nothing, not a single share at the current niggardly prices. Perhaps we'll even buy if we have capital left over. You'll see, those cutthroats the River Rich will be buying all the shares they can lay their greedy hands on from desperate speculators who've been caught with their breeches down."

Carl peered at her out of dark, cadaverous eyesockets. "Adversity excites you, doesn't it?"

"Living excites me. Meeting adversity head on and prevailing. We're not destitute; you Majorses are given to such melodrama. Don't worry, Chris, you'll continue with your schooling, we'll see this trouble through with style."

"I believe you, Callie," Carl said. "The bridge will be our rock, our refuge, our rescue. *Your* bridge, Callie."

"The bridge . . ." Bruce said tonelessly and drank from his glass. "Everything else is gone."

"Be grateful for the bridge," she said. "Chris, if you expect to be the *femme fatale* at the Halloween Dance tomorrow night, you'll have to stop looking like a lemon, such a wrinkled sourpuss."

On Saturday night, she warned Bruce and Carl, "This is an important night for Chris. Don't spoil it for her by whining to Ham, he's lost in the crash, remember, same as you. Don't poison his good nature with your drunken self-pity. Go on, the two of you. Go to your rooms and sleep it off."

Chris was grateful. "Thank you, Callie. I want it to be a special night. How do I look?" She did a pirouette. The full skirt of her red chiffon gown ballooned around her slim legs.

"Like a temptress. Red excites men." She appraised the plunging neckline. "But your gown would be exciting in bridal white."

The girl was crestfallen. "I wish it was a bridal gown."

"You could be a bride tomorrow if you weren't such a mule. Promising yourself to one man all these years. A man who—" She bit it off deliberately. The thought was long rooted in Chris's own mind.

"A man who doesn't want me," Chris said miserably. "Oh, Callie, but Ham does want me, I'm certain of it. He acts like a man in a cage. We reach out to each other, but we never really touch. It's always there between us, a barrier."

"You could have Ham like that." Callie snapped her fingers under the girl's nose. She didn't believe it for a moment, a sinister urge drove her to bedevil Chris.

Chris would have done the devil's bidding to win the man she loved. "How, Callie, tell me how? I'll do anything, you know I will."

"The trouble is, Ham knows it even better than you or I. Since the day you first laid eyes on him, you've been wearing your heart on your sleeve. Ham thinks he can have you any time the whim suits him. If it ever suits him. What you must do is spoil the image he has of you. Shake up his smug complacency."

"How can I do that?"

"Show him he's not your whole existence. That you have eyes and desire for other men."

"Ham's not the jealous type."

Callie gripped her by the shoulders, shook her gently. "It's born in all men, they're possessive creatures. If Ham believes he's losing you, he'll want you all the more. You do as I say, and everything will work out for you and Ham."

"Callie, tell me what I must do."

"You had beaus in high school, before he came into your life. Bruce told me the line of boys waiting to sign your dance card at your senior prom ran halfway around the gymnasium."

The girl's eyes shone almost as brightly as Callie's. "The most wonderful night in my life."

"The belle of the ball. Of course it was wonderful. You can recapture that wonder, Chris. You haven't forgotten how to flirt, no woman does. You're beautiful, Chris. In that dress you'll dazzle all the men tonight. Be cool to Ham. Aloof. Spread your favors around. Make him jealous, Chris."

Callie's confidence heartened Chris. "Yes, make him jealous. Oh, will I ever make Ham jealous tonight!"

"Good girl!"

Chris threw her arm around the older woman, cheek to cheek. "Thank you, Callie. Thank you for being such an understanding"—she hesitated—"sister. . . . I used to think of you as my sister when Bruce was courting you, and then—"

"I married your brother and came to live at Wheatley."

"Yes . . . I'm sorry," she said with humility. "I was jealous of you, Callie. I resented your strength. I told myself it wasn't strength, that you were a selfish, willful, ruthless woman who would stop at nothing to get your own way."

Callie laughed softly. "But you were right, you see, I will do anything to get what I want. The means and the ends are one. To see it otherwise is a fool's delusion."

Chris stepped back and appraised her with uncertainty. "I don't think I'll ever be as close to you as once I'd hoped we'd be. Sisters. No one can. Trying to reach the real person inside you, Callie, is like threading a maze. There may be times again when I'll hate you. But after what I saw today, you'll always have my respect. Bruce and my father sniveling like frightened children over their calamities, it shamed me to see them behave so, once-proud men. Only you were strong, Callie. You wiped their snotty noses, slapped their bottoms, and pulled this family back together again. If only I could be strong like you. I'll try tonight, I promise you."

"I'm very flattered, Chris." She bit her underlip, bothered by the confusion of her feelings toward the girl in the new light of the candor with which Chris had expressed herself. "Chris, about tonight, sometimes one can assert oneself too strongly. Perhaps—"

The moment was lost as the door chimes clanged.

A toll, Callie thought.

"That must be Ham!" Chris said. Her face lit up, the serious talk with Callie out of her mind.

Still bothered, Callie stood at the open front door and watched them descend the broad steps to Ham's car. No pickup truck tonight, Chris noted gratefully.

"You bought a new car?"

"Naw, it's secondhand." Acquisition of material objects embarrassed him for some reason. "I bought it from Ray Noonan after Walt fired him last week. There's been no orders for slate come in two weeks, since all this mess has been stirred up on Wall Street. I paid Ray more than she's worth, but he's got to have something to tide him over this dry spell. I hear your father and brother were hit bad by the stock market crash, Chris?"

"Same as everyone." She moved closer to him on the front seat and snuggled up against his arm. "But we'll come through it all right. We have the bridge to fall back on. So do you. Most important, we've got Callie. Nothing can get the best of her."

He was silent. Driving out of the gate onto the road, Ham was aware of a strangeness about Chris. One moment she was close to him, warm and affectionate. Then, without any reason he could fathom, she was drawing away from him, sitting stiff and prim against the door on her side.

Chris regarded him guardedly. She had almost forgotten Callie's advice.

Ham had been inside the Clinton Presbyterian church twice in his lifetime. He had attended a supper at which box lunches were auctioned off to the boys and men, and the high bidder for a given box got to eat it with the female who had prepared it. Ham had spent fifty cents to share his supper with fat Mary Sparks, who had bad breath and pimples. The other time he'd gone with his mother and father on Armistice Day the year after the war to a memorial service honoring the American dead.

For the Halloween dance the large rectangular meeting hall in the church basement had been decorated by the children of the Bible class with appropriate posters and cutouts of witches, black cats, and pumpkins. Garlands of corn husks and straw festooned the lighting fixtures and the bandstand at the front of the hall. At the opposite end of the room was a long table laden with sandwiches, salads, fruit, and an immense punch bowl. Camp chairs, one against the other, were lined up along the side walls.

Ham had no intention of attending the Halloween dance at all until a night in early September when he had picked up the Campballs' mail along with his own at the post office and driven it out to their farm. Lucy had come out to the car boldly and invited him to escort her to the affair. He'd said the first thing that came to his mind: "Sorry, but I already have a date."

The same night he had mailed the invitation to Chris. Lucy Campball intimidated him with her blatant sexuality. With chaste Chris he felt secure. He loved Chris. Not in the way she wanted to be loved, but she didn't force the issue as a girl like Lucy would be bound to do. Ham was resigned to his impotency. Cursed since that hot Indian summer afternoon six years before when he and Callie had murdered his father.

Murder most foul . . .

Resigned was a passive word. The truth was, although Ham was too removed from the forest to see the trees, that he savored his affliction with the consecration of a saint.

One day he had come in from the fields and found Chris waiting for him in his bed.

She flung off the sheet and exposed her nakedness. "Love me, Ham. I've wanted you for so long. I need you so, my darling."

She was so beautiful, tears welled in his eyes, blurring the vision of her breasts and loins beseeching him. He turned his back on her.

"Chris . . . please . . . don't do this. . . ."

"All right, I have no pride. Think of me as whore and harlot, I don't care. All these years I've saved myself for you, it isn't the normal way of life. I want to be used, Ham. A man and woman who love each other the way we do, it's right they should be together. Joined in every way."

He shook his head and lied to her. "Chris . . . I don't love you. It wouldn't be right. You mean too much to me to . . . to 'use,' as you put it."

She began to cry softly. "I don't believe you, Ham. You do love me. You *do*! You've told me so many times you love me."

He heaved his broad shoulders and sighed. "Yes, but not that way. You're very dear to me, but—we were both so young—I didn't know what love was all about. I'm still not certain."

In his uncertainty she grasped at hope, faint hope. "I won't give up on you, Ham Knight. You may not be certain, but I am. *I love you.* And love's contagious. But for now, why can't you accept me as a woman. Any woman. Ham—" There was a terse intake of breath. "Have you ever—you must have had a woman? Ham . . .?"

Pain and humiliation scalded him. "Yes . . . I've had a woman," he replied. Head bent, he left the room and closed the door behind him.

The next time he saw Chris, they pretended the episode had never occurred. Sometimes with Chris he had the odd sensation that the two of them were suspended in time. Like the adulterous lovers he had read about in Dante's *Inferno* who were punished in hell by reliving the day of their sin over and over again through eternity. For he and Chris, too, time was spellbound.

Ham was puzzled by the transformation that came over Chris on the drive to Clinton. He glanced over at her.

"I like your dress."

She arched her eyebrows. "Do you really? I didn't think you'd noticed."

"It's hard not to notice you in that dress," he said, eyeing her *décolletage.*

Chris threw open her coat and thrust out her breasts. "You think it makes me look like a hussy, don't you?"

"I didn't say that."

Her laughter was bawdy, a key she had never struck before, not with him anyway. "Well, maybe I want to look like a hussy tonight."

Ham pondered, was the change in her a portent that their static relationship was about to bestir itself at last?

Her disregard for Ham was even more pronounced once they were at the church hall. When they were dancing she showed more attention and animation to the other men in the set than she did to Ham. It was customary for the four couples who made up each square set to dance together until intermission. As the program progressed, Chris and Jake Spencer—she was the "corner lady" to his left—joined in an ever-bolder flirtation.

Jake Spencer was big man in the fast crowd that Lucy Campball ran with. A blond man with a pasty complexion and mean blue eyes. The sleeves of his red-checkered shirt were rolled up to exhibit his muscles. When he wasn't showing off fancy new steps in the middle of his square, which elicited scowls from the old traditionalists, Jake stood, hip slung, with his thumbs hooked in the waistband of his Levi's, beating time with the steel tap on one boot to the dizzy interplay of fiddle, bass, and banjo.

. . . The two head ladies cross over,
And by their opposites stand . . .

Looking across the square at Chris, Ham tried to catch her eye, but she had eyes only for Jake. He might have been a stranger to her, she was that indifferent.

The two head gents cross over,
Please do as I command.

Ham joined her on the other side and whispered, "You and Jake know each other long?" It was very casual, but her heart quickened. He was jealous!

"Oh, I knew him in high school. He's matured a lot since

then. Very sophisticated, don't you think?"

Ham made a guttural, uncomplimentary sound deep in his throat.

Now honor on your corners,
And salute your partners all . . .

"I hear he drives a new Dodge. What business is he in? It must be good. At the refreshment stand he flashed a roll of bills as big around as this." She made a circle with her hands.

Recalling what Walt Campball had said about Jake, Ham answered with malicious satisfaction, "I guess the crash hasn't hurt the bootleggers any."

"Oh, I don't believe that about Jake. He's a real gentleman."

Take your corner lady,
And promenade the hall.

Jake Spencer took Chris away from him and Ham was paired with a pretty redheaded girl in a gingham dress. Jake and Chris, just ahead, were a handsome, graceful couple, Ham conceded grudgingly. The intricate skipping two step in the processional around the perimeter of the dance floor posed an obstacle for his own big feet. The awkward stance, man and woman crossing arms in front, her left hand in his right hand, her right in his left, vanquished him altogether. Jake and Chris danced in fluid rhythm, as one, while Ham was in constant competition with his partner. Once he almost knocked her off her feet with a hip check.

"All rest!" the caller shouted, and the couples stopped and clapped in appreciation for the musicians.

The column broke up as dancers sought out their own partners. Ham thanked the redheaded girl and apologized for his clumsiness. He looked around for Chris, but she and Jake had disappeared.

He looked around the hall over the heads in the crowd and finally saw her at the punch bowl with Jake Spencer. Heat stung his cheeks. He told himself it wasn't jealousy. All the times he had argued with Chris because she wouldn't date other men. It was her undeserving rudeness that rankled Ham, so unlike her.

He stood on the sidelines observing the two of them. Jake ladled punch into paper cups and escorted her through the press at the refreshment table to a cozy corner. Hand spanned possessively across the small of her back.

The more Ham spied, the more disgust he felt. Chris was behaving like a giddy schoolgirl, gushing and giggling at everything Jake said. Fluttering her eyelashes and tilting her head coyly that way and this way. They were standing close together and Jake's impudent blue eyes were feasting on all the bare flesh exposed by the cut of her gown.

When Jake took a flask out of his hip pocket and spiked their drinks, Ham had to stifle an impulse to interfere. It was out of line, he knew, Chris was twenty-four years old, a woman. She had a right to drink liquor if she chose. It was her choice of drinking partners that worried him.

Two of Jake Spencer's cronies joined them. One was Ray Shuffelmeir, a squat, burly fellow with a round face and kinky red hair. A telephone lineman, Ray was notorious for his bad-tempered drinking bouts. His nickname was "Mad Man," an apt title sodden or sober. "Mad Man" Shuffelmeir was the only sport in Saratoga County who owned an automobile with screen doors.

The third man was Leon Ballard, a small, skinny man with sharp features and beady eyes. He had been arrested in 1921 for sneaking into the girls' room at Clinton High School and exposing himself to a terrified student who was seated in one of the booths.

"Ham Knight! How are you, boy?" Followed up by a clout on the back that jarred his teeth.

Ham looked around and recognized the gangling buck-toothed youth who had sat alongside him in mathematics class, his last term at Clinton High.

"Buck Evans! Say, it's good to see you again."

They shook hands and exchanged amenities. Five minutes, no more, until Ham excused himself.

"I have to find my date."

He looked back to the corner, but Chris was gone. Ham made a full circle of the room, but she was nowhere to be found. Nor were the three men in whose company she had last been seen.

While Chris and Jake Spencer were talking in the corner, Chris kept sneaking looks in Ham's direction. He was angry with her, she could tell, the way he glowered at them. When she let Jake pour whiskey in her punch, he looked so furious, she almost had to laugh. For the first time in their relationship, Chris felt she had some power over Ham. The desire to wield it goaded her on. She put a hand to her forehead.

"It's stuffy in here, Jake. Let's get a breath of fresh air."

His hard eyes were amused. "Why, sure, that sounds like a fine idea. See you later, boys." He nodded to Roy and Leon, but Chris, in turning, missed his sly wink.

Walking up the stairs in front of him, Chris experienced a prickling along her spine. A warning intuition that went unheeded.

On the church porch, they stood at the railing overlooking the dark parking lot. Chris folded her arms across her breasts.

"It's chilly. I should have taken my wrap," she said.

Jake laughed softly. "I know a better way to warm you up." He stepped behind her and put his arms around her. "Now, ain't that better than your old wrap?"

She tried to make light of it, afraid to make a scene. "Really, Jake, I'm not cold."

"I'll bet you're not."

She grasped his wrists and tried to remove his arms, but he was too strong for her. "Please, don't. Someone will come out and see us."

Ham! She wanted to make Ham jealous, but if he saw her like this in Jake's arms, he might think she'd invited it.

"No law against a feller and his gal doing a little smooching, is there?"

"I'm not your girl. Let me go." He reeked of whiskey and tobacco and sweat.

Jake relaxed his hold on her so that he could move around to face her. "How's about a little kiss, Sheba?"

His mouth sought her lips, but Chris was too quick for him. She ducked under his encircling arms and broke loose. Ran for the door. Leon Ballard blocked the entrance, hands braced on the frame on either side.

Chris uttered a muted shriek. Panicked. That was her undoing. She whirled, ran down the steps and around the side of the church, her goal the side entrance. In her panic, she chose the wrong side of the building. Ran square into Ray Shuffelmeir's outstretched arms. In the moonlight he looked like a grinning gargoyle.

She tried to scream. A hand slammed over her mouth, smashing her lips against her teeth. His other arm clamped powerfully around her waist. Tears of pain and terror blinded her. Their three dark forms surrounded her. Phantoms in a nightmare. This wasn't happening to her. She'd soon awake.

Voices filtered into her numbed consciousness. Dim, remote, unreal voices.

"Let's get her into the car. Come on, quick now, 'fore that dumb boyfriend comes looking for her."

She was floating in the air, hardly conscious of the hands on her arms and legs. The big hand clamped over her mouth and nose was suffocating her.

She was on the floor of a car, the back seat. Pushed down. A foot planted on her back. The hand was removed from her mouth and she could breathe again. Everything was spinning. She shut her eyes to keep from getting dizzy sick.

"Okay, Leon, give her the gun."

A car engine revved. There was the sound of flying stones kicked up by spinning rubber, and they were on their way. A lurch, a bump, Chris was jostled back against the seat. The foot was lifted from her back, and a voice spoke to her.

"How're we doing, sweetie? You can come up now, if you promise to behave."

She twisted her head around and looked up into the leering face of Jake Spencer. She got up on her knees. Couldn't speak at first. Gulped in air.

A flask was shoved at her. "Here, have a little snort, Sheba. It'll put you in the mood."

"Where are you taking me?" she asked with mounting fear.

"Seeing as you were so finicky about someone seeing us smooching on the porch, I figured we'd go someplace where it's real private. Come on up here and sit between me and Ray, sweetie. We'll all get acquainted." Hands lifted her under the arms. She fell back on the seat between the two men.

"Oh, please," she moaned.

Jake cackled. "Get that, boys, she's begging for it. She can't wait. *'Oh, ple-e-e-e-ese!'* I spotted you as a sheba, honey, the minute you walked in that dress. Vo-do-de-o-do!"

Chris pushed Ray's hand off her thigh. "You stop that! I'm not going anywhere with you—you bums."

"Oh, now we're bums," Jake chortled. "You hear that,

boys? Drop the act, Sheba. The minute you set eyes on me, you started licking your lips for it. Your boyfriend, he's the bum. The bum's rush, you sure gave it to him."

"You don't understand," she wailed. "I was just trying to make him jealous."

That made them hilarious. People passed on the road took them for a trio of country youths with nothing more mischievous on their minds than a night of innocent merriment.

Jake put a powerful arm around her, pinning her arms to her sides. His free hand fondled her breasts. "Is that what you were doing all night, making him jealous? And all the while I thought you was showing off those pretty little titties to tell me something. Now, it's time for you to stop playing games with me, Sheba. You ain't fooling anybody. I've met your kind before, you little prissy cock-teasers, you're all the same. You shove it in a feller's face like a bitch does to a hound dog. Then when he comes to get it, you pretend you don't know what he wants." He mimiced her in a falsetto voice, " '*It's so stuffy in here, Jake. Let's get a breath of fresh air.*' Females, they're a caution, and that's the truth, ain't it, boys? They make out they don't want it same as we do, so the next morning they can look into the mirror and tell themselves it wasn't their fault what happened. No, their little pussies weren't itchy one bit."

Chris threw back her head and howled like a frightened animal. "Oh, no, please don't touch me like that. Please let me go! Stop it!" She bucked and twisted as Jake's hand slipped inside her bodice. On the other side, Ray slid his hand up under her dress, pried apart her clenched knees. Her outcries were muffled by a hand over her mouth again. She bit the hand, it pulled away.

A savage curse. "You bitch, I'm bleeding!"

He punched her in the face. Excruciating pain blinded her. A red curtain of pain. Fading into black oblivion.

The black brightening to gray as she regained consciousness. Gray fog lifting gradually. She opened her eyes slowly, striving to bring the world back into focus. She was lying on a thick furry rug in front of a fireplace, red and orange flames licked over the gnarled logs.

She let out a sigh of enormous relief. So it had been a nightmare. She was in the Knight house. She had fallen asleep on the bear rug in front of the warm, relaxing fire in the grate. She was with Ham.

"Ham?"

She reached out, feeling for him. Turned her head slowly away from the fire and looked around the room. A pair of man's legs. Ham's legs. Ham's boots with steel toes.

Steel toes!

Her eyes flew up to the smirking face of Jake Spencer standing over her.

"I didn't want to start without you, Sheba," he said. His face was hot and ugly with lust. It was only then that Chris realized she was naked. She doubled up, crumpled, covered herself with her hands. Pathetic reflex of chastity sanctified all of her twenty-four years.

"Oh, no!" she cried out in anguish as he began to unbutton his pants.

"This is what you've been waiting for all night, Sheba," he said hoarsely. He dropped his pants.

Chris screamed and shut her eyes. She was lost. All hope dead. She did not resist him when he rolled her over on her back, spread her thighs, straddled her. Crying quietly, she tried to tell him what a monstrous deed he was committing.

"Please don't do it to me. I never have before. No man ever has. I've never had a man. Never wanted a man other than him. Oh, Ham!"

Her whole body spasmed with the pain and she screamed.

"Ham! I'm sorry, Ham!"

"Jesus!" Jake marveled to the other men awaiting their turns. "It's on the level. She never did before!"

Chris was still missing at the end of the intermission. Ham went searching for her. He looked everywhere inside the church. Behind the altar. The organ loft. All the way up the spiral staircase that led to the belfry. He borrowed a flashlight and went outside to prowl. Shining his torch in darkened cars in the parking lot. Calling her name until he was hoarse. The empty, lonely sound of his voice echoing back to him from the hills around.

Chris-Chris-Chris-Chrisssss.

He went inside and made inquiries about Jake Spencer and the other two. The girl Jake had danced with told him, "I heard Ray tell Sheila Gordon they were leaving early 'cause something unexpected had come up." Her grin underlined the innuendo. "What's the matter, Jake steal your girl?" She put a hand on his arm. "What do you say, you and me make some whoopee, sweetie?"

"No thanks." He turned his back and walked away.

She stomped a foot and stuck out her tongue at him. "What's he so highfalutin about?"

Ham had exhausted all other options. There was no course left but to spread an alarm. He left the dance, got into his car, and drove to the nearest gas station.

"Fill 'er up," he told the attendant and went into the office to use the pay phone. He gave the operator Wheatley's number.

Callie picked up the phone.

"This is Ham. Is Chris home yet?"

"Of course she isn't home. Isn't she with you? What's happened?"

He told her, and surmised, "I thought Jake Spencer and his friends might have brought her home."

There was a long silence at the other end. Finally Callie said, "I think we'd better phone the sheriff. I'll attend to it. You get back here as fast as you can."

Ham arrived at Wheatley a little before midnight. Carl and Bruce were in a vicious humor. Pacing the floor in the sitting room. Chain-smoking. Drinking steadily. Ham refused a drink and sat down on the couch.

"Sheriff Adams and two of his deputies are out looking for Chris," Callie advised him. "If they can't find her, the state police will have to be notified in the morning. All we can do is to wait."

They waited until three o'clock. When the door chimes sounded, Ham startled; he'd been dozing. They all rushed into the hall. Bruce flung open the door, recoiled from the sight of his sister propped up by an officer on each side. She was a grisly sight.

"My God!"

"Oh, no!" cried Carl.

"What did they do to her?" Ham recoiled.

"It's clear what they did to her. Who did it?" Callie demanded.

Chris was conscious but she did not appear to recognize them or where she was. Her eyes were as blank as the blue-glass marbles in a doll's face. Her hair was wild and soiled with vomit and blood; so was her torn dress. She was barefooted. There was caked blood on her mouth, her top lip was split. A purple bruise stained her swollen cheek on the right side.

"Who did it?" Callie repeated.

Samuel Adams, a portly man of thirty-five, was the sheriff of Saratoga County. He'd won the Bronze Star in the war with the military police. His present post he owed in large measure to the Majorses. It was Carl who had persuaded him he could put his military background to better use than baking bricks in the Majors kilns. And Carl who had prevailed upon Senator Wayne Harrison to be Sam Adams' mentor when he first broke into politics. His debt was a big one. No one appreciated it more than Sam himself.

He took off his wide-brimmed cavalry hat, patted his sparse brown hair.

"It was Jake Spencer." He glanced at Ham. "You were right about that. It's all we could get out of her so far. You can see she's in a state of shock. They took her to a cabin, the three of them, and—" He looked down at the floor. "No need to go into that now. They're drunk and ugly. Soon as we leave here, we'll track 'em down. Don't you worry, sir," he said to Carl. And to Callie: "Ma'am, do you want my deputies to help her upstairs?"

"Yes, thank you. Bruce, wake Maude and Jane. Tell them they're wanted to help upstairs right away."

Before the deputies took Chris upstairs, Carl embraced her. He was crying and his voice was full of pain.

"My darling, baby, it's going to be all right. You're safe now in your own home again, we'll take care of you." He kissed her bloody abused face, stroked her hair, petted her as if she were a child.

The girl gave no sign that she understood what he was saying, that she heard him at all. She appeared to be oblivious of everything and everyone around her in this familiar hall, no longer familiar. Shut off in a private world of her own where no intruder could gain admission.

"They shouldn't be hard to round up," Sheriff Adams speculated. "We found your daughter wandering in a daze on the Lake Shore Road. There's a lot of summer cabins up at the lake. I figure Spencer and his crew are holded up in one of 'em. Far as we can make out, they got so drunk, they all passed out, and that gave her a chance to get her clothes and scat. Probably don't even know she's gone yet. Yup, they'll be sitting ducks.

Soon as we have them in tow, I'll let you know. You can come over to the county jail in the morning and sign a complaint."

"No complaint, Sheriff." It was Callie standing on the balcony above them. Her voice had a hollow ring in the nave of the tall hall. All eyes lifted to her figure on the balcony. The elevation made her a dominating presence.

"We don't want to sign any complaint, do we? Carl? Bruce?"

The sheriff blinked. "Ma'am?"

"Not sign a complaint?" Bruce stared at her in bewilderment. "Let those three get away with what they did to my sister? Are you crazy?"

"The point is, Chris *is* your sister. Carl's daughter. Is that what you want for her? Her picture on the front of every newspaper from Saratoga to Lake George? Yellow-journal accounts of all the lewd acts she was forced to perform with those degenerates. *In lurid detail!* Chris made to describe those obscenities on the witness stand!"

"Enough!" Carl held up a restraining hand. He turned to Bruce and the sheriff. "She's right. We can't put Chris through that ordeal. It's bad enough that she's been through it once. But not again in court with the news jackals howling after her."

"But we just can't sit back and let Spencer and his thugs get away with this outrage," Bruce objected.

"That's right, Mr. Majors." Sheriff Adams supported Bruce. "A crime has been committed. Rape. Assault. I'm obliged as a law officer to apprehend those felons and see to it that they're prosecuted and punished for the crime."

"Not if we don't press charges," Callie contended. "For all we know there was no crime. It could be in the girl's imagination."

"You're talking nonsense, damnit!" Bruce yelled. "All you have to do is look at the condition she's in."

"That isn't the issue, Bruce. The point is, the sheriff has no case without a complaint. Legally there's been no crime committed."

The sheriff scratched his head, befuddled. "I don't know, Mrs. Majors. It doesn't seem right." He appealed to Carl and Bruce. "You really want to pretend those bastards—pardon the language, ma'am—didn't beat and rape your daughter, sister?"

Bruce started to reply, but Carl beat him to it. "Under the

circumstances, Sheriff, I don't think we have much choice." A note of the old authority fortified his voice. "Sam . . . I want your solemn word of honor that none of what you saw and heard tonight will go outside this house. I'm holding you responsible for your two deputies as well. You understand?"

The sheriff had nothing to consider. Carl Majors was his patron. He had been a good friend, and, if antagonized, he could become a powerful and dangerous enemy.

"If that's how you want it, then that's how it has to be. You have my word, sir. I'll vouch for Helmer and Saxon too. They're good lawmen, and loyal."

"Thank you, Sheriff," Callie called down. "Good night. I must see to Chris now, poor girl." She went off down the hall.

When the sheriff and his men departed, Carl, Bruce, and Ham went back into the parlor.

"I think I'll have that drink now," said Ham. "It's been quite a night."

Carl placed a hand on Ham's back. "We can all use a drink. You'll spend the night here, of course. It's too late to go back to Knightsville now."

"I guess so. Maybe I can see Chris tomorrow morning before I leave. I have to make sure."

"Make sure of what?" Bruce half-filled a water glass with bourbon.

"I know Jake Spencer was one of them," Ham said with vengeance, barely able to control his wrath. "I have to make sure about Shuffelmeir and Ballard, that they were the other two. Before I settle the score . . ." It trailed off ominously.

"I've been thinking the same thing myself, Ham." Bruce downed his whiskey in one gulp and hurled the glass into the fireplace. "It's driving me mad knowing what those brutes did to my sister and having to let them get away with it. Count me in, Ham."

"Bravo!" Callie clapped hands, standing in the archway. "It's reassuring to discover that some men still value family honor and personal pride. And you, Carl?" It was a challenge.

The old man tugged at his mustache, looking uncomfortably from Bruce to Ham to Callie. Gave a curt nod, drew himself erect, clenched a fist in the air. "It would be some consolation to bash in their cowardly faces."

Bruce walked to the server and poured himself a fresh drink. "We'll decide what to do about those three tomorrow."

"Tomorrow?" Callie put the spurs to him. "Tomorrow's for the pigeon-hearted. Why put off till tomorrow what can be done tonight? What *should* be done tonight. Jake Spencer and his friends may make plans of their own tomorrow when they sober up. They may decide to run."

"She's right," Bruce concurred. "They'll expect us to file charges against them. Rape is a very serious offense in this state. Twenty years in jail or more. That prospect can whip a man to run a long way."

"But we don't know where to find them," Ham said.

"Oh, you'll find them," Callie assured him. "Chris has been babbling, she's delirious, but some of what she says makes sense. We know the sheriff found her on the Lake Shore Road. She keeps talking about an iron deer. It gave her a terrible fright when she escaped from the cabin. In the moonlight it looked real."

"An iron deer," Carl mused. "I know the place. Whenever I drive past, I can't help thinking what a monstrosity it is on a small lawn."

"Let's go, then." Bruce downed his drink and poured himself another. He was high on alcohol. Ten feet high. Invulnerable. Indestructible. Omnipotent. His blood was singing in a wild course through his veins and arteries. He led the way out into the hall, swaggering. They dressed in coats taken from the guest closet.

"You must have arms," Callie told them.

"Guns?" Ham didn't go along with that. "My fists are all the weapons I need against scum like that."

"Aye, lad," Carl agreed.

"Don't be fools!" she reproved them. "Scum like they are seldom go unarmed. One or more will have a pistol or a knife."

"Spencer is bound to have a gun." Bruce sided with her. "Remember, he's a bootlegger. We'll take shotguns."

He went down the hall to the den and removed three guns out of the weapons rack. He armed his father and Ham each with a double-barreled Remington shotgun and a fistful of shells. In the crook of his arm, he carried his favorite Winchester pump-action gun.

Callie stood at the open door watching them hurry down the steps to Ham's car parked in front. She waved as they drove away. Not that they could see her in the darkness. It was a personal salute.

Salute to what? Her forehead puckered. She closed the door and stood there with her hand clutching the brass knob. The metal cool on her sweaty palm. Head downcast, staring at the swirls in the wood's grain. There were patterns in good wood as there were in clouds. Omens of the future read by soothsayers. It was clear in the grain, this picture. A death's head.

She went into the den and sat behind the desk. Picked up the phone and gave the operator Wayne Harrison's private number in Albany. The assembly was in session, he'd be there.

His voice came to her, thick and sibilant from sleep. "What do you want at such an hour?"

"There's been a terrible tragedy here, Wayne. I'd appreciate it if you could come to Wheatley right away. You're needed."

"You must be mad!" He was fast collecting his faculties. "I'm speaking on the floor at ten tomorrow morning."

"This is more important, Wayne."

"And what is this matter that's so important?"

"I don't wish to discuss it on the phone."

"I'm not going anywhere until I can judge for myself if the cause warrants it. Has anything happened to Carl or Bruce?"

"Not exactly," she evaded. "Look, Wayne, how would you feel about discussing your little Troy episode on the phone?"

She could hear the taut intake of his breath over the wire. Silence lasting one heartbeat, and then in resignation: "I'll be up there as soon as possible."

"Thank you, Wayne." She put down the phone and sat there motionless. Worrying her bottom lip with her sharp teeth. After a while she smiled.

They rounded a sharp bend and the car's headlights swept across the iron deer on the lawn. A regal buck with one front hoof raised, his metal carcass green with moldy fungus. A spike had been broken off the left antler. The cabin appeared dark and deserted. Ham drove on until it passed out of view and parked at the side of the road.

The three men disembarked from the car and checked their weapons. Ham made double sure that his gun's safety was on. He didn't want to shoot anyone accidentally, even Jake Spencer.

They walked back to the cabin, keeping to the short grass

at the side of the road to muffle footsteps. Stopped at the edge of the clearing in which the cabin stood and surveyed the dark building.

"They're asleep or gone, that's for sure," Ham said.

Bruce cursed softly. "They'd better not be gone. Not after I've got myself all worked up for this."

Ham shivered, not from cold. He half-wished they were gone. There was an aura about this group he was part of that made him uneasy. The tension was palpable. He could feel it, the way he could feel his heartbeat accelerating with each step closer to the confrontation. A viable force driving them toward a destiny that all of Ham's instincts rebelled at.

Bruce leading the way, they circled around to the rear of the cabin. Steps led up to the back door. They creaked, and Ham's heart raced faster. Bruce tried the doorknob. He looked back at Ham and Carl. His expression was demoniac in the moonlight. A man possessed, Ham thought.

"It's unlocked," he whispered.

The door opened inward and they moved single-file into the kitchen. Bruce inched his way across the back room to avoid bumping into things and giving their quarry an alarm. He moved through a doorway into another room. It was blacked out, but he could make out the dim outline of a fireplace with coals glowing faintly in the grate. He ran a hand over the wall on his right, feeling for a light switch. Smooth paneling. He shifted the gun and explored the wall on his left side. Found it.

He whispered to his conspirators. "All right. Heads up, here we go!" He snapped the switch the light burst over the room, painful to the eyes.

Jake Spencer was sprawled on a rug in front of the hearth. Ray Shuffelmeir and Leon Ballard were asleep back to back on a daybed against the far wall. A table in the middle of the room was a clutter of bottles, glasses, and mounded ashtrays. Jake was clutching an empty beer bottle in one hand even as he slept.

"Wake up, you scurvy sons of bitches!" Bruce shouted. He held his Winchester at the ready.

Jake opened his eyes and shook himself the way an animal comes awake. He brought up one hand slowly to shield his eyes.

"What the hell you shouting about, Ray?" he asked drowsily, not yet comprehending what was happening.

Bruce crossed over in two strides and kicked him in the side. "On your feet, Spencer!"

"Jesus!" the blond man howled in pain. He grabbed his side and rolled away as Bruce aimed another kick. He struggled up on his knees and raised the beer bottle defensively. His expression was flabbergasted as he looked from one to the other with fear and cunning.

"Who are you guys? What do you want? This dump belong to you? Okay, so we were drunk and broke in here to sleep it off. My cousin has a place looks just the same as this." He rubbed his side and frowned. "You had no cause to kick me like that, mister." The placating whine in his voice was out of respect for the shotguns they were carrying. If they had been unarmed, Jake reflected bitterly, he would have already brained the bastard who'd kicked him with the beer bottle in his right hand.

"He's mine, Bruce," Ham said. He handed his gun to Carl and advanced on Jake.

The shock of seeing Ham Knight sobered Jake and brought his alcoholic hazy thoughts into sharp focus. His mean little eyes darted in a frantic search for the girl.

"What the hell's going on around here?" He shook his head and thumped the heel of one hand against his forehead as if he hoped to light up the dark blank spaces in his memory.

"She's not here, Jake. She got away while you were asleep." Ham brought up his fists, belt-high, and spread his legs. "Now get up and take what's coming to you."

Jake sat back on his haunches, fingers closing more tightly on the bottle's neck.

"She?" He feigned ignorance. "Ain't no 'shes' in this crowd, as you can see."

"Stop lying, Jake. You brought Chris Majors here tonight by force. Raped and beat her."

Jake gaped at him, eyes and mouth wide open, playing the losing game to its pointless end. "Now, listen here, mister, you have made one *big* mistake and you'd better watch yourself." He yelled to the men on the couch. "We don't know nothing about any girl, do we, fellers?"

Both men were awake, though barely. Ballard lay immobile on his back, staring at the ceiling, trying to put his mind in order and make sense out of this improbable happening.

Shuffelmeir propped himself up on one elbow, head braced in his hand. He yawned and spoke in a groggy voice.

"Girl . . ." He gazed dreamily around the room. She was gone. Truthfully, Ray was uncertain. Could she have been a figment of his doped imagination?

"Get up, Jake, or I'll kick your teeth in right where you are," Ham barked.

"Okay . . ." Jake threw his left hand into the air, conceding defeat on that front. "So there was a girl here. I didn't want to say it because it makes her look bad. Look, Knight, you must know the score? You saw the way she was playing up to me all night at the dance." He glanced at Bruce. "You ask him, mister. She gave him the old heave-ho, went for me real big. Isn't that so, Knight? Listen, if she said we made her come here, she's a lying whore. She begged us to bring her out here. She was drooling for it. That's the hottest piece I ever—"

The blast from Bruce's Winchester at such close range flung him back across the hearth, head bent over one andiron grotesquely like a chicken with a twisted neck. The heavy buckshot had almost cut him in half. Abdomen and waist were mangled chopmeat.

"You filthy lying beast. A rattlesnake's worth more than your life." Bruce walked up and spat on the dead man.

Ham and Carl were speechless. In Ham the numbness in him gave way fast to horror.

Bruce scowled at him. "Why are you looking at me like that, Ham? Isn't this what we came here for? I mean, *really* came to do? To exterminate a nest of vermin!"

Ham backed off, shaking his head. "No, Bruce. No!" He denied it vigorously. "Not to kill! They deserve to go to jail, but you refused to press charges. You and Callie." He sensed *her* presence acutely in this dreadful miscalculation. Was it miscalculation?

"*You* were the one who started it, Ham," Bruce accused. "It was your idea to avenge what they did to my sister."

"Bruce, it isn't true! A thrashing was all I had in mind, you know that."

"Are you sure, Ham?" Before Ham could deny it, he addressed Carl. "Well, what are you waiting for, Father?" He swung the shotgun on the two men cringing on the bed. Ballard and Shuffelmeir were wide awake now, sitting petrified with their backs flat against the wall. Straining against the pine boards, hoping for a desperate miracle that would let them escape through one of the knotholes in the wood.

"The gun, Father. Use it," Bruce said in a voice as flat as the cut a digger's spade makes in a new grave.

Carl looked down at the shotgun cradled in his arms. It was an alien object.

"Use it . . . ?"

"You damned fool! You old fool!" his son raged. "If they're let go to talk, it'll be our doom. All of us. Chris, you, me, even Ham." He flung an arm at Ham. "You're involved in this as much as any of us. An accessory. Remember, it was your idea. *Father, use the gun!*"

"No! I didn't touch her! I don't want to die!" Crazed with terror, Leon Ballard leaped off the bed and ran for the kitchen.

As calmly as if he was leading a flying mallard, Bruce followed the man's mad dash with the muzzle of his Winchester. His trigger finger tightened. The charge hit Ballard, framed in the doorway, and lifted him off his feet. He hit the floor spread-eagled on his face.

In the split instant before the windowpanes and glassware in the room stopped rattling from the blast, Carl emptied both barrels of his shotgun into the man on the bed. He later claimed it had been an involuntary flex of his finger triggered by the backlash of Bruce's shot. But there wasn't bourbon enough in all of Saratoga County, the whole world, to convince him of the logic of that poor deceit.

It was a quarter before noon on Sunday when two official county cars turned into the main gate of Wheatley estate. They drove up the long circular drive and parked in front of the Georgian mansion. Sheriff Adams got out of the first car and walked back to speak with his two deputies.

"I'd better go in alone for now," he told them. "This is going to be a very sticky business. The Majorses and the Knights between them pretty much own this district. You just don't go around charging people like them with murder."

"Well, there ain't no doubt about who killed those three up at the lake," Ben Saxon, the driver, said. "They must have gone up there after 'em as soon as we left the house. That's why they wouldn't press charges against Spencer and his gang. All the while they were planning to take care of 'em themselves." He took out a cigarette and struck a wood sulfur match on the brim of his cavalry hat. "Just between you and me, Sam, they did us a favor. We've been trying to nail that bastard Spencer on likker charges for months now. I'll bet between 'em those three have been hauled in thirty, forty times on one complaint or another. I say good riddance."

"No loss to this county they're dead, Ben," Adams conceded. He gazed stern and thin-lipped at the house. "But the law says otherwise. Nobody, not even a Majors or a Knight, can set himself up as judge, jury, and executioner." He hitched up his Sam Browne belt and took a deep breath. "Well, here goes, men. I'll call for you when I want you."

"You want us to bring in the cuffs?" the other deputy asked.

The sheriff wiped a hand across his face, undecided. "I suppose they should be treated like any other lawbreakers. But . . . Hell! No, I can't humiliate Carl Majors that way. He's done a lot for the sheriff's office."

He turned and walked up the broad front steps with heavy footsteps.

Callie Majors opened the door for him, all sweetness and smiles. "Good morning, Sheriff Adams. My, isn't it a lovely morning. I haven't been out yet myself. Please come in."

"Morning, ma'am." Adams removed his hat and came into the front hall. Being greeted by the Majors woman unnerved him. She acted so damned cheerful. Almost as if she'd been expecting him to stop by for Sunday coffee and buns.

"You're looking chipper for a man who's been up half the night, Sheriff."

He fumbled with the hat held in two hands in front of him, avoiding her intent gaze. "I've felt better, Mrs. Majors. Being here this morning doesn't make me feel so good." He glanced up. "Ma'am, where is your husband and old Mr. Majors?"

"Why, they're in the sitting room. We have company, but you're welcome to join the group, Sheriff. You may know the gentlemen."

She was mind-boggling, this woman; he grasped for the right word. She was unnatural, apart from the women of the region. He suspected there might not be another like her anywhere. He followed her across the hall to the sliding doors that closed off the wide archway into the sitting room. Callie flung them apart and motioned him to enter.

They were grouped around the huge fireplace whose

sweep covered twenty feet of wall. Carl Majors. His son, Bruce. Ham Knight. And two other men who looked familiar to him. Halfway into the room he recognized them. State Senator Wayne Harrison and the district attorney of Saratoga County, Walter Edwards. Their presence here on this of all mornings was a consternation to Adams.

The red ruby eyes of the widespread eagle on the brick mantle glittered with hostility. *How dare you intrude on this august gathering?* it seemed to say.

Carl Majors's complexion was the same hue as his gray pinstriped banker's suit. He looked like death. Good reason. Bruce Majors was dressed in riding breeches and polo shirt, and wore a white silk scarf knotted at his throat. A society sportsman with nothing more grave on his mind than an invigorating canter before lunch. The sweat beading on his forehead, the tic at the side of his left eye, and the wet circles spreading down from the armpits of his white shirt betrayed him.

The senator and the district attorney wore blue serge suits, attire fitting such a pair of distinguished advocates.

Ham, the sheriff noted, was wearing the same blue blazer and white slacks he had worn the night before. He looked like a young Atlas bearing the weight of the world on his rounded shoulders.

The tone of this meeting was set as soon as the sheriff entered the room. Senator Harrison was their spokesman.

"Sam, by God, boy, it's good to see you again." He came forward, right hand extended.

Sam . . . boy . . . The practiced familiarity of a nobleman to his serf.

"Morning, Senator. It's a surprise to see you here, you're looking fit." He nodded toward the D.A. "Mr. Edwards . . ." His gaze came to rest on Carl Majors. "Mr. Majors, I think you know why I'm here?"

Carl met his gaze squarely, lips pressed tight-shut in a bloodless gash.

Senator Harrison, so at ease, so jovial. The confident barrister with an open-and-shut case. He answered, "If you're collecting for the police fund, Sam, I'm sure we'll all be happy to contribute."

The sheriff's ears burned like frostbite. He didn't care to be toyed with, even by a state senator.

"I don't find much humor in any of this, Senator." He glanced from Harrison to Edwards. "If Mr. Majors wasn't expecting me, you two gentlemen wouldn't be here. Carl Majors, I'm here to question you about those three murders happened in that cottage on the Lake Shore Road. The men who attacked your daughter."

"What's this?" Senator Harrison gave Callie a theatrical double-take. "Chris looked fine at breakfast, positively radiant."

"I'm sure I don't know what the sheriff is talking about, Senator," Callie said lightly.

The red was spreading from the sheriff's ears, across his face and down his neck. It required all his self-restraint to be civil.

"Mrs. Majors . . . Senator . . . last night my office received a call from this house, from Mrs. Majors herself, saying that Christine Majors had been abducted by three men. I went out myself with two deputies, Ben Saxon and Willie Helmer, to search for her. We came upon her on the Lake Shore Road all dirty and bloody, her clothes half torn off. She was in a state of shock, but she was able to tell us that three men took her from the Halloween dance at the Clinton Presbyterian church to a cabin where they beat and raped her. We brought her back to the house and were going out back to the lake to pick up the men, but Mrs. Majors here said no. They refused to make any charges. Ain't that so, Mrs. Majors?"

"You must have dreamed it, Sheriff." She seemed amused.

It was too much, his temper flared. "Ma'am, I hate to say this, but you're lying!"

The senator drew himself up to his full height of six feet four inches and balled his fists on his hips. His voice was cold and intimidating.

"*Don't* say it, Sam."

Adams was shaken. Things were going even worse than he had expected. He entreated Carl. Bruce. Ham. "Mr. Majors . . . you, sir . . . Mr. Knight . . . tell him the truth."

The three were silent.

"They've told me everything, Sam," said Harrison.

"I'd like to hear them speak for themselves."

"That won't be necessary. I speak for them all. My law firm represents both the Knight and Majors families in various capacities. Harrison, Walsh and Pierson, our offices are in Albany."

Adams made a move to turn. "Senator Harrison, I think I'd better get my deputies in here. They're waiting in the car outside. They were witnesses to everything that happened here last night."

Callie spoke up brightly. "Ben Saxon and Willie Helmer, did you say, Sheriff? The names are so familiar. Oh yes, I saw them on a list my husband has on his desk. Bruce, what is that list anyway?"

Bruce Majors was standing in profile at the fireplace, one hand resting on the brick mantel. A stage pose. He cleared his throat, licked his lips and spoke his lines as from a script: "At that emergency meeting we held at the bank last Friday . . ."

"My husband is a director of the Clinton National Bank, Sheriff, but of course you know that," Callie prompted from the wings.

Bruce went on: "Due to the economic disaster that has overtaken the country, the bank is forced to call in certain loans and foreclose mortgages that are in arrears."

"That's the list," she said. "What a shame for those poor souls who lose house and property in these sad times. I don't envy my husband and the other directors the responsibility of making that difficult decision. It's a little like playing God." She pointed a condemning finger at thin air. "You are doomed!" Pointed again in reprieve. "You will be spared!"

The sheriff stared at her. "Who else is on that list, Mrs. Majors?" he asked with irony.

For the first time District Attorney Edwards spoke up. "I am, Sam," he said in a soft voice. He stood up, tugged down his vest, took out his gold pocket watch, frowned.

"It's getting late," he said. "I suggest we stop this fencing match and get down to business."

Senator Harrison repressed a smile. Edwards had a pompous Colonel Blimp quality about him: a silly brush under his nose and thick-lensed spectacles that magnified his round blue eyes. But he was anything but absurd in a courtroom. Relentless in his prosecution of criminal justice. His command performance at Wheatley this Sunday morning as devil's advocate was one of life's small tragedies.

"Walter is right," the senator said. He addressed the Majorses and Ham. "Would the four of you be so kind as to retire for the present? The district attorney and I would like to confer with Sheriff Adams privately for a few minutes."

"Of course," said Callie. "Carl, Bruce, Ham, we'll leave these gentlemen alone."

When they had left, closing the door behind them, Sheriff Adams felt more at ease. And adamant.

"Don't think I don't know what's going on here," he said. "They think they own this county, the high and mighty Majorses and Knights."

"They do." Senator Harrison removed three cigars from an inside pocket of his jacket and offered one each to Adams and the D.A. "Any of you gentlemen care for a drink? I know I do."

Adams said no and continued speaking, bellicose and worried. "They don't own me!"

"Don't they?" Harrison spoke with his back to them, as he stood at the server in the bay window mixing drinks. "What about the next election? You figuring on retiring after this term, Sam?"

Adams had enormous admiration for Senator Harrison. Not the fawning respect that petty bureaucrats affect toward the political princes who patronize their careers. He had believed until this moment that Harrison was an upstanding legislator and a man of unimpeachable integrity and honor. He felt wretched being witness to this scene, listening to him mouth deceits and sophisms. Hearing the clay underpinning crack and crumble.

"No, I ain't retiring, and I don't need their help to win. I've been a damned good sheriff here for six years, the people like me, and it's the people who'll reelect me. Not the Majorses and the Knights."

Harrison came back and handed him a drink he didn't want. "No, drink it, Sam, you'll need it before we're through here."

Adams accepted the drink and put it down on a table. "Far as I'm concerned, we're through right now."

"*You* may be through with everything, politics included. The people may elect you, Sam, but it's the party who puts you on the ticket. If you can't be realistic and reasonable about this affair, I tell you quite frankly, Sam, I'll do my best to have you drummed out of the party. And I'm not particular how it's done." He nodded to the district attorney.

Edwards took the cue. "We've all done things in our lifetimes that we'd just as soon keep swept under the rug. Right, Sam?"

"Oh, Christ!" The sheriff heaved his big shoulders, feeling the weight the D.A. was bringing to bear on him. Four years before, he'd gotten mixed up with a woman who had taken a lake cottage for the summer. Her husband came up on weekends, but there were occasions when business problems kept him in New York. She was a restless, lonely woman with hot blood. On the first night they met, Adams went to bed with her in her cabin. The relationship lasted most of the summer. Until the husband surprised them one Saturday night on a weekend when he was supposed to be in the city.

Adams managed to get out the back door without the other man getting a good look at him. The wife didn't fare as well. Her husband beat her so unmercifully that she had to be hospitalized. He was arrested and booked for assault and battery. At his interrogation he produced a set of keys on a ring that he claimed the unknown seducer of his wife had dropped in his hasty flight.

Walter Edwards had been present. So had Sheriff Adams. There was a tiny penknife affixed to the chain, and if you looked at it closely you could make out the initials S.A. Edwards knew that knife well. Whenever the two of them conferred on a police matter either at the D.A.'s office or at the sheriff's office, Adams invariably would clean his fingernails with the small blade. A nervous habit.

After the interrogation, the district attorney sauntered over to the police captain's desk and picked up the keys.

"Mind if I borrow these, Captain? They don't constitute relevant evidence in the case, but I'd like to see if my investigators can locate the owner. Not that we need him as a witness. The evidence is *prima facie*. Just a hunch, that's all."

The captain was grateful to have the D.A.'s office relieve him of that routine detail of the case.

The sheriff and the D.A. left police headquarters together. In the parking lot, Edwards put a hand on Adams's shoulder. Without expression he said, "Sam, on second thoughts, maybe you'd be the best man to follow up on this key thing." He took the keys out of his overcoat pocket and dropped them into the sheriff's hands. Adams mumbled something unintelligible, foolish, gazing down at the keys in his open palm.

The D.A. got into his car, and before he drove away, he winked. "Be good, Sam. And hell, man! If you can't be good, just make sure you don't get caught."

What the hell! Adams wasn't surrendering his scruples, his sense of duty to a job he took so much pride in, and the self-respect it gave him without a fight.

"Walt, don't do this to me and to yourself. Senator Harrison, hear me out before you decide to go through with this whitewash. . . . It's not as if they had committed some misdemeanor. Hell, I know young Bruce was a hellion when he was in school. He got off with things any other lad would have spent time in the pokey for. All right, the Majorses rate certain privileges in this county—"

"In this state," Harrison said with emphasis.

"So, in the state. We all know there'll always be different laws for the rich and the poor. I accept that bitter truth. But murder! Three murders! In cold blood. No matter what you say, Senator, you know it as well as I do. Last night Carl Majors, his son, and Ham Knight went out after those fellers who raped the girl. They went with guns, and they used those guns. God! You ought to see the mess out in that place. Like a slaughterhouse."

"A slaughterhouse," Harrison repeated it, exploiting the imagery. "Well . . . that's what a slaughterhouse is for, killing animals. Jake Spencer, the other two, they were no better than animals. Worse."

Adams looked at this big, tanned handsome man in scorn tempered with pity. Appearances were deceiving. He looked free from the vulnerabilities of small men like himself. Quietly he asked, "I wonder what kind of list they have your name on, Senator?"

Harrison turned away and walked back to the server to refill his glass.

It was the district attorney who held the final trumps in a game that had been stacked against Adams before the sun rose that Sunday morning.

"There's another matter to be considered, Sam, that wouldn't be altered, even if you and I and the senator himself got noble and bore personal witness against the Majorses. There'd be a trial. A man avenges his daughter's dishonor—his sister's dishonor. That's the unwritten law with mountain people, river people. It has been since the beginning of time.

The Bible. *An eye for an eye.* You remember that gandy dancer back in '26, you brought him in, Sam? He cut the throat of a traveling man he caught with his fourteen-year-old daughter in the barn. Statutory rape? Like Hell! She was the whore of Clinton High. It took but ten minutes for the jury to exonerate him, right? And here you are talking about prosecuting big folks like the Majorses. I'd be laughed out of court. Carl, Bruce, and young Ham would be heroes." He passed gas. "They'd get off even if they didn't own us. I'll lay you ten to one we couldn't pick a jury in these parts that more than half didn't depend on Majorses or Knights for their livelihoods. Life. The kilns. The quarry. Working their farmlands. Or like your deputies, Sam —and me—who are defaulting on their mortgage payments in those hard times and managing to keep the roof over our heads by the grace of God . . . and of Majorses and Knights. . . . Face up to it, Sam, we bring these three to trial for murdering those shits who raped Chris Majors, we're slitting our own throats, we're wasting the taxpayer's hard-come-by money, and they'll go free in spite of it."

Sheriff Adams picked up the drink the senator had poured him. He peered dismally into the glass.

Ben Saxon's philosophy: *"I say good riddance!"*

Senator Harrison was standing over him, solid as the mountain peak visible through the front window across the river. Knight slate.

"What say you, Sam?" No longer intimidating. Wayne Harrison knew the game was won.

He bowed his head in defeat. "The Majorses have been getting away with murder in this county for years, so why should I concern myself about a few more bodies. Sheriff Thomas, he held this job for twenty years before I beat him out of it. The office was like home to him. He'd find the damnedest excuses to come in, sit down, put his feet up on the desk, and talk. Later, when he took to drink, he'd talk too much. There was this woman—"

"Sam!" Walter Edwards warned him. "That's enough!"

The sheriff heaved his meaty shoulders. "All right, Walt . . . I say good riddance." He tipped the glass up and drank down the scalding bourbon.

Outside in the hall, Callie had one ear to the closed door. With the sheriff's surrender, the meeting was at an end. She straightened up, smoothed down her skirt, and walked back quickly to the study where Carl and Bruce were pacing in suspense, like prisoners awaiting the verdict of a jury.

On Monday morning the Clinton *Herald* ran the headline and page-one story:

LOCAL RUM RUNNER SLAIN IN ALL SAINTS' EVE MASSACRE

On Saturday night Jake Spencer, long suspected by the police as a trafficker in illegal whiskey imported from Canada, and two companions, Raymond Shuffelmeir and Leon Ballard, were found dead in a cabin on the Lake Shore Road. The grisly murders, reminiscent of the bloody Saint Valentine's Day Massacre in Chicago last year, are thought to have been committed by professional killers brought in from Chicago or New York by a rival bootleg ring. . . .

Callie put down the paper. Her expression was triumphant. *"All's well that ends well,"* she said.

Carl was sprawled out on the couch, glass in hand, the bourbon decanter standing on the floor within easy reach. Drunk before noon, as had been his custom for months.

"What a hell of a way to put it. Three men dead, my daughter half out of her mind upstairs from the horror she's been through." He paused to slurp from the glass. "And you can say "All's well that ends well.' My God!"

"You might be sitting in the electric chair, you and Bruce," she said. "And without your precious bourbon. Honestly, Carl, sometimes I imagine that glass is an extension of your arm."

"It might be more merciful than sitting here thinking about what we did to those three boys. I'm afraid to shut my eyes at night because I can see them as clearly as if I was standing in that room. Bloody. Mutilated." He shuddered and drank deeply. "Their ghosts will haunt me till my dying day."

"Ghosts . . ." She was amused. "An invention of your puritanical Protestant conscience. . . . You won't drive them off with bourbon, Carl. Spirits nourish spirits. How poetic are homonyms. Your specters gain substance from intoxication."

Carl lifted his eyes to the ceiling. "How long has that doctor been up there with her?"

"Twenty, thirty minutes, no more."

"It seems like eternity."

It had been decided on Sunday, after the convocation with the law had been joined and won, that Chris should not be attended by a local doctor. Before Sheriff Adams departed he had warned them, "Best to keep that girl under wraps. If it should get out what's happened to her, folks just might put two and two together."

Chris was not in need of urgent medical attention. Her physical infirmities were superficial, aches and bruises, a cut lip. Callie and Cook and Jane Hathaway had bathed and salved her wounds and put her to bed. She had rested quietly all day Sunday. Too quietly, like a vegetable, lying flat on her back, with her fair hair spread out on the pillow, her wide blank eyes fixed on space. Nothingness. Serene as a doll. She could not or would not speak except to reply to simple questions that could be answered by a yes or no.

Senator Harrison suggested a consultation with his personal physician in Albany. They could depend on his discretion. He promised to phone Dr. Paul Frantz that night when he returned to the capitol.

Dr. Frantz arrived at Wheatley at eleven o'clock on Monday morning. A dignified old-fashioned gentleman who wore an opera cape and high silk hat. A small, pixyish man with cotton-ball sidewhiskers and pince-nez glasses on a gold chain. His faint accent was Viennese.

He spent an hour with his patient, then came downstairs to consult with Carl and Callie in the living room. Bruce had gone to Troy to see what could be salvaged out of the wreckage of the Majors Brick Company precipitated by the crash.

The doctor had cool regard for Carl and his glass and bottle. He addressed himself to Callie.

"Madam, I have made a thorough examination of your sister-in-law. Her heart and lungs are sound. Her temperature is normal. Her reflexes . . ." His forehead creased and he rubbed his chin. "Her responses are a cause of concern to me. Naturally, we must consider how Miss Majors has suffered, mentally as well as physically. Her present state may be a delayed reaction to the traumatic experience she underwent.

We will watch her very carefully in the days ahead. My hope is that the wounds up here will heal in time"—he tapped the side of his head—"and that she will enjoy a full recovery."

"And if she remains in her present state?" Callie wanted to know. "This remote inner world she's shut herself away in, what then?"

"There is a small, but excellent sanitarium up in Saranac. . . ." He noted their expressions and held up a hand. "No, not for consumptives. A friend of mine is the director. Dr. Ignace Lerner, one of the most eminent psychologists in this country, in the world."

"You think my daughter is insane?" Carl asked, near tears.

"Insane is a layman's word, Mr. Majors. The spectrum of mental disorder is as wide and varied as the nature of physical disease. Two patients came to see me one week with what appeared to be an identical complaint. A wart on the neck where the starched collar rubbed. One I removed by simple surgery in the office. The other man had to be operated on for cancer. I hold no hope for him." He sighed and rubbed his hands together. "Let us pray that Miss Majors has the 'wart,' *nicht wahr?*"

"Germans are honest men, so the Bard said, Doctor. My father-in-law and I are both very grateful to you for coming all this distance."

He pulled on his gloves. "When Senator Harrison explained the circumstances to me, I had no choice."

"So few of us do," said Carl. He picked up the bottle. "Can I offer you a drink, Doctor?"

"No, thank you, sir," he answered with Teutonic stiffness. "I enjoy my daily *schnapps,* but not so early in the day. Good day, sir."

Callie escorted him to the door. "When will you see her again, Doctor?"

"The end of the week, perhaps next Saturday. There is nothing I can do for her that you can't do, medically speaking. I will check her reflexes, and, hopefully, her responses will be more positive than they were today. If you observe a significant change in her attitude, phone me at once." He took a card out of his wallet and handed it to her. His eyes narrowed behind the rimless lenses. "What you said in the other room, about Germans being honest men?"

"Shakespeare . . . *The Merry Wives of Windsor.*"

He tilted his head to one side, examining her with curiosity. "Yes . . . I see. . . . Well . . . I think maybe I am not being so honest with you before. . . . The truth is, madam, I am deeply concerned about Miss Majors. More so than I intimated to you and her father. I have a strong background of clinical psychology myself. In the old country, I was a student of Sigmund Freud's at the University of Vienna. I'm not qualified to practice psychiatry, but—"

"What is your unofficial diagnosis of my sister-in-law's condition, Doctor Frantz?"

He lowered his head and pursed his lips. "I fear this withdrawal, as you call it, this retreat from reality, may be progressive. Are you familiar with the term 'catatonia'?"

"Yes, I looked it up in one of the medical books in the library this morning. Catatonia—the 'living death.' " Tickled by his bemused expression, she quipped, "You could say I, too, studied under Freud, Doctor."

He chuckled and shook his head. "You are a-a"—lost for words—"shall we say a 'highly unusual woman,' Mrs. Majors. I think I can see now why the senator holds you in such high esteem."

There was a riddle in her smile. "Can you now, Doctor? . . . Oh, Doctor, one more thing: do you think there's any chance she may become pregnant? Three men, I hate to imagine how many times."

Dr. Frantz took her hand and patted it with gravity. "My dear madam, that is a matter to be determined between her and God."

Callie chewed on her underlip as she closed the door behind him.

"Between her and God," she said to herself. "Oh, no, Doctor, there are some concerns in this brief life far too important to trust to God."

That night she spiked Chris's bedtime hot milk with a potion Wayne Harrison had given her during their affair at Lake George to ensure it would not end with Callie pregnant. An oversight in his relations with Evelyn Hardy that had cost him dearly.

On Tuesday Chris was strong enough to get out of bed and sit in a chair on the open deck above the front porch in the sunshine, swathed in blankets. The wind off the river was chill in November. The swelling on one side of her face was subsiding and the discoloration was fading. But there was no improvement in either her mental or emotional condition visible to Callie. On the encouraging side, there was no evidence of the progressive catatonia of which Dr. Frantz was apprehensive. She was able to feed herself and attend to her bath and toilet needs, and she continued to respond to uncomplicated queries:

"Are you hungry, Chris?"

"No."

"Are you tired?"

"No."

"Are you afraid, Chris?"

Tight-mouthed. The vapidness worsening.

"Chris, Ham is here. Do you want to see him?"

It was the first time since the sheriff and his deputies had brought her home on Sunday morning that Chris gave any sign that she wanted to break out of this prison of "self" in which she was confined. Her head came up. Her lips moved.

"She's trying to speak," Jane Hathaway whispered to Callie. "What is it she's trying to say? I can't make it out."

Callie studied the girl's mouth, imitating her, forming the sounds with her own lips. "Ha . . . Har . . . Harm . . . No, that's not it." Her mind lit up. "Ham! She's trying to say 'Ham'! Come on, Chris, you can do it! Say it! Ham!"

Chris nodded her head. Swallowed twice and got it out: "Ham . . . Ham . . . Ham."

Callie laughed and put an arm around her shoulders. "Good girl. Jane, tell Mr. Knight he can come upstairs. Miss Majors will see him now."

Downstairs in the sitting room, Ham was alone with Nate. This six-year-old boy, living proof of his crime. With each passing year the resemblance he bore to Ham became more marked and Ham's guilt became more oppressive. Guilt compounded by his involvement in the three killings up at the lake. Guilt piled upon guilt.

He stood convicted and the Hudson Valley was his prison. His only hope of freedom was to leave Knightsville, put half the distance around the world between him and this land where everything and everyone was a macabre reminder like the black bands mourners wear around their arms.

"Ham, what *really* happened to Chrissie?" Nate kept repeating like a broken record.

"She got hurt, she fell, I think. I wasn't there." Ham walked to a window and opened it wide, took deep breaths. Being alone with the boy always brought on a choking sensation.

"But you took her to the dance, Ham. I heard Mama and Papa talking. They said some fellows hurt her."

Ham wiped a sleeve across his face. "That's right. I forgot. Chris was horsing around with these fellows, you know how we do sometimes on the beach, you, me, and Chris. She fell and hurt herself."

The boy came over to stand beside him, tugged at his arm. "She acts funny, Chris does. Like she's asleep, only her eyes are open. I speak to her and she acts as if she doesn't hear me."

Ham shriveled up inside. *Dear God!* He stood condemned for this too! She had flirted with Jake Spencer to make him jealous, Callie had said so. *Callie! That witch!* But no, he couldn't shirk the blame.

Five years Chris had loved him selflessly. His fault was not that he could not return her love like a a man. His crime was in not telling her the truth. He had turned away from Chris once too often.

He dropped a hand on Nate's shoulder. "Chris will be all right, you'll see. Don't worry, Nate."

With a shy clumsiness, much like his own, the boy rubbed against him, a puppy craving for affection. "I'm glad you're my brother, Ham. I love you."

Ham's throat constricted; it was a while before he could speak. He kept patting Nate's shoulder until it passed. "I'm glad too," he said hoarsely.

Jane Hathaway stood in the doorway watching them in silence, enjoying the poignant scene. Jane received strange vibrations from Ham and the boy whenever they were in a room together. Strong currents of emotion she could not fathom.

Ham sensed her presence and looked. She nodded self-consciously.

"Good morning, Mr. Knight. Mrs. Majors says you can see Miss Chris now if you like."

"Thank you, ma'am. I'll be right along." He faced the boy, bending low so that their faces were level, and put both hands on his shoulders.

"Nathaniel . . . That was your grandfather's name too, you know. He would have loved you so."

"My grandfather?" Nate thought it was very funny. "My father's name was Nathaniel. You should know that, Ham, he was your father too. Grandfather's name was Cyrus. Oh, wait until I tell Callie and Chris. I'll bet that will make her sourpuss go away, old Chris. She'll have to laugh."

Ham was stunned. He had never made a slip like it before. A sure sign. Time for him to escape. He glanced at the doorway, fearful that the governess had overheard, but Jane Hathaway was gone.

He spoke to Nate. "Don't tell anyone what I said, please, Nate? They all think I'm silly enough as it is. Imagine a grown man forgetting his own father's name!" His laughter was dry and bogus.

Nate laughed along. "All right, Ham, I promise I won't tell on you."

"Good boy." He ruffled the boy's hair. Straightened up. "Now I have to go up and see how Chris is."

"Play with me later, Ham?"

"I'm sorry, Nate," he said with real sadness. "But I don't have time. You see, I have a train to catch at Knightsville station at three this afternoon."

The boy was curious. "Where are you going?"

"On a business trip. Like your father, he's always going off on trips, isn't he?"

"Sure." The boy grinned. "I wish I could come with you."

"So do I, Nate. So do I. Good-bye, son, good-bye."

He walked out of the room and up the curved stairs. Callie met him the hall outside Chris's room.

"How is she?" he asked.

"I think a little better. . . . She spoke your name."

"You make her sound like a child learning to talk."

"That's what she's like. Up until now it's been just two words. Yes. And no."

Ham was worried. "I thought the shock would have worn off by now."

"The doctor thinks it goes deeper than that. A wound to her mind that won't heal overnight."

"That's terrible." He braced one hand against the wall.

"It's all my fault, but that can't be helped now. I only wish there was some way to make it up to her."

"You were born to be nailed to a cross, Ham," she said with malice. She crossed her arms and smirked. "Since you're so set on making it up to Chris, why don't you marry her?"

He wanted to smash her face. He wanted to fasten his hands around Callie's throat and choke the life out of her. He might have too, if Jane Hathaway had not interrupted. She came out of Chris's room.

"She's waiting for you, Mr. Knight."

Although he had been prepared for the encounter by both Nate and Callie, Chris was worse than he had imagined. A pretty, vacuous puppet.

She seemed pleased to see him.

"It's the first time she's smiled since it happened," Callie said, behind him.

He walked to Chris and took her hand. "Are you feeling better?"

"Ham." The voice flat and mechanical. She clutched his hand in both of her hands.

"How are you feeling, Chris?" He bent to look into her face.

"Ham."

Her strangeness made him uncomfortable. "Chris . . . I'm sorry about what happened at the dance."

"Ham-m-m-m-" An animal howl of bottomless despair that raised his hackles. Her head fell forward and she wept. The tears fell like rain on his hand. Suddenly she let go of his hand and pushed him away so hard he almost tripped. She howled, a rising crescendo of hysteria. Beat her fist on the arms of the chair.

"*Ham!*" It was an indictment.

He whirled and ran into Callie. He shied off, struck a small table with the side of his knee, and sent it toppling over. A glass, a pitcher of water, medicine bottles crashed to the floor.

Demoralized, he fled the room, passing the startled governess who came running up the hall from the stairs.

"What is it?" she asked excitedly. "What's happening to Miss Majors?"

Callie, pursuing Ham, called to her, "See if you can calm her down, Jane. Give her one of the red pills. Hurry!"

She caught up to Ham outside the house at the bottom of

the front steps before he could get into his pickup truck.

"Wait, Ham. You mustn't blame yourself for the way she carried on. I can't believe it. She was so eager to see you. I can see how upset you are. I'm sorry. Honestly, I am."

"It doesn't matter." He leaned on the fender of the truck with both hands. "I shouldn't have come here in the first place, but I thought—" He dismissed whatever thought he'd had with a wrench of his head. "The thing is, I came to say good-bye. She won't have to see me again. None of you will."

Callie was dumbfounded. "Good-bye? What are you talking about?"

"I'm leaving Knightsville."

"Don't be ridiculous! You can't leave Knightsville."

"Who's going to stop me?" He backed off, a beast at bay, as she stalked him around the truck.

"Your roots are planted too deeply in this place, Ham. Knightsville. It's as much a part of your flesh and blood as that boy in there." She thrust an arm toward the house.

"Stop it! You want him to hear?"

"Does the idea of Nate knowing terrify you so much?"

He got into the truck and slammed the door.

"You coward!"

He gave the engine too much throttle in his agitation and flooded the carburetor. He slumped over the wheel, a captive audience to her tirade.

"Everything you own is in Knightsville, your share of your father's estate. What about the house, the farm, the quarry?"

He laughed in scorn. "It'll be my parting gift to you and Nate. Now it's all yours. That's what you've been plotting for since the day you met my father, isn't it?"

"You fool!" She slammed the flat of one hand against the door. "We could have had so much together. The three of us."

"No, the three you'd have is Carl and Bruce and me," he taunted. "That's what you really mean, Callie. You've got this mania for owning things and people. It's too late for Carl and Bruce, they're dead men. Me? I'm still on my feet, like them consumptives up at the Saranac, sick to death but alive and walking. And I'm walking!" He tried the ignition again, the motor turned over three times, caught, and held.

"Where are you going?" she yelled as he raced the engine to drown her out. "I might have to reach you by telephone or telegraph. You're third heir to the Knight estate. Your signature's required on certain documents, you know that."

"I told you, it's all yours." And spitefully: "Don't thank me, Callie. From what I hear on the radio and read in the papers, it ain't worth anything so much any more. I mailed a letter to the lawyers, turning my share over to you and Nate. Signed by me and notarized, so it's proper and legal. Goodbye, Callie."

"No, Ham! Wait!"

The truck slid away from her outstretched hands and she fell on her knees in the dust.

"You poor fool!" she shouted after him.

She picked herself up, brushed her hands, and went back into the house. Nate came down the hall from the kitchen with a slab of hot pie in his hands.

"Has Ham left yet?" he asked.

"Yes, he was in a hurry. Did he say anything to you about going away?"

"Yes. Ham said he had to go off on a business trip the way Papa does. When will he be back?"

"A business trip . . ." She mulled on it. "A business trip, that's where he's off to, of course." She put an arm around his shoulders. "I don't know when Ham will be back, my heart. He may be gone some time. Now, while he's away, you and I must see to it that the Knight house and lands are kept trim and tidy for him."

"Oh boy! That'll be swell, Mama. I'll show Ham I can do a man's work same as he can. Then maybe he'll let me come to live with him and help him run the farm."

She pulled him tighter to her, holding his face on her breast to hide her brooding expression. "You want to leave me, Nate? Don't you love me anymore?"

He laughed and gave her a bear hug. "I love you more than anything, Mama. I meant the three of us would live together, you, me, and Ham."

Her face brightened. "Well, there's plenty of time to think about it, son."

Something amused Nate. "Son. . . . that's what Ham called me before. . . . Son . . . I wonder why?"

"I don't see anything funny about it, Nate. Mr. Perkins calls you 'son' all the time," she said serenely.

"Oh, yeah. . . . It just sounds funny 'cause Ham is young."

On her way upstairs to see how Chris was, Callie mused,

"Ham will come back. His heart and soul are here."

When Callie entered the room, Chris was as stoical as she had been before Ham's untimely visit. Staring at some tranquil scene with her mind's eye. Blind to the real world around her. Mouth lifted at the corners, the hint of a secret smile.

"She's fine now," Jane Hathaway assured her. "I didn't even have to give her the red pill. She came around as soon as he was gone. Poor Mr. Knight, he meant well. I wonder why she reacted to him that way?"

"Oh, it was an odd quirk. I'm sure it'll pass. You can go now, Jane, and thank you for your help. Nate is waiting for his grammar lesson."

For the past few years there had been no real need for Jane Hathaway's services as nurse and governess to Nathaniel. He was a strong, big lad, with a streak of independence and determination inherited from his mother. She had been kept on at Wheatley because of Callie's disinclination to enroll him in the public school. Miss Hathaway had a state certificate to teach the lower forms.

Carl and Bruce were against it and so was Ham himself.

"He should be in school with other children his age," Bruce argued. "It's unhealthy for a boy to spend all his time with grown-ups, and when you consider the example we at Wheatley set, it's more the folly."

She sniffed. "You'd have my son take backwood clods such as Jake Spencer and his ilk for models?"

"Why must you cite extremes? There's more decent people in these parts than bad apples like Jake Spencer. I grew up here, so did Ham."

"Oh, yes, you two are noble examples indeed."

"I'll overlook the sarcasm."

"Bruce, you know what I mean. Anyway, the Brewster children come down to Wheatley in the summer. So do the Atwoods. And Cook's nephew, he spent a week here last June."

"It's not the same, Mama," Nate declared. "All the kids around here make fun of me for not going to school. I want to go Clinton on the school bus like everyone else does."

"We'll see . . . maybe next term." She picked up her knitting, indicating that the discussion was over.

"Promise me, Mama." Nate stood before her, arms folded across his chest, feet spread. A pose copied from Ham.

She flushed in anger. "No, I won't make any promises. Do

you know a school bus skidded off the highway last winter and two boys were crippled? Now, would you like that to happen to you, son?"

"Oh, Mama!"

Carl looked up from his newspaper. "Yes, Nate, and I read an airplane crashed into a house in Texas while the family was eating supper and killed them all. Perhaps we should eat supper in the cellar as a precaution, eh, Callie?"

"I'm going to school next term, and that's settled!" Nate's temper flared. He stamped his foot and stalked out of the room, swinging balled fists, jaw thrust out resolutely.

"Nate! You march back here right away, young man!" she called sharply.

He paid no heed. Callie started to rise, then sighed and slumped down again. "He's headstrong, that's all," she told herself, not Carl or Bruce. "It's the age."

Carl and Bruce looked at each other in amazement. Little Nathaniel had defied her and come away unscathed. A small miracle. And an omen.

After Jane Hathaway left to look for Nate, Callie dropped on her knees before Chris in her chair. She took the girl's limp, cold hands, looked into her blank eyes.

"Chris, I'm sorry about Ham. I can't understand why seeing him upset you so." She detected a nuance of expression, a tautness around the mouth and nostrils. "Ham's gone, but don't you worry, he'll be back. His heart and soul are imprisoned in this land. Dear, it will be all right again between you two, you'll see." She patted the marble hands and stood up. "Dear Chris, you must believe me, I never intended anything like this to happen. I never wanted any harm to come to you, Chris."

Chris looked up and fleetingly the woman inside the shell appeared to Callie, like a face glimpsed behind a curtain moved by a gust of wind.

"*You liar!*" She spat it out. The final words she would ever speak to Callie.

That night at the supper table, Carl announced, "I heard on the radio that Mr. Hoover said, anyone who lacks confidence in the basic strength of the American economy is a fool."

"It's Mr. Hoover who's the fool," Callie said. "I think from now on we'll keep the revenues from the bridge in the den safe."

Bruce put down his fork and stared at her. "Are you getting soft in the head, Callie? Keep that kind of money here, in the house? In times like these when we need every penny of interest we can get on our cash?"

"Bank interest? You and Mr. Hoover, you're both soft in the head. We can't count on income from the kilns, the quarry, or the farms, not in the near future anyway. It will take every penny we can scrape together to maintain the Knight and Majors property and holdings. Handly phoned this morning. They want 25 percent higher margin on those shares we bought last February."

"We can't manage it. It would be throwing good money after bad. We'll have to sell and take the loss."

"Out of the question," she said with an air of finality that tolerated no dissenting opinions. "I told him he'd have our check before Friday. I also ordered him to buy an additional five hundred shares. It's at rock bottom. It has to go up, that's certain."

"What!" It was an exclamation, not a question. "This time you've gone too far. You-you-you-" he spluttered helplessly.

Old Carl was laughing softly behind his napkin. "Give her credit, Bruce. The girl has guts. Right alongside old J. D. Rockefeller. They say he's buying up shares from his bankrupt friends like there was no tomorrow. The old thief."

"That's a game only the very, very rich can sit in." Bruce moped. "All right, what's done is done, but this business about keeping money in the safe. It's pure nonsense."

"Is it?" she asked. "Why do you think the brokers are calling for more margin? Because the banks are recalling the loans they made to the brokers. All the extravagant speculation that's been going on so many years. Men, no, boys, with the ink still damp on their business school diplomas, only had to have a letterhead printed up and any bank would loan them money. Now those loans are being called in. Hah! They're locking the stable after the horse has been stolen. That money is gone. Not just bank money. They were loaning depositors' savings. No, thank you, from now on, our money stays where we know it's safe."

Bruce appealed to his father. "The woman's crazy."

"Like a fox, she's crazy," Carl said. "She's got a point about the banks. The banks, the brokers, the investors, they're like the tigers in the story *Little Black Sambo.* I'll vote with Callie."

In May of 1930 President Hoover announced that "we have now passed the crisis . . . the worst is over."

Callie derided the statement. "Governor Roosevelt says the worst is yet to come."

Bruce railed: "That hypocrite! He wants the federal government to put men to work on public work projects, and to hand out free money to the unemployed. He calls it unemployment relief, that's just a fancy term for socialism."

"You'd rather have it Mr. Mellon's way, our distinguished Secretary of the Treasury," Callie chided. "Liquidate! Liquidate! Liquidate everything. He thinks it would be a healthy thing—*healthy,* mind you—if the economy went down to rock bottom. Mellon says, 'People will work harder, live a more moral life. Values will be readjusted . . .' The fatuous ass."

The nation's economy had spiraled up year after year during the Roaring Twenties, on "an irreversible course," so the optimists prophesied. And then in three short years it plummeted. "An irreversible course," said the pessimists. Sage seers all.

In the middle of 1932, there were 12 million Americans unemployed, 25 percent of the total working population of the United States.

In Knightsville, as in many small towns along the Hudson River and along other rivers throughout the land, there was virtually 100 percent unemployment.

The quarry was closed. The Majors brick kilns were closed. The New York Central Railroad cut road gangs to the bare bones. It was common to see a full train of cars roll through Knightsville coming from or going to New York with a handful of passengers. Once the Albany Special pulled into Grand Central Station empty. Not a single fare.

Callie was shocked to see one of her tenants on a line in front of one of the two Salvation Army soup kitchens that had been opened in Clinton as the Great Depression worsened. When she questioned him, the man said he walked six miles along the riverbank to Clinton every day with his two sons to get food for the family, two adults and four children.

On almost every street corner there were men and women selling apples donated by a Western apple growers association. Five sales a day purchased twenty-five cents' worth of food, sufficient to provide a starvation diet for a family of three.

She ordered Sam Perkins, the handyman, to drive her to the nearest market, where she ordered the manager to fill the big touring car with milk, eggs, bread, meat, and fresh vegetables. On the trip back to Knightsville, she had to sit in front with Sam, the back was overloaded.

The evidence of depression was in melancholy evidence along the highway and the length of Knight's Road. Shacks and homes boarded up, abandoned. Deserted barns, parts of barns really, dismantled by desperate neighbors, who were still clinging to a precarious existence in the river valley, for firewood. Diehards who would not give up the dignity and privacy of a family unit to scavenge with the less sensitive mobs, men, women, and children, who were migrating to shantytowns on the outskirts of big cities where the dole was more liberal and reliable and there was an outside chance of getting work. Communal living in squalor, all pride killed.

Some of the factories and mills that had closed down for lack of business or because the banks had called in their loans and foreclosed their mortgages were reopening in shabby guises. Paper mills or garment lofts financed by unscrupulous profiteers. They offered to pay one dollar per day to males for a ten-hour day, half that amount to girls and women. Their hiring shacks were cliqued up long before the sun rose. It was better to be exploited than to be dead of starvation.

That afternoon Callie was patron to twenty families who were tenants on Knight Land.

For most it was the first meat, eggs, bread, and milk they had enjoyed in the same day for over a year. When the supplies had been dispensed, she ordered Sam to drive her to the Campball farm. Callie had one of her rare humanitarian impulses. There were four times as many to be fed and clothed in Knightsville and its environs. Many of the children she had seen in the dreary poverty-stricken hovels were barefooted. Others wore sneakers that didn't match, or bedroom slippers; threadbare shirts and trousers, hand-me-down dresses that were too large or too small.

Susan Campball's blue eyes opened wide, as wide as eyes deepset in fat rolls could open, when she saw Callie Majors on her front porch. She dried her hands, red and raw from lye soap, on the soiled apron that spanned her enormous belly and waddled to the door.

The Campballs were part of a fortunate minority of the river people who were eating almost as well as they had before the depression. Money was tight for Walt, as it was for everyone, the butcher, the baker, the banker, the broker, but they managed to live off the produce of their small farm and feed a dozen kin, less fortunate, with the surplus stores.

His stewardship of the Knight enterprises over the last two years had become little more than a title. The quarry was closed down. The farmlands lay fallow after a bad year, when 70 percent of the crops had failed.

The Clinton National Bank had advised Callie to sell all of the Knight acreage in the valley. They had an interested buyer, an anonymous speculator, one of the River Rich. She spurned the offer and any other future offers.

"Cyrus Knight would rise out of his grave and smite me down for such treachery. Sell Knight land? Land irrigated by Knight sweat, blood, and tears? Never!"

Bruce tried to reason with her. "Our financial position is critical. Holding on to all the stock costs us a fortune. There's the upkeep on Wheatley and the Knight place. Taxes. Maintenance costs on the kilns and the quarry while they're shut down. If that damned farmland lies fallow another year, we'll lose it to the bank anyway."

Callie would not be swayed. "Never. It's a trust I can't betray. Knight land, and it'll stay Knight land, I'll see to that!"

She kept the land and she kept Walt Campball on to oversee it. More the warder of a graveyard, he reflected, than a manager. He considered himself lucky to have employment, even at half-pay.

"Mrs. Majors, what a nice surprise to see you," Susan Campball greeted her. "Do come in."

Susan was suddenly conscious of her dirty apron. "Oh dear, excuse my appearance, Mrs. Majors. I've been making soap, it's such a messy job." Flustered, she whipped off the apron and stuffed it down inside the umbrella stand in a corner of the hall. "Come into the parlor and sit down. I'll make us a nice cup of tea."

She reminded Callie of the waltzing elephant she had seen long ago when the orphanage sisters had taken them to a traveling circus. Bustling around the room with the ponderous grace allotted to stout persons, opening the blinds, fluffing the pillows on the couch, dipping one knee ludicrously as she made a hand flourish at the room's company chair. "Sit down, ma'am."

Mrs. Majors.

Ma'am.

Everywhere Callie had visited this day, she had been received with humility. Servility. Even by Susan Campball.

She recalled the first time she had met the Campballs, not long after she had moved into the Knight house. The poisonous glint in the blue pig eyes.

"So you're Callie Hill?" she'd said. Her look had said, *"I know what you're up to, you brazen little slut!"*

The poverty of the times was evident in every aspect of daily existence. The bread lines. The apple vendors. The decaying buildings. The barefooted children. And above all else, it was evident in the poverty of human spirit.

Fawning over her as if she was Lady Bountiful: she held them in contempt for it. Yet it was the solemn obligation of a patron to be patronizing. *Noblesse oblige.* They were her people. Her children.

She smiled warmly at the obese peasant woman. "Thank you very much, Susan, but I don't have time for tea. Is Walt home? I have a project for him."

Walt was summoned from the barn. He came in a hurry, arriving out of breath and red-faced from the exertion. Smoothing back his thinning hair with his hands and profuse with apologies. The Scottish burr in his voice thicker than she remembered it in more prosperous days when he had sat down at the dining-room table at Wheatley with them to review the balance sheets, pipe in hand, a snifter of brandy at his elbow. Assured and self-respecting, an important man in an important position. A man with the means to indulge in creature comforts plucked out of that magic treasure trove, the Sears, Roebuck Catalog.

A trusted and prized employee and friend. Today he lived by the grace of their philanthropy.

Callie related how she had given food to the twenty families in Knightsville that day. "I never realized before that conditions were this bad, Walt. Driving along Knight's Road and through town, it looks like half the folks have moved away. Sam says they've gone where food and work are easier to come by. I won't have that, Walt, our people starved out of their homes and property. Here's what I want you to do. Survey all the homes in Knightsville. Note how many there are in each family. What income, if any, they have. How badly they're deprived of clothing, household staples, the bare necessities. Then you and I'll sit down a day a week and make a list. You'll drive to Clinton in the truck and make the purchases. Charged to me. To be doled out, say, every Tuesday morning. The head of each house will receive his family's share at the big Knight barn. What do you think of my idea, Walt?"

"It's mighty generous of you, Mrs. Majors." He dropped his eyes. "I know things have been bad for you people at Wheatley too."

"We'll manage, Walt, as long as we have the bridge."

"Yes . . . I hope so. . . . But are you sure this give-away plan of yours won't be too much of a load for you?"

"We do what must be done, Walt. It's not a matter of *can* we do it? It *will* be done." She stood up and pulled on her gloves. "I have to rush off now. My son is bringing some school friends home for supper."

"Young Nate, oh, he's a handsome boy!" Sue gushed. "I saw him just last week. He was helping Walt clear out the south meadow and Walt brought him back to lunch. He's the spitting image of his brother, Ham." She chuckled. "Lucy said she was going to wait and marry him when he grew up. Isn't that something?"

"Very amusing." Callie was anything but amused. Bruce had told her that Lucy Campball was walking the streets of Clinton. Increasing numbers of girls and women were resorting to the "oldest profession" because the army of unemployed men was now competing with them for menial jobs that heretofore no self-respecting male would have accepted.

"I've been meaning to speak to you about Nate, Walt. Don't hesitate to discourage him from coming over here so much. I'm sure he must get in the way."

"Nate, in the way?" Walt was fond of the boy, he always had been. "That lad's a born farmer. He's big and strong for his age. The truth is, I have to step to keep up with him."

"I'm glad you feel that way, Walt, but he does spend too much time on this side of the river. It's beginning to interfere with his schoolwork."

"You're right, that won't do." He was quick to please her wish. "You tell him I've decided to let the north meadow go for a while, so I won't be needing him this week. Good grades come before cutting hay."

"Thank you, Walt. Don't forget, as soon as you make up that list, you come to Wheatley and we'll sit down."

There was a wistful quality in his voice. "Sit down, like old times, won't it be, ma'am? Saturday was our day to go over the books."

She patted his arm. "There's an inch of dust on those books, Walt, but don't look so sad. This slump won't last forever." With deliberate casualness: "By the way, have you heard from Ham lately?"

"Well . . . there was that one letter I told you about when he joined the merchant marine. From time to time, we get a postcard from one of them far-off foreign places. I save the stamps for my nephew." He was flushed and uncomfortable-looking, shifting his weight from one foot to the other, rubbing his chin nervously. "You know, Mrs. Majors, I would have given them to Nate except—" It was painful for him to say.

"I know, Walt," she said curtly. "Except you don't want Nate to know that Ham writes to you and never sends as much as a postcard to his own family. Thank you, Walt, I'll be on my way."

Susan and Walt came to the door with her. Impulsively the old woman took one of Callie's delicate gloved hands in both of her red swollen hands with sausage fingers, brought it to her mouth, kissed it.

"You're a very good woman, Callie Majors," she said with strong emotion. "Thinking of Knightsville's poor and hungry. Old Cyrus Knight, he would have been right proud of you."

"Well . . . I—I—" It took Callie aback. "Thank you very much, Susan, they're generous words. I'd like to think that Cyrus Knight would approve of me."

I've been called a lot of things in life, but I never expected to hear anyone call me that: A Good Woman!

When she arrived back at Wheatley, Jane Hathaway admitted her. "You were gone so long, madam, I was beginning to worry."

"Yes, it's been a tiring day for me, Jane. But very rewarding." She looked into the empty parlor. "Where is everyone? At this hour my father-in-law never ventures more than ten feet from the liquor cabinet."

Miss Hathaway suppressed a smile. "Mr. Majors senior went to bed right after lunch and is still upstairs."

"My husband?"

"With Miss Chris, madam. He spends so much time with her now that he's—" She checked herself.

"Now that he's not working. That's all right, Miss Hathaway. Mr. Majors has enlisted in America's growing army of unemployed. Too bad we're in between wars. The government could put uniforms on them and, overnight"—she snapped her fingers—"instant full employment."

Miss Hathaway's horsy face seemed to lengthen more. She'd lost two brothers in the Great War. "Oh dear, Mrs. Majors, I hope we've seen the last of war. Mr. Wilson vowed it was the war to end all wars."

Callie dismissed it as culpability. "Politicians' promises have as much worth as brokers' scrip. Besides, there will always be war, the people love it."

Miss Hathaway clapped her hands to her cheeks. "What a terrible thing to say, madam."

"It's true. Coriolanus said it all: *What would you have, you curs, That like nor peace nor war? the one affrights you, The other makes you proud.*"

"I don't know the gentleman," the nurse said stiffly. "But I don't think much of his cynicism."

Callie laughed and patted her arm. "Pay no attention to him, Miss Hathaway. He was just another hollow politician. I think I'll look in on Chris and my husband." She started up the stairs.

"He's such a devoted brother," Miss Hathaway praised Bruce. "You seldom see such closeness between a brother and sister anymore."

"A good thing, too, it is," said Callie under her breath.

She was fascinated by the curious relationship that was developing between the siblings since Chris's return from the Lerner Sanatarium at Saranac. She had spent three months there undergoing psychiatric treatment and had improved up to a point. Her speech and behavior were that of a child of six or seven. She progressed no further, and Dr. Lerner conceded he could not achieve better results at this stage of her illness.

"If we push too hard, she may lapse back into classic paranoia. She's willed herself back to a time in her life when all the world was solid and safe and her family lavished love and protection on her. We can only watch and wait and look for a chink in the rampart she's built around herself. Then we may break through."

Chris worshiped Bruce as she had worshiped him when she was a child. Her big brother. She would sit cross-legged on the floor at his feet when he read the paper or listened to the news on the radio. Gabriel Heatter: "*There's good news tonight . . .*"

But the good news invariably was a forlorn hope mealy-mouthed by President Hoover or one of his cabinet: "*We can now see the daylight at the end of the tunnel.*"

She'd sit there like a purring cat, rubbing her cheek on his knee, his hand idly stroking her sleek blond head, both of them oblivious to reality. Chris in her safe fantasy world. Bruce in his world of alcoholic dreams.

She'd yawn like a cat, head thrown back, pink tongue licking out. Then she'd ask in her simpering little girl's voice, "Brucie, will you tuck me in and read me a story?"

"Of course, dear," he'd reply. "You have Miss Hathaway call me when you're all ready for bed."

Later, when Callie retired and passed Chris's bedroom it was common to see Bruce fast asleep on top of the covers of his sister's bed with Chris snuggling into his encircling arms.

The gardener was pruning the trees close by the house the afternoon Callie returned from her mission of mercy in Knightsville. The buzz of his saw deadened her footfalls on the stairs and in the upper hall, and the sound of the knob turning as she pushed open the closed door of Chris's room.

Bruce was embracing his sister on the bed. Kissing her eyes, her cheeks, her lips. His hand was inside her robe, fondling her breasts. The two of them too lost in their rapture of each other to be aware of Callie. She withdrew and closed the door silently.

She walked down the hall to her own room. Sitting in front of the vanity mirror, she engaged in sober self-interrogation.

How do I feel about what I have just witnessed?

Detachment. Nothing more, nothing less than if I had discovered him with another woman. Indifference.

But she's his sister. Incest!

It's a gentler deed than murder.

Now that she was confronted by the fait accompli, it struck her that this consequence had been inevitable since the night of the shootings. Carl said Bruce had been a cold-blooded killer; that he had never believed his son was inhabitated by demons so savage and vengeful. When a man kills for a woman, he gives a part of himself to her as intimate and intense as a carnal embrace. That Chris was his sister mattered not. Bruce had pledged himself to her when his finger pulled the trigger on Jake Spencer. Rightfully Ham should have been the avenger, but Ham had shrunk from the momentous commitment.

Bruce never came to Callie's bed again. A divorce by unspoken mutual consent. His new alliance with his sister went deeper than sex. It pitted them against Callie and her son, Nate. An unequal contest if ever there was one. Fated by gradual erosion to second-class status within the family structure—Bruce and Chris reduced to poor relations, Carl the patriarch, a prostrate king on a chessboard.

Nate too young to fathom all the interplay of power, will, and personality. Recognizing weakness and strength with the instinct of a canny pup, quick to exploit them. His respect for his stepfather in constant decline until nothing remained in him for Bruce but disgust and pity. He had once loved Chris almost as much as he loved his mother and Ham. But when she persisted in her grotesque masquerade, a grown woman acting like a spoiled six-year-old brat, Chris became repellant to him. He avoided her. He pitied her.

On June 27, 1932, the Democratic party opened its nominating convention for the presidential elections the following November. It was the general consensus that the man who headed the ticket, whoever he might be, would beat President Herbert Hoover, renominated by the Republicans chiefly because historical precedent favored the incumbent. This incumbent wore his record for the past four years in the presidential office like a scarlet letter.

Twelve million unemployed; 25 percent of the total labor force. Five thousand banks had closed their doors. Wall Street lying as fallow as the fields in Knightsville.

The Democratic champions who aspired to put the coup de grace to Hoover and twelve years of Republican rule in the United States were legion. Among the elite, William McAdoo, former President Wilson's son-in-law; Newton Baker, Secretary of State under Wilson; Governor Harry Byrd of Virginia. The front runner, as projected by the party's inner circle, was

"Cactus Jack" Garner of Texas, the Speaker of the House of Representatives. The "dark horse" candidate was Franklin Delano Roosevelt, the governor of New York State.

"A crippled president?" was the question posed by many. "What kind of an image would the world have of a leader incapable of standing on his own two feet?"

The same Democrats had asked the same question when he threw his hat in the ring for the governor's race.

Dark horses who win Derbies must have ingenious jockeys. The same is true in politics. Such a man was Joseph P. Kennedy, Boston millionaire financier and a volatile force among the attending delegates. A man heralded for his business and political acumen and his sense of perfect timing, he had seceded from the market at its highest peak. His detractors insinuated that rats possessed like instincts in the case of sinking ships. No one could deny, though, that Joe Kennedy knew how to pick a winner, although he claimed that "making winners" was more his style. History would record his boast was closer to the truth.

It was Kennedy who jockeyed FDR to victory in the stretch. Callie inscribed important events in her Shakespeare volume the way people of her age and culture kept family registers in their Holy Bibles. The prominence of certain dates enriched by time. Periodically, she'd review them, underscoring a name, a day, a mark. The final record would show one inscription in neat, meticulous script.

Joseph P. Kennedy.

Underlined three times.

They met at a Labor Day reception in Albany, as guests of Senator and Mrs. Wayne Harrison. As soon as the Majorses arrived, Bruce excused himself and headed for the gentlemen's lounge. Callie was on to his game. He'd shut himself in one of the toilets and fortify himself for the trial that socializing had become with deep swallows from his hip flask.

Red-jacketed black waiters circulated among the guests with silver trays borne adroitly on one upturned palm. Callie took a shell glass of grape punch, set it down untouched on a table, and swept the room with her eyes. She saw Wayne Harrison coming toward her, head and shoulders above the crowd.

He took her hands. "Callie, I've been looking for you."

"We just got here."

"Where's Bruce?"

She smiled. "Need you ask?"

"I had better get to him before he gets bashed. Joe Kennedy wants to talk to him about the company."

"Who's Joe Kennedy?"

"A Boston financier."

"The company isn't for sale."

"Joe isn't interested in buying it. He's optimistic about the resurrection of this country once his man is in the White House."

"Oh, *that* Kennedy. The one who got the nomination for Governor Roosevelt. I told you that gentleman had the look of kings, do you remember, Wayne?"

"I remember."

"Do you think he'll be elected?"

Senator Harrison steered her off to one side by the elbow before he replied. "I'm certain of it. I can't afford to be overheard espousing the enemy's cause. I'd be excommunicated from the party for treason."

"Why don't you change parties then?"

"It's odd you should say that. My father-in-law has been proselytizing to me lately. He's very close to Franklin Roosevelt. If the governor gets elected in November, he's promised Senator Clement a key post, maybe in the Cabinet. The senator is trying to persuade me to recant my Republicanism and get on the Democratic bandwagon. Roosevelt is not a man to be bound by party nepotism. If the best man for a job is a Republican, he'll get the appointment over a less qualified Democrat. It seems he's impressed by my record here in Albany."

"And so he should be. Will you take a post if it's offered to you?"

"It will take some thinking."

"Don't think too long, Wayne. I have the idea that Mr. Roosevelt would take undue delay as indecisiveness. I don't believe he courts men of indecision."

"Well put, ma'am," a voice behind her said. "He's got to get off the dime and soon."

She glanced back over her shoulder and saw a thin, sinewy man of medium height with reddish sandy hair and glasses. A nondescript man was her first impression. His speech was foreign to this part of the country, all the vowels flat and elongated.

"Joe, we were just talking about you." The senator was pleased. "Callie, this is Joe Kennedy I was telling you about. Joe, meet Mrs. Callie Majors."

From all she'd heard about him, she had expected Joseph Kennedy would be a more compelling figure. His smile was toothy and infectious. She did not offer her hand, but he took it anyway in both of his, pressed it warmly.

"So you're the lady with the bridge. The infamous Mrs. Majors. I'm delighted to meet you."

Callie raised her eyebrows at the senator. "What slander has this man been spreading about me, Mr. Kennedy?"

"Oh, the senator's not my source. It's the governor whose toes you've trod on."

"You mean to say Governor Roosevelt is still stewing because I wouldn't sell the state my bridge?"

"He's got a long memory, the governor, but there's more to it than that, Mrs. Majors. It seems you've stolen a march on our next president with your own 'New Deal.' "

"My 'New Deal'? Whatever is he talking about, Wayne?"

Senator Harrison laughed. "He must mean the little welfare state you've established in Knightsville. Mr. Roosevelt's intent is to emulate your measures on a nationwide scale. Food and clothing to the needy, unemployment relief. Create new jobs on the federal payroll. Subsidize farmers."

"Funny, I think of it as philanthropy," Callie mused.

"It's a question of semantics," Kennedy declared. "If I, a private individual, donate a million dollars to the Salvation Army to distribute among the poor and the indigent, that's charity. But if the President of the United States gives away federal money, that's socialism, according to President Hoover and Mr. Mellon."

"Call it what you will, Mrs. Majors is the prettiest commissar I've ever seen. Long may her fiefdom flourish."

"I'd drink to that if someone would spike the insipid punch." Kennedy grimaced at the purple liquid in Callie's goblet. "That's another Republican corpse Mr. Roosevelt is going to lay to rest. Prohibition . . . You know, Mrs. Majors, if half of what our friend here tells me about you is true, you're the world's most remarkable woman."

"Never believe anything a politician tells you, Mr. Kennedy. They're all looking for votes."

He nodded. "Well, Senator Harrison won't get my vote until he comes to his senses and realizes that he's been playing on the wrong team."

Still holding on to Callie firmly with one hand, he put his other hand on Harrison's sleeve. "A losing team that's destined to warm the bench for a lot of years to come. That's not for you, Wayne. You've got to be out there on the playing field making body contact. That's what the game is all about. Playing your ass off." The large, strong yellow teeth were bared. "I beg your pardon, Mrs. Majors. I get carried away when I'm excited. Games have a heady effect on me. Football. Cards. Playing the market. Politics, now there's the greatest game of all, the highest stakes. *Power.*"

His hands tightened on them. Callie had the odd sensation she could feel the power pulsing through him into her, tingling all the way up her arm like a mild electrical charge.

Pow-wahrr . . . his New England twang resonating with emotion. The devotion of a high priest addressing his God.

Callie was delighted. The visible stature of this man was only the tip of the iceberg, she sensed. She answered him puckishly. "There's nothing to pardon you for, Mr. Kennedy. The metaphor is most apt. It takes strong language to make a strong point: *'Playing yawh awss awff.'* " Her mimicry of his speech was broad yet perceptive.

They all laughed, and Joe Kennedy laughed the hardest.

"Mrs. Majors, I like you," he said. His hands were on them all the while. Primal organs of communication. Their argot more beguiling than the facile deceits and dissemblings of the tongue.

"And I like you, Mr. Kennedy." Head bent slightly to one side, she fancied him with her fey, oblique smile. Her free hand dipped down, flipped up her skirt, and she made a little curtsy. Callie was as fluent as he at body language.

"Well, it's plain you two can get along without my company," Harrison joked. "Mrs. Harrison looks as if she could use some support with the ladies of the W.C.T.U. If you'll pardon me." He turned and moved off through the throng.

"You and Wayne must be very good friends," Joe Kennedy said. "I can't think of many he would have trusted with the confidence that he may jump the party line."

"Senator Harrison is an old and dear friend of my husband's family."

There was a hint of whimsy in his eyes as they took her measure boldly, up and down. "But you're a dearer friend. I somehow doubt he would confide the same in Carl or Bruce."

"I didn't know you were acquainted with my husband and father-in-law," she said, skirting the pitfall he was leading her into.

"I've had business dealings with the Majors company in the past. I'd like to expand the association in the future to everyone's profit. I want those kilns back in operation, so we get the jump on our competitors. Once the Democrats are in control of the government, this country is going to kiss the old depression good-bye. Construction, that's where the big boom is going to kick off."

"*If* Governor Roosevelt gets elected," she baited him.

"He'll get elected, you can count on it. I make it an absolute rule never to back losers."

"Is it true Roosevelt wouldn't have got the nomination without your backing?"

"It was touch and go for a while. Franklin and Cactus Jack were doing a balancing act on a very touchy seesaw. It all came down to how the California delegation would vote."

"Yes, but William Randolph Hearst pulled the strings that controlled the delegates from California, and he was publicly for Mr. Garner. How did you persuade him to change his mind?"

"He owed me a large favor. Some years back I helped a friend of Bill's out of a jam. John Hertz. A group of Wall Street bears tried to raid his Yellow Cab Company. But a lady such as you wouldn't know about the invidious machinations of the stock market, or care less."

"Now, that's a narrow view for a tycoon such as you, Mr. Kennedy," she said with an arrogance that matched his own. "They circulated rumors that the company was in trouble, sold short to drive down market value of the stock with an eye to buying it back later for a sou. You bamboozled them by placing bogus buy and sell orders for the stock from all over the country. You bluffed them out."

He let go of her hand, backed off a step and appraised her, a connoisseur taking a second look at a canvas with newly gained insight. Right hand folded over his chest, braced under his left elbow. Chin resting on the clenched knuckles of his left hand.

"That was stupid of me, Mrs. Majors. You probably know as much about the market as I do."

She opened her pocketbook, and removed a cigarette from a silver case.

"That's not true, and you know it." She closed her bag and put the cigarette in her mouth. "If it were, I would have gotten out when you did."

He lit her cigarette with his lighter. "Not necessarily. There's more than one way to skin a cat. You'll come out fine if you can dig in and hold the line until the game's over for the Republican team. The market is going to rally from this slump, take my word for it."

She found his sporting metaphors droll. "Hold the line, what game is that?"

"Football. I like it best because it's the game most like life. A rough-and-tumble contact sport. Man to man, and the weak man gets his face ground into the mud. Every boy should play football as soon as he can walk."

"You have sons, don't you, Mr. Kennedy? I can't remember how many children Senator Harrison said you had.

"Four sons. Joe Junior, he's the firstborn. Then there's John, Robert, and Teddy. They all play football, except Teddy, he's the baby."

"With a competitive nature like yours, Mr. Kennedy, I'm surprised that it's not you at the top of the Democratic ticket rather than Franklin Roosevelt."

He moved closer and put his arm around her, his hand splayed on the small of her back. "To tell you the truth, Mrs. Majors, it's being coach of the team that most appeals to me. This campaign I'm just getting my feet wet. It's a warm-up, you might say, for the 'big game' ahead."

She eyed him quizzically. "And what big game is that?"

"The day my son Joe Junior runs for president of the United States."

He was perfectly serious, she did not have the slightest doubt of it. "And the other boys, what about them?"

He flashed the yellow, toothy grin. "Why, a good coach always has a couple of good subs to back up his quarterback. We never know in life, do we, Mrs. Majors?"

"We never know," Callie reiterated. "I wish you'd call me Callie. I feel as if we're good friends. I'm like that about people. Some I've known for years, I'll never be friend to. I've only just met you, but it seems as if I've known you for years."

"I'm the same way, Callie, and you call me Joe. Listen, if you ever get to Boston, my name's in the phone book."

She smiled. "I've never been there, but suddenly it's a city I've a desire to see. . . . Joe, Wheatley is only a short drive from Albany. If you and Bruce are going to do business together, you should visit with us before you go back to Boston."

Twice Joseph Kennedy was a weekend guest at Wheatley. The first time was a week before the election day that saw Franklin Delano Roosevelt poll over 22 million popular votes and score a landslide sweep in the electoral college, 472 to 59 votes over incumbent Herbert Hoover.

His second visit was on December 13, the day after the run on the Clinton National Bank.

In the four months between Election Day and Roosevelt's inaugural on March 4, 1933, the nation was in a limbo of uncertainty, literally in a state of suspended animation.

The governors of twenty-two states ordered all the banks closed down until the new president assumed office, fearing that the psychology of the nation, impaired by the Wall Street crash and three years of subjugating depression, might collapse altogether under the trauma of "changing horses in midstream," as the Republicans had predicted throughout the campaign if Roosevelt were elected. This irresponsible and unwarranted action served the very end it had been implemented to ward off. It scuttled the last vestige of confidence the American people still had in the monetary system. All over the country, thousands converged on banks to withdraw their life's savings.

The run on the Clinton bank commenced right after noon on Friday. The Board of Directors convened for an emergency meeting at one o'clock. Bruce Majors arrived early, shaved and sober for the first time in two weeks.

It was decided to resort to a delaying tactic as a stop-gap measure. The bank would close at three o'clock and would not reopen until nine o'clock on Monday morning. A forty-hour reprieve to enlist help at the state and federal levels and from private financial institutions. They were grasping at a straw.

One week before, the Bank of the United States had closed its doors in the worst bank failure in history. Even the most optimistic director held out small hope that anything but a miracle could save the little Clinton bank.

Bruce said as much to Callie and Joe Kennedy as they sat before the blazing logs in the sitting room drinking hot toddies, which Callie had concocted with the purpose of generating a little holiday spirit and cheer. She refused to allow the mood of gloom pervading the house to spoil Nate's Christmas.

"Joe is a maker of miracles," Callie observed. "What about it, Joe, can you conjure up a miracle to save the Clinton bank?"

He lay back in his easy chair gazing at the big brass eagle dominating the room. Uncle Sam appeared more benign than usual, with the twilight softening his ferocious countenance.

"There is no such thing as a miracle," he informed her. "If you take an outrageous gamble and it succeeds, then it's a miracle. If it fails, then you're a bloody fool." He sat up and looked at Callie. "I can offer you a gamble that could save the bank. Would you care to hear it?"

"Before I hear it, let me ask you a question. If you were me, would *you* take the risk?"

Without hesitation, he told her, "Yes, I would."

"Then it's settled, I'll do it. Now, tell us what we're going to do."

He asked Bruce, "Did you draw out your personal funds before the bank closed on Friday? You and the other directors?"

Bruce was red in the face. "No . . . not exactly. We discussed that possibility, but the majority of us voted down the motion." His self-conscious manner made it plain how Bruce had voted. Not with the majority.

"All right, how much cash do you have on hand and how much more can you raise by Monday morning?"

Callie answered the question. "I've been keeping the revenue from the bridge in the house safe for two years now. I lost my trust in banks when they began to call in loans from speculators they never should have loaned money to in the first place."

He chuckled; she pleased him in almost every sense. Women of beauty, sophistication, and quick wit could be charming companions, but they were insubstantial, helpless creatures under stress. The thoroughbred syndrome. Not this Majors female. The facade she wore disguised a hardy, practical, resourceful woman of the earth.

"Good girl, well, how much?"

"Ten thousand, maybe a little extra."

"There would have been double, triple that amount if she hadn't wasted it on those ungrateful peasants across the river," Bruce complained.

She demolished him with a single cutting stroke. "We must keep the peasants alive at all costs, my dear, if only to produce the grain without which men of leisure could not enjoy their daily bottles of whiskey, my 'noble' husband."

"Ten thousand will do very nicely," Kennedy assured them. "Now here's what I think you should do. . . ."

On Monday morning, when Callie and Bruce drove up to the Clinton Bank at a quarter before nine o'clock, the line-up at the front entrance stretched down the block and around the corner.

A fine figure of a woman, so elegantly clad, stepping out of a chauffeured car was bound to be an object of attention, even among people so grievously preoccupied as the worried depositors at the Clinton National Bank.

There were shouts of indignation when she marched right up to the front of the line.

"Hey, lady, back to the end of the line!"

"You gonna wait like the rest of us to take your money out of the bank."

"What does she think, she's got special privileges 'cause she has a car with a chauffeur?"

Callie pretended to be bewildered. She touched her gloved fingers to her lips and asked, "This is the withdrawal line, isn't it?"

"What did you think it was, dearie?" A stout woman wearing a babushka tied over her gray head threatened Callie with a formidable elbow in the event she made an attempt to crash the line.

"I'm not withdrawing, I'm depositing." Callie opened the large paisley bag slung over one arm and displayed its contents, stacks of neatly bound greenbacks. Fives, tens, and twenties. "See, there's more than ten thousand dollars in here." She walked up the line, showing off the money to a score or more of gawking onlookers.

An elderly man wearing a bowler and a dark overcoat with a velvet collar that had seen better days addressed her. "Madam, you must be out of your mind depositing your money in this bank. You might just as well dump it into the Hudson

River. Better yet, distribute it among the needy souls on this line."

"That's pure nonsense!" Callie lifted her voice to reach all the ears she could. "You must be out of your mind taking all the rubbish you hear on the radio and read in the papers as gospel." She took Bruce's arm. "Here, ask my husband. He's a director of this institution. Do you honestly believe we would deposit money in the bank, if there was any chance of it failing? No! My husband would be inside right now, making sure he got our savings out safely before you get yours. . . . Haven't you heard the latest news? President-elect Roosevelt has announced that all the banks in the country that have closed will reopen the same week he takes office. And that every depositor's savings will be guaranteed by the federal government *to the penny!*"

She took up a position on the top of the front steps, opposite a short man at the head of the column. "All right, I'm forming a depositor's line. Anyone has to be a fool to give up three months' interest on his savings these days. That's all you'll be accomplishing if you withdraw your money now. In another three months you'll only be putting it back in and kicking yourselves in the ass for acting so foolishly."

". . . *Kicking yourselves in the ass* . . ."

As Callie described it later: "It struck a pure chord. You could feel the tension break the way a crystal goblet shatters when Caruso hits a perfect high C."

A cadenza of laughter played down the line of people, around the corner, to the end, and rippled back again.

"Hey, lady, you're all right!"

"She *is* right. What am I doing here, anyway?"

"Thanks for kicking *my* ass, lady!"

The tight little army that had besieged the bank since before dawn that morning broke ranks. By the time the doors were opened to the public at 9:05 A.M., no more than a score of diehards pressed their determination to withdraw funds. Six converts were lined up behind Callie on her fanciful "depositors' line."

On March 4, 1933, Franklin Delano Roosevelt was inaugurated as the thirty-second president of the United States.

True to his promise, he submitted his Emergency Banking Act to Congress on the first day it convened, March 9. It was passed into law in the record time of eight hours.

On the evening of March 12, a Sunday, FDR delivered the first of his to-be-famous "fireside chats" to the American public on radio.

Will Rogers, ex-rodeo cowboy, who had gone on to fame as the foremost humorist of the twenties and thirties in vaudeville, radio, and motion pictures, as a provincial critic and commentator on American politics and politicians wrote of that speech: "The president took up the subject of what's been happening to the banks, and what he intends to do about it and made everybody understand it, even the bankers."

On Monday morning the banks reopened, and by Wednesday the stock market began to rise. President Roosevelt received a second vote of confidence from the American public when a federal bond issue was oversubscribed on the first day it was issued.

Walt Campbell summed up the general feeling of the "forgotten man" to whom President Roosevelt had pledged his "New Deal": "He gave the country back to the people."

The last time Callie met Joe Kennedy was at Saratoga Racetrack in the summer of 1934. She was alone. He was sitting in a box with newspaper tycoon William Randolph Hearst and movie actress Marion Davies. He was panning the grandstand with field glasses between races when he saw her standing at the rail, marking her form. He excused himself and went down to her.

"Joe! What a delightful surprise." She offered her cheek.

He took both her hands and kissed her.

"Callie Majors, why didn't you let me know you were going to be here?"

"I didn't know myself until yesterday. Bruce is away, and my son is at camp." Her smile disappeared. "I'm worried sick about it. It's the first time he's been away from home."

"That's no way to talk. Camp will do him a world of good. You don't want a mama's boy tied to your apron strings all his life. Not you. You're not the common run of women, Callie."

"Of course, you're right." She managed to look cheerful for him, but it was a mask. "Anyway, Nate has a mind of his own, and he had his way in this."

"Ah-ha! That's what's really bothering you, isn't it? You're used to getting your own way in everything, giving orders.

Your nose is out of joint because in this matter the boy dictated to you. I know that feeling well. My son Jack, he's seventeen, and he's got a mind of his own too."

She changed the subject. "Congratulations, Joe. I read about the president appointing you as Chairman of the Securities and Exchange Commission. What do you do?"

"The SEC will be the watchdog of the stock market. No exchange can operate in the United States without our license and they must register all the securities they deal in with the commission. In short, our job is to make sure that the old manipulators like me are cleared out of Wall Street."

"Yes, your appointment stirred up quite a fuss."

"A fuss? You put it mildly. An uproar is what it stirred up, and it's still echoing in the halls of Congress and the canyon of Wall Street. The problem is FDR thinks and acts so far out in front of the pack, that it takes the rest a while to catch up with him. I'm the best man for the job, and that's not ego speaking, although I've got plenty of it. If the house wants to make sure a game is honest, the surest way is to hire the biggest card shark in town to run it. He knows all the tricks in the book, can spot a stacked deck and a bum shuffle. It's no job for an honest man in an ivory tower. Well, enough of me, what have you been up to?"

"Nothing very interesting. We were snowed-in most of the winter. And so far it's been a lonely, boring summer. I was up at Lake George for a week the end of June. I don't think there were more than a dozen people staying at the Sagamore. The porch, you remember how the old hens used to gaggle and cluck out there. On Sunday afternoon I counted two men and three women, all over ninety if they were a day. Half-blind and all with earphones. I could have sunbathed stark naked on the beach and no one would have noticed me."

"I would have noticed you." He gave her hand a squeeze. "It's the same way down in Miami. A ghost town. Recovery won't come overnight in this country, Callie. After all, the Republicans took twelve years to foul up the economy. We can't expect the Democrats to put it right again in one hundred days, a year, or even two. Incidentally, if you want to invest in Florida land, you can get in on a gold mine. There's miles of ocean frontage going for peanuts. In ten or twenty years they'll be paying gold nuggets for it."

"I don't know, Joe, it's taking all our capital to hold on to what we've got. All that property, Knight's and Majors', the taxes are staggering. I'm beginning to think Mr. Gould is right. This man Roosevelt likes to play Robin Hood, feeding the poor by robbing the rich."

"I'll have to tell that to Frank, he'll get a good laugh. There's one secret his illness taught him, how to laugh at himself. Most men fail because they take themselves so seriously. Hell, life's one big game. A great game, the greatest game there is, but a game. And when it's over, the rich man and the poor man cash in their chips and enter the pearly gates as equals. But seriously, is there anything I can do to help? A loan?"

"No, thank you anyway, Joe, we'll manage. Spread thin, but holding together. The market is rising, the Dow Jones is back to one hundred, and if it keeps up at this rate, in another year we'll be able to sell shares to ease the strain."

He was thin-lipped and solemn. "Let me give you a piece of advice, Callie. The first thing you should sell is the Majors Brick Company."

She frowned. "That's contrary to the advice you gave me when we first met. You were enthusiastic about the brick business then, its future in the post-depression building boom. And business has been good this year."

He shook his head. "Sales figures mean nothing. What counts is how many bricks are delivered and paid for. You'll feel the backlash next year. You see, when Majors stated its intention to go public, the SEC did a thorough check on the company. It's a mess, believe me, Callie. Backlogged orders that will go down the drain by default. Complaints from customers about the quality of the product. Some of your oldest outlets are going over to Kelly in Philadelphia."

Callie leaned back against the rail and brushed a lock of hair off her temple. "I'm not all that surprised, Joe. It's Bruce, isn't it?"

"I hate saying it, but yes, it's Bruce. I like the man, but he's weak. The crash and the depression were too much for him. There's no place in big business for weak men."

"Gutless is the word you want," she said. Her eyes were hard. "I'd hoped that Gardner would work out. For years now Bruce and Carl have been mere figureheads. Gardner runs the operation."

"Gardner won't because it's not his business. A company

is like a ship. If there's no one at the helm, it will founder and sink. You'd be surprised how sensitive workers are to that lack, that there's no one to crack the whip and lead them. Majors Brick is plagued by inertia, carelessness, inefficiency, and even dishonesty. The books are crooked as hell. The SEC couldn't possibly approve of your application to issue common stock. I shouldn't be telling you this off the cuff, but you're a good friend. Sell out before it's too late. You give me the word, and I'll find you a buyer and see to it that you get the best price." He winked. "I have quite a bit of leverage in transactions of this sort, you understand."

"It's you who's the good friend, Joe." She kissed his cheek. "We'll sell the company. It won't be easy to convince Bruce. The company is in his name, but he knows how much it means to Carl."

"Of course. When a man founds a business and nurses it from infancy to maturity, it's like parting with a child to give it up."

She shut her eyes and Nate's image was vivid before her. "I never thought of it that way. It may be harder than I thought."

He looked back at the grandstand. "The next race is about to begin. Come up and meet my host, William Randolph Hearst."

She followed his gaze, fixed on the man and woman sitting in a prime box just above the starting gate.

"That Mr. Hearst, the one who owed you the favor. Yes, I'd like to meet him." The man was watching them through binoculars.

In the box, Hearst increased the magnification of his glasses. Focused on the blond woman in conversation with Joseph Kennedy. She was breathtaking. Her eyes lifted, stared straight at him. He could see into them as though she was standing at arm's length. Green, brilliant, piercing. Like looking into the sun. He blinked and put down the binoculars. Rubbed his eyes.

His companion asked, "What's the matter, Bill, get something in your eye?"

"Yes, yes . . . that's it." He massaged his eyelids with his fingers.

Something in those eyes. . . .

Joe Kennedy took her elbow. "Then come along." She resisted him. "What is it?"

She bit her underlip. "I really would like to meet Mr. Hearst. Who is that with him?"

"You'll like her, she's a movie actress. Miss Marion Davies."

"Hearst's mistress." She shook her head. "No, I don't think so."

It put him off balance. "I don't believe it, you a prig! Because the woman—"

She cut him short. "No, no, it's not what you're thinking." She pressed her hands together and touched her fingers to her lips, head bent. "She's always been one of my favorite actresses. I've seen every movie she's ever made. . . ."

"Well then?"

"I know her—every role she's ever played. She's all those women . . . some of them sweet and virtuous . . . some whores . . . some sweet . . . some sour. . . . She's best when she's wicked. . . . The truth is, I don't care to know what she's like in the flesh and blood. On Celluloid she's mysterious and eternal—I don't want to be disappointed. Mortals are so pitiful and minuscule, so insignificant. You said before, Joe, that all of us must enter heaven as we entered life. Naked, penniless, and identical. That will come soon enough. It's essential we maintain a few illusions." She took his hand. "My best to Mr. Hearst and Miss Davies. Tell them I had to hurry off because of an important phone call . . . my son. . . . And thank you, Joe, for everything."

He pressed her hand and stooped to kiss her cheek. "I hope Bill is taking all these loving pecks in. We'll be a scandal tomorrow morning on the front page of the *Journal.*"

She feigned distress. "Oh dear! Would he be such a cad?"

He laughed. "He wouldn't dare!" He stared at her, hard and searching. "You baffle me, Callie, how you baffle me. You're a jigsaw puzzle, of the kind you can never put together and swear the maker planned it that way. It's why you're so alluring, I suppose. Next to games, I've always been fascinated by puzzles. . . . Good-bye; let me know what you decide to do about Majors Brick."

The following weekend Callie told Bruce about her meeting with Joseph Kennedy in Saratoga. She spared him nothing.

He stood up, ran his hands through his thinning hair and walked to the liquor server. His hands were trembling so, the decanter chattered against the rim of the glass.

"All right, I'll admit it, I'm a failure. Goddamn, it's so easy for him to criticize. If I had half his capital, I'd pull the business out of the hole it's in."

"No, Bruce." She plunged the blade in deeper and twisted it. "If you were half the man he is you might, but even if you had twice his capital, you'd still run it into the ground. You never were cut out for leadership."

He downed the drink and poured a second with a steadier hand. "Then why the hell don't you run the company yourself? You run everything else around here. Sometimes I get the feeling you even run Wayne Harrison."

"Don't be silly."

"Have you had an affair with him, is that it? Is that why he's afraid of you?"

"What would you care if I had?" She sneered. "Unless it would be envy to be in my place. Half a man."

"Stop! I won't stand for—"

"Shut up, I'm speaking! You contemptible degenerate. Did you think you could hide from me that you were a fairy before you married me?"

"You rotten bitch!"

"The only way you can feel like a man is with your own sister!" She ran the blade clean through.

He screamed at her, gibberish, animal furies. Hurled the drink at her. She stepped out of its path and it crashed against a table, scattering shards of glass and ice over the spreading stain on the Persian carpet.

Bruce grabbed the poker from the side of the fireplace and advanced on her with it poised to strike. She held her ground, arms folded underneath her breasts, expressionless.

"What are you going to do? Murder me the way you murdered Jake Spencer and his friends? You believe they'll let you off a fourth time? You and your drunken father would have fried in Sing Sing if it hadn't been for me. Wayne Harrison wouldn't have lifted a finger to save you if I hadn't prevailed upon him. Go on, here's your chance to pay your debt to the state, long overdue. The electric chair is waiting, Bruce."

"Jesus!" He took one, two steps, faltered. The poker wavered. Cocked full back, and in that instant he almost succeeded. Her eyes held his like magnets. Arrested by field of force around her. He lowered the poker, let it slip through his fingers. Sank down on his knees and covered his face with his hands. He cried like a woman. Distraught, hysterical sobbing that wracked his frame.

Callie walked to the server, poured whiskey into a glass, and brought it over to him. "Here, drink this, and stop sniveling. Get up and wipe your nose before the cook or Miss Hathaway comes in and finds you in this state."

He took the glass obediently. "Thank you." He choked on the warm liquor.

She whacked his back. "You're a worse baby than your sister."

Carl came home from the sanitarium the last week in August. "Dried out" was an apt metaphor for the excruciating regimen that brought an alcoholic back to sobriety. He was shrunken, wrinkled, leathery as a prune. An ugly caricature of the virile rakish dude who had driven to her wedding in the big Mercer with red-spoked wheels and two cases of champagne on the back seat.

He didn't touch a drop of alcohol for six days. He was barely recovered from delirium tremens. Rid of the devils that had been tormenting him in his wakeful hours, but at night, when the mind's defense were at low ebb, the fiends would slip back into his unconsciousness and plot his nightmares.

Not the crawly terrors that had stalked Joe Hill after his drinking bouts in the final years before he died.

Callie would hold his head in her lap and comfort him as if he was the child, not she, while he shrieked and slapped at the figmentary spiders on arms and legs and face.

Carl Major's tormentors were ghosts. Jake Spencer sitting cross-legged at the foot of his bed, crying out to Carl to help him as he tried to shove coils of his intestines, all agleam like snakes, back into his rent belly with bloody fingers.

The expression on Ray Shuffelmeir's face when he pulled the trigger. Vanishing before his eyes. Face, head, pulverized. Gray matter bright with blood spattering the pine boards. A chunk of jawbone embedded deep in the wood with a flap of skin fluttering from it like a gay pennant.

His screams curdled the blood and bristled the nape. A clarion that would wake the whole household, even the servants on the ground floor. Bruce would stay in the room with him until he was fully awake and calmed down.

On the sixth night, Callie came out of her room, belting

her robe, as Bruce hurried down the hall.

"Go back to bed," she told him. "You look like death. I'll take the watch tonight."

He was grateful to her. Half in a drunken stupor from the quart of scotch he had swilled down between dinner and bedtime, he staggered back to his sister's room. He'd spend the rest of the night with Chris, soothing the terrors that Carl's fits induced in her. She'd roll up in a ball, pull the covers over her head, and lie there trembling.

Callie went in and woke Carl. He sat up, awake but still possessed by gory visions. He clapped his hands over his eyes and shouted at them, "Leave me alone, you bastards! You're dead. Go back to your graves."

Callie stroked his head and crooned to him, "Hush, hush, Carl, they're fading now, aren't they?"

He shivered, groaned, mumbled an incantation she couldn't make sense of, went limp. His hands came away from his face and he looked up at Callie. Poets called the eyes the windows of the soul. Not Carl's eyes. His looked into the pit of hell.

"Why won't they leave me alone?" he asked her.

"It's you who won't let them rest in peace. You keep summoning them back to punish you." She sat down on the bed. "Let's talk awhile to get your mind off the spirit world. Would you like a drink to wash down the taste of your bad dream?"

"You know I'm not supposed to. The doctor said . . ." He distrusted her, but his terrible thirst respected no rhyme nor reason. "Do you really think I could?"

"One drink, there's no harm in one drink. I've seen you down a bottle and not even feel it." She patted his hand. "I'm not as hard as you think I am, Carl. I know how badly you need a drink to steady you. It will help you to go back to sleep. I'll be right back." She rose and left the room, closing the door silently behind her.

Carl lay back and stared up at the light in the ceiling. Two moths were doing a dance of death around the glowing bulb. Of moths and men.

He was wary of Callie, her unwarranted solicitude. Torn out of deep slumber by his ravings, she'd come to him sweetly. Stroked his hair, calmed him. And now she was fetching him a drink of whiskey, of all things. Callie of all people! He was wary.

All day she'd been berating them, Bruce and he, for resisting her. She wanted to sell the Majors company. *His* company. It was one contest he vowed she would not win.

Bruce had rallied to his impassioned appeal: "We must stand together on this, son. She mustn't have her way. You and I, we've lost everything that makes a man a man. Pride, dignity, our self-respect. She'll not deprive us of the only thing of value we have remaining. For almost a century, the name Majors has been a symbol of quality the length of this valley, all over the United States. 'A Majors brick, the best that money can buy.' It's more than a slogan, it's a trust. Our name meant something, and it will again, we'll see to it, you and I. Together we can do it. Put the company back on the tracks. We'll do it if it costs every cent we have, every thing else we own. Remember, madam," he said to Callie, "you don't have your pretty hands on the Majors estate yet. Not while Bruce and I are alive!"

Unexpectedly, she had turned her back on them and left the room. It was the first time in Carl's remembrance that Callie had ever quit a fray without uttering the final word.

Yes, he was wary. He was alert, roused from his torpor, rallying to the pump of adrenalin through his veins. Attentive to her every word and action when she arrived back in the room with two glasses in one hand and a decanter in the other. All smiles.

"I'm going to join you in a nightcap. It will help us both to sleep." The smile faded. "You know, Carl, I've bad dreams of my own of late. About my mother, imagine that? I can hardly remember what she looked like."

"Your mother . . ." He watched her pour the amber liquid into the two crystal glasses. "Why should you have bad dreams about your mother?"

She handed him a glass. His longing for the taste of bourbon was unbearable, but he held it untouched, she noted. Pressed the question: "This bad dream, what is it?"

She sat down on the foot of the bed and drew her knees up under her, folding the robe and silken gown demurely about her legs.

"It's a recurring vision. I dream I am a witness to her murder."

The whiskey glass went ignored. "Her murder? Why would you dream that? Your mother went away."

She sipped her whiskey, studying him intently over the rim

of the glass. "We don't know that. No one saw her leave Knightsville. She disappeared without a trace, my father told me so."

The whiskey was splashing over the sides of the glass, wetting his shaking hand. A drink would have steadied him, but he did not drink. Licked his dry lips instead.

"How was your mother murdered?" Amending it too quickly: "In this fanciful dream of yours?"

She closed her eyes and touched her eyelids. "I see her like Ophelia spread-eagled in the shallows beneath a willow with pale water shimmering over her paler face, lending to it a guise of life. Her hair too, fanning out and fishtailing in the eddies, seems alive. But when I look into her dark eyes, wide open, I see death. Mirrored in her fixed pupils I see death. And as I bend closer death becomes her killer. And the foul deed is mirrored in her dead eyes as in a witch's crystal ball."

"And who is the man, anyone we know?"

"So far I've only seen him from the rear. I cry out to him to stop, and as he turns his head toward me I awake. One time I won't wake up and then I'll see him."

"Christ, that's horrible!" He jerked the glass to his mouth and swallowed the contents.

She picked up the decanter from the floor beside the bed and leaned forward to refill his glass. Poured half as much into her glass. "This is so good. It warms the belly and sooths the mind. Does it exorcise the devils, Carl?"

He stared into the golden elixir, cureall for all the ills of mankind, so he'd thought once. Cureall for nothing. An idiot's delusion. Anesthetic deadening the body and mind to pain. Fugitive pain, waiting patiently to claim the debt with interest.

His answer came delayed. "They feed on it and thrive."

She held up her glass to the light. "See how it sparkles." Brought it to her nose. "Glorious aroma." Put the tip of her tongue into the whiskey. "Hmmmmm . . . a potion that titillates all the senses. Small wonder it becomes a habit." She sipped and rolled the tart liquor around in her mouth.

Mesmerized, he followed suit, drank deeply.

"Carl, did you and my mother ever drink together the way we are now?"

A ghost of a smile formed. Bittersweet memory of ghosts. "Your mother and I . . . we drank champagne. How well I remember a time in Albany. . . . Let me see, it was Fourth of July—ahhhgggh!" He gagged, dismayed at what he'd confessed.

Her voice was sweet, cajoling. "Why did you pretend you never knew my mother?"

"I—I—I didn't mean—you see, it's not the way it sounds—your mother—I—I—" His tongue tied itself up in confusion.

"Champagne in Albany, Carl. Is that where the affair began, in Albany?"

"I was only one of many, you must believe that, Callie." He drained the glass and held it forth. She filled it. "She was a vixen, your mother. A beautiful creature. You're not like her in appearance, but you have her magic. Black magic. The gift of power."

"Why did you kill her, Carl?"

He recoiled, spilling whiskey on the front of his nightshirt. "Kill her? You must be mad."

"Something Sheriff Adams said the Sunday after those three were killed and he came here to charge you and Bruce. *'The Majorses have been getting away with murder in this county for years.'* "

"A figure of speech."

"Not the way he said it. He was going to make it clearer, but the district attorney shut him up. Walter Edwards knows too, doesn't he, Carl?"

He put the glass down on his bedtable and cradled his bowed head in his hands. "I would never have harmed a hair on Kitty's head, everybody knew that. I loved her. I wanted her to divorce your father and marry me. I'd have given the child my name, though God only knows if it was really mine. She'd wenched around before I met her and she could have been carrying on behind my back."

"The child?" She was unprepared for this disclosure. "My mother was pregnant? By you? I don't believe it."

"It's the truth." Tears streamed down his cheeks. "I begged her to marry me. She was a fever in my blood, the same as you. Kitty wasn't as purposeful as you and her goals were less ambitious. She valued her freedom. She didn't want to be bound to anyone or anything. Neither me, nor your father, nor you."

"You're a liar!" she snarled. "My mother loved me very much. My father told me so."

She had told that lie to herself over and over in the orphanage until she came to believe it.

What Tom Hill had said was, *"Your mother cares for no one in this world but herself."*

"Believe what you want, Callie." Carl sighed and wiped his eyes with the sheet. "I offered her marriage and she refused. Her terms were that I had to arrange and pay for an abortion and pay her ten thousand dollars afterward so she could run away from Knightsville. She was going to New York. She wanted to become a stage actress. I believe she would have succeeded, she was like you in that respect. Once she set her mind on an objective, she wouldn't rest until it was hers. She used to say that life was a game of chance. This time she took one chance too many. She lost the game on the doctor's table."

"The abortionist killed her." For the first time in her life she knew the true meaning of the Bard's *"cold fury."*

"He was no butcher. A reputable surgeon indebted to me for a sizable loan. He was a compulsive gambler. The operation was a success, but she died of heart failure. She had a murmur, she joked about it once when we were making love." He cringed under her glare. "I—I'm sorry."

She bit her lip so hard she could taste the blood, metallic, earthy flavor. Her nails cut into her palms.

"What did you do with her after she was dead?"

He grabbed the glass on the table with both hands, emptied it. Held it out to her. "Please . . ."

She filled it again. "What did you do with my mother?

He groaned and shook his head. "He said if she was a woman without kin who might report her disappearance to the police, he could make 'certain' arrangements. I was in a panic. She'd had this row with your father the week before. He came near to killing her and he was jailed. As soon as she got the money from me, she was leaving him. So . . ." He drank more whiskey to fortify himself for the admission. "I—I told the doctor she was a drifter without any family ties that I knew of." He squeezed his eyelids tight together to shut out the sight of her face. "Next morning she was found downriver near Newburgh with the identification of some derelict he'd lifted from the hospital morgue. The authorities there made queries about missing persons up and down the river. Ben Thomas, he was sheriff in this county then, a canny man, he went down and had a look at the corpse. He recognized Kitty but didn't say so. Ben came straight to me. I paid him for his bad memory, enough to retire and spend the rest of his life fishing and boozing."

"Murderers!" She threw the decanter at him. It missed his ducked head and crashed against the wall. "Worse than murderers! Monsters! My mother! You cut open her belly, then you dumped her in the river as if she was refuse. A human being. *My mother!* I'll cut out your heart and devour it raw and bloody!" She screamed and hurled herself at him, fingers scratching like cat's claws. Raked his face four bright red slashes along each cheek.

Carl found strength in terror. He pushed her away from and leaped out of bed, fled the room, down the hall, down the stairs. He stopped in the reception hall, turned and listened. No sign of her pursuit, the house was silent. Groping blindly in the darkness he found his way into the sitting room and to the server. He opened it and took out a bottle. He couldn't see the label, it made no difference. With a clear and shining purpose in his mind, he set off for the kitchen.

Upstairs on Carl's bed, Callie lay prone, her hands clenched into his pillow. Motionless. Eyes staring at the puddle of whiskey on the bedtable from the broken decanter. It trickled down the side of the table and dripped onto the floor. With a lethargic metronome beat:

tuc . . . tuc . . . tuc . . .

Abner Dalton was standing the late watch in front of his tollbooth at the Knightsville side of the bridge. A produce truck had paid the last quarter more than an hour before. A slow night, and Ab was restless. It had been a hot day, in the mid nineties, but the breeze off the river cooled the valley fast after the sun went down. The full moon loomed large over the wooded hills behind the Knight property. A burned-orange hue that meant more hot weather for the next day.

Ab stooped and picked up a flat stone. He bounced it on his big callused palm, reared back, and pitched it far out over the Hudson. It left his sight in the dark. Seconds passed. Then a spout of water marked where it hit. A bull's-eye of concentric circles widening on the luminous surface of the river.

"Good shot, Ab!" a voice came to him from somewhere on the bridge.

He strained his eyes at the figure halfway across. Obscured by the shadow of the superstructure, a patchwork of moonlight and dark. At first he believed it was a woman wearing a white flowing dress. But the voice had come from a male. Walked closer to him, Ab saw it was a man clad in a nightshirt. Old man Majors.

"Good evening, Ab. That was a mighty fine throw, but you'll never beat George Washington. He scaled a silver dollar across the Hudson."

"Thank you, sir." Ab knew he had his rivers mixed but he didn't take exception with him. Carl Majors, in a nightshirt with a bottle in one hand, drunk as a skunk as usual. "You oughtn't be out in your nightclothes, barefooted like that, Mr. Majors. You'll take a chill."

"Take a chill, yes, you're probably right, but the matter of my health is an academic issue right now."

"Sir?"

Carl laughed oddly and offered Ab the bottle. "Here, have some warmth and cheer."

Ab hesitated, wondering if he would incur the wrath of that Majors woman if he humored her tipsy father-in-law. He decided to risk it and took the bottle. He tipped it up and drank a healthy swig, wiped his mouth with the back of his hand.

"Thank you, Mr. Majors. A nip sets well about this time. Now you better mosey back home before they find out you're not in bed and come looking for you."

Carl glanced back at the dark mass of Wheatley crouched on the bluff like some predatory monster out of the past.

"Yes, we wouldn't want that to happen." He took the bottle from Ab and held out his other hand. In the palm was a silver quarter glinting in the moon's rays. "Here, I wanted to give you this."

The toll-taker's mouth went slack. "What's that for?"

"The toll fee, naturally." His laughter was sardonic.

"Madame is strict about it, you know that. Every man, woman, or child who sets foot on her bridge pays the price. No exceptions, not even an old fool like me out for a stroll in the good night air." He inhaled deeply, let it out.

"Ah-h-h-h-h, this sweet Hudson Valley ozone, now I'll miss it."

"You going somewhere, Mr. Majors?"

"As a matter of fact I am, Ab. A river voyage, that's what I'll soon be off on."

"Up the Hudson?"

"No, not the Hudson. A somewhat more tempestuous river, Ab. The Styx, have you heard of it?"

"It sounds familiar. It's not in this state."

"No, not in this state." He slapped the coin into Ab's hand and clapped his shoulder. "Here's your fee, and now I must be off. Good luck, Ab."

"Yes, sir, thank you, sir. Good luck—I mean good night."

He watched until the staggering man was absorbed into the kaleidoscopic patterns of the bridge's masts and cables painted by the moon. Smiled ruefully, shook his head, and went into the tollbooth to deposite the quarter.

When he reached the middle of the span, Carl sat down cross-legged on the planking. The long carving knife he'd taken from the kitchen was stuck upright in the wood where he'd thrust it on his way across. He grasped the stag-bone handle and jerked it free. He positioned it with the blade turned inward, his hand firm around the hilt. He put the bottle to his mouth, tilted his head back as far as it would go and drank. Kept drinking even as he drew the cutting edge of fine-honed Sheffield steel across his throat.

There was no pain. Briefly he was unsure he had accomplished his purpose until the blood welled up in his throat, melding with the whiskey, choking off his breath. He toppled over gently on his side. One eye on the crack between two planks. The life's juice, dark and gleaming in the moonlight, ran freely over the wood, dripped down through the crack into the smooth-flowing water far below. He could see the droplets strike. One by one.

. . . *drip* . . . *drip* . . . *drip* . . .

He closed his eyes in peace. Eternal peace.

Nathaniel came home a week early from camp to be present at his grandfather's funeral. The Majors family crypt was in a cemetery built for and by the Hudson River Rich. It seemed to Callie it displayed more Italian marble than what remained in all of Italy. Cupids. Angels. Cherubs. Crosses. Christ. Christ in marble in every direction as far as the eye could see. The landscaping was as unreal-looking as the statuary, grass, trees, and shrubbery all too green and manicured. An atmosphere suited more to a museum than a burial grounds. She preferred the impoverished little graveyard behind the Knight house with its slanted headstones, blighted grass, and somber weeds.

She cut her eyes at Nathaniel standing beside her as the Reverend Wilson Woolcot read the invocation outside the tomb. Tall and broad for his eleven years. So much like Ham the day she had seen him grieving at his mother's burial. The same dark good looks, brooding eyes, and strong jaw. The way he carried his body, like Ham.

As if he could read her thoughts, Nate said to her, "He should be here."

"Who?"

"Ham. We're his family. A family should be together in time of trouble." He even sounded like Ham.

"We didn't know where to reach him. He's at sea, no doubt. I'm sure he'd be here if he had a way of knowing."

"No, he wouldn't." His jaw squared and anger clouded his face. "Ham's a bastard!"

"Nate!" she whispered. "Someone will hear you."

"I don't give a damn! I hate Ham. I hope he never comes back here again."

The duality of the Majors family was apparent to the other mourners, friends, associates, employees, who had come from up and down the Hudson River to pay final respects to Carl. Bruce with his arm around his sister, pressing her close to him. Her pretty empty face registering nothing more than a childish curiosity and awe about the ritual. A trace of petulance as well at being forced to leave her warm, cozy room and make the long, uncomfortable car trip to this foreboding place.

A yard apart, Callie and Nate. She clinging proudly and possessively to her son's arm with both hands.

". . . No one who knew him could find an unkind word to say about Carl Majors. A good man. A moral man. A generous man. . . ." the syrupy claptrap of the Right Reverend Woolcot poured forth unremittingly.

Her eyes sparked with contempt behind the black veil. *He was a son of a bitch! A good man! A moral man! My ass!*

He got exactly what was due to him. Murderer. Not that Spencer and the other two mattered to Callie. He'd killed her mother! A son of a bitch to the end. He couldn't even take his life with any grace or consideration for his kin. He had been purposefully vindictive in this final living act. Cutting his throat and bleeding to death like a stuck pig out in public. On her bridge! Inviting embarrassment and scandal on his loved ones. Loved ones! Hypocrite!

She touched her handkerchief to her eyes, but her smile was hidden behind the black veil. He'd done it to spite her, the old bastard, but she would have the final laugh. Callie had issued strict orders not to scrub clean the planks stained red with Carl's blood. The blood would stay there until it washed and wore away. Until it did, those grisly marks would lure ghouls from miles around, eager to pay a quarter toll to see where a famous man had died by his own violent hand.

PART 3
Fraud & Malice

Walter Campball adjusted his spectacles, lit his pipe, made sure his bottle of apple brandy was within reach, braced his elbows on the kitchen table. Letter writing was a ceremony for Walt. He had to mobilize his forces, to contend with it in the same way he armed himself for church on Sunday mornings. He frowned at the sheet of paper, tapped the nub of his Waterman fountain pen on the blotter, testing for leakage; daughter Lucy had sent it to him last birthday from New York City. Heaved a great sigh and bent to his task.

December 14, 1936

Dear Ham,

I don't know when you will get this letter. When you wrote last you said you expected to leave the U.S. Dayton *after it returned to New York, so I am sending this in care of the main offices of the United States Lines. I'm sure they will forward it to you wherever you are.*

Things go on here in the valley as usual, not much better or much worse than they have since you left. I keep hearing on the radio that the country is doing fine again and stocks have been on the rise ever since President Roosevelt took office. I expect it's true. The people elected him again by the biggest vote in history. His New Deal to help the forgotten man must be working, but as Mrs. Majors says (you know her and her quotes), all men are born equal only some are born more equal than others. Same thing with the forgotten man in these bad times. Some are more forgotten than others. That's how it is with us here in Knightsville. The hard fact is conditions haven't improved hardly at all in the past four years. I guess we're too small to matter. Big farms and big business get a lot of help from the government, but us small potatoes have been left to rot in the ground. And you know what, Ham, the government isn't all to blame. Even if they was to help, there's no one left here fit to work the land. The young started to leave Knightsville back in nineteen thirty, like yourself, and they keep on leaving. They want jobs that pay well and where you don't have to dirty your hands and break your back. I can't say I blame them. Our own Lucy is living in New York. She's a cashier in a restaurant and studying shorthand at night. I'm glad for her. It's the same with the railroad. The New York Central can't find local men to work the road gangs. The ones who'd take the jobs are too old like me. I'm lucky. Your stepmother Mrs. Majors keeps me on, even though there's nothing much for me to do. And what work gets done is mostly due to your stepbrother, young Nate. God! You ought to see that lad. He's the spitting image of you when you was his age, only bigger, I think. He does the work of two men. Trouble is it would take ten men to keep the acreage in proper shape. The weeds and bugs are beginning to get the best of us. Mrs. Majors has decided to sell the north and the east meadows next spring.

Things haven't been going well over at Wheatley either. Bruce is in a private nursing home, permanently, I think. It's his liver, from all the drinking he was doing. And Jane Hathaway retired and went back to Elmira where she came from. Chris was getting to be too much to take care of, especially after Bruce wasn't around to help. Now it looks like Mrs. Majors is going to have to put her away. It sure has been a tragic family. In every way. I think I told you in my last letter about her selling the Majors Brick Company. The quarry has been closed down since before you left Knightsville. Nobody wants slate roofs no more, I guess, not when the tar shingles cost so much less.

We get the government welfare here. It just about feeds you if you don't mind leaving the table with a gnawing belly. We'd all be much worse off if it wasn't for Mrs. Majors. When you add her dole to what the welfare gives, you can live pretty comfortable. I don't get welfare, of course, because she pays me a salary. Like I told you before, the salary is more honestly a dole too. Last month the bank sent Sheriff Adams around to evict Lou Martin from his house for faulting on his mortgage payments. Lou barricaded himself inside with a shotgun and a squirrel rifle and told them to go to hell. I don't know what would have happened if Mrs. Majors hadn't told the bank people to let him be. The Knight estate holds first and second mortgages along with the bank on most of the property in and around Knightsville. The people of this town are sure beholden to that Majors woman.

Nate and I try to keep the old Knight homestead in condition. Last winter the side porch roof collapsed from all the snow. Come summer we painted the place inside and outside. The barn's boarded up. Last year we sold the last of the livestock off. It's funny, houses and land are like people. When they're not used they go to seed.

Ham, I know it ain't my business to lecture you on how to treat your family. You never made no secret how you felt about her! *You're a fair man, and I know she must have done something to you none of us can know about to make you feel so strong against her. But the boy, Nate, the two of you are blood kin. Before you left here he thought the sun rose and set on you. In the beginning after you were gone, he talked of nothing else except what you and him were going to do when you came back to Knightsville. He aimed to live here with you in the Knight homestead and work the farm with you. What I'm saying is, Ham, you could have kept in touch with him, a note or a card at least. How do you think he feels knowing an outsider like me gets letters from you? In the beginning I hid the fact you wrote me, but that wasn't fair, not for as many years as you've been gone. I had to let them know you were alive and well. You'd be surprised how much interest Mrs. Majors shows about you. Now young Nate, he's a different story. Now he acts like he don't want to hear, and when I take over a letter to read, he goes out. He never mentions your name anymore, that's how bad his heart is broken, Ham. Can't you find it in your heart to be kind to him? Whatever his mother has done to you in the past, Ham, Nate is innocent. He deserves better from you. I'm sorry if I have stuck my long nose so deep into your business. Aunt Sue sends her love, she has lost weight and looks younger every year.*

As ever,
Uncle Walt

P.S. You wouldn't believe Mrs. Majors. She doesn't age at all. She's as beautiful as the day she married your father, God rest his soul, and almost as youthful. They say that means a person is without sin. Or maybe it should be without conscience.

August 1940

Dear Ham:

I hope you do not succumb to your natural loutish and childish bent to discard this letter without bothering to open it. You must

admit throughout all the years you have been away from Knightsville, I have faithfully respected your desire to disassociate yourself from me and from our son. Yes, Ham, the time for pretending is past. You are like Enobarbus who said to Cleopatra:"The truth should be silent, I had almost forgot. . . ."I won't let you forget it, Ham. Nathaniel is your son as well as mine. If time has treated you as well as I remember you, you could be twin brothers, as everyone believes you are.

I write in part to tell you that Walter Campball is dead. He died in Nate's arms in the south pasture mending a fence. It was quick and merciful. Susan has nothing to worry about as I will continue to pay her Walt's full salary as long as she lives.

I don't mean to sound like a magnanimous grande dame. It's just that the country seems to have turned its back on these poor little river people, notwithstanding King Franklin's welfare state. That's what a good many people are beginning to call Mister Roosevelt. Knightsville folks and others in the same predicament in like Hudson hamlets are fast becoming the poor white trash of the north. It's wretched because they are fine, proud, God-fearing people. I can see you smiling at my sanctimonious rhetoric. Desist. The God they fear, as well as the King Franklin they worship, doesn't even know they exist. Their destiny, the destiny of Knightsville is in my hands. An irrevocable trust invoked by your grandfather, Cyrus Knight. Yes, Ham, I have assumed the full burden of a responsibility which by all that's fair should be borne by you. I am loyal to the heritage that you disavowed. Just as you have disavowed your son. You self-righteous pharisee.

I have made these people mine, they look to me for everything. It's been neither easy nor cheap. Despite the good showing our shares have been making on Wall Street these past five years, the income is not extravagant. I sold the brick business, I guess Walt told you that. And this past spring I finally let Mr. Roosevelt have his way. My bridge now is the property of New York State. The price was fair. Nevertheless, it was a personal sacrifice for me. Other people can't understand that, and I don't expect you to either. It was my *bridge. I let them have it because there was no other way. To keep faith with your grandfather, to preserve his trust, his monument. Knightsville is a monument to him. To all the Knights. You too, Ham. It's time you acted like a man and stopped running away from your debts. Run, run, run, rabbit run! The only time you displayed any manhood was with me. And becoming a man with me frightened and ashamed you. The hour has tolled for you, Ham. All Knightsville awaits your return.*

Affectionately,
Callie

It was eight months before her letter caught up with Ham Knight. It had been lying in the dead-letter bin in the San Francisco branch office of the National Maritime Union since he had quit the sea. A chance meeting in a bar on Fisherman's Wharf with a friend who clerked there put him on to it. Otherwise he'd have passed through on his way from Mexico to the Klondike and history would have been shaped differently. Ham told himself that, but never really believed it. Fate is the hunter, and the letter would have stalked him down one way or the other.

On August 12, 1941, Ham stepped stiffly down the steps of the Pullman coach he had boarded in New York the night before. His arms and legs were sore and cramped from trying to sleep doubled up on a hard wicker seat. His faded seabag was slung over one shoulder. He gripped the metal handrail as the car bumped to a stop, rattling and groaning in all of her outworn parts, and swung himself down to the ground. His foot made firm contact. Something akin to a shock went up his leg. It had been eleven years and nine months to the day since his last contact with the good earth of Knightsville.

Hector Jones, the stationmaster, was grayer and thinner and tackier than Ham remembered him. Once he'd strutted about in his billed cap and blue uniform with the brass buttons like a drum major. He still wore the cap, the bill was cracked, the blue serge worn off. Frayed blue denim trousers and a blue workshirt, both bagging on his gawky frame, simulated the uniform.

"Well, hot damn!" he exclaimed, displaying his uneven, blackened teeth in a cadaverous smirk that made Ham shiver. "Ham, boy, you been away a long time." He wrung Ham's unresponsive hand.

Ham looked around. Alva's store looked the same. The bench in front spaced with old men smoking and gossiping. He couldn't see the creek alongside the building, but he heard the water rushing over the boulders.

"Seems like yesterday I got on the train," he observed. "Nothing has changed that I can see."

"And nothing's likely to change if you had stayed away ten more years. Twenty. More. All what's left in Knightsville is the likes of me and Alva. Old Walt's dead, and we're not far behind him."

"Come on now, Hec. I guess Alva must be sixty, a few more years maybe, but you can't be over fifty-five."

The stationmaster slapped his leg and cackled. "Boy, I'm only forty-nine!"

"I'm sorry," Ham apologized.

"Don't be, I look it. It's this town. Knightsville ages you fast. The land of the brave and the home of the free," he clowned; it was gallows humor. "The land of the doomed and the home of the dead."

The words were superfluous. His smile had said everything there was to say. His death's-head grin.

Ham walked across the bridge. The tollbooth was gone. Halfway across, a boy was fishing at the rail. No proper pole, just a coiled line in his hand looping down in a broad parabola to the river. Ham put down his seabag and lit a cigarette. The towheaded boy squinted around at him.

"Got a butt, mister?" he asked.

Ham grinned. He was ten or twelve at the outside. "Your ma know you smoke?"

"Sure. My brother smokes and he's younger than me."

Ham shook his head and gave the boy a cigarette. He offered him the pack of matches but the boy shook his head.

"Save it till later. Girl next door lets me feel her up if I let her smoke it with me."

Ham was not amused. He picked up the bag and went on. Everything he had seen since he got off the train reeked of decadence. Everyone, even the children. They were ratty in behavior and appearance. Audacious and scrounging.

He walked up the winding road that ran past Wheatley. The wrought-iron pickets needed paint. So did the gate. He stopped to examine the bronze plaques inlaid in the brick colonnades flanking the drive. One read:

WHEATLEY—In memory of Tobias Wheatley.

The other:

MAJORS—The Name in Bricks

He walked up the circular drive toward the house. It had been freshly painted, yet it bore the stamp of elegance in decline. Slates missing on the roof. The porch roof sagged. Birds' nests under the eaves. The front steps needed repairs. He paused at the gap in the hedge and looked up the garden path in the direction of the bluff. Callie was standing up there looking out across the river. He wasn't surprised. Intuitively he had known she would be there as he approached the house. He went through the hedge and up the path to the bluff. Walt had written that her beauty never faded. It was true. Her profile was a cameo set in blue satin sky. Her golden hair streamed back in the wind off the Hudson the way it had the day they had first come to Wheatley in Carl Majors's open touring car. She wore a loose sweater and a tartan skirt with knee socks and loafers. Looked as young as the screeching, dewy-eyed young females thronged up at the box office of the Paramount Theater when he had walked east to Grand Central Terminal from his hotel. Some had waited all day, he'd heard, to claim choice seats for the stage show that featured the current singing idol of America. An emaciated Italian youth with a pock-marked face who held on to the microphone when he performed, ostensibly for support.

Although he stepped softly on the grass, she sensed his presence with the same empathy that had prompted him she would be on the bluff before he saw her. She turned.

"Ham, so you finally got here." Spoken in the tone of a hostess greeting a tardy guest. She had been planning this reunion for a year. Never abandoning hope that he had received and read her letter and would in time return to Knightsville.

He put down the bag as she came toward him. "I got your letter back in April, it took some time to catch up with me. No, that's not right, I caught up with it."

"It doesn't matter, you're here." She put her hands on his shoulders, stepped up on her toes, and kissed his cheek chastely.

He had expected this confrontation would be awkward, but it was not. His wound had mended neater than he would have deemed possible. Layered over with tough scar tissue that deadened feeling.

"You're looking well, Callie."

"So are you, dear." She touched his cheek, tan and leathery from exposure to the sea, sun, and wind. Ran her fingers across the graying hair at his temple. "You look older."

"I am older."

"Older than your years, and I mean that well. I like the way you look. You're a man." She stepped back, folded her arms, craned her head from one side to the other, inspecting him with approval.

"It was your letter that brought me back," he said. "I'm not given to introspection, but that letter of yours stimulated this gray matter"—he tapped his skull—"as it had not been stirred up in some time. Ever."

"I'm pleased to hear you see things my way." She had not anticipated this unconditional surrender. She expected if he came at all he would be truculent, resentful, defensive, a bull on a tether with a ring in its nose.

His smile formed slowly, a lazy, sprawling, flippant smile. "I'm pleased that you're pleased."

Furrows marred the smooth skin between her eyebrows. He was making sport of her, she sensed it; it put her on her guard.

"Yes, Callie, I read your letter and a flash of insight struck me, a bolt of lightning. Suddenly it was revealed to me in that flash what I must do. My responsibility to Knightsville. To the people living here. To Nate, first and foremost. Unsatisfied obligations that no decent man could turn away from."

She could find no fault with what he said. It was the cryptic way he said it. The duel of words was going in his favor. He was toying with her.

"You've changed, Ham," she said. "Not your appearance, I don't mean that. I don't know what it is about you." She paused and touched a finger to her lips, bit her lip. "*Nor the exterior nor the inward man resembles that it was.* So spake the Prince of Denmark. Yes, I do know the why of it at least. Something *big* has happened to you, hasn't it?"

His smile was remote from her, the present. "I saw the world. All four corners. By sail, rail, and shanks' mare. Calluses on my butt and feet thick as armadillo hide. That's it. I got thick-skinned all over." He tapped his head again. "In here too. . . . My thoughts are no longer so transparent as they once were. I've been used by experience, and I've made use of it."

Ambiguity seasoned with irony, it made her uneasy, watchful. "Are you making fun of me?"

"*Me* make fun of *you?*" He affected a sorrowful, wistful look that was not altogether successful in submerging the mischief he was working on her. "Whatever are you talking about, dear Callie? You summoned me here, and here I am. It's as simple as that." He threw out his hands with the flourish of a magician demonstrating to his audience that he has nothing up his sleeve or under his cloak.

"As simple as that," she repeated. She couldn't refute him. "Did you come straight here from the depot?"

"I walked up to have a look at the house. It's going to hell, the house, the farm."

"Nate and Walt kept it up as best as they could before Walt died. Now with Nate away at college most of the year, I've been paying hands from the village to look after things."

"The hands you hired are so preoccupied with their own misfortunes, they can't be bothered with anything else."

"It gives them the pride of earning their keep," she explained. "I find something for all of them, the ones I've been supporting through this depression. Sewing, painting, patching, chopping firewood." She was fazed by his reaction.

"Made work, like the old men pushing brooms and leaning on shovels in the WPA. There's no pride or satisfaction in that kind of work. It mocks you. Look, I'll whip that place into shape. Repair the house, slap on a coat of paint. The barn too. There's still good farmland there and I intend to farm it. The graveyard needs a scythe put to it, and then weeding. I can't even see the tall gravestones in the Knight plot. . . . Don't worry, I won't can the men you have marking time over there. They'll stay on and work under me, only now they'll do real man's work."

Callie was impressed by this "new" and "different" man who inhabitated the body of Ham Knight. Not overwhelmed. No, he could be dealt with, and he *would* be dealt with in a way to meet her ends. With a caution and respect uncalled for in her manipulation of his predecessor.

There was an air of mystery about him now that fascinated and excited Callie. Ham living back in Knightsville. Ham and her and Nate. Was it such a twisted fancy to imagine the three of them living in the big white house as a family?

Something else about Ham excited her. His new vitality. The proximity of him aroused her sexually as she had not been aroused in years. *Waiting for Wayne on the dock to transport her off to their island of paradise.* She pictured Ham's hard, muscular body.

She brushed back her hair with her hands. "You can move in as soon as you like. It's clean and the linens have been closeted and wrapped to keep out dust. If you like, I'll drive you over there now. It's not easy for a man to make a home out of a house closed up all these years. It takes a woman's touch."

His response was polite and distant. "Thank you kindly, but it'll be easy for me. A bachelor finds his own way of doing things."

Their eyes met in a silence, each counseling with his or her private thoughts.

The spell is broken. Her witchery is powerless.

His impotency is cured, I feel it. He's as good as in my power.

"Nate . . . is he back in college yet?" he asked. "I can't believe so much time has passed. Little Nate, old enough to go to college."

"Nate's old enough to go to war," she said bitterly.

It came as a jolt. Ham had registered for the draft himself but did not expect to be called up because of his classification. Merchant mariners were exempt from military duty. If he remained inactive they would change his classification, but they drafted the young men first, a sergeant he had met at a San Diego bar had told him. The young men. Like Nate. His son.

"He doesn't think it's worth starting the new term at Yale," she went on. "Some of his classmates have been called up already. They say King Franklin will get us in the war soon, and that it will be a long war. I almost think the young fool is eager to be drafted."

"If he feels that way, why doesn't he enlist?"

"Don't talk like that!" Her sharpness startled him. "Not in front of him, at least. It's been his idea to do just that."

"The boy has sense. A man who enlists can pick his duty. Army, navy, marines, along with whatever specialty he chooses in his branch of service."

"It's all the same in the end. He'll be sent off to die in a foreign war."

He didn't recognize her, not this voice of doom, it couldn't be issuing from the person of Callie Knight Majors. Indomitable. Indestructible. Invulnerable. Immune. That was Callie, all of them. Now here she was like any other American mother worrying about her son. How prosaic.

"In the first place, not every serviceman gets shot at. More don't than do. It takes an army of paperworkers to field an army and a navy. But why look for danger where there isn't any? We're not in the war yet. We may never be."

"I've been in touch with Wayne Harrison, he's one of Roosevelt's top advisers. Wayne is favored to be the Democratic presidential candidate in '44, you may have heard."

"If Roosevelt steps down."

"Don't be an idiot! A fourth term?"

"You always said he was the stuff that kings are made of."

"So I did. . . . My reason for consulting Wayne is this: if Nate is determined to get himself into the service, the best course for him is to seek an appointment to West Point. That way he'd be safe for four years, even if we do get into war."

Ham had to applaud her wiliness. Nate would do his time in the academic environment of the military academy, training how to become an officer and a gentleman. No foxholes, no bullets. It would be almost as comfortable as matriculating at Yale. And only a short drive from Wheatley.

"It may not be as simple as you think for Nate to get into West Point. Boys from all over the country compete for the appointments. They're not up for political grabs."

"Rubbish! Wayne will make the necessary arrangements, he's assured me of that. The problem is to persuade that stubborn mule of mine to do the sensible thing. Perhaps you can help me convince him, Ham."

"Perhaps, we'll see."

Perhaps that flaw, that hint of vulnerability he'd detected in Callie earlier, was like a knot in a pine board, tougher than the grained wood around it when the ax or saw was put to it. The power was still there, no doubt about it. To "own" a man like Wayne Harrison, confidant to presidents and kings, it took some doing. He wondered about the hidden strings she pulled to manipulate this man of honor, elder statesman, future presidential prospect?

"Come, Ham, it's time we were getting back to the house. I'll tell Maude to set another place for supper. She's still with us, the only one of the help. Jane's retired. Old Sam is dead."

"Uncle Walt kept me up on the local news; twice, three times a year he wrote. By the time I got his letters, it wasn't news, I guess, except to me. I'm sorry about Carl, Walt, Sam too." He walked with her back down the garden path. "How are Bruce and Chris?"

"Not well, Ham. They both had to be hospitalized. Bruce

has cirrhosis of the liver, he's the luckier of the two. A year at most is what the doctors say he's got. Poor Chris. When Bruce had to be put in the nursing home, what little mind she had was snapped. They were"—she bit her underlip—"very close in these last years. Her health is good, and she could live another thirty years. It's a fine place she's in, the best that money can buy, but it's a living death. She's a vegetable."

"It must be expensive with both of them in hospitals all this time?"

"Expensive . . ." She brushed a lock of hair off her forehead with the back of a hand. "As fast as the income from the Majors and Knight estates comes in, it's paid out one way or the other. This past year I've had to draw on capital to balance the books."

He put a cigarette into his mouth. "This charity program you've set up for all of Knightsville, I'm sure there must be some way—"

She interrupted him, annoyed that he would have the cheek to even hint. "Cut back on what I'm doing for *our* people in their time of need? It's out of the question." She cast a sidelong suspicious glance at Ham. "You told me you'd come back to satisfy your responsibilities here in Knightsville?"

He looked her in the eye, unblinking. "It's true, and I intend to live up to every letter of that promise."

"I see." He made her ill at ease as no one else had in her rememberance. The remote, enigmatic part of him that was a stranger to her. The Ham she could no longer touch.

Guardedly she told him, "That letter you sent to the lawyers before you left, I never took advantage of it. Your share of your father's estate is still intact. The only use that was made of the letter was to confirm my power of attorney to make decisions in your absence in administrating your holdings. You can assume those duties personally now."

It came as a surprise to Ham that one so avaricious would have acted altruistically when, after all, he had renounced his share of his own free will.

"That was very generous of you, Callie. I thank you, I truly do." Was it possible that the years had effected changes in her as they had in him? He was alarmed at the sudden fierce compulsion he had to believe that they had.

As they neared the hedge she stopped short, bent over slightly from the waist, and clutched her abdomen with one hand. He saw the fleeting spasm of pain across her face.

"What is it?" he asked. "Don't you feel well?"

She straightened up quickly, squared her shoulders, and resumed her pace. "It's nothing, Ham. Female problems. I'm fine now."

He let it pass. "I'm looking forward to seeing Nate. Is he at the house now?"

"I imagine so." She put a hand on his arm. "Ham . . . don't expect the boy to welcome you as the prodigal son. Leaving the way you did, so abruptly, letting him believe you were coming back again soon, it was a terrible blow to Nate. The years you didn't write, not one letter, have been a chronic pain. Don't expect too much, Ham."

"I promise you I won't. I don't. In time I may be able to make him understand, but I won't push the issue."

She looked at him quizzically. "Why should you care if he understands, Ham? You never cared before. When he was a child, you always kept him at arm's length, as if he was a leper."

He jammed his hands in his pockets, threw back his head and looked up at the sky. "Callie . . . what was it you quoted before? Let's see if I have it right: *Nor the Exterior nor the inward man resembles that it was.*"

His cunning bothered her. Cunning was the word for him tilting at her with her own lance, slinging back quotations at her. She would have to be on her guard with Ham.

He blew smoke into the air, a cotton puff that lost itself in the flowing clouds above.

She frowned at him. "Ham! You're smoking! You always disliked smoking, remember those hateful cigars of Carl's?"

He laughed softly. To himself. Shutting her out of his private amusement.

They went into the house through the front door. "This place could use some work on it," he observed.

"I know. The trouble is finding qualified carpenters and roofers and masons. The good ones who settled here with your grandfather and father have either died or migrated to the cities where there's work to be found."

"Then Nate and I will learn how to perform these jobs ourselves."

"Nate and you?" Once more she experienced an inexplicable pang of anxiety.

"Sure, that is, if he's serious about quitting college. I've mastered a few manual skills in my travels. The sum of them should do to get us by with the simple tasks required here and across the river. Nate was eager to work with me before I left, now I'm eager to work with him."

She was about to answer when the boy appeared, far down at the end of the hall, standing in the kitchen doorway. He filled it, height and width. Ham marveled at how his son had grown, though Callie had prepared him for it.

"Nate, come see who's come to visit," she called to him.

"Come to stay, you mean." Ham walked in his direction. "You were this high when I went away, Nate." He held his hand level with his chest. "Now you're a man. A bigger man than I am, it looks to me."

The handsome face changed as precipitously as the blue sky above the valley with the onrush of a dark and angry summer storm. He whirled without a word and left by the kitchen door with long, stiff strides.

"Nate . . . wait!" Ham called to him.

Callie came up behind him and put her hands on his broad shoulder blades. "I warned you, Ham. Let it pass. He'll come around in time, it's quite a shock to him seeing you."

"I've got to talk to him. You wait here, Callie."

He followed Nate. Down the sloping lawn to the beach. Ham paused a moment at the edge of the sand. The youth was standing on the end of the dock, looking out across the river. Legs spread wide, arms bracketed tensely on both sides. Fists bunched. A posture of belligerence if he had ever seen one. He made his approach slowly, speaking in low, affable tone, the way he had moved in on shy, pugnacious stallions when he was roping wild horses in New Mexico.

"I don't blame you a damn bit for what you're thinking about me right now, Nate. It was a rotten thing I did, leaving here the way I did. Lying to you that I was coming back soon. Real courage comes hard for the young." He snorted in self-mockery. "Hell, I wasn't all that young, was I. Well, maybe not, but I sure was more cowardly than you are now. No lies for you. You're giving it to me straight. I am one son of a bitch and you hate my guts this minute. You won't always feel that way, Nate. I'll make it up to you—hell! There I go with more lies. How can I make up for all those years? Never letting you know where I was, what I was doing, not one damn lousy penny postcard! I know, Nate! I know how you must feel. All I ask is that you give me a chance to make up a little bit of what I owe."

He was up behind him now on the dock. He dropped one hand on Nate's shoulder.

He came around swinging with both hands. Shouting, *"You don't owe me a fucking thing, you bastard!"*

Ham parried the right with his left forearm, slipped inside the wide left hook and chopped his right fist, short no more than six inches, hard on Nate's jaw. The youth went flying spread out back into the river.

Ham dropped down on one knee and held out his right hand as Nate surfaced spitting and snuffling near the ladder. Solemnly he said, "Among other gems of wisdom I've learned in my travels and intend to pass on to you was this one here: never lead with your right, man."

He saw the muscles twitching at the back of Nate's jawbone and the corners of his mouth. Straining not to laugh. It was a beginning at least.

Nate spurned the hand. "I can make it up by myself. I'm not a kid."

"Indeed you're not." Ham moved back to show he was going to respect Nate's aloofness. Touching him too soon had been a liberty pre-empted.

"All I ask of you, Nate, is that you listen to what I have to say. You can keep on hating me if you want. I'm not asking you to speak to me. But please listen. You know, your mother says that everything there is to learn about life is in Shakespeare's works. She's right. The sum total of what he's written *is* life. It's life talking to you. You can always gain for yourself if you listen to what another man has to say. Any man."

Nate wiped the water off his face with his hands. Combed it out of his thick black hair with his fingers. Jogged on his left foot to rid his ear of a water bubble. "I'm listening," he muttered grimly.

"First let's go upstairs in the boathouse and get you some dry clothes. Is there any whiskey up there yet?"

"Yeah, I guess so. Mother entertained the Harrisons down here over Labor Day."

A wave of nostalgia broke over Ham as when he stepped into the room. The pegged decks. Binnacle. Franklin stove. All so familiar to him, as if he and Chris had sat kissing on the bunk a week before. No more time than that.

"Poor Chris." He hadn't meant to say it aloud.

"She doesn't feel or care about anything, so the doctor said," Nate called back from the small side room where he was changing. "She gets good care where she is. It's better than if she was still here. It got so I couldn't bear to be in the same room with her, look at her. She was so—so—"

Ham was disappointed. "You loved her once. Do you believe it's right to stop loving a person because he or she loses an arm or a leg, or grows old, or gets sick the way Chris did?"

"No, you don't understand. I still love Chris, she was like my own sister. Even now I think about her some nights and I want to cry. But I don't want to be with her. She's so"—he found his word this time.—"pitiful. I pity her so."

"I do understand." Ham walked to the panoramic window and looked out on the river with a heavy sadness in his breast. *You look like me,* he thought. "You're more like your mother than I imagined."

"How's that?"

"To her pity is the basest of all emotions. To be the object of pity is the most abominable of all conditions in human suffering."

"I can't explain it. I just know what I feel." Nate appeared, pulling a sweatshirt over his head that matched the baggy woolen trousers he had found in one of the lockers.

Ham went over to the little bar on the wall. "Will you have a drink with me?

"Only if there's a beer in the refrigerator. It's new since you left. The door under the sink."

Ham discovered a dozen bottles of beer in the cold cubicle under the sink, with assorted bottles of soda.

He opened one for Nate and mixed a scotch and water for himself. Nate pushed the glass aside he'd served with the beer and drank it from the bottle.

"You'd make a natural merchant seaman," Ham observed.

"That's what you did when you left here, you went to sea. Uncle Walt told me." With a baleful glare: "He read me your letters for a while. But it got so it only made me mad to hear what you had to say to *him!*"

But not one word to me! It was a bone caught in his throat that he could neither swallow nor spit out.

Ham cast down his eyes in humility. "I want to say this now. You think I ran away from Knightsville. From your mother. From you. I cared so little for my birthplace and my people that I forsook you all as dispassionately as I'd discard an old pair of shoes, that's what's eating at you, isn't it?"

"Why then, Ham? *Why?*" They confronted each other across the narrow bar counter, two men poised to Indian wrestle.

A memory of a day long past when a boy and a man had done the same, a brawny forearm pitted against a white, puny stick, pretending.

"I beat you again, Ham!"

"I was running away, but not from you or Callie or Knightsville. It was *me* I was running from. The idiot's game, trying to escape from one's shadow." He sensed Nate would interrupt and held up his hand. "No, wait, hear me out. There are skeletons tucked away tidily in the closets and attic of that old house across the river. One by one, they've got to be brought out into the open and dusted off. You'll hear their bones rattle, Nate. Bear with me, I need time. I never was one to plunge head first into cold water. I've got to get wet by degrees. Coming back here was the first step in that journey, I'm ankle-deep at least. Trust me. Please." He risked some intimacy now, reached across the bar, and put a hand on Nate's shoulder, a firm grip. Their eyes met.

"I don't know why I should. You talk in riddles I can't fathom. It's—it's that I—" Nate raised a hand and groped as if to snatch his meaning out of thin air.

"The thing is you *feel* the answers to the riddles are true and meaningful to our relationship." Ham said it for him.

The tension in him began to wane, Ham could feel it where his hand lay on Nate's shoulder. It was reflected in his face, no longer scowling and defensive.

"Something like that, I guess," he conceded. "All right, Ham, I'll trust you."

Ham offered his hand. Nate pressed it hard. "I'm glad we're friends again, my . . ." Ham paused. "My brother. . . . All right, there's plans to be made. Your mother says you want to drop out of college?"

"It's that or be drafted. I thought I'd beat them to it and enlist. Mother doesn't like the idea, naturally. She's made Wayne Harrison agree to appoint me to West Point, but I'm not sure I want that. I'd feel like a draft dodger, the worst kind, taking an appointment away from some deserving fellow who wants a military career. I certainly don't." He shook his head wonderingly. "Mother, she's fantastic, isn't she? I'd like to know how she managed that. He's not the kind of man whose arm twists easily." A shadow crossed his face. "It's better that I don't know how she did it."

Well, well, Ham thought, his son was deep. Deeper than most his age. Ham himself would never have doubted his mother in any concern. "Mother" to him had meant blind loyalty and infinite love. No faults, no vices in her. Nate was wiser, more perceptive, he knew his mother was human. The last person she'd want to expose her fallibility to, the irony. Nate's mind was keen, like her own . . . *there's the rub.* After all, he was her son too.

"I could get you into the merchant marine with my connections. It would keep you out of the service."

Nate smiled for the first time. "No, thank you, I get seasick in a rowboat. Besides . . . I don't want to get out of serving, Mother aside. I'm no better than any other man, why should I deserve special favor?"

Ham viewed him with a crooked smile. "You'll have to stand up to your mother, that's not easy."

Nate's smile was short-lived. "Do I ever know it. When you cross her, it's inviting a long crusade. She hates to lose."

"I don't think she ever has, not to my knowledge at least." He lit another cigarette, offered the pack to Nate, who shook his head.

The boy stared, rolling the beer bottle back and forth in his palms, his expression morose. "Oh, I've won a few battles; she was set against me going away to school. Still, they were inconsequential triumphs. In this . . . well . . . I just don't know."

"Don't fret about it now, Nate. You'll need all your strength to meet that test when it's upon you. All right, if you decide to drop out of college, you and I can find plenty to occupy us here at Wheatley and across the river before winter comes. There's a lot of work to be done, house repairs, the barn over there needs painting bad, and the land. Hell, boy, we're going to break our humps to get it ready for seeding next spring."

Grinning like a pumpkin, Nate reached over and cuffed his hand around the nape of Ham's neck. "Working together, the way I always planned it as a kid. Hell, brother, my mind's made up. Good-bye, Yale!"

"We'll drink to it," Ham said and raised his glass.

It was not as bad as he had anticipated it would be settling back in the big white Knight homestead. The skeletons he'd told Nate about made their presence felt, but that was part of why he had come back. To exorcise the ghosts. The worst of it was when he and Nate were inspecting the old barn. It smelled of mildew and rot. They climbed up to the loft and it hit his eye with an impact that almost toppled him back off the ladder. The pitchfork!

As clearly as he had that indelible Sunday afternoon, he could see his father, God's wrath stamped starkly on his face, towering above him with the pitchfork.

Nate noticed. "What is it, Ham? You're so pale."

He wiped a hand across his eyes and the apparition vanished. "I saw a ghost," he murmured.

Nate laughed his hearty laugh that Ham so envied. "More likely you saw a rat, there's some big ones took over here since the barn's been boarded up."

Ham's initial undertaking as the tenant of the farm was to summon the three *caretakers*—he deliberately italicized the word when he addressed them—to the house.

"You haven't been taking care of anything that I can see," he told them sternly. "All right, as of now you're off the WPA. Off the dole. You'll earn your pay or I'll find three that will. Now, any man who's afraid of work had better step forward now."

Lem Campball, cousin to Walt, couldn't believe his eyes or his ears, that this authoritative man who reminded him of his World War I drill sergeant was the shy, quiet, awkward youth he had regaled with war stories on the Campball front porch, who blushed when Lucy made eyes at him.

"What are you gawking at, Lem?" Ham demanded.

"Nothing." He swallowed. "I was just admiring how you've changed."

Ham nodded curtly. "I've changed all right, and now I've a mind to make some changes in Knightsville. Tell me something, Lem, how is it a strong, capable fellow like yourself has been doing token work all these years? You don't look over forty-five or six."

Lem Campball was a tall, stooped man with snaggled teeth, scraggly blond hair, and a lean horse face. He twisted his cap self-consciously. "No offense, but I'm forty-three."

"All the more reason you should be doing man's employment instead of behaving like a retired septuagenarian with a government pension."

"There ain't no other jobs in Knightsville," Lem whined.

"He's right—" Art Frisbie caught himself before he called him "Ham." "Yes, sir, *Mr.* Knight. Hasn't been honest work in these parts since the *de*-pression."

"Maybe it's that you haven't bothered to look since the *de*-pression, could that be it?" Ham chided. "Maybe this lad's mother has been playing the bountiful queen for too long. I'll pick up that hot chestnut when the work to be done right here has put some callus on my hands. And my arse," he added with a faint smirk. "I expect I may get the toe of a certain lady's pump planted back there before our problems in Knightsville are resolved."

After Ham dismissed them, Nate looked ill at ease. "It's not my place to interfere, Ham, but don't you think you stomped too hard on them? They're honest, decent men."

"You're right, and honest decent men deserve to be respected and to respect themselves in turn. Listen to me, Nate, here's a bit of knowledge you won't have to learn the hard way I did. I was twenty-four years old when I left Knightsville. Twenty-four, and I had never earned a dollar in my life. I know what you're thinking, I worked hard around this farm all my life, first for my father, then when he died for myself. But it's not the same as breaking free and standing up on your own two feet. I mean, all my life the money was there in the bank, in securities, in property. It was mine just the same if I worked or sat on my ass in the shade. I remember the first paycheck I got as a seaman. I cashed it, and when I walked out of the bank with that roll bulging in my back pocket, I felt damned good. I swaggered down the street with my sailor's rolling gait, and I knew there wasn't anything in the world that I couldn't reach out and get. I went into the first bar and ordered a beer." He smacked his lips. "Best brew I'd ever tasted. Then I ordered a hamburger, it beat the prime sirloin we used to cut from our own stock. I bought a pair of shoes from Thom McAn, they felt as soft as glove leather. You understand the point I'm trying to make? I'd earned them swabbing decks and polishing brass and standing watch in pitching seas in the dead of winter, so cold the flying scud glued my eyelids tight and turned my fingers into icicles. I was my own man. On my own. Alone. I didn't need an inheritance to make it in the world." He thrust his thick forefinger into Nate's chest. "One of these days you are going to have to take your own cut at life. Prove yourself. Some to the world but chiefly to yourself. There's the pride. It makes a man feel good to be respected by his peers, but there's no short cuts to winning. First, he's got to build self-respect. It's why I laid into Art and Lem and Stan the way I did."

"You laid it onto *her* pretty good too," Nate said slyly. " 'Bountiful queen'; if she heard that, you'd get that kick in the arse sure as hell."

Ham nodded gravely. Callie was not a laughing matter. He was in no great hurry to force the showdown from which there was no evasion.

"Your mother might have been a Knight by birth, the way she craves power."

Nate came to her defense. "You believe that's why she goes on helping the poor of Knightsville, because it gives her a sense of power?"

"Why else would she do it?"

"That's not fair, Ham. She's given a lot to the people around here. It was more expense that she could afford, I heard the lawyers and accountants telling her that only last July."

"What's money except the currency to purchase power? Power is always expensive. If you value it so much, you'll pay any price to make it your own and keep it. My mother used to accuse my father of the sin of pride, the pride he took in Knightsville. That the Knights were the founders and the 'proprietors' of a village he viewed as their personal feudal estate. She felt the opposite was true, that in reality it was the village and villagers who *owned* the Knights."

Ham was content to rest his case for the present. Let Nate ponder on the notions he'd introduced. He trusted Nate's inquisitive mind to lead him to the right conclusions.

On his part Nate was intrigued by all of Ham's philosophy. Skeptical of some of it, but he kept his doubts to himself.

The days and weeks that followed demonstrated to Nate that Ham was a sounder philosopher that he had allowed.

The three hands seemed to profit enormously from Ham's indoctrination. He was a hard taskmaster, but fair, as quick to praise as to criticize. By the end of September, Lem, Art, and

Stan were putting forth the combined effort he demanded of them, with some extra output on their own initiative. Thriving on the new industry he had fostered in them.

"It's new and exhilarating to them," Ham explained to Nate, "because Knightsville has been in suspended animation for so long, they've forgotten what it's like to have a future."

By mid-November the repairs and painting were completed on Wheatley and the Knight house, inside and out. The barn was shipshape, vivid against the green grass in its fire-engine-red bright coat. The fields were all plowed. And Ham had bought two milk cows, six hens, and two horses for a start.

He decided it was time to start proselytizing in earnest. He began by preaching his faith at the general store in the evenings where a fair sampling of the people still attended the ceremony of the night express thundering through on her way from Albany to Fort Edward. The high point of the excitement was when the handlers in the postal car slung the canvas mail sacks off. On the fly, churning up clouds of dust in the dry weather as they tumbled over the ground, brought up short by the wooden split-rail fence along the parapet above the stream.

A signal for the men and women to gather inside the store and wait for Alva Lampbert to sort out the letters. Children pressing around the penny-candy counter at one side of the store, dirty fingers and snotty noses on the smeared glass. Wide, serious, sorrowful eyes fixed on the treasure of sweets that few had pennies to buy anymore.

Incoming mail was made up mainly of circulars and long-overdue bills from Sears and Montgomery Ward. The balance from sons and daughters who had the good sense and good fortune to be free of the stagnation that was Knightsville.

Alva Lampbert and his wife, Rena, were both stringier than he remembered them. Shrunken too. Old age for them like the potion in Alice's bottle. They'd keep diminishing until they were nothing.

One night he confronted Bill Miller, one-time blacksmith, his magnificent physique all bloated with lard and beer.

"I've got a job for you, Bill," Ham said. "I want new shoes on my two horses. The dealer I bought them from outside Clinton, he's looking to hire an all-around hand for his stables. From what he told me, the job would fit you to a T."

The big man puffed up like a bullfrog and his face turned

fire red. His tongue was tied in knots. "Well . . . that's . . . that's . . . I sure am grateful . . . but . . . that-er-ah . . ." He went into a fit of violent coughing.

"What's the matter with you, Miller? You look and act like a schoolmarm who's heard an indecent proposal."

The people laughed and moved in closer. Alva cackled and called from behind the postal window, "Indecent is what it sounds like to old Bill. A job like that, he'd have to take the train to Clinton, stay sober ten hours a day, and work up a sweat. He's got to get off the welfare because he's got a job. It's worth more to him sitting on the bench out front guzzling beer. Between the welfare check and the dole that Majors woman hands out."

"You're content to live on handouts all the rest of your life, Miller?" Ham chastened him. "A lackey to the duchess in that mansion across the river."

"I'm no lackey," Miller bridled, but with pale fire. "Mrs. Majors is a nice, kind lady. She treats us right."

A voice jeered from the back of the group around them. "Wasn't that you last week I saw polishing her car out front? She drove over here and found Billy asleep on the bench. Gave him a slap with her riding crop and told him to get the lead out and spruce up her buggy. And did you ever jump, Billy boy!"

He was mortified, he could hardly speak. The mousy voice emanating from the big man produced hilarious laughter. "She didn't slap me. She had to poke me to wake me, that's all." He looked over the head of the crowd. "You, Danny Stiles, you're a fine one to talk. Last July we was playing penny ante in Alva's back room and she phoned and told Alva to send Danny right over there, she had a task for him. He lit out so fast, he forgot to cash in his chips."

Miller's tormentor was squelched and withdrew from the fray. Old Charley Sills, who had been one of the best mechanics in the county before he became unemployed seven years earlier when the factory where he was chief millwright shut down, rubbed the back of his neck and said with understandable self-consciousness, "Let's not trade insults, boys. After all, there isn't a man, woman, or child in this store who isn't beholden to Mrs. Majors. When she wants a favor from someone, she gets her way. That's only right, we owe her that."

Ham laughed in derision. "Beholden? Is that what you call it? You hear me, all of you, Callie Majors owns this town lock, stock, and barrel. She owns *you,* Bill Miller, and *you,* Danny Stiles, and *you,* Charley Sills. Owns the lot of you just as sure as any medieval duchess owned her fiefdom. In the old days it was the only way of life. A poor peasant pledged himself to some rich lord or duke in return for a parcel of land to work, some seed to plant and protection from rogues and bandits. He became a serf to his benefactor. Serf, that's from the Latin, it means 'slave.' "

He heard indignant protestations from all around him, but in their faces Ham saw promise. The shamefaced expressions that might be worn by an audience of men and women whose clothing was made to vanish by a mischievous sorcerer. Eyes averted from each other's nakedness. A pose they couldn't hold indefinitely. They were going to take a long, intent look at themselves pretty soon now, if he'd judged right.

Charley Sills caught up to him outside the store on his way back up the hill.

"Ham, you got a minute to spare?" he asked.

"Sure thing, Charley. Walk along with me up to the house and I'll buy you a drink."

"What you said tonight about Mrs. Majors owning this town, all of us. Hell! Ham, I don't want to be a slave to anyone." He placed a hand on Ham's arm. "But you don't know what it was like at the worst of the depression. No work, no money, no food. When a man sees his children starving, it breaks him. His manhood is scarred. Like a dog who's been whipped by a bad owner. When it's had too much of that ill treatment, let even the kindest hand reach out to it and its tail goes between its legs. I, this whole town, Ham, we've come through a bad whipping. It's been comfortable letting the welfare and Mrs. Majors look out for us."

Ham stopped, faced him, and took him by the arms. "Charley, the depression is over. You can get work if you want it. You've got skills that are in great demand these days."

Charley touched his gray hair and his white mustache. "A man my age, I'm sixty-three, you're dreaming, Ham."

"Charley, you've got to think and act in the present, not the past," Ham remonstrated with him. "All these young men the government is drafting into the service. They've got to be supplied with guns and planes and tanks and ships. There are defense plants being built all over the country, they're sprouting everywhere like dandelions. On my way up the valley from

New York, I counted a half dozen. The papers are filled with 'Help Wanted' ads, pages of them. They need top-grade mechanics like you, Charley. Tell you what, I'm going to look into it for you."

The old man's eyes were brighter than any pair he'd seen in this dreary town since his return from exile.

"Ham, I'd sure be grateful. I swear to you, it's always shamed me living on the dole the way I've been all this time." His voice cracked. "To work again with tools, it'd be like laying with a woman again after being in jail. God bless you, Ham!"

"You still want that drink, Charley?"

"Thanks, but I think I'll pass it up, no offense, please, Ham." He tittered. "I want to break the news to Mildred."

Ham stood in the middle of the dirt road—it was dark now—looking after Charley quickstepping off in the direction of his home. He breathed in deeply of the crisp autumn night smelling of pine and looked up at the evening star, a scintillating gem in the navy sky.

"The world keeps turning despite you, Callie." He lifted one hand high in a fanciful toast. "To you, World *ad infinitum.*"

He marched on home whistling the "Beer Barrel Polka."

A fanciful toast to a fanciful world that would end one month after, on a Sunday in December. The seventh of December in the year Nineteen Hundred and Forty-One Anno Domini. A pretentious proclamation worthy of a momentous date.

The new world was upon mankind. A mad-whirling tornado of chaotic change and revolution in which no one thing caught up in its frenzy would ever be the same again. The shape of nations and continents. The very air man breathed. Nothing. Cities would vaporize in balls of fire and mushroom clouds would scatter their ashes in the heavens. Men would plant their flags on the moon. "Reaching for the stars," no longer poetry but science. All in a score of years and five.

Within one week after Japan unleashed its bombers in the "day of infamy" at Pearl Harbor, the United States was at war with the axis powers, Germany, Italy, and Japan.

Charley Sills was working as a government inspector in a defense factory that produced armored tanks and vehicles, forty miles down the Hudson. He boarded up the house he and his wife had lived in for forty years and moved to a new apartment near his job.

The thirties had ushered in the exodus of the young from Knightsville. World War II set their mothers and fathers free.

Ham, out of his own pocket, inaugurated the first bus service from Knightsville to Clinton, where a mammoth aircraft plant was under construction.

Before the New Year every able man and woman over sixteen and under sixty-five was self-supporting.

That Christmas there was little "peace and good will" on the planet. Less of it at Wheatley, where the bad blood that had been fermenting between Callie and Ham since his return to Knightsville boiled over on Christmas Day. She had invited him to feast on the skewered bird. Her real motive was to skewer him.

He sensed the tension as soon as he arrived. Callie and Nate were drinking eggnog in front of the cold hearth. He looked from her to the eagle spread over the mantel, decided they made a bellicose pair. Nate's expression confirmed he was in for a fight.

Right off Ham blundered into a trap. He rubbed his icy-stiff fingers, held them up to the flames that were not there.

"Why don't you have a fire, the day is perfect for it? Ten below and it's snowing again."

"Because there's not one man in Knightsville who'd chop me firewood, thankless louts. Bill Miller, Dan Stiles, they're all alike." She mimicked Bill: " 'I sure wish I could do that favor, ma'am, for you, but I don't rightly see I got time. I'm working a double shift on Christmas Eve.' " Her voice trembled with outrage. "My money was good enough for him last Christmas!"

"Mother, that's not fair," Nate protested. "Why should Bill Miller chop wood for us when he's working sixty hours a week as it is? Besides, I wanted to chop the wood, but you wouldn't let me."

Ham went over to the server and poured himself a tall scotch. "Why are you angry with Bill Miller and the others in Knightsville? Because for the first time in years they've got work that pays well? Not only in dollars but in self-respect."

"Self-respect!" She spit it out with distaste. "Oh, how I rue the day I wrote you the letter that brought you back here to stir up these simple folks against me. Me who saw to it that they had food in their bellies and a roof over their heads all during the depression, and long after that. Ungrateful curs!"

"Curs," Ham said dryly. "Like the old blue-tick hound used to be here at Wheatley, you fed and housed him. He was so grateful, I remember, how he'd shimmy up to you on his belly, tail wagging, and lick your feet. Is that the kind of gratitude you expect from humans?"

"Don't patronize me, you hypocrite." She paced up and down before the fireplace, an angry tigress. "The only reason you came back here was to turn the people against me. All that self-righteous pablum you've been feeding them."

He stirred his drink with a finger, licked the finger dry, peered at her challengingly. "Pride and self-respect, honest work for honest pay, you figure there's something treasonous about favoring such principles?"

"You've even got them believing I'm sapping their manhood like some Salem witch." She sneered. "There never was a man among them in all of Knightsville!"

Nate made matters worse by speaking up for Ham. "Mother, you make it sound as if Ham himself declared this war just to spite you."

She did a thing she'd never done before. She slapped his face. An impetuous act, which for a split second made strangers of them. To strike a stranger. To be struck by a stranger. Ham read it in their dazed faces.

It passed and Callie reached up and put a hand to Nate's reddening cheek with tenderness. "Nate . . . son . . . I didn't mean . . . I—I—please, I'm sorry."

"It's all right, Mother." He gripped her wrist firmly and removed her hand from his face.

"You're vexed with me," she said.

"No I'm not. Stop apologizing, for God's sake!" It was her atypical contriteness that was intolerable.

She turned to Ham. "You're even trying to turn my son against me, I know what you're up to, Ham."

"You're out of your mind, Mother." Nate ridiculed her.

Ham laughed. "Nate, I think your mother could use another eggnog to settle her down."

Callie clenched her fists against her thighs, her nails biting through the wool skirt into flesh. The momentum of her wrath was lost. Worse, she'd lost face. She'd been outmatched by the two of them. *Father and son posed against the mother.*

"I have eyes and I have ears, I know what you're up to." And *that* she determined would be the final word on the subject. For now. "No more eggnog, Ham, will you fix me a bourbon and water, please?" She was the mistress of Wheatley; Ham would find that out to his regret.

Ham and Nate went out to the shed after they had finished eating and split some logs, in the face of Callie's objections that Nate would chop off an arm or leg.

"He handles an ax better than I do." Ham scoffed at her misgivings. "Besides, the two of us need to work off all that turkey, mashed potatoes, and stuffing, not to mention the pies. You give the cook a hand with the leftovers."

The logs, wet with snow, snapped and complained in the beginning, spitting coals against the screen, but Ham coaxed them with a bellows until the flames leaped high into the chimney. They had their coffee and brandy there, chairs pulled up close on the hearth to enjoy the warmth.

It began innocuously; cataclysms have a way of creeping up on those they doom.

"You'll be nineteen in a few months," Ham commented. "And from what I hear, now that we're at war, the selective service boards are gobbling up you young fellows before the ink on your classification cards are dry. Don't play it too close, Nate; if you have a mind to enlist, do it before your birthday."

"Nate won't be drafted, nor will he be enlisting." Callie reigned over him with a superior smile. "He's going to West Point. Tomorrow I'll phone Wayne in Washington and tell him to make the arrangements."

Ham looked at Nate with narrowed eyes. "I'm surprised to hear that." His tone said he was disappointed too. "You led me to think that appointment would be the last option you'd choose."

Nate sat forward in his chair with his forearms braced on his knees, staring straight down at the rug. His face was flushed.

"Mother wants me to accept it," he said in a small voice.

"I know that, but what do you want to do, that's the first consideration?"

"Don't confuse the boy," she said. "He's made up his mind."

"Has he? Nate, did you decide this or did your mother?"

"Stop it, Ham!" Temper detracted from her beauty, nostrils pinched together, lips thin and bloodless. "I won't have you badgering Nate about this. He's made up his mind."

"Then let him speak for himself, Callie. Look at me, Nate."

She rose from her chair. "I'm warning you, Ham!"

He ignored her. "Nate, why did you change your mind about that appointment? You told me you wouldn't take it because you didn't want special favors. You'd serve your country like all the rest, you said."

Nate lifted his head and met Ham's questioning gaze. "It's true, I want to enlist," he blurted out miserably. "She won't let me."

"Nate! That will be all, the issue is closed." She clapped her hands imperiously.

"The queen has spoken." Ham leaned back in the chair, crossed his legs, regarded her with distaste.

"*No,* Mother!" Ham was on his feet, towering over her slight figure.

Goliath menacing David, Ham thought wryly, the giant was doomed without support.

He turned to Ham. "Nag, nag, nag, it's all she'd done the past few weeks. If I have to hear once more what my duties and responsibilities to her are and to this goddamned pygmy dynasty she's so obsessed with, I'll go mad!"

"Nate! How dare you!" She raised her hand.

"I do dare! Go ahead, slap me again, it will make it easier for me!" he defied her.

Instead she pressed the back of the hand to her flushed forehead. "Don't talk like that to me, son. You'd think I had been an unkind, unloving mother when all these eighteen years the worst punishment I've ever done to you is to smother you with love."

Nate laughed harshly. "You hear that, Ham, she boasts about it? Smothered with love, at least you're honest about that, Mother."

"I'm always honest."

"Are you, now? You call it honesty, how you tricked me into compliance about the appointment? Listen to this, Ham. I asked her last week what she wanted for Christmas. She answered in the coy way she has that, since it was my last Christmas at Wheatley before I went into uniform, the gift should be a special one. I agreed. She made me promise on my word of honor that I'd please her in this one request. I did.

Now you can guess what she asked for, I was a fool not knowing."

"Her request was that you accept the appointment to West Point. Look here, Nate, men of honor aren't bound by pledges won by trickery. Your mother speaks so righteously about duty and responsibility, I've gone that route with her myself. All right, I'll tell you where your first duty lies, it's to yourself. Say the hell with the appointment and enlist. That's what *you* want to do, isn't it?"

"Yes."

She turned away from her son and folded her arms. Her voice was calm now. The flat brassy hush that heralds the approaching storm at sea, Ham felt it.

"You don't see what he's doing, how could you, Nate, his hidden motive. . . . He's goading you to throw away your life the way he did, to run away."

"You're wrong, Callie. I've talked to Nate some. I told him why I'd run away, to find myself. The reason he's got to get away from this place and *you* is to save himself. Don't get trapped here, lad, flee before it's too late."

"You told him *some?*" The irony was unmistakable. She was ready now. To unleash the ultimate weapon that would destroy Ham. She did an about-face with military precision. "He lied to you, son. Ham Knight ran away from Knightsville because he couldn't bear the sight of you and me."

Nate was shaken. "What did you say?"

"He despises both of us, Nate. It's fitting, Ham's a mariner too, though not as ancient as Coleridge's. He wears an albatross around his neck, yes, you and I are the effigies haunting his conscience."

Nate appealed to Ham. "Has she gone daft? Can you make any sense out of her gibberish?"

Ham remained silent, bemused, fingertips pressed to the point of his chin.

"Gibberish, is it? Go ahead, Ham, you've talked to Nathaniel *some,*" she taunted. "Talk to him of it all. See, son, he's tongue-tied. Don't you remember, when you were a child, how you adored your big brother, Ham? How you chased after him, and rarely caught him? He was always running, even then. *To get you out of his sight!*"

Nate was light-headed as the rush of memory overwhelmed him. He rubbed his eyes with his fingers. He *did* remember. Hurt so often by Ham's rejection. He shook his head to clear it, looked at Ham sitting so silent, not disputing her accusations.

"Ham, why don't you say something?" he implored.

"Because there's nothing he can say," Callie gloated. "There's nothing your *father* could possibly say to deny what I'm telling you."

"My *what! My father.* I must be going mad, I thought I heard you say Ham was my father." His nervous laughter flirted with insanity.

"Your father. Ham is not your brother, *he is your father.*" She enunciated every word. Pleasurably. "This paragon of virtue you revere. Whose words you cull as if they were gems of wisdom. This man of honor, when he was two years younger than you, he lusted after his father's wife. Day and night, week after week, until the power of his passion finally broke down my resistance. Yes, I was seduced and I lay with him even while his father was working in the fields or snoring in his bed." She raked Ham with her blazing eyes. "That's how you were conceived, my son. By Ham, not his father, Nathaniel. You're Ham's son!"

Nate backed away from her, overcome by nausea and revulsion. He could hardly speak, his throat was so clogged with emotions. "Good God! What kind of an evil fiend are you, to say such things? I've always known you let nothing stand in your way when you seek a goal. You can bend steel to your will if you set your mind on it. I can forgive your wiles, chicanery, deceit, even your falsehoods. You're dear to me, Mother. But this time you've gone too far. This monstrous lie you're saying." He groaned. "Mother, Mother, to say that Ham—" His eyes swung around on Ham. "Ham . . . she doesn't know what she's saying, she's unbalanced by the fear I'll leave her. . . . Ham . . . ?" The contradiction he wanted so desperately to see in Ham's expression, to hear him say she was lying, was denied to Nate.

"It's true, Nate. I'm your father. There's a question about who was seduced and who was the seducer, but that's an inane point, anyway." He stood up. "And as your father I'm telling you, get free of her. Be grateful to your mother for this, son, it's because of her that I came back to Knightsville to discharge my responsibilities."

"Damn you! Damn you! Damn you!" she screeched. She threw herself on Nate, sunk her nails into his sleeve. "See! See! You can see what he is, son. He admits everything. A man who'd fornicate with his own father's wife, what kind of a degenerate is he?"

Nate looked down at her. Looked *down* on her. She cringed from the abhorrence mirrored in his eyes.

He spoke in a graveside whisper. "What kind of a degenerate is *he?* . . . And what about *you,* Mother? *Mother!*" He uttered it like a curse. He brushed her hands off his sleeve with the contempt he'd show a crawling insect.

"Nate! Wait!" She reached out to him.

He backed away from her, whirled, and ran out of the room. Callie started after him, stumbled to her knees, and pressed both hands to her waist. Squeezed her eyes shut tight and moaned.

Ham went over to her, bent down, and put his hands on her shoulders. "Are you all right?"

"Get out of this house!" she mumbled through gritted teeth.

"Callie . . . you brought this on yourself. In damning me you damned yourself. You must have realized that."

"Get out!"

It reverberated through the house. Echoed from the high nave of the center hall.

out . . . out . . . out . . . out

He left her crouched in the parlor, took his coat and hat from the guest closet and departed into the snowy night. Ice pellets punished the backs of his hands and his face like fine game shot.

Ham went home, built a fire, and poured himself a half tumbler of apple brandy from the dusty jug his father had stored in a corner of the pantry for as long as he could remember. He stood by the window over the sink looking out across the graveyard where Nathaniel and all the other Knights rested.

Rest in peace. Did his father?

The graves and markers were buried deep in white, except for the two tall gravestones marking the place where Cyrus and

Emma were buried side by side. Snow reached up to the bronze plaques.

Ham walked into the parlor and sat on the couch before the fire where he had first kissed Chris Majors. Poor mad thing. He sipped his applejack and stared at the hypnotic flames.

He watched the blazing logs shrink and fall apart, heap the grate with glowing coals. He never closed his eyes, yet a part of his brain must have slept, for abruptly the clock on the mantel was striking two and someone was pounding on the front door. He put down the empty glass and jumped up, curious to see who would call on a stormy night such as this one at such an hour.

It was Callie. Her face was a pale oval in the fur hood crusted with ice crystals.

"You look distressed, has anything happened?" he asked, concerned by her agitated appearance. "Is it Nate?"

She rushed past him into the parlor. "Where is he, Ham?"

He shut the door and went after her. "Nate? Here?"

"Don't lie to me! It isn't enough that you've come between Nate and me. Now you've taken him away."

"Callie! I swear, I haven't seen Nate since I left Wheatley. Are you sure he's gone? Did you look everywhere in the house? The boathouse, I'll bet that's where he's at!"

"No, I thought of that, I've looked everywhere." She walked past him into the hall, her eyes darting suspiciously up the stairs, down the long hall, across the hall into the dining room. "Are you being truthful, Ham? Please! I beg of you, if you know where he is . . ." Emotion choked her, her hand flew to her throat.

"Callie, I don't know where he is. I'd think this is the last place you'd expect to find him after what he's learned about the two of us tonight. . . . Is his car gone, did you think of that? He may have driven to Clinton, the plows are keeping the highways reasonably clear."

She shook her head. "His car is in the garage." She was close to panic now. "Ham, my God! He wouldn't go off on foot in this blizzard?"

The same glum thought had occurred to Ham. In his despondency over the truth he'd heard from Callie's lips, he might have renounced everything. He had a frightening vision of old Carl Majors dragging one foot after the other over the rough planking of the bridge, marching to his own execution.

He walked back into the parlor with Callie on his heels.

"Ham, what are we going to do?"

He picked up the phone. "I'd better call the sheriff's office. No, wait, did you look in his closet, his drawers?"

"I didn't think."

"All right, there's one possibility to be looked into before we bring the law in on this. I'll phone the depot."

With the onset of war it became a government regulation that the railroad had to keep a man on duty at every station along the line around the clock. It was a common occurrence for passenger trains and slow freights to be diverted onto sidings to permit troop trains and freights carrying military hardware to speed through to their destinations.

He reached the new man hired as assistant to Hec Jones, the stationmaster. "Did you have a passenger leaving Knightsville any time tonight? You know young Nathaniel Knight, don't you?" A pause and then with finality. "I see. Thank you very much." He put the receiver back on the hook and turned to Callie.

"What is it? He was there, I can read it in your face."

"Yes, Nate was at the station."

"Come on, we'll go and get him." She started for the door. Ham caught her, held her arms.

"No, Callie, it's no use. He's not there anymore. Ed Peters flagged down the one forty-five to New York for him. He's on the train. With two suitcases, Ed said."

"No-o-o-o-ohhhh-owww!" She threw back her head and howled like a she wolf torn from her cub. He had seen Callie cry only one other time, the day Nate had almost drowned in the river.

"Carrying on like this won't help." He tried to calm her. "Accept it, Callie, he's a man. He's made a man's choice."

Her green eyes were enormous, magnified by the tears, dark as the sea. "*No!* Not by his own choice. It's your doing, Ham! You came back to Knightsville to destroy us, my son and me, with some twisted notion that if you obliterate the two of us you can wipe away your own guilt!"

"That's your twisted notion, not mine."

"It's true! You and your obsessive guilt. That sanctimonious image you have of yourself, Christ on the cross would suit you fine. Penance and atonement, you wear them like a cassock, such saintly pride. Saint Ham! Let me *go!*"

Ham held firm to her wrists. "I will when you stop acting like a madwoman. It's what drove Nate away, and sure as hell it's not going to bring him back."

"You contemptible ninny, all these years carrying around your grand ennobling guilt. You fatuous monk. You didn't kill your father. You had nothing to do with it. It wasn't God that sent him to the barn that afternoon. It was *me!*"

"You sent my father to the barn? How could you?"

"That morning I mentioned to him, quite casually, that you'd been taking some girl into the hayloft every Sunday after dinner."

He felt nothing at first. Numb in body and mind. "You told that to my father, *knowing* he'd come up there and find you and me?"

"I planned it perfectly, didn't I, Saint Ham?" She tormented him. "So you see that halo you've earned from all the years of penance and atonement is made of fool's gold. Fool! Fool!" She spat in his face.

Rage boiled up like lava in him, erupted, all reason left him. His after-memory of the scene made up of fragments, a jigsaw puzzle with pieces missing. He ripped her coat off. Buttons flying everywhere. Her dress? The tattered remnants good for nothing but dustcloths. Blood streaming down her face from nose and mouth. His last clear point of view was looking down at Callie, kneeling over her, with his hands encircling her throat, pressing down hard on her windpipe. Mortal combat. Eyes locked. No fear, no plea, no submission in her green feline irises.

Startled by the sight of one white breast loose of the torn brassiere. The nipple rose red and turgid. His grip on her throat relaxed.

One hand moved down the curve of her shoulder, fingers stroking the satin flesh stretched tight over her collarbones. Powerless to influence his hand. Her breast was a magnet, pulling at his hand. His hand covered it. The nipple sharp against the sensitive skin of his palm.

"Ham . . ." Her voice soft and coaxing. She took the unbroken strap of the brassiere and slid it down over her shoulder, baring the other breast. Lifted both arms toward him in supplication. Breasts bunched together, inviting him. Her hands caressed the back of his neck. The downy hair curling at the nape bristled.

Her bruised, bloody mouth smiled. "It's only fair, Ham. You took Nate away, now you're here in his place."

"No!" His voice tremored.

"Yes, love me, Ham."

"I *hate* you!"

"Love, hate, there's no more than a spider's thread between the two. You want me, don't you?"

His head bobbed up and down, a doll with a spring in its neck. "I want you."

She clasped his face and pulled it down to her face. Her mouth opened to receive him. Bloody lips soft and moist on his, smelling and tasting of metal. Iron in the blood.

Her hand between their bodies, expertly opening his pants, extracting his penis, swollen and rigid.

Big as life!

The jest of a whore he'd laid in Hong Kong, the only English she could speak.

"Big as life, Yank-ee."

He tried to get up on his knees to pull off his pants.

"No, don't spoil it," she cooed in his ear, nibbling the lobe. "Now's the time, not one moment longer."

She positioned him and lifted her hips to take him in. A mighty roaring in his ears, filling his whole body like air rushing in to satiate a vacuum. Erotic magic dispelling the curse. Nathaniel Knight, his father, was buried at long last.

The next day Callie moved out of Wheatley and in with Ham in the big white Knight house on the hillside. It was ironical. Callie had harmed herself far more than him when she turned the secret weapon that he had fathered Nate on Ham. Ham had delivered himself into her hands in a like manner. Since his return he had kept himself aloof from Callie, resisting all of her enticements to join in any meaningful relationship with her. His celibacy had been his strength, a weapon to keep her at bay. But flesh had betrayed him, just as Callie's cool, keen logic had betrayed her.

In the weeks and months that followed, she was as charming, loving, tender, and as nagging and bitchy as any normal wife. Callie kept her own house.

"I've had enough of servants," she professed. "This is the way it was when I first came here. I want to do things for you, Ham, and for our son when he returns from the army. Oh, he'll be back, Ham, I know he will. Like you, Ham. You came back."

"I came back . . ." he repeated flatly. He wasn't so sure about Nate, but held his tongue. Let her keep her illusions. There was a pathetic quality about her he'd never recognized before. Thin spots in her once impervious armor where the flesh was vulnerable.

A sadistic side to him, he realized with a twinge of guilt. He relished probing into those chinks, making her suffer. Her great phobia was that Ham would board the train one day as he had before, as Nate had, and leave her alone. He fed the fear slyly.

"I'm getting restless," he'd say. "Maybe I'll run up to Albany for a few days."

"I'll go with you," she'd say. "I don't want to be alone here. You're all I've got now, Ham. I've never been so alone in all my life."

He was tempted to tell her, "You alone? You have everything you ever wanted, all that you dreamed about when you were in that orphanage. Land, money, two big houses, one a mansion fit for any of the River Rich along the Hudson. Your own town, even if it doesn't suit your fancy that way it once did. You even have your own graveyard. No, not the Knight cemetery, Callie. *Knightsville.* You're as good as buried now!" But again he held his tongue. She was too pathetic.

During his first year in the Air Force, Nate mailed them four letters. The first began:

> Dear Mother and Ham,
> I can't think of you as a father yet; I suspect I never will. Right now I don't want to talk about the truths you revealed to me the night I left. I don't want to even think about them, it's too painful. I can understand now why you ran away from the truth, Ham. Quite frankly, for the present, I must detach myself in every way I can from the two of you. I would prefer not to open this frail channel of communication, but Ham, you taught me how cruel and selfish it is to cut yourself completely off from those who love you. Radical surgery. I know you love me, Mother. Ham, you too. I, for my part, don't hate either of you for the wrongs you have done in the past. I don't feel anything at all. I'm still numb from the shock, I guess. Meanwhile, I'm keeping a diary, more of a journal really. It starts back

when I was a child, as far back as I can recollect. In fact, it goes back much further than my birth date. Bits and pieces of family gossip and reminiscences picked up from mother, Ham, Bruce and Chris, even strangers. The Knights and Majorses are not strangers to the people of Saratoga County, and by keeping my identity to myself, I've acquired quite a few juicy tidbits about this tribe. Some apocryphal, no doubt, but the truth in most of the tales is easy to separate.

> I like the air force. I don't think I have the emotional stability to become a pilot, so I am setting my sights on being a navigator. I always was good in math, and this work is fascinating, like solving puzzles, I was good at them as well. I should really edit some of these run-on sentences. I try to keep my journal in better literary form. . . .

Callie rhapsodized for weeks after that first letter arrived.

"I told you, Ham. He's forgiven us, oh, I knew he would. He loves me as I love him. Mother and son, we're bound together forever."

Ham was silent.

Callie wrote her son a letter every day and two on Sundays.

"What can you find to say to him anymore?" Ham asked her with amusement.

"Oh, I send him grist for his mill, his journal. I wrote ten pages last week about my recollections of the orphan asylum."

Ham laughed. "You honestly believe he's going to put that in his diary?"

"It's not a diary, it's a journal, a family history, I would imagine."

Ham sighed. "Then for all of our sakes, I hope he burns it."

The last letter they received from Nate before he was shipped overseas depressed Callie. The sight of the ominous APO number in the upper left-hand corner of the envelope. The contents confirming her apprehensions.

> . . . We don't know where we're going, but it's bound to be somewhere in the thick of the action. Now that Africa has been invaded, Europe will be our next stop, and soon, I'm betting . . .

Another paragraph had a more subtle unsettling effect on Callie:

> There's a girl I've been seeing a lot of. I think very highly of her, and I think you will too when you meet her. Next summer she intends to spend a week's vacation at Lake George and she promised to stop in and visit you on her way. . . .

Callie frowned and bit her underlip, tapping with a finger on the sheet in her lap. "A girl, I wonder where he met her?"

"Probably at the USO," Ham ventured. "One of the girls who entertain the soldiers at canteens, they're volunteers."

"Yes, and I know what type of girls volunteer for that sport. . . . You know, it's probably a good thing the army took him out of *her* clutches!"

Summer came and went and the *femme fatale,* who Callie had believed posed a threat to her precious son, did not put in her promised appearance in Knightsville. Nate did not mention her either in his letters from England.

> I'm a full-fledged navigator now. Note the rank, Second-Lieutenant Nathaniel Knight. I can't tell you what our duty is, that's security, but my job is to see our bombers get there and back again as the crow flies. . . .

Callie's health began to fail in the summer of 1944, a dramatic transformation. It seemed to Ham she aged more that one summer than in the twenty years preceding it. He saw a certain symbolism in her decline, a form of justice too. Her youth and beauty had been sustained by feeding on the lives of those around her. Body, mind, and soul. She had bloomed while Knightsville wasted away. Now with Callie's withering the town was resurrecting itself.

Retribution?

The medical diagnosis was less poetic. Ham came in one day and found her writhing on the kitchen floor in agony. She was under observation in Clinton General Hospital for three days. The tests and X rays left no doubt. Cancer of the stomach in the terminal stage. The doctor told her she had ulcers and Ham went along with the fraud. But Callie knew the truth. Sickness hadn't dulled her keen faculty for looking past the words and masks that those about her presented to glean their secret thoughts.

"I won't die until my son comes home," she vowed. "I want his love and his forgiveness to warm and comfort me in my cold dark journey into eternity."

Ham believed her. The specialist had given her four months at most to live. Six months after that she was alive, no, she existed. A mummy with parchment stretched over the bones. The morphine she ingested each day could kill an elephant, the druggist told Ham. Yet it did little to relieve her suffering.

Daily she went into the little graveyard behind the house. Hardy weeds encroaching from the plots around it were slowly destroying the once-tidy rectangle of green fescue. As the cancer was destroying her. Ham put the scythe to them weekly, but it only delayed the inevitable—like Callie's medicine. The marble stones in neighboring plots were chipped and green with mold, some toppled over, uncared for and unvisited.

Ham would stand at the kitchen window watching as she read excerpts aloud from Shakespeare and the Bible. *An atonement to my father,* he mused. *His* Good Book.

"One day we'll all be together here," she said to Ham when he came out to help her back to the house. "You and I and Nate all together." Her eyes turned up to him, the last remnant of her life and beauty, still clear and pure green as clean seawater.

"We will, Callie. We will." He lifted her shrunken, bony hand and kissed it.

She was in the graveyard the day the telegram came. Ham knew what it was before he opened it with trembling fingers. From the War Department.

"We regret to inform you that Second Lieutenant Nathaniel Knight . . ."

He sat down on a kitchen chair and stared at the yellow sheet. Lethal yellow sheet. In this household Nate had been alive until the instant he unfolded the telegram and the words leaped off the page. He stood up, walked to the window, and looked out at Callie kneeling beside his father's grave. She wasn't praying. She never prayed. This day it was the Bible clasped to her breastbone. Her breasts had withered up.

"I can't do this to her," he said to himself.

He crumpled the telegram in his hand, walked stoop-shouldered through the hall to the parlor, and dropped it in the fireplace. He lit a match, put it to the paper, then drew back.

"I must," he said, and blew out the match. He picked up the telegram and smoothed it out.

It was a day like the day they had buried his mother. The sun shone intermittently. When it was hidden by the dark clouds that scudded over the sky like sleek hounds, the wind blowing off the Hudson chilled his back. It was bleak overhead as he came up behind her.

"Callie . . ." It was difficult for him to speak.

She turned her head slowly and looked up at him. "I heard the bell. Who called?"

"It was a Western Union messenger."

Her lips parted. Her eyes fixed on the rumpled telegram he was holding out to her. She recoiled from it, clasped the Book tighter to her body.

"I'm not interested in any telegrams," she said in a whisper barely audible.

"It's from the War Department, Callie."

"Stop! I don't want to hear it!" She threw down the Bible and put her hands over her ears.

He kneeled down and took her wrists. He'd never been gentler. He pulled them away from her ears.

"Callie, we can't pretend this way. It's terrible. Hateful. The night my mother died, I came out here and threw rocks at God. I feel like doing it again now. It must be faced. Nate has been killed in action."

She shook her head until he thought it would fly off her frail shoulders. "No, no, no! It's not true. They must have got the names mixed. Nate's alive!"

"Nate is dead and we have got to accept the fact."

He caught her before she collapsed, held her in his arms. The frail tortured body so racked by her sobbing, he was afraid she would come apart, turn into fine dust. He gathered her up in his arms like a Raggedy Ann doll, she weighed no more than a rag doll. He carried her into the house and up the staircase. He took her into her bedroom and placed her down softly on the bed. Covered her with a quilt. She had stopped crying. He couldn't be sure, but her mouth was shaped in a way that it crossed his mind she could be smiling.

"Ham, I'm very tired," she said.

He put a hand on her brow, parched with fever. "Sleep, dear, it's time."

He bent and looked into her eyes. The light was flickering, soon it would go out. Bent lower, kissed her on the lips.

Her smile was real now.

"I think I'll write a letter to Nate as soon as I awake."

He pulled the quilt up to her chin and left the room. He went out into the backyard. Looked across the graveyard. Wind whipped high grass around his grandfather's marble stone. The sun was out. He looked up at the sky. Stooped, picked up a round stone. Hurled it as far and high as he could into the heavens.

A black cloud eclipsed the sun.

A Beginning

The captain's fingers touched the cold marble, Ham Knight's headstone; a voice called from in back of him.

"His date's not been fixed yet."

He looked behind him, saw the ghost of Nathaniel Knight. How he'd looked the day Amanda was buried.

White hair and beard, wild in the wind, gave him the appearance of Michelangelo's God on the Sistine Chapel's vaulted ceiling.

The captain stood up and faced him. Enjoying the astonishment and disbelief visible on the older man's face. More than one ghost in this graveyard.

The captain glanced down at the stone marker. "You must be him, then?"

"Yes, I'm Ham Knight." He approached the captain with slow caution, one hand outstretched like a blind man groping his way along.

"I saw you from an upper window. Even at that distance it was remarkable, the resemblance. My God, man! Are you real or a specter of this senile brain?"

The captain smiled. "I'm real enough. Here." He offered his right hand. Ham gripped it, looked him up and down.

"It's incredible. Who are you?"

"Ham Knight."

"Yes, I'm Ham Knight." Ham was impatient. "It's you I want to know."

"I said, Ham Knight. I'm Ham Knight too." A pause. He said it. "Grandfather."

"Grandfather!" Ham exclaimed. His voice shook with emotion. "Who put you up to this masquerade? What's your game? I'm not amused, young man. Out with it before I lose my temper." He tried to withdraw his hand but the captain held it fast in both of his hands.

"It's no game. I came all the way from Texas to find out if you were still alive. You and my grandmother." He turned his head and surveyed the even rows of marble sentinels guarding the Knight graves.

"She passed on years ago," Ham told him. He drew the back of his left hand across his moist eyes. "I have no grandson. My son died in the war when he was still a boy."

"No boy, a man. My father. Nathaniel Knight the Second."

"My son, *your* father?"

"Yes, I'll tell you everything, but first, is that bar open?" He nodded at the big Knight house, hotel now. "You look as if you could use a drink, and so could I."

"Yes, I think a bottle is more what I need."

They made their way back through the cemetery to the parking lot.

Ham fixed him sternly, bushy white brows suspicious hoods. "You claim your name is Ham?"

"My mother named me. She knew how much he loved you."

"Your mother, who is she?"

"She was Jenny Doyle. She's dead too. When I was in Vietnam."

"When did she marry Nate?"

"She didn't. They were going to when he came home, but fate said no. My father was shot down over Germany in 1945."

Ham frowned. "If what you claim is true, you're illegitimate?"

The captain smiled, tongue deep in cheek. "Does it bother you? From what I've heard, the Knights don't shock easily. Or shouldn't anyway."

"What shocks me is that you kept yourself a secret to me all these years."

"I didn't know. Not until two weeks ago. It's a long story, wait until we're settled with a drink."

They entered the building through a rear entrance, went

along a short hall to the lobby. Danish modern, chrome and naugahyde, the uniform decor of second-rate hotels across the country.

"This place has certainly changed," the captain mused.

Ham was intrigued. "You sound as though you were here before?"

"In a way. I know this house almost as well as I knew the ranch where I grew up in Texas. My father wrote about this house, about you, his mother, all the Knights and Majorses."

A glimmer of understanding came to Ham. "Ah, yes, his journal. I laughed when he wrote us about his keeping a journal, but his mother was infatuated."

"Yes, there are reams of her letters with his papers." He held his hands apart, measuring the depth of the pile. "Once I began to read, I never stopped until I had finished the last page. Forty-eight hours of reading, my eyes were close to falling out."

Ham was perplexed. "Just two weeks ago, you say, is that when you first came into possession of these papers?"

"That's right. My mother never let on that he had any family but her."

"But why?"

"Because she was ashamed and frightened. It was wrong of her, she knew it, her guilt became almost too much for her to bear alone. She intended to tell me when I was old enough to understand, but then the older I got the more impossible her dilemma became. It was only in the last letter she wrote before her death that she mustered the courage."

They entered the cocktail lounge, the dim rosy illumination simulating coziness, disguising the dirty tablecloths, fake pine walls, and vinyl paneling. Ham led him to a corner booth. The waitress, blond and leggy, swivel-hipped, wore black mesh hose and a red mini-skirt that hung no more than an inch below her crotch.

"What'll it be today, Mr. Knight?" she asked. Her voice dropped an octave when she spoke to the captain. "Anything I can do for you, soldier?" Pressed her hip against his shoulder.

When she was gone, Ham told him, "Sarah has an eye for you. You can have her if you want. She's free, like so many of the young liberated females today."

The captain chuckled. "I've noticed."

Ham leaned across the table, huge shoulders hunched,

hands folded in front of him. "Your mother was ashamed and frightened, and that's why she kept silent?"

"Yes, the things my father had told her about the Knights and Majorses, what he wrote in his journals, I must confess you don't come off exactly as the normal American family. You might have inspired Poe or Shakespeare, but you terrified the timid farm girl who was my mother. She intended to visit Knightsville the summer my father went overseas, then she found out she was pregnant."

"It wouldn't have mattered. She should have told us."

The captain sighed. "What could have been . . . the saddest words in the language. She was afraid his mother, that *Majors* woman, would eat her alive if she found out her precious son had knocked up a wench from Texas. From what I've read she must have been an intimidating woman, my grandmother. Was she as wicked as she's made out to be?"

Ham rubbed his jaw, reflecting. "I thought so once." His mouth twisted. "The devil *her*self as that Ms. Steinem would phrase it. I don't doubt that if she had been born in seventeenth-century Salem, they would have burned Callie for a witch. *They.* The Nathaniel Knights. The Ham Knights. The Carl Majorses. The Bruce Majorses. It's a sad condition of human nature that man feels compelled to blame his weaknesses and shortcomings on forces outside of himself, beyond his control. Scapegoat demons, ah yes, I am blameless because I am possessed by the *devil.* The truth is, Callie had no supernatural power to bewitch. She waved no magic wand over my father and me or the Majorses, Carl and Bruce. The incontinence, the violence and brutishness, the fraud and malice, they were in us repressed all along. The part she played was in recognizing our capacities for sin—if you want to label our frailty of spirit and flesh as such—and abetting them. From my present advantage she seems not the witch I once credited her to be. She was a woman.

"Oh yes, strong, determined, willful, grasping, self-possessed, and arrogant, proud of her beauty and intellect. But a woman, human, all too human, of the earth. I think sometimes that if I had been stronger in the beginning, not so content to stand in the shadow of my father, a seventeen-year-old infant sucking his thumb, then perhaps Callie . . ." He dismissed the futile tack with a flourish of his hand. "What's past can't be altered. Do you know, near the end, I pitied her."

The captain grimaced. "What punishment that must have been to Callie. To have become an object of pity."

"You saw the inscription of her gravestone: *"This judgement of the heavens that makes us tremble, Touches us not with pity.'* " Ham swallowed the burr in his throat. "Now that I've learned about you, I pity her even more. How she would have adored his child. Your mother was cruel to keep you to herself."

"She rued that decision when she was older and wiser. But to a frightened eighteen-year-old, pregnant and unmarried, the safest course seemed to stay on the farm with her parents and let the neighbors think she'd married him before he shipped out and then was tragically widowed." He lit a cigarette. Ham took out a cold pipe and chewed on the bit thoughtfully as the captain talked.

"Her whole life was a tragedy, my mother. Her lover killed in World War II. Her son shot down over Hanoi twenty years after."

"You dropped the bombs that killed all those thousands of people?" Ham asked in a flat tone.

"No, I was a fighter pilot, a Phantom jet." He scrutinized the dour brooding countenance across the table. It was a "countenance," not an ordinary face. "What would you think of me if I had dropped bombs?"

Ham looked cryptic. "Oh . . . I suppose it would occur to me that blood will tell in the end."

"That isn't very flattering. You're an honest man, I knew you would be exactly the way you are. I like you, Grandfather —or would you prefer 'Ham'? That could be confusing, two Hams, we'd end up talking to ourselves."

Ham smiled. "It'll take some getting used to, but 'Grandfather' suits me. *You* are going to take some getting used to. My grandson . . ." He shook his head. "I still don't believe it."

"It's not real to me either. Look, about the war, I'm honest about things myself. Dropping the bombs, or flying cover for the bombers, it's all one and the same, a dehumanizing job. I paid for my part in the war, those seven years I spent in North Vietnamese prison camps. The 'Last Circle of Hell,' that's what we called the first compound where I was penned up. . . . To get back to my mother, she had two heart attacks while I was in prison. The last one in 1970 was almost fatal. It was then that she decided to tell me the truth. She turned over my father's journal and all the letters to her sister, my Aunt Kate, with a letter she'd written to me. I arrived back in Texas on the fifth of this month, and that's when Kate gave it to me, my heritage." His mouth twisted.

The waitress brought over their drinks, applejack for Ham and bourbon and beer for the captain. This time she brushed his face with a breast as she bent over him. She swished her bottom at him as she turned, a brazen beckon. He was beginning to get interested. Ham touched his arm.

"You're going to lay her, I can tell."

"I may. If I decide to stay."

Ham looked down moodily into his glass. "I guess it's been a disappointment to you. Knightsville, that is. Not the way it was in your father's journal. This old house, a cheap honkytonk motel. A whistle-stop for those bound someplace else. A rundown amusement park. Amusement, why do they apply that term to all the sad lonesome holes like this one?"

"Well, it isn't quite what I expected," the captain admitted. "I don't understand. Do you run this motel? The amusement park?"

"Yes, that's what I've been doing for the last eight years. And from the expression on your face, Captain, I can tell you understand even less now. You see, there's a gap of twenty-eight years in Nate's journal. After Callie died, things kept running downhill. I never had much head for figures or business. She managed all of that for both the Knights and Majorses for so many years, when she got sick and died, I had no knack at all. Taxes on the property doubled, tripled, still going up. Income on our investments was next to nothing during the war. Debts piled up. Bruce Majors died soon after Callie. But Chris is still alive. Over twenty years in that private sanitarium, you must have read about that. Well, it got so bad at one point, 90 percent of my income went to pay her bills." He shook his head. "Those charlatans. But what else could I do? It would be criminal to commit her to a public institution after the kind of care she's been used to up at Saranac. I had to sell Wheatley and the Majors property on the other side of the river back in '52. In the bad market of 1963, 'most everything else went. Let me tell you, when that fellow walked in here one day that summer and offered to set me up in this deal, it sounded pretty good. They've got a chain of these places all over the United

States. The White Knight Motel Corporation. There's irony for you, did you see that damned fool plaster monstrosity set up in the park?"

The captain grimaced and ground out his butt. "It's a relief to learn it wasn't your inspiration." He looked up the ceiling, touched the wall, craned his neck around the barroom. "I wouldn't be surprised if maybe something could be done with this place. You know in Texas we have motels that *are* motels."

Ham laughed. "Bigger and better, everything in Texas, ain't that so?"

"I can teach you a thing or two."

"Oh? you're thinking of staying on for a while, after all?"

The captain gazed at Sarah, the waitress, bending over to pick up a napkin, showing off her pretty backside.

"It still has local color, Knightsville."

Ham's eyes twinkled. "You watch that girl, Captain. She's like Callie in many ways, I guess it's why I hired her."

"Oh, it's a pleasure watching her." He placed a hand on Ham's arm. "Grandfather, you have got yourself a new bartender. This one makes lousy drinks."

"You're hired." Ham laughed and called to the waitress. "Hey, Sarah! Bring us another round. Make it doubles. My grandson's come home."

A couple came into the bar by the street entrance. In the brief seconds the door was open, they could hear the music in the distance with the grinding of the merry-go-round.

> *And when she passed away, I cried and cried all day.*
> *Alone again . . . naturally. . . .*

The song reminded Ham for some vague reason of young Ham's mother whom he'd never known. He experienced a pang of grief for the faceless woman his son had loved and made pregnant.

"My mother named me. She knew how much he loved you."

He was glad it was dark in here, so the captain wouldn't see how close he was to tears.